The Ivanov B
Book 1

The Last Hope

Gateli Yozrel

Copyright © 2025 by Gateli Yozrel

All rights reserved.

No part of this publication may be reproduced, stored in a retrieval system, or transmitted in any form or by any means—electronic, mechanical, photocopying, recording, or otherwise—without the prior written permission of the author, except in the case of brief quotations embodied in critical reviews or articles.

This is a work of fiction. Names, characters, businesses, organizations, places, events, and incidents are either the product of the author's imagination or used in a fictitious manner. Any resemblance to actual persons, living or dead, or actual events is purely coincidental.

Cover design by Gateli Yozrel

Independently published

ISBN: 9798314290941

For information, inquiries, or permissions, contact :

Lifrel.bookz@gmail.com

For all the women who have overcome the obstacles and the darkness of this world and have risen above it…

Content Notes

This novel is a dark romance that explores intense emotional and psychological themes. It includes depictions of physical and emotional abuse, trauma, sexual violence (non-explicit but implied), captivity, PTSD, and complex moral choices.

While the story is ultimately one of resilience, healing, and unconditional love, some scenes may be distressing to sensitive readers.

Discretion is advised.

This story in mature and unsuitable content for young audience.

Synopsis

He was her last hope. She became his deliverance.

Trapped by one of the most ruthless men in the Italian mafia, Selina isn't living—she's merely surviving. Until the night she runs, her son clutched to her chest, hunted by the very monster who once claimed her.

Her only chance at freedom? Nikolai Ivanov—a cold, calculated Russian mob boss with a soul as scarred as hers. Taking her in means igniting a war between empires. But in the shadows of betrayal and power, something dangerous sparks between them: a connection forged in pain, defiance… and forbidden desire.

As secrets unravel and alliances crumble, Selina must choose: confront the demons of her past—or lose herself in the chaos of the underworld.

Selina & Nikolai is the first book in **the Last Hope series.**

Prologue

"Start over from zero."

A trembling breath escaped from between my bloodstained lips. Standing on a chair, I clutched my skirt, gathered between my fingers. My gaze drifted away from the reflection of myself—distorted by tears in the large mirror of the room—and settled on the photograph of a little boy. *My little boy.*

The chill of the iron rod struck my shins once again, and yet another sigh of pain escaped me.

My baby slept, silent; my baby slept, silent…

The same words looped endlessly in my head as I felt the blood flow steadily toward my feet.

"One," I whispered in a weak voice.

The taste of blood, the smell of blood, the sensation of it trickling down my skin made me want to vomit.

My wounds, my scars, my tears, my cries—they all made me want to vomit.

The cold bit into my burning skin once again.

"Two."

His scent, his touch, his voice made me want to die.

His apologies, his gestures, his gifts—offered in a bid for forgiveness after striking me—made me want to die.

"Three."

But my baby slept, and I had promised him that we would play together tomorrow—I could not die.

"Four."

I could not abandon my baby to these monsters; I had to fight. I had to keep fighting, just as I had for the past eight years.

"Five."

For my baby. For my son.

I would not give up—

Not until my last breath.

Chapter one
Nikolai

"Six !" Ivan shouted as he dashed across the lawn, arms spread wide. Dimitri and Emre chased after him, their cries echoing his. *"Moy bednyy paren'* (my poor fellow), it's high time you teach your cubs to run," laughed Grigori—my eldest brother—as he patted my back and trotted off to join his sons.

I grumbled and sank onto the bench, reaching for my water bottle. Six to two—I'd seen some shitty scores, but this time we truly outdid ourselves with my boys. I muttered another Russian curse before taking a deep gulp, just as my sons approached, dragging their feet. Mikhail, my twelve-year-old eldest, grabbed his own bottle before slumping beside me, his face dark and breath ragged. He unleashed a string of Russian insults before sipping again. I couldn't help but smirk behind the towel I retrieved from my bag as I watched my nine-year-old twins follow in turn. Alexei immediately buried himself in the book tucked in his sports bag, while Andrei pulled out his tablet from under the bench and launched a cartoon about horses.

Teach them to run ? First, they'd have to understand the very purpose of sport—and why we organized these matches every year, I thought, draping my towel over my shoulder. Grigori snickered at the sight of me but fell silent when his sons, Ivan and Dimitri, leapt onto his back and flipped him onto the damp grass. He shoved them off, then toppled them in turn, tickling them mercilessly. A heaviness settled in my chest as I watched them. There was a time when things were like this with my boys—a time darkened by my choices, my mistakes. I closed my eyes to fend off the bleak thoughts, trying to dispel that red vision that had haunted me for four long years.

I sighed and began searching for my jacket when I froze—Roman, the youngest of our four siblings, was sneaking up behind our eldest. A mischievous smile spread across his face as he clutched a bucket of water. What a *mudak* (idiot). It seemed our yearly football tournament was about to end with the "murder" of my little brother at the hands of my eldest.

That idiot always pulled a dirty trick during every match; just the other day, he nearly got a taste of Sasha's baseball bat—our third brother. Fortunately for him, Roman ran fast. "He's gonna get himself killed," said a monotone voice behind me. I glanced over my shoulder and saw Sasha leaning against the wall, eyes on his phone, brows furrowed.

"Don't overdo it—he's just going to get wet, nothing dramatic," I said, loosening the fuchsia cleats Roman had given me for my last birthday. Of course, I'd never wear them, but that idiot had rummaged through my suitcase meant for Italy and swapped my pair with those… things. "Not any worse than the time he put horse manure in your sneakers," I added, recalling our match two years ago at our estate in Russia. That day, he didn't even pull out his baseball bat—instead, he brandished a semi-automatic, forcing us to repair the backyard fountain without our sister-in-law noticing.

I heard Sasha muttering behind me, tossing his towel to the ground. "The problem isn't that he's going to get wet—it's what he's going to get wet with, *moy brat* (my brother)," he said bitterly. I froze and slowly raised my eyes toward Roman, now just a few steps from Grigori. "What the hell is in that damn bucket, Sasha ?" I asked darkly. "I saw him circling the stables on his way back from my car—especially around the water troughs," he replied, referring to the stables near the field we'd rented in Rome.

"*Blyad'* (damn)… you mean the troughs where the little ones played around… and did their business ?" Sasha merely nodded, wiping his forehead with his jersey before returning to his phone.

Damn.

"Greg !" I warned—but it was too late. Grigori looked up, his eyes full of confusion that vanished the moment Roman doused him with the bucket's contents, grinning like a fool. A deathly silence fell over the field as my sons abandoned their activities, their eyes fixed on their uncles. Grigori's lips moved rapidly—no doubt unleashing a stream of curses—as he slowly turned and shot Roman the deadliest glare in our family's history. Roman still stood behind him, the bucket held high over Greg's head.

"Roman," Grigori growled. "*Moy brat*," Roman replied innocently. "What the hell was in that bucket, *moy brat* ?" demanded Grigori, under the heavy stares of his sons who had also been splashed. "Water, *moy brat*… and perhaps something more," Roman dared to snicker. "You bastard, I'm gonna kill you !" roared Grigori, leaping up like lightning. Roman tossed the bucket over his shoulder and made the best getaway of the century, sprinting as the chase began across the field.

"Fifty bucks if he catches him," mocked Ali, our associate, collapsing beside Mikhail and me. My son made a sound of disapproval before pulling out a laptop—God knows from where—and showing us several graphs. "The odds of Uncle Grigori catching Uncle Roman are slim, based on probabilities calculated from the past few months of similar pursuits," Mikhail explained calmly. I examined the graphs and nodded, while Ali gave me a baffled look. "He's right—Roman runs like an Arabian thoroughbred," I confirmed. I pulled out four vests from my sports bag—tossing one onto Mika's head, another to Alex, sliding the third over Andrei, and slipping the last onto myself—just as my phone buzzed again. I grimaced at the flood of missed calls and messages, all from the same person.

Loud shouts drew my attention, and I muttered a curse as my brothers ran toward us. I yanked my twins' hoods to clear the path, only to fall on my backside with the kids in my arms. Roman leapt over the bench, dodged Sasha—who barely glanced up—and bolted toward the exit. Grigori followed, though less gracefully, crashing into Sasha and soaking him before tearing after Roman. Sasha threw aside his phone and nearly ripped off his jersey in disgust, hurling it after Roman while cursing him. And as if by divine justice, Roman tripped over Dimitri's cleats and slammed flat onto the grass. "Looks like your odds were off, *evlat* (kid)," teased Ali, bumping Mikhail's shoulder.

"There are things in life we cannot control, Ali *abi* (big brother)—these things simply happen. We must learn to accept them and turn them into strength," Mikhail replied, eyes on his screen, his voice steady. I watched him typing furiously, he hated using the computer without his glasses, which he'd left at the hotel. Each of my sons was so different. Mikhail, calm and organized on the surface, ready to explode at the smallest trigger, reminded me of myself—though he often overturned everything in his path. Alexei, detached, immersed in his books and puzzles, reminded me of Sasha—quiet and sharp. And Andrei, the most expressive, spent his time outdoors, especially with the horses. We used to have a bedtime ritual of sharing stories—now, those moments had grown rare.

"I got you, you little shit !" roared Grigori, pulling me from my thoughts. Roman tried to get up, only to slip. Grigori grabbed his jersey and threw him down again— but ended up tangled in his son's cleats too. Roman crawled away on all fours, groaning. Grigori rose again, panting, ready to continue the chase—until he stopped, staring at someone ahead. Roman crouched behind that someone, smirking.

"Nearly forty years old and still chasing your brothers, *aşkım* (my love)?" asked Elif, tossing her dark hair and placing a hand on Grigori's chest. "Elif, what are you doing here, *moy kotonok* (my kitten)?" Grigori asked softly. Roman, Sasha, and I grimaced at his sudden tone change. "What ? Am I not allowed to watch my husband beat his brothers senseless ?" Elif purred, stepping closer. I stifled a laugh as she grabbed Roman's ear— without breaking eye contact with her husband—lifted him to his feet, smacked his shin with her stiletto, and shoved him toward the exit. The idiot tripped again before finally reaching the damn door.

"Elif, my Elif, shall we head back to the hotel now ? Come on, *moya lapochka* (my little darling)," Grigori murmured. Elif rolled her eyes and pushed him aside with her fingertips. "*Aşkım*, call me after your shower, alright ?" she said, tapping his cheek then she circled him, adjusted her jacket on her shoulders, and beckoned to her sons. "Mama ! Mama!" Dimitri cried, running to her, "oh, my angel, come here," she said, embracing him as he proudly described his goals. Ivan joined them, showing off bruised knees. Greg touched Elif's shoulder, but she brushed him aside again, "Elif, shall we go, *moya lapochka*?" he tried.

"Grigori Ivanov, how dare you leave our sons in soaked jerseys in this chill ? Want them to get sick ?" she scolded, finger pointed at him. The mighty head of the Bratva actually took a step back and began to stammer. Ali chuckled behind me as Sasha left, shaking his head. Andrei slumped against my chest, staring longingly at Elif and her boys. I clenched my jaw and held him tighter—but he pulled away to escape back into his cartoons. Sighing, I helped Alexei up. "Come on, let's go home." Mikhail packed his laptop and said goodbye to his cousins, followed by his brothers. I slung my bag over my shoulder and waved to Ali.

"Are you sneaking off, brother ?" Grigori asked suddenly, stepping in front of me, hand on my shoulder. The 'sneak-off plan' had failed. I growled, trying to step around him, but he stopped me again. "When are you going to stop running, Nikolai ? When will you talk to us ? We're your family—we want to help you and your sons," he said. "I have nothing to say. I don't need help—we need no one," I snapped, pulling free and raising my collar.

As I passed Elif, I hugged her briefly. She caught my hand, pressed her finger to my forehead, lifting my head. "Keep your head high, Niko—eyes on the horizon. Don't miss your sunrise," she whispered, I closed my eyes and nodded before squeezing her hand and walking off. "Don't be late tonight ! Seven o'clock in the lobby !" Greg called behind me. I waved once and stepped into the air of Rome to join my sons in the car.

Chapter two
Selina

"*Cazzo* ! (Fuck !)"

I let out a pained moan as I swung my foundation brush and bent over the lever, pressing my palms against the cold marble of the bathroom counter. I lifted my eyes toward my reflection, and a sob escaped me at the sight of the painful bruise on my cheek that I could not cover. I looked up to the ceiling, my lashes fluttering to prevent the tears from falling and ruining the makeup I was barely managing to apply. I snorted and jumped when I heard a soft knock at the door, holding my breath.

"*Mamma ?* " asked a small voice behind it.

I sighed in relief, unlocked the door, and let in my ray of sunshine. He slipped into the room, and I quickly locked it again. I took him in my arms and grimaced at the pain that surged through my body as I set my son on the counter and smiled at him while brushing the bangs from his forehead. "Why aren't you dressed yet, *Angelo mio ?* (my angel)" I asked softly. "My jacket is in my room, but I can't tie this !" he complained, holding out his bow tie. I laughed, lifted the collar of his shirt, and tied the little bow tie before straightening his collar. "There you go, my love," I murmured, smoothing his shirt. "Thanks, *Mamma*," he whispered, wrapping his arms around me tightly, rubbing his nose against my ear—just as he always did. *I love you*—that's what it meant. We shared these little gestures to communicate.

Speaking our feelings aloud was impossible, dangerous under this roof, so we had created our own language.

He stepped back, studied my face, and gently placed his warm little palm against my aching cheek, making me shudder. "Does it hurt, *Mamma* ? " he asked so innocently that it shattered my heart. I shook my head, pressed my lips together, took his little hand, and kissed his palm. "Not at all, *Angelo mio*. Don't worry." He stared at me for a few seconds and then nodded, though I knew he didn't truly believe me. He was almost eight—old enough to see through my lies, yet too young to grasp the full horror of what he endured.

Suddenly, someone began drumming on the door, making us both jump. My son threw himself against me, clinging so tightly it made me wince. "*Mia dolce* ? (my sweetheart ?) Are you ready ?" asked the man on the other side, his voice gruff. I wrapped my arms around my son, gently massaging his neck—*It's going to be all right.* "Selina ?" the voice called again. I shut my eyes, burying my face in my son's neck—*go away, go away, go away*—as the blows resumed, shaking the very walls. "Unlock this damn door, Selina ! Open up ! Selina !"

My baby grabbed my wrist and squeezed it twice—our code. *I'm afraid.* I sniffled, stepped back, and cupped his face in my hands, rubbing my nose against his—*I'm here.* "Selina ! I swear, if you don't open that door, you'll pay for it, *mia dolce* ! Do you hear me ?" I lowered my son from the counter and turned toward the door. My whole body trembled as I closed my eyes, drew a shaky breath, and flung the door open—only to come face-to-face with my worst nightmare.

His eyes swept over my body, and the satisfaction gleaming in them made my skin crawl. He reached out to caress my unmarked cheek, brushing my cheekbone as he leaned in closer. "You're beautiful, *Cara mia* (my dear)—more beautiful than any of my dreams," he whispered, pressing his nose against my temple. I choked back a sob and began to count in silence : *uno, due, tre, quattro, cinque, sei…*

A groan escaped me as he yanked violently on my freshly styled hair, "but it seems your makeup is a bit light, or perhaps…" he muttered, tightening his grip as his lips brushed my bruised cheek, "you did it on purpose, leaving some traces, huh?" I shook my head, clenching my teeth, barely restraining the urge to spit in his face. I pressed my lips together and stood on tiptoe to ease the pain. "Leave *Mamma* alone !" cried a small voice behind me, Antonio glanced past me, a smile curling his lips. "Rafael, son, were you there ?" he asked. At last, he released me, stroking my hair one last time before stepping around me toward my son.

"You're so handsome, just like me," he laughed, bending down to scoop the boy into his arms—but Rafael dodged him and snuggled against my legs, "*mamma…*" I lifted my eyes toward the monster who haunted us, straightened my chin, and pulled my son close. Antonio stared at us, a slow, smug smile spreading across his lips. He slid his hands into the pockets of his tailored trousers and approached us with calculated, deliberate steps. I did not lower my gaze. I did not bow my head. On the contrary—I stood tall despite the pain in my back, the fear that constricted my breath, the tremble in my limbs. I stood tall. And I knew—it irked him. I knew it annoyed him that I refused to cower, that I would not grovel. He leaned forward, lowering himself to my level with that damn smile I longed to rip from his face.

"Hurry and finish your makeup, *Cara mia*. The guests have started arriving. Being late when you're the host is not acceptable for a Rasili." "I'm not a Rasili," I spat, without hesitation, my voice as sharp as the cold fury boiling inside me. He chuckled and straightened, never taking his eyes off me. "It won't be long, *mia dolce*. It won't be long," he murmured, tucking a lock of hair behind my ear with a deceptively gentle gesture. He kissed my cheek—right over the bruise—making me whimper in pain despite myself, then strolled out of the room whistling.

I stood frozen until the door closed behind him, carrying his darkness with it. I leaned against the frame and sighed, gently wiping my cheek with a trembling hand. "*Mamma?*" I looked down at my son, who stared up at me with glistening eyes—eyes that shone in a way I despised. I crouched beside him and smiled, stroking his dark hair. "It's okay, *Angelo mio*. It's okay," I whispered. "Come on, go fetch your jacket and wait for me in your room. I'll come get you, okay?" He hesitated for a moment, watching me with those green eyes so much like my own, then nodded and ran off.

I stood up, leaning against the wall as I tried to steady my cotton legs, pressing myself to the marble and groaning in pain. It would be all right. It had to be all right—for my son. I picked up the brush again and resumed covering the marks my nightmare had left on my skin—even if it could do nothing for the ones he had left on my soul.

I gripped my son's little hand as we sat in the back of the black sedan. I watched the city of Rome pass by beneath my eyes—for only the second time in eight years. The first had been when I arrived in Roma, when I had been forced to come, and I had seen the city through a window, just like today, before finding myself locked away in that gilded cage. The car eventually stopped in front of the grand five-star hotel where the Rasili insignia shone brilliantly. I felt my son snuggle closer to me, gripping my wrist twice—*I am afraid.*

I kissed his hair and gently massaged his neck. *It will be all right.* Antonio's door opened, letting in a draft, I shivered despite the mild Rome air and jumped when mine opened. I gazed at the towering building, people streaming inside, and I began to feel the stress creeping in. It had been eight years since I had last gone out in public, eight years since I had been trapped in the monster's lair. A shadow appeared above my door, forcing me to slowly lift my eyes and I met the gaze of that very monster. Antonio extended his hand, urging me to come down. "Come on, *Cara mia.*" I clenched my jaw, restraining myself from biting his damn hand, and simply ignored him as I descended on my own. I stood up straight, smoothed my rose satin dress with trembling hands, and helped Rafael out as well, taking his hand in mine and turning toward the hotel entrance—but a firm grip stopped me.

"Don't do anything stupid, Selina. Don't make me regret this decision. Don't you dare disappear from my side, understood, *mia dolce* ?" he murmured, his lips brushing against my ear, making me shudder with disgust. I merely nodded and let him do as he pleased. He slipped my arm under his, and we walked toward the entrance, where his men held back the numerous journalists trying to question him and snap blinding photos. I felt panic rising—all that noise, the chaos. I tried to quicken my pace, clutching my son, as Antonio almost dragged us along the ground, moving forward without a single glance at us. We finally entered the lobby, leaving the chaos behind, only to find ourselves among the sharks who fixed their attention on us. For even though I had been locked away in a cage for years, I had lived among the most dangerous of sharks—those who spent their days boasting about their exploits and projects, believing I did not understand their words.

None of the people in this room knew me, but I knew most of them—I knew their strengths and weaknesses, their secrets… things that could destroy them, truths that could ignite wars between the great families of the *Cosa Nostra*.

Chapter three
<u>Nikolai</u>

I watched as my twins joined their cousins near the playground in the reception hall where the Rasili gala was taking place, while Mikhail went to sit beside Elif without even glancing around, his eyes fixed on his phone. I glanced at my watch—8:00 PM, one hour late. I grimaced, hoping Grigori wouldn't notice our tardiness, but a heavy hand on my shoulder crushed that hope instantly. "Well, well… isn't this my little brother—the one I told to be in the hotel lobby at exactly 7:00 PM? " Grigori growled as he appeared in my field of vision. I merely shrugged, grabbing a glass from one of the trays circulating through the room. My brother never took his eyes off me as I downed the drink in one go. Under his persistent gaze, I finally sighed and nodded toward Andrei, "Andrei locked himself in the bathroom. He didn't want to come out," I murmured as I set the glass on an empty tray.

Grigori's shoulders slumped as he glanced at our sons, who were seated around a table coloring. He shook his head gently and sighed. "Maybe you should take him back to a shrink ? " he suggested, still watching the children. "Already did—just last week. She said they're not progressing anymore, that he doesn't say a word," I replied. "Maybe a vacation would do you good ? " "Maybe," I said simply, fully aware that it wouldn't help. Andrei's situation wasn't a whim. Even if his brothers showed it less, I knew they had all gone through the same thing. Since they discovered the truth a year ago, everything had changed between us. Nervously, I scratched my jaw while scanning the hall, recognizing most of the guests still streaming in—making me growl. I hated crowds ; too many people meant too much risk, especially in our world. Having my children, my nephews, and my sister outside the safety of our estate set me on edge. My eyes quickly found Marcus near the entrance, David by the playground keeping watch over the kids, and Igor stationed outside. We had brought only a few men, since we were all present—and more than capable of defending ourselves.

"Rasili's still not here ? " I asked my brother as I scanned the room. The Rasilis were one of the three major families that made up the Italian mafia, and Antonio Rasili was the son of Capo Fernandez Rasili. After years of war between the Italian and Russian mafias, an understanding had finally been reached sixteen years ago—thanks to my brother and Capo Marino. "Not yet. He's making us wait," Grigori growled, loosening his tie.

I sighed and made my way to our table, collapsing between my sister-in-law and my son. I leaned over his shoulder to glance at his phone. I raised my eyebrows, trying to make sense of the article he was reading—something about AI. Suddenly, my phone vibrated in my pocket, dragging me out of my confused concentration. I groaned at the name flashing on the screen. "She won't stop until you answer, you know ?" my son muttered quietly beside me. "I already know what she wants, and the answer is no," I replied. "She's our grandmother. Of course she wants to see us." I gave him a puzzled look, raising one brow, "but that doesn't mean we want to see her," he quickly added, turning back to his phone.

Across the table, Elif shot us a glance over her glass, her dark eyes glowing with compassion—the same look that had helped me stay afloat when she first joined the family. She had married my brother seventeen years ago, shortly after our parents died, and helped us learn to live again. She had been a ray of light in my brother's life—and not just his. Despite a rocky start (Grigori as emotionally rigid as a tree, me caught in a teenage crisis at sixteen, and Sacha and Roman still just kids), Elif had managed to take charge of our chaotic group at only nineteen, after an arranged marriage—and she never gave up on any of us. She truly was the maternal heart of the family—the one we all turned to when we needed grounding. It was no surprise Grigori turned into a teddy bear around her. My brother really was a lucky man. He sank beside her, took her hand, and interlaced their fingers before leaning in to whisper something that made her burst out laughing. "She drives him crazy," said Sacha as he sat down next to my son, "he doesn't seem to mind," I replied with a shrug. "Better not, for all our sakes," Sacha added gruffly. I nodded. A moody Grigori was trouble—but an upset Elif ? That would be our downfall. She was the glue that held us together, even in our darkest moments—calm, kind, and stronger than steel.

My jaw clenched as a rush of memories struck me—blood on my hands, on my shirt, the stench of gasoline, the screams...

"Nikolai," a voice murmured behind me.

My arm tightened around the still-warm body of the woman against me, her blood soaking into my clothes, while my free hand remained clenched around the cold weight of my weapon. The stench of gasoline made me want to retch—it was everywhere : on the furniture, the walls, the floor, mixing with the blood and the sound of a crying baby. I didn't react when a hand settled on my shoulder ; I didn't react when a woman crouched beside me ; I didn't react when her fingers gently slipped into mine, prying the gun away. It was only when she cupped my frozen face in her warm hands, brushing away tears I hadn't even realized were falling, and looked into my eyes that I recognized her. "Elif," *I breathed.*

"Yes, it's me, Niko. It's going to be alright, it's going to be alright," she whispered firmly, her expression serene.

I rubbed my face with my hand, head bowed, trying to anchor myself in the present—but the same scream echoed in my mind, over and over again, a sound that had haunted me for seven long years.

"Why?! Why?!" a woman screamed on repeat.

But her voice faded beneath another, gentler one.

"Keep your head up, Niko. Eyes on the horizon, so you don't miss the sunrise—your sunrise, understood?" Elif's voice echoed through my thoughts.

I slowly shook my head, drew a deep breath, and straightened up, trying to regain control. But I froze the moment my eyes landed on a woman who had just entered the hall. My gaze swept over her figure—she wore a long satin dress in a delicate pink hue that reminded me of the sky at dawn. Her long, wavy brown hair spilled over her back, cascading to her waist. Her delicate face was framed by high cheekbones, and her full lips moved softly as she spoke to the little boy beside her. Her green eyes, framed by long lashes, shimmered with light. A tightness gripped my chest as she lifted her eyes and looked around hesitantly, stepping inside with an expression of lost uncertainty. A sudden urge to go to her surged through me, and I clenched my fists to hold myself back.

I slumped back in my chair and let out a low Russian curse as Antonio Rasili appeared behind her, slipping his arm around her waist and placing a hand on the boy's shoulder, startling him.

Married and a mother—great eye, Nikolai, nice.

Sacha, sensing my shift in mood, followed my gaze. "Looks like Rasili finally decided to show his face," he murmured. "I can't stand that bastard," he added, taking a sip from his glass. "Totally agree," I muttered, swallowing down a wave of jealousy. Rasili leaned in and kissed the woman's temple, tightening his grip around her waist. I growled under my breath and turned away.

Lucky bastard.

I refocused on my phone, scrolling through emails and replying to the urgent ones. I sighed at the latest technical report from one of our ships—an engine failure, a code signaling trouble with the weapons shipment. *Damn it.* "And here come the Ivanovs," a voice with an Italian accent announced. I looked up and met a pair of green eyes—deep, forest-like. She widened them in surprise before quickly glancing away. I cleared my throat and tucked my phone away without standing, unlike my brother, who rose to shake Rasili's hand.

"I welcome you," Antonio said, looking at each of us in turn. He shook Grigori's hand, then turned to Elif. "Madame Ivanov," he greeted, extending a hand to her. That alone was enough to put all of us on edge. If there was one thing we couldn't stand, it was outsiders laying a hand on our women or children. Grigori wasted no time—he slipped his arms around Elif, pulling her against him and effectively shielding her from Antonio's reach. "And may I present my magnificent wife, Selina, and our son, Rafael," Antonio declared with pride.

Selina.

He gently nudged her forward with a hand at the small of her back—as if offering her up to a pack of wolves. Which, quite literally, he was. Selina took a few tentative steps, her posture rigid, as though his touch unsettled her—or maybe that was just my imagination. "Welcome," she said softly, extending her hand to my sister-in-law, who took it without hesitation and squeezed it with a smile. Despite the gentleness of her voice, it struck me like thunder crashing between my legs, unleashing a wave of intrusive thoughts—ones in which she moaned my name in the dark. *Fuck, Nikolai, pull yourself together.*

At that moment, Dimitri came running toward his mother, waving the drawing he'd just made. Elif smiled, praised him, and held him by the shoulders, gently turning him toward the Rasili. "And here's my little second, Dimitri—Dimitri, look, it's Rafael," she said, introducing the two boys. "Hi !" Dimitri exclaimed in perfect English. Rafael pulled his hand from his father's grip and slipped behind his mother's legs. She ran her hand soothingly along the back of his neck, and when her eyes flicked up toward her husband, fear shimmered in them—a fear that awakened something primal in me, something I'd thought reserved only for my own.

"Forgive him ; he's a bit shy," she offered, her voice soft as she turned back to us, her shoulders slumping. Our eyes met again. Her doe-like gaze lingered longer than it should have. Before I even realized what I was doing, I was on my feet. I clenched my fists inside my pockets and walked steadily toward her, stepping behind Dimitri and placing a hand on his shoulder. "It's nothing," I said. "Dimitri just gets a little too excited sometimes. Nikolai Ivanov." I extended my hand toward her, our eyes locking.

"Nice to meet you," she said, she placed her hand in mine, and I took it in a grip that was firm but gentle, frowning at the fragility and thinness of her fingers—but even more at their coldness. My entire body tensed as I lowered my gaze and caught sight of faint marks along her wrist, exposed by a slightly rolled-up sleeve. I turned her hand subtly, catching a glimpse of more on the inside. Her shiver told me she'd noticed. She quickly pulled her hand away, hiding it behind her back and turning again toward her son.

"Well, I hope you have a good evening. We're off to greet our other guests," Antonio announced as he grabbed his son's hand and wrapped an arm around his wife's shoulders. They walked away toward another table. But Selina's glance over her shoulder didn't go unnoticed. "Did you see what I saw ?" Elif asked beside me, her eyes still fixed on Selina. I nodded slowly, unwilling to speak, afraid my voice might betray the fury burning in my chest.

"A problem ?" Grigori asked as he drew his wife into an embrace. "No," I said, my eyes never leaving the little family weaving among the tables. "Let's enjoy the evening. Tomorrow's return will be rough—we've got trouble with one of the shipments." I sat back down. Sacha cursed under his breath, shooting me an annoyed glare as Grigori sank back into his seat with a sigh. Elif gently caressed his arm. "It's nothing. The other three ships have reached the delivery point, and I'm sure we can calm the clients about the delay," she said. "You mean you'll calm them, *moya dorogaya ?* (my darling) " my brother teased, lifting her hand to kiss it.

My gaze wandered again, searching for Selina, but I saw only Antonio and his son, whom he dragged behind him. I squinted, watching the little boy squirm in resistance. Antonio's features hardened, and he scooped the child into his arms, whispering something in his ear. The boy immediately stopped struggling. "*nana! nana!* " (Dad ! Dad !) a voice shouted. My heart skipped as I recognized Alexei's voice. My eyes followed him as he ran toward me, David close behind. I stood so abruptly that my chair wobbled. Sacha caught it just in time as Alexei reached me, and I crouched to grasp his small shoulders. "*nana*, Andrei left. He was crying," he said, his voice stern. *Fuck.*

"Why ? What happened, Alexei ?" "One of the kids kept asking where our mom was… so I hit him," he replied, looking everywhere but at me. "I was busy separating Alexei from the other kid. I didn't see Andrei leave," David added. I took a deep breath, trying to calm the storm of rage rising within me. Elif appeared at my side, her hand gently brushing Alexei's hair. "Keep an eye on him, please," I said in a low voice as I stood. I scanned the hall—no sign of Andrei. I cursed again and strode toward the lobby.

Chapter four
Selina

His touch made me want to rip off my own skin, despite the dress covering me. I tried once again to pull away from his hand resting at the small of my back, but it was useless. I exhaled softly, feeling Ivanov's gaze burning into my back. He had seen the marks. He wasn't supposed to. And if he told Antonio ? A shiver ran down my spine, and I gripped my son's hand tighter, holding onto him like a lifeline. That heavy gaze didn't leave me, and if Antonio noticed, he would kill me. I wanted to grab my heel and throw it at that damn Russian's face. What the hell was his problem ?

Antonio's arm coiled around my waist like a snake, and I lifted my eyes to him. Without taking his gaze off his conversation partner, he leaned down toward me. "You should take a trip to the bathroom, *mia dolce*, to touch up your makeup," he whispered against my ear. He pulled back, smiling as he gently pushed me toward the exit. My eyes flicked to my son, who was already watching me with worry as I stepped away. "Don't worry, *Cara mia*, I'll keep an eye on our son," Antonio said cheerfully. Tears pricked my eyes, and I clenched my jaw as anger burned inside me. He knew. He knew I would never escape without my son. He used him as a leash, one he had fastened around my neck, keeping me at his feet. The helplessness suffocated me. I wanted to scream, I wanted to hit him, I wanted someone to see me, to see what I truly was. I wanted help.

But I did nothing—nothing except nod, throwing one last glance at my son, who silently begged me with his eyes. I smiled at him gently and walked toward the hall on trembling legs. I entered the restroom, smiled at a little girl who was leaving, and waited a few seconds to make sure I was alone. I placed my bag beside the sink and looked at my reflection, grimacing as I saw a mark beginning to show on my neck. With a shaky hand, I opened my bag, took out my foundation, and began applying it. I didn't even feel it coming when it escaped my lips—a sob. My whole body trembled, my cheeks dampened, but I kept covering the marks that would never truly disappear.

I set the brush down, grabbed a tissue, and roughly wiped my tears away, ignoring the physical pain. That kind of pain had long become secondary. I had learned to block it out, accepting that I abandoned my pride and honor with each hit I took. My only reason for living was my son. My son, who was currently alone with our tormentor. I grabbed the brush again and started applying makeup to my face, thinking only of returning quickly to my baby. I finished reapplying my makeup, calming down little by little. I took one last look at my reflection to make sure no marks were visible, grabbed my bag, straightened my shoulders, and stepped out.

I walked stiffly and quickly down the hallway toward the hall when something crashed into me. I let out a cry and found myself on the floor, a small body sprawled across my lap. I lowered my gaze and found myself face-to-face with a little boy, his eyes brimming with tears, nose red, lips trembling, and shoulders shaking with sobs. Suddenly, he buried his face against my stomach, wrapping his arms around me. I froze, unsure what to do as he continued crying into me. I looked around, but I didn't see his mother, in fact, I saw no one at all. We were alone. I placed my hand on his back, rubbing it gently, then slid my fingers through his hair—it was shorter than my son's, who had slightly longer, curly locks. My hand drifted to his nape, squeezing gently, *it would be okay.*

He lifted his little face, sniffling softly, and his eyes found mine again. I smiled at him and wiped away his tears, just as I had wiped mine only moments ago. "Hey," I said softly.

"Hey," he replied in a small voice, making me laugh. "Do you think we can get up ?" I asked him. He stared at me a few more seconds through his tears, then nodded. I helped him to his feet and groaned as I rose as well. He kept his head down, shoulders slumped, and wiped his nose on his sleeve, making me smile again. "Wait, here, take this," I said, pulling a tissue from my bag and handing it to him. He hesitantly took it and blew his nose. I ran my fingers through his hair, smoothing it down as he gradually calmed.

"Did you get hurt ? Is that why you're crying ?" I asked him gently. He shook his head softly, sniffling again. I frowned, quickly scanning him, but I didn't see anything alarming. "It's… Mom…" he sobbed. "Oh, did you lose your mom ? Don't worry, we'll find her. Come," I said, holding out my hand. But he shook his head again, though he still grabbed my hand. "Dad said Mom left, that she's not coming back, but that she's watching over us from where she is." I froze, my eyes widening as I understood what he meant—or rather, what he couldn't say, what he couldn't understand. I pressed my lips together and squeezed his hand, trying to comfort him. To my surprise, he squeezed back and snuggled against my legs the way my son did. I hugged him in return, rubbing his back.

"Your dad is right, *angelo mio*. No matter where she is, a mother always watches over her child," I reassured him. "Really ?" he asked, looking up at me with big, hopeful blue eyes, I brushed his hair from his forehead and nodded with a smile. "Of course. Mothers never abandon their children. I'm a mamma, too. Our duty is to protect our children." My eyes welled up with my own words. To protect my child. But I had failed at the very foundation of my duty as a mother.

What kind of mother was I?

"Really?! You're a mom?!" the little boy exclaimed, his eyes shining with hope. I nodded, though I felt a twinge of unease at his growing excitement. "Would you be my mom, too?" he asked excitedly. I stared at him, mouth slightly open, stunned. I felt whatever was left of my shattered heart break even more—a little boy, barely older than my son, asking me to be his mother when we didn't even know each other's names. "What? Me?" I whispered, perplexed, he nodded eagerly, tightening his grip on my hand.

I tilted my head, biting my lip, emotions and thoughts swirling inside me. I searched for the right words to explain that his request was impossible—when a deep voice made us both jump. "Andrei !" I looked up and instantly recognized the deep voice. My gaze locked onto the handsome Russian whose name escaped me. His brows knitted together as he saw me holding Andrei.

The little boy turned to him and ran toward him, bouncing on his feet, his sobs and tears already forgotten. "Dad ! Dad! " he cried, jumping into the man's arms. He caught him effortlessly, lifting him with ease. I watched his strong arms wrap around the small body, inhaling his son's hair with closed eyes. And my thoughts drifted immediately to my son. He would never have a father who held him like this. Never have a worthy man to look up to as he grew.

I tensed as the little boy jumped down from his father's arms and rushed back toward me, pulling his father along behind him. "Dad, look ! I found a mom !" he exclaimed, grabbing my hand. I stared at him, and he returned my gaze with so much hope that my chest tightened. Slowly, I lifted my eyes to the man before me, feeling uneasy—and whatever breath remained in my lungs vanished when I saw that his pensive gaze was already fixed on me. He took a few more steps in my direction, and I tried to back away, but my legs refused to move, as if my feet were anchored to the floor. He kept moving forward until our bodies were separated only by his son. I lowered my head as a dark fear crept in, preparing myself for the worst. What if he hit me for being near his son ? What if he thought I had planted the idea of a new mother in his child's head ? What if he told Antonio ?

I shuddered, squeezing my eyes shut when he raised his hand. I waited for the hit. I waited for the familiar pain. I waited for a shout—mine or his, I didn't even know. But nothing happened for long seconds. Nothing except a light touch under my chin that made me shiver. He pressed gently, and I lifted my head, my eyes still firmly shut. "Look at me," he murmured against my face, his scent filling my senses—the sea and pine trees, things I hadn't seen or smelled in so long.

I slowly opened my eyes, and my gaze met icy blue ones. When I had seen them for the first time in the reception hall, they had reminded me of icebergs—cold and calculating. But now, as he looked at me with this deep stare, they reminded me of a clear summer sky—warm and soft. "I... I saw him crying. I just wanted to help," I murmured hesitantly, feeling my lips tremble as he closed his eyes and exhaled deeply. His hand left my chin, glided down my arm, and finally grasped my free hand, lifting it between us. His blue eyes studied my hand, and I whimpered when he gently squeezed my wrist. I tried to pull away, but he held firm, sending me a warning look—not one that frightened me as I expected, but still, I stopped resisting.

He pulled up my sleeve, his fingers brushing over the violet bruises, making me tremble. I felt my cheeks burn as I sensed him observing me through his lashes while Andrei clung to me. "Is it your husband who did this to you?" he asked in a low voice, his eyes turning cold again—turning back into icebergs. "He is not my husband," I nearly shouted, my voice laced with hatred, and I froze, startled by my own reaction. I bit my lip, avoiding the Russian's gaze. "How—"

"*Mamma!*" my son's voice suddenly echoed down the hall. I lifted my head, and my blood turned to ice as I saw Antonio standing at the end of the corridor, watching us with a crazed look in his eyes. He let go of Rafael, who had been squirming in his arms, and the boy rushed toward me. I yanked my wrist away from Ivanov and stumbled backward, hitting the wall behind me. My breathing became erratic as my son threw himself into my arms. I picked him up, whimpering at the pain in my back, and he buried his face in my neck, rubbing his nose behind my ear, *I love you*. I hugged him tighter, kissing his hair, gently swaying him.

"Mr. Ivanov, is there a problem ?" Antonio asked in a calm voice that made me want to break down in sobs. This was bad. "I found a mom !" Andrei shouted again, making me grimace. The fear gripping me was so visceral that my limbs started to go numb. "What ? No ! She's my *mamma* !" Rafael protested, leaning toward Andrei. I let out a small cry as I felt him slip from my grip, dragging me forward, but a strong arm wrapped around my waist while another caught Rafael, lifting him higher. I looked up and found myself lost in that summer sky again, warming me, stopping my trembling. I calmed against the heat of the man holding my son and me.

"Selina !" I jumped, the warmth disappeared, the summer sky vanished. Cold seeped back into my limbs as I stepped away from the Russian's hold. "Come here," Antonio ordered, shoving his fists into his pockets. I turned to my son, still perched in Ivanov's arms, unable to look at the man himself. I held out my arms, and Rafael immediately snuggled into them. I tried to step back, but Ivanov's arm remained wrapped around my son. I froze, pleading with him through my eyes to let go. After a few seconds of silence, he finally did. I took a step back, then turned to walk toward Antonio—but Andrei clung to my dress. "No ! Mom ! Don't go !" he cried, sobbing. I closed my eyes, exhaling softly as a tear escaped, falling to the floor along with the little boy's desperate whimpers.

"Andrei, that's enough. Come here," Ivanov said behind me, though he did nothing to pull his son away. "Selina, hurry up. The guests are waiting," Antonio said, taking a few steps toward us. I forced myself not to step back as Rafael clung tighter to me. Finally, Ivanov grabbed his son despite his protests, lifting him into his arms. I walked toward Antonio, and before I could say anything, his hand wrapped harshly around my forearm. "Have a good evening, Mr. Ivanov," he said in that eerily calm tone as he dragged me behind him. I didn't dare look back, despite the burning gaze I could still feel on me. My heels clicked against the marble as I tried to keep up with Antonio's fast pace.

My stomach knotted when I saw that he was heading toward the elevators instead of the reception hall. A sob escaped me when he shoved me inside, and my back slammed against the elevator wall. Rafael started crying loudly against me and I stroked his neck, straightening up with a whimper, *it will be okay.* It had to be okay. For my son. To protect him. The elevator climbed to the top floor. Antonio paced the small space like a caged lion as I trembled like a leaf, trying to soothe my son.

The ding signaling our arrival rang in my ears like a gunshot, making me jump and this time, Antonio grabbed me by the back of the neck, dragging me down the gold-and-silver-decorated hallway. He unlocked a door and shoved me inside, slamming it behind us. We found ourselves in a large suite with multiple rooms. My heart raced, nausea gripped me as I sniffed quietly, trying not to scare Rafael. "Rafael, leave us. Go to a room and lock the door," Antonio ordered, prying him from my arms and setting him down. My little one shook his head frantically, clinging to my legs, "no ! I want to stay with *mamma!*" Antonio watched us with dark eyes, his jaw clenched, hands gripping his hair, ready to explode. I crouched beside Rafael, cupping his face with a small smile despite my blurred vision from the tears, "*Angelo mio,* go inside and wait for me, okay ?" He shook his head again, hugging me, rubbing his nose behind my ear, *I love you.* I sobbed uncontrollably now, tears flowing freely, "me too, *Angelo mio.* I love you too," I whispered, holding him close. "Enough, Rafael ! Now !" Antonio yelled.

I separated myself from my baby, gently pushing him toward one of the rooms. He gave me one last look, his green eyes—so much like mine—shining with tears, before slowly closing the door behind him with a sniffle. And then, everything happened so fast, I let out a cry when Antonio grabbed me by the hair, yanking me to my feet. I bit my lip hard to stop more screams from escaping—to stop my son from hearing, to stop giving the monster the satisfaction. He pressed his nose against my bruised cheek, tightening his grip, making me whimper. His other hand wrapped around my throat, squeezing harder and harder. "Ah, Selina, Selina, Selina… So, you flirt with my enemies ? In dark hallways, behind my back ? Did you dare betray me, *Cara mia* ?" he shouted into my face.

I squeezed my eyes shut, shaking my head despite the pain his grip caused. "I just wanted to help the boy—he was crying. His… his father came after, I swear," I whimpered, trying to justify myself. His hand slapped across my face so violently that I collapsed to the floor. The pain was so intense that the world blurred, and the familiar taste of blood flooded my mouth, worsening my nausea. He yanked me back to my feet. I had lost one of my heels, my dress had slipped, leaving one shoulder bare, and strands of hair stuck to my bloody lips. His fingers clamped around my jaw, squeezing so hard that my teeth sank into my own skin. He slammed his forehead against mine, making me groan, "*Mia dolce*, you want to be another boy's mother, huh?" he spat in my face. I tried to speak, but only pitiful whimpers escaped my trembling lips. I tried to shake my head, but my body was paralyzed, tears flowing freely, mixing with the blood. "He touched you. That Russian bastard touched my wife," he growled against my lips, his grip shifting from my throat to my left hand—the same hand Ivanov had held just moments ago.

"Was it this hand he touched, *Cara mia* ? This hand that belongs to me ?" he asked, tightening his hold on my wrist. "No, no, please," I whispered, and his eyes gleamed with pleasure at my words. He nodded slowly, released my jaw, and grabbed my index and middle fingers. Our eyes locked as a twisted smile stretched across his lips, and before I could say anything else, he twisted my fingers—breaking them. A scream ripped from my throat, but his hand muffled it, cutting off my cries and sobs. The pain made black spots dance before my eyes. I felt myself slipping into unconsciousness, but the agony dragged me back. Antonio finally released me, and I collapsed to the floor. I clutched my wrist with my uninjured hand, cradling it against my chest. I sobbed, I whimpered, I hurt—I hurt so much. "Where else did he touch you, *Cara mia* ? Huh ? Your arm ?" he taunted, stepping toward me again. He was going to break my arm next, my arms, my legs, and then my face. I closed my eyes, praying, thinking of my baby in the room next door. I flinched when two soft knocks sounded against the door, I lifted my eyes as the monster moved toward the entrance. I struggled to my feet, my legs shaking, trying to reach the bathroom. I had to lock myself in. I had to get to safety.

I grabbed the handle, crying so hard that my lack of oxygen made my head spin. I pushed the door open, but before I could step inside, he yanked me back by the hair and threw me to the floor. I cried out, curling my injured hand against me. The sound of heels clicking against the cold marble floor made me lift my head. I met the icy gaze of Alia, standing over me in her designer heels. She sighed and turned to her cousin, who was pacing a few steps away like a caged animal. "Seriously, Antonio, how are we supposed to cover this up now?" she asked in an exasperated voice. I closed my eyes, sobbing at the humiliating words. She talked about me as if I were just a broken doll that needed to be patched up and repainted. How could a woman ignore the suffering of another woman? How was that possible?

"She deserved it! She deserved it! She deserved it!" he repeated over and over, pacing like a madman. "Enough, Antonio! The guests are looking for you. We need to go," Alia said in her soft voice as she walked away. He was going to leave. He was going to leave me alone—at least for a few hours. But my relief was short-lived when I heard him striding toward me. He wrapped his fingers in my hair, lifting my face from the floor to his level. "We'll finish what we started when I return, *Cara mia*. If you want a second child so badly, then you'll have one," he whispered, smiling, his pupils blown wide. He released me roughly, my cheek slamming against the marble and I whimpered. My fingers throbbed so much I could barely breathe, barely think.

The front door slammed shut behind them, and I heard them talking outside. I already knew there was a guard stationed by the door. I pushed myself up, gasping from the pain, biting my lip so hard I forgot it was already split. I whimpered again, leaning against the bed, taking slow breaths to steady myself. I had to get up. I had to immobilize my fingers. I had to clean myself up. I had to see my baby—he must be terrified. But I couldn't. I couldn't move. I couldn't do anything. Eight years was a long time. A very long time.

I rested my head against the mattress, closing my eyes, humming the lullaby I sang to Rafael every night. Tears rolled down my temples, dampening the silk sheets. I rocked myself gently, clutching my injured hand to my chest, praying. Praying for help—any help. Praying for someone to get my son out of here. *Nothing more. Please.*

I woke with a start when someone touched my broken fingers. I screamed, my eyes meeting light green ones, paler than my own. "Sienna?" The young woman—*my little sister*—sniffled, wiping her tears, nodding as she stroked my hair. "It's me, it's me, Selina, I'm here," she whispered, taking my uninjured hand and kissing it repeatedly. "I'm here, *mia sorella* (my sister), I'm here." I frowned, struggling to comprehend what was happening. I tried to determine if this was just a dream, an illusion caused by the pain. "Am I dreaming?" I asked weakly, blinking rapidly. Sienna let out a sob, more tears spilling down her cheeks, "I'm sorry, Selina. I'm so sorry. This is all my fault, everything is my fault." She curled up, resting her head against my lap, her face buried in her hands. I placed my hand on her back, stroking it gently.

I must have been dying. This must have been God's final mercy—letting me see my little sister one last time, letting me smell the bleach scent clinging to her. Bleach ? I lowered my gaze, noticing her uniform—similar to the hotel staff's. I glanced toward the door and gasped when I saw a man lying unconscious in the small hall. "This... this isn't a dream," I whispered, my body freezing. I turned to my sister in shock. "Sienna ! What... how...?" I tried to lift her face, forgetting about my injured hand. Pain surged through me. I groaned, throwing my head back. Sienna jolted upright, eyes wide. She reached for my hand, but I shook my head, pulling it away.

"What are you doing here, Sienna ? How did you get here?" I asked, my eyes darting between her and the entrance, terrified that Antonio could return at any moment. "No time ! We have to leave !" she exclaimed, suddenly standing. "We have to what ?!" I growled, trying to push myself up by leaning on the bed. Sienna grabbed my arm, helping me stand. "Rafael !" I called out, turning toward the room where he had locked himself in. "He's sleeping. I checked on him when I arrived," she reassured me, guiding me toward the bathroom, "we have to leave, Selina, but first, we need to take care of your fingers," she said while rummaging through the drawers, looking for anything that could help.

She cursed under her breath, making me smile despite the situation. It reminded me of our childhood—she had always had the worst temper. She finally placed a roll of bandages and three pens next to the sink, then gently took my wrist, making me whimper. She sniffled, carefully positioning the pens—one on each side of my fingers and one in between. I let out a sob, gripping the cold marble counter for support. My sister reassured me, slowly wrapping the bandage around my fingers and the makeshift splints, immobilizing them. "It's almost done, Selina. Just a little more, hold on a little longer. I'm getting you out of here," she said, taking a deep breath, fighting back her own tears. Once the bandage was secure, she grabbed some cotton pads and started cleaning the blood from my lips and chin, then my makeup. One glance in the mirror was enough to see the damage.

I had had worse. I had felt worse. My lower lip was swollen, my right cheek already darkening into a deep purple, as was my left cheekbone where he had slammed me into the floor. "This will have to do. We don't have time to waste," she said, rushing back into the bedroom. I followed her with unsteady steps. She threw open two sports bags I hadn't noticed before and pulled out a pair of blue jeans, a white blouse, a white cardigan, and sneakers. She laid them on the bed before taking a child-sized pair of pants and a light sweater from the second bag. "I don't know if this will fit him… I— I only saw him once when he was a baby," she muttered as she moved behind me, beginning to loosen the laces of my dress. She helped me slip out of it carefully, mindful of my injured fingers, leaving me in my underwear.

I felt her freeze behind me, her fingers barely brushing over the marks on my back, making me shiver. "What are you doing, Sienna ? He'll never let us leave. Even if we get out of here, he'll find us in no time," I tried to reason, slipping my arms into the blouse she handed me. "And we can't leave, Sienna. You know that. He still has the evidence." She quickly buttoned my blouse, then grabbed the jeans and helped me into them as well. She gently pushed me onto the bed and pulled out a pair of socks tucked inside the sneakers. "Don't worry. I've planned everything. Since the moment I found out this gala was happening, I've been preparing for this."

I whimpered as pain shot through my fingers. Sienna finally finished lacing my shoes, then pulled the hair tie from her wrist and swiftly braided my hair. She grabbed the child's clothes and rushed into Rafael's room. "*Mamma ?*" My angel's weak voice reached me from the other room. I got up and followed them, trying to compose myself. "I'm here, *Angelo mio*, I'm here," I reassured him, stepping toward the couch where he had fallen asleep. He was now only in his undershirt. Sienna tried to help him put on his sweater, but he dodged, bouncing on the seat. His face lit up when he saw me, but his smile quickly faded when he noticed the marks on my face and my bandaged fingers. "*Mamma !*" he exclaimed, jumping from his perch. I winced when he crashed into me, his little hands brushing against my injured fingers. "Does it hurt, *Mamma ?*" "No, not at all, my love. I'm fine," I reassured him, stroking his hair. "Let Aunt Sienna help you get dressed, okay ?"

"Aunt Sienna ?" he asked, looking up at me with wide eyes. "Yes, it's me, *Pulcino mio*," Sienna introduced herself, stepping closer. "Would you let me help you get dressed ? We need to go." "We're leaving ?! Really ?! Without him ?!" he asked, his voice full of hope. I remained silent, unable to find the words. I didn't want to give him false hope. "Of course. Just the three of us," Sienna declared firmly, without hesitation. "But you have to get dressed first, okay ?" Rafael nodded eagerly, then joined my sister, letting her help him change quickly. Sienna then rushed to the entrance, stepping over Antonio's unconscious guard, whom she had somehow managed to knock out.

She cracked the door open, peering outside. I grabbed my son's hand and followed my sister, hesitating. Once she ensured the coast was clear, she opened the door wider and gestured for us to follow. I froze at the sight of a laundry cart filled with linens outside the door. I looked at my sister, confused, but she gestured for me to get in. "This will never work, Sienna…" I started to protest, but she shot me a sharp look. "Shut up and get in, Selina ! The cameras will be back online soon. Hurry !" she urged. I didn't hesitate any longer. I tried to lift Rafael inside, but Sienna grabbed him before I could. I climbed in after him, lying down with my son in my arms. Sienna covered us with several sheets and I heard her close the bedroom door before she started pushing the cart.

I tried to hold back a whimper as pain pulsed through my fingers. I sniffled, burying my nose in my baby's hair. I heard the elevator doors open, and she pushed the cart inside. We started descending. The elevator stopped once, and I tensed when I heard one or more people step in before we continued downward. Rafael snuggled closer to me, and I stifled a scream when he pressed against my injured fingers. I clamped my hand over my mouth, smothering my groans. "Sorry, I hit my elbow," Sienna said calmly from outside. The elevator stopped again before continuing downward. "We're almost there," my sister murmured.

We came to another halt, and this time, Sienna pushed the cart outside and after a few moments, she stopped and lifted the sheets covering us; come on, quickly," she said, bending down to grab Rafael. I climbed out of the cart, glancing around. We were in the hotel's boiler room. "This way. A car is waiting outside," she informed me, heading toward an emergency exit with my son in her arms. I followed them on shaky legs. The pain in my fingers was becoming unbearable. I was sweating, struggling to breathe slowly. Sienna opened the door with her back to let me through. A black car was parked just outside, an unfamiliar man behind the wheel. I froze.

"Sienna…"

But she was already opening the back door, securing Rafael in his seat. She motioned for me to get in, but I hesitated, looking at the driver. "Don't worry, Selina. I trust him," she reassured me, her eyes pleading. I finally climbed in next to my son, still wary as Sienna settled into the front passenger seat, and the car pulled onto the road. I glanced through the rear window, watching as the hotel faded into the distance. The weight on my shoulders began to lift. But the fear was still there—stronger than ever, more visceral than ever. I pushed it down. I held my son close and buried it deep. For him.

Chapter five
Nikolai

Andrei wouldn't stop crying. We had all tried to calm him down—even Elif couldn't do it. He kept asking for the woman from earlier, Selina. I closed my eyes, rubbing my beard. I had let her go. I hadn't wanted to, but I had to. Andrei was my priority. Right now, we didn't even know how long it would take to get our 'ship' back on track. This was not the time to turn the Italians against us, even if it was an idiot like Rasili. I knew I had made the right decision in letting her go. But then why did I feel like this ? A weight I had never experienced before had been crushing my chest ever since I watched them leave. "Come on, Andrei, that's enough," Elif soothed him softly against her chest. "No, I want mom," he sobbed against my sister-in-law's neck. Alexei hadn't left his side, holding his hand tightly.

Grigori placed a firm hand on my shoulder, squeezing lightly. "We should head home," he said. Sacha nodded in agreement, getting up and clapping me gently on the back. I nodded as well and slowly stood, Mikhail got up and handed me my jacket. I thanked him and quickly put it on before helping Dimitri, who was struggling with his own. "Come on, Roman called the cars," Sacha signaled. I reached for Andrei in Elif's arms, but he wriggled free and ran straight to Mikhail, slipping under his arm. My eldest son held him close and walked toward the exit. I sighed and followed them, my thoughts drifting to Selina's little boy, Rafael. The moment I had held him. The way he had clung to me—just like my sons did after a nightmare. I searched for them with my eyes, but I never saw them again after we crossed paths in the hallway. After I let them leave with Antonio.

Speak of the devil—he walked into the hall just as we were leaving, now accompanied by a young woman, but his wife was nowhere to be seen. That weight in my chest turned unbearable. A cold sweat trickled down my back as a strange sense of dread gripped me. What had he done to his wife? A light pressure on my forearm made me glance down, meeting Elif's confused gaze. She nodded and joined Grigori, who was speaking with Rasili and the woman beside him. I followed, stepping behind her discreetly. "I'm glad you enjoyed the evening, Mr. Ivanov. I wish you a safe journey home," Antonio said, shaking my brother's hand. "I would have liked to say goodbye to your wife as well. Where is she?" Elif asked, a polite smile on her lips—one of the most insincere I had ever seen.

Rasili tensed, his eyes flicking to me, dark and hostile. I simply offered him a slow smirk, my hands buried deep in my pockets. His jaw clenched, his body tilting forward as if ready to lunge at me—which, for some reason, I silently prayed for. I wanted him to. I wanted an excuse to rearrange his damn face. But, of course, the woman at his side stepped in. She pressed a perfectly manicured hand to Antonio's chest, pushing him gently back. Then she turned toward Elif, mirroring her smile, which pissed me off even more. I sensed Sacha tense behind me. If I felt protective of Elif, it was nothing compared to what Sacha and Roman felt.

Our mother had died when Roman was just five years old, and Sacha barely ten. They had been too young, Grigori and I had been old enough to handle it, but our younger brothers had been lost, struggling to adapt to life without a mother figure. Then, as if by some miracle, Elif had arrived. She had bulldozed into our lives, tearing down every wall we had built around ourselves. She had reached Sacha and Roman when they had shut down more than ever. When we had all drifted apart, she had pulled us back under the same roof, around the same table. To Grigori, she was the love of his life. To me, she was a sister. But to Sacha and Roman, she was a mother. I didn't even want to imagine what they would do for her.

The woman clinging to Antonio's arm stepped between us. "Selina is taking care of Rafael. The little angel wasn't feeling well, unfortunately," she explained in an irritatingly sweet voice. Then she lifted her brown eyes to mine, her smile stretching wider. She ran her fingers through her long blonde hair, and I barely held back from rolling my eyes. Thank God Elif stepped in front of her, blocking her view, making me smirk. Always playing the shield. "Excuse me, but may I ask who you are… Miss ?" Elif finally said, her voice carrying a sharp edge. Sacha chuckled under his breath. "Oh, forgive my lack of manners. Alia Rasili. I'm Antonio's cousin. A pleasure," she introduced herself, extending her hand. A twisted sense of satisfaction washed over me as I watched Elif glance at Alia's hand with disdain before completely ignoring it and turning to Grigori. "*Askim* (my love), I'm exhausted. Let's go," she murmured, wrapping her arms around him. This time, Sacha's chuckle was anything but discreet. I had to elbow him in the ribs to shut him up. "*Moya lapochka*, let's go right away," Grigori agreed without hesitation, guiding her toward the exit—forgetting even his own sons, who, like lost ducklings, scurried after them.

Sacha simply nodded, picked up Andrei and hoisted him into his arms, then grabbed Alexei's hand before heading outside. I pushed Mikhail to follow them, and he did, leaving me alone with the Rasili family. I took a step forward, a smirk tugging at my lips as I caught sight of the various bodyguards subtly closing in around us. "What happened to your boy, Antonio? I hope he's alright?" I asked, my jaw tightening, searching for any sign—anything at all—that might tell me where Selina and her son were. "He had a stomachache. Nothing—" "I wasn't talking to you," I cut off the girl who was desperately trying to get my attention. "What business is that of yours, Nikolai?" Antonio asked, stepping closer, all pretense of politeness gone.

He wanted to hit me. Every part of his body was screaming for it. And I was just waiting for him to try. My hands slipped out of my pockets, ready to make him swallow his own teeth—but, of course, it wasn't going to happen.

"Mr. Rasili! Mr. Rasili!" A man shouted, running toward us—one of his guards. He bent down, whispering something in Antonio's ear and the moment he heard it, Antonio took off toward the elevators, his cousin following him, though she didn't leave without throwing me a glance over her shoulder. Every fiber of my being screamed at me to follow him. Something was happening. Something to do with that woman, those bruises, and the little boy who had clung to me like I was his last hope. "Nikolai!" Grigori called from the exit, motioning for me to come. "Hurry up, Andrei won't stop crying." I shut my eyes, groaning as I ran a hand down my face. I turned on my heel and headed outside, leaving behind the trembling, mesmerizing woman and the boy who had held onto me.

Selina

My fingers hurt so much that it made me dizzy as the airport slowly came into view. I gently stroked my son's hair as he slept on my lap. My eyes shifted again to my sister, sitting in the passenger seat, constantly making calls and sending messages. She spoke in English, Italian, and what I assumed was Russian while putting away the makeup she had used to cover my bruises. I had asked her several times where we were going and, more importantly, how we were getting there, but she just kept telling me not to worry, that she was taking care of everything. My gaze drifted toward the driver, who hadn't spoken a word in the two hours we had been on the road. He hadn't even looked at us, keeping his eyes firmly on the road. "*Mamma ?*" my son called in a sleepy voice. "Yes, *Angelo mio*, I'm here," I answered, kissing his head as he groaned and shifted, sitting up. "Where are we ?" he asked, leaning between the two front seats. "We're at the airport, *Pulcino mio*," my sister replied, turning in her seat and ruffling Rafael's hair. "The airport ? With real airplanes ?" he exclaimed, more excited than ever. "Of course they're real airplanes," Sienna confirmed with a nod. Watching my son interact so freely, without fear, with someone other than me stirred an emotion I had never felt before. Seeing him talk without hesitation, without looking over his shoulder, made my heart ache in ways I couldn't explain.

He had spent his entire life locked inside four walls, no matter how large they were, with no one but me to keep him company. The fact that he had never gotten to experience what every child should broke me more than anything. No matter how much I had tried to entertain him, to distract him from the horror of our reality, I couldn't shield him from everything. The way he had hidden behind my legs at the gala, unable to meet people's eyes, let alone speak to them, had been one of the hardest things I had ever had to witness. I had never felt so powerless. "Here," Sienna said, handing me two passports. I took them with furrowed brows, and my eyes widened as I opened them. "Nina Lebedeva, Vlad Lebedev," I read aloud. "What is this… Sienna, what's going on?" I demanded. She shrugged, showing me hers, which read "Alina Lebedeva," before slipping it back into her bag. "Did you really think we were going to leave the country with our real names? That bastard would find us in no time. Besides…" she said, digging into her bag again before pulling out two caps and a pair of sunglasses, "…put these on. We need to avoid the cameras."

I shook my head, struggling to process everything that was happening. A few hours ago, I had thought I was going to die, and now, here I was, about to board a plane to… I didn't even know where. "Where are we going, Sienna? At least tell me that." "Somewhere safe for now, before taking a boat to where we'll actually be living," she responded vaguely, still not giving me a specific location. "Sienna," I warned, narrowing my eyes at her. A small smile tugged at her lips as she chuckled softly, "I missed you scolding me like that," she said, still focused on the road. The slight tremor in her voice didn't escape me, making me blink rapidly to hold back tears. She reached out her hand, still not looking at me, and I took it, squeezing it tightly. My son nestled against me, sensing my sadness. "We're almost there," the driver announced in English, speaking for the first time.

I put on the cap my sister had given me, letting a few strands of hair fall over my face. I helped my son put his on, and he smiled up at me, his eyes shining with excitement. The car came to a stop near one of the airport entrances and Sienna stepped out quickly and helped Rafael down. He immediately jumped into her arms without hesitation. I stepped out as well, groaning as I clutched my injured wrist against my chest. My legs trembled, and I leaned against the car, sighing softly as tears escaped despite myself. A tissue appeared in my field of vision, and I glanced up at the driver, who had also stepped out. He still didn't look at me, his gaze fixed on the airport entrance. "*Grazie* (thank you)," I murmured, taking the tissue. I wiped away my tears and winced at the pain from touching my bruises. I quickly straightened up when I saw my baby approaching, skipping excitedly.

"Come on, *mamma*! Let's get on a plane!" he exclaimed, grabbing my hand and tugging me toward the airport. I whimpered at the pain shooting through my shoulder. "Easy, *Pulcino mio*. Let's go," my sister said, picking him up after hugging our driver and handing me a bag she had retrieved from the trunk. I followed them inside, glancing one last time at the driver as he got back into the car. The only things I noticed before my sister called for me to hurry were the scar beneath his left eye and his Asian features. When we reached the check-in line, Sienna handed me two tickets with our fake names. "Sochi," I read with a frown. "Isn't that in Russia?" I asked, looking up in confusion. She nodded, pulling Rafael along as the line moved forward. "Are you sure that—" "shut up," she cut me off. "Be careful what you say," she murmured, giving me a warning look. I scanned my surroundings anxiously, half-expecting Antonio to appear out of nowhere and drag me back by my hair to my gilded cage. My stomach knotted as our turn arrived. We handed over our passports, and after a brief check, we were finally cleared to go. I let out a relieved sigh, squeezing my son's hand.

After half an hour of waiting, we finally boarded. I took a seat by the window, with my son between me and Sienna, who sat by the aisle. My son's warm little hand slid into my ice-cold one, squeezing twice. I tore my gaze away from the window, still expecting to see the monster storming onto the tarmac. My eyes landed on my son, his big green eyes watching me like a fawn. I smiled, kissing the tip of his nose. "Don't worry, *Angelo mio*. It's over. We're free," I whispered, my voice trembling as a tear slipped down my cheek. "Yes, you're free," my sister repeated, wiping my tear away. But the guilt in her eyes made my heart ache even more. I squeezed her hand gently. "We all are," I said meaningfully. She only smiled before looking away, fastening her seatbelt. I closed my eyes, sinking into my seat, trying to forget the pain. Trying to forget the monster still hunting us.

"*Mamma!* Look! It's the sea!" Rafael exclaimed, pressing his face against the window as we flew over an endless stretch of blue. I smiled softly at his excitement, his little hands gripping the armrest. "Yes, I see it, *Angelo mio*. It's beautiful." "Can we go there? I want to touch it, *mamma*, please! Do you think it's like in the cartoons?" he asked, bouncing in his seat. I felt Sienna tense beside me, and the weight of her gaze on us was heavy. "You… you've never seen the sea, *Pulcino mio*?" she asked gently, her voice barely above a whisper. Rafael tore his eyes away from the window to look at her. "No, but now I will, thanks to you, Aunt Sienna!" he beamed before turning back to the view, completely oblivious to the effect of his words. My sister sank into her seat, her fingers gripping the armrests. I heard her breathing change—fast and shallow—and my chest tightened as I watched her stare blankly ahead. "Sienna…" I began, reaching for her hand, but she pulled away abruptly, standing up so quickly it startled me. "I… I need to freshen up. I'll be right back," she muttered, avoiding my gaze before hurrying toward the back of the plane.

I wiped away the tears that escaped despite myself and winced as I moved my injured hand. A glance beneath the bandages made my stomach churn—my fingers were swollen, the red turning to an ominous purple. "Excuse me, ma'am, please fasten your seatbelt. We are beginning our descent," a flight attendant told me with a polite smile. I returned the smile and nodded, watching her walk away. "Alright, *Angelo mio*, time to buckle up. We're about to land," I told Rafael, kissing the top of his head. He nodded enthusiastically, but when I tried to secure his seatbelt, my injured hand made it impossible. Frustration rose in my chest—I couldn't even buckle my own child in. Two hands appeared, fastening his seatbelt swiftly before doing the same for mine. I glanced up to see Sienna settling into her seat, fastening her own belt, her eyes slightly red from crying. "Sienna," I whispered, "this isn't your fault. It never was." She shook her head tightly, lips pressed together, her eyes fixed straight ahead. "It's all my fault. All of it." "No ! You defended yourself ! You—" "enough, Selina. Let's forget about it," she shut me down in a quiet, defeated voice. I said nothing more, just squeezed my son against me.

Once our passports were checked, we headed toward the exit. Rafael was still half-asleep, his little body heavy in Sienna's arms as she hurried toward the main doors. I adjusted my cap, struggling to keep up with her pace. I was so exhausted that my legs barely cooperated. Sienna had promised we'd soon be somewhere safe, that I just had to hold on a little longer. A loud cry suddenly cut through the crowd behind me. I froze. A small figure appeared between the throngs of people, running straight toward me. "Mom ! Mom !" I barely had time to process the words before Andrei Ivanov crashed into my legs, wrapping his little arms around them. I didn't fall—miraculously—but I stood there, utterly frozen. I looked down at the boy, his bright eyes sparkling with excitement, a wide grin stretching across his lips. "I found you, Mom."

"What...?" I stammered, completely lost. "Andrei !" a voice called out, and I recognized the man approaching—an Ivanov, one of the brothers. Andrei turned excitedly toward him. "Uncle Sacha, look ! I found my mom !" I met Sacha's gaze, and his expression shifted from confusion to something more intense as he stepped closer. "You're Antonio Rasili's wife. What are you doing here ?" he asked, gripping Andrei's shoulders as if to pull him away. But the child struggled against his hold. Panic gripped me. He's going to call Antonio. They're going to hand me over. I tried to back away, but he suddenly grabbed my injured wrist, making me cry out in pain. "I asked you a question—what happened to your hand?" My chin trembled as I searched desperately for an escape. I tried to pull away, but his grip was like iron. Then, like a whirlwind, Sienna appeared in my vision. I didn't even have time to warn her before she slammed her fist into his face, then immediately followed with a sharp strike to his throat with her elbow. Caught off guard, he released me, stumbling back with a groan, coughing. Sienna grabbed my good hand and yanked me forward. "Run !" I stumbled after her as we pushed through the crowd. I spotted Rafael waving at us from the back seat of a car, already strapped in. Sienna practically threw me inside, shoving me next to my son before jumping into the passenger seat. "Drive !" she barked at the driver. The car surged forward, tires screeching as we merged into traffic. I looked over my shoulder, heart pounding and there, through the airport doors, I saw them.

Nikolai Ivanov, clutching his son against him, watching us. Two icebergs staring straight into my soul.

Chapter six
Nikolai

"Oh my God, I can't believe I missed that !" Roman laughed, slouching on the couch, while Sacha paced behind him, an ice pack pressed to his jaw. "Sacha got his ass handed to him by a woman half his size !" I groaned, rubbing my face, my head on the verge of exploding between Roman's laughter, Sacha's grumbling, and most of all, Andrei's crying from upstairs, where Elif was trying to console him. "Roman, shut up ! And Sacha, are you sure it was her ?" I asked, standing up, my body tense as a bowstring.

"Don't take me for a fool, *moy brat*," my brother snapped. "It was Antonio Rasili's wife. And that *malen'kaya gadyuka* (little viper) if I get my hands on her…" he growled. I sighed and walked toward the floor-to-ceiling window overlooking the vast garden and the pool below, with the sea stretching beyond. Sochi had been our mother's favorite city, which was why our father had built this massive estate here for us to live in. We had spent a lot of time here, even though we frequently traveled back and forth to the U.S. for business—mainly California, our primary base. From there, we controlled Arizona and New Mexico, handling the western region, while Smirnov and Kuznetsov, two loyal *Bratva* factions, managed our territories in the East, spanning from South Carolina to Louisiana, including Florida. Unfortunately, our northern territories were less extensive, with only Montana and Minnesota under our control—and they were risky, surrounded by Italian vermin.

"She was injured," Sacha suddenly added, silencing Roman's laughter. I felt my blood pressure rise as I turned to face my brother. "Injured ?" I asked. "Yeah, her fingers were broken, I think," he replied, tossing the ice pack onto the marble table Elif had custom-made before sitting down. She was here, in Russia, with her son and she was injured, her fingers broken. My jaw tightened as I massaged the back of my neck, pacing back and forth just as Grigori entered the room, hanging up his phone.

"Ali said Rasili left the party early, disappeared after we left, and his cousin took over hosting the guests," he reported, shoving his hands into his pockets. "Probably off looking for his wife. I hope this doesn't cause problems for us…" "we need to find them," I said without even thinking. My three brothers immediately looked at me, confused by my sudden concern. "You're not listening when I speak, *moy brat*. I say 'no problems,' and you say, 'let's go find Rasili's wife !' " Grigori growled, throwing his hands up. "Now is not the time to piss off the Italians, Nikolaï!"

"Piss off the Italians ? That son of a bitch broke that woman's fingers, Grigori ! And worse, I saw the marks on her arms last night. Elif did too…", "I know," my brother cut me off. "I'm not blind, *moy brat*. But that doesn't mean her husband was the one who hurt her. Maybe she ran away to be with her lover. Maybe her marriage to Rasili was arranged, and she fled. There could be a hundred reasons ! Let's not get involved !" I shook my head, turning away. Do nothing ? Just because I didn't want trouble. And then what ? Look at myself in the mirror and still call myself a man?

" Then don't get involved if you don't want to, *moy brat*. But I'm going to find them," I said, grabbing my jacket from the chair and heading for the door. But Grigori grabbed my arm, stopping me. "Don't do anything stupid, Nikolaï," he growled. I wrenched my arm free, clenching my jaw, and pushed past him, heading for the exit, Sacha and Roman following close behind.

"Are you sure this is the address ?" Roman asked, his head poking between my seat and Sacha's behind the wheel. We all stared at the rundown building, its flickering neon sign barely spelling out motel in Russian. "My sources are reliable. They're here, with the kid," Sacha replied, rubbing his jaw. "They also sent me the fake identities they used to travel." He handed me his phone. I took it and examined the three photos with their corresponding names—Nina Lebedeva. I zoomed in on the picture. She looked much younger, barely in her twenties. "Only one way to find out," I said, opening my door and stepping out, my brothers followed as we made our way down the narrow alley leading to the motel entrance. "Stay outside, Roman. Let me know if you see anything," I ordered.

"No way, *moy brat* ! I'm not missing Sacha getting his ass kicked again," he retorted, but quickly fell silent under the dark looks Sacha and I shot him. Sacha and I stepped inside and headed straight to the front desk. "Good evening, miss. What's the room number for Alina Lebedeva ?" Sacha growled, spitting out the name. The young girl—no older than eighteen—looked up from her phone and froze. Two well-dressed men like us must have been a rare sight around here. "I... I can't give you that information. It's confidential and against—" "Come on, don't waste our time. You're going to give me that number one way or another," Sacha murmured menacingly, leaning over the counter. The girl shrank into her seat, eyes wide. "203. They arrived a few hours ago," she blurted out, pointing toward the staircase at the end of the hall.

"Thanks. Have a good night," I said, striding forward without another glance. I grimaced at the foul stench as we climbed the stairs to the second floor and stopped in front of Room 203, Sacha nodded at me, and I knocked. No answer. I knocked again, harder this time. A few seconds later, the door creaked open, revealing a small boy with green eyes. He looked up at us, his gaze darting between Sacha and me, then widened in recognition. He took a step back, trying to shut the door, but I stopped him. "Rafael, *Angelo mio*, wait..." Selina Rasili appeared behind her son, her face bruised. Our eyes met, hers widening, while mine dropped to her bandaged fingers. Rafael rushed behind his mother, clutching her legs as she stepped backward, her chest rising and falling rapidly.

I stepped inside cautiously, hands raised in a non-threatening gesture, like trying to approach a frightened kitten. "I won't hurt you," I murmured. Selina shook her head, eyes shining with unshed tears. She lifted her uninjured hand in a plea, stopping me in my tracks. "Please... don't tell him. Please," she begged, her voice trembling. A heavy weight crashed onto my chest, stealing my breath. But worse than that, rage coiled deep inside me at the sight of her countless wounds. "No, I won't—" "Selina !" a female voice shouted as a blonde woman burst through the door, panting. Her gaze landed on Selina and the child before shifting to me, then to my brother. "You !" she hissed, her face contorting with recognition. She clenched her fists and swung at Sacha, lightning-fast—but he caught her wrist before the punch landed. "Once, not twice, *malen'kaya gadyuka*, (little viper)" he growled, yanking her toward him and twisting her arm behind her back, pinning her against the wall.

"Sienna !" Selina cried from behind me, and only then did I realize I had instinctively placed myself in front of her in a protective stance. "Sienna ? A pretty name for such a venomous snake," Sacha sneered, tightening his grip as she thrashed. "Let me go so I can show you how a snake really bites !" she spat, kicking at his shins. Sacha let out a pained grunt, then wrapped a hand around her throat, pressing against her artery. "Don't hurt her ! Please, don't hurt my sister !" Selina pleaded, clutching my arm. I looked down at her tear-streaked face and clenched my fists, "don't worry. He won't hurt her—she'll just pass out," I reassured her. Roman appeared in the doorway just as Sienna went limp in Sacha's grip, his phone pressed to his ear. "Grigori says there's an issue with the shipments—" he began, then froze, taking in the scene, "what the hell is going on here ?"

"What's happening ?" I asked, not moving from my place, still gripping Selina's trembling hand. "We need to get back. There's a problem with the deliveries, and I spotted Vassili's men lurking nearby," Roman replied, shoving his phone into his pocket. It wasn't unusual for Vassili's men to be in the area—hir prostitution business reached even the darkest corners of the city. What was unusual was our presence. We needed to leave before we drew too much attention. "Let's go. Pack your things," I told Selina, finally releasing her hand. She hesitated, clutching her son protectively against her, but quickly obeyed when she saw Sacha heft her unconscious sister over his shoulder and head for the exit, muttering curses under his breath. Roman followed behind, snickering as he asked if this was the same woman who had punched Sacha that morning. Selina gathered their few belongings into a small bag, her son trailing her like a lost duckling. Every time she winced from pain, likely from her injured fingers, I had to stop myself from stepping forward to help. Instead, I stood by the door, waiting patiently. She finally joined me, her son still avoiding me. I grabbed the bag from her hand without a word and motioned for them to go ahead. We descended the stairs quickly, making our way back to the car where Sacha and Roman were already waiting.

I stepped into the living room, followed by my brothers—Sacha carrying the still-unconscious woman in his arms, and Roman attempting to engage Rafael in conversation while the boy clung to his mother. Grigori was pacing behind Elif, who was seated on the couch, trying to calm him down. Her eyes widened when she saw us, and she immediately stood up. I was the first to step through the archway into the room, and I was the first my brother saw by the bay windows. "There you are, *moy brat!* Rasili called about—" But he stopped talking the moment the others followed me inside. Sacha placed Sienna on the couch under Elif's stunned gaze, while Roman stood frozen behind Selina and her son. "*Blayd!* Are you fucking kidding me, Nikolaï?!" Grigori roared, storming toward me, but Elif quickly stepped between us, pressing her hands against his chest to hold him back. "Calm down, *askim !*" she said firmly. "Calm down ?! Calm down ?! We're about to start a new war with the Italians after everything we've been through, Elif!"

"What are you talking about ?" I asked, stepping forward. "You'd know what I was talking about if you weren't busy chasing after another man's wife!" my brother snapped, his glare making me grit my teeth. "Rasili called, saying his wife and son were kidnapped, and he asked if we knew anything ! The man is looking for his wife everywhere, like a rabid dog…" "I am not his wife !" The sudden outburst in that soft, trembling voice made all of us turn. Selina stood there, her expression just as shocked as ours, and her face quickly turned crimson. If she hadn't been covered in bruises, with a busted lip and that unmistakable fear in her eyes, I might have found it beautiful. "You said the same thing last night at the gala. What do you mean, you're not his wife ?" Selina didn't respond. She simply lowered her head, clutching her son against her legs.

"It doesn't matter whether you're his wife or not, young lady. You're the mother of his child, and that has been the case for almost ten years ! You have to go back to—" "Grigori, enough !" I growled, my gaze locked onto the mother and son who flinched at my brother's words. She lifted her head and met my eyes. "They're not going back to Italy." Her chin began trembling, and I clenched my fists to stop myself from reaching for her. My brother grabbed my shoulder, pulling me back, his jaw tight. "Come on, Greg, let's get some air, *askim*," Elif said, throwing herself onto her husband's arm and pulling him toward the sliding doors leading to the garden. Grigori tried to resist but quickly gave in when his wife flashed her infamous 'bunny eyes' at him. They disappeared between the freshly trimmed hedges.

"*Mamma ?* Are we going back to the monster's lair?" Rafael whispered in Italian to his mother. Selina immediately crouched beside her son, shaking her head gently and offering a small smile. "No, *Angelo mio*, we are not going back there," she reassured him, caressing his cheeks. I crouched beside them. "Your mother is right, little man. You're not going anywhere. You're safe here." "Here ?" Selina repeated, her eyebrows drawing together. "Yes, here," I answered in English, standing up, forcing her to look up at me. "Absolutely not," she said, shaking her head vigorously. "I don't trust you. Your brother wants to contact Antonio." She stepped back slightly. My jaw tightened at the accusation and I stepped toward her, lifting a hand to grab her arm, but she flinched violently. "No ! Don't hurt *Mamma* !" Rafael shouted in English, suddenly punching my thigh.

Selina tried to restrain him with her free hand, "Rafael, *Angelo mio*, calm down." But the boy refused to stop. I bent down and grabbed his small arms, lifting him to my eye level. The sudden movement surprised him, and he stopped struggling. "Listen to me, boy, because I'll only say this once—I will never hurt your mother, nor will I ever hurt you. Never." I kept my voice firm but soft, locking eyes with him. "Do you understand ?" his green eyes—so much like his mother's—widened, and after a second, he nodded. "Good," I said, setting him down and ruffling his hair, "and I hope you understand as well that you're staying here," I added, looking at Selina, who now seemed utterly lost.

"Absolutely not," another voice echoed—this time from the woman sitting up on the couch, groaning. "Sienna!" Selina exclaimed, rushing toward her sister. Sienna swayed dangerously, and before she could fall, Sacha grabbed her arm to steady her, a concerned look on his face. "Don't touch me, you !" She tried to pull away, but she was too weak. Selina hurried to her bag, which I had left near the entrance, and pulled out a syringe, placing it on the coffee table. "What is that ?" Sacha asked, frowning, "insulin. Sienna is diabetic," Selina answered as she removed the cap from the needle. "Diabetic ?" Sacha repeated, his jaw tightening as he helped the pale and trembling woman sit down. Selina lifted her sister's skirt and injected the insulin into her thigh through her stockings with practiced precision. "It'll be okay, Sienna. I gave you the injection, you'll be fine," she reassured her, rubbing her leg gently. Sienna nodded weakly, offering a small smile before letting her head fall back against the couch, her lips trembling. Sacha remained beside her, his fists clenched, his eyes glued to her.

"What's going on ?" Elif asked, stepping back into the room alone. She quickly moved toward Selina, "is she okay?" "She'll be better in a few minutes," Selina answered as she groaned softly, bumping her injured hand against the couch. "What have you done with your husband, little *kotenok* (kitten)?" Roman asked sarcastically, emphasizing the nickname Grigori always used for Elif. She turned her head sharply toward my younger brother, a dark glint in her eyes. "I buried him in the garden. If you don't want to join him, shut up, *mudak*, (idiot)" she replied with an exaggerated smile.

Roman grimaced and raised both hands in a sign of surrender. "And you, are you okay ?" Elif asked Selina next, gently pushing strands of hair from her face and wincing at the sight of her numerous bruises. Selina looked up at my sister-in-law, her eyes shimmering with emotion, "*Oruspu çoçugu !* (son of bitch)" Elif swore in Turkish, brushing her fingers lightly over Selina's bruised cheek. Selina blinked, her eyes shining with unshed tears, "she needs a doctor for her fingers. Sacha, call one—" "No need. I already found one. He was supposed to meet us at the motel before you kidnapped us," Sienna grumbled, pushing herself up now that she had regained some color.

Sacha pushed her back down firmly but gently, "don't get up," he ordered through gritted teeth. She shrugged off his hand, "*Ne trogay menya, ublyudok!* (Don't touch me, you bastard)" she growled in Russian, her accent slightly off. "You speak Russian," Sacha remarked, surprised—something that rarely happened. Sienna ignored him and stood, grabbing her sister's hand and Rafael's, "let's go." "You're not going anywhere," I stated simply as Sacha and Roman blocked their path. "You're safe here," I repeated, stepping closer, locking eyes with Selina. "Safe ?" Sienna scoffed. "Don't take me for a fool. I know exactly who you are—Ivanov." She scanned each of us, "Grigori Ivanov, the eldest, head of the Russian mafia. Nikolaï Ivanov, his right-hand man." She turned to me with disdain. "Sacha Ivanov, the devil's lawyer. And the youngest, Roman Ivanov, the family's mad dog" her words made Sacha groan and Roman chuckle. "And let's not forget the mastermind behind keeping this family standing for years—Elif Ivanov," she added, glancing at my sister-in-law.

"I like her," Elif said with a smirk. "You're well-informed," Sacha murmured darkly, stepping closer. To her credit, Sienna didn't back down. "I prefer to know my enemies," she retorted. Their stare-down lasted a moment before I put an end to it, noting Selina's pale face and how she clutched her injured hand. "Enough. Roman, get a doctor. Elif, have something prepared for them to eat," I said, removing my jacket. Sienna looked ready to argue, but I raised a hand, silencing her. "Antonio Rasili called my brother. He suspects you're here, probably because of our exchange last night," I said, glancing at Selina, "you won't be safe in that motel. And your sister needs help urgently. So stop being selfish and think about her." Sienna stiffened, her glare faltering. "Don't talk to her like that ! She's only doing what she thinks is right—she didn't save me out of selfishness !" Selina defended her, glaring at me as she squeezed her sister's hand. I met her gaze, intrigued by this newfound fierceness. "I'll show you to your rooms. Follow-me." I turned toward the white marble staircase leading to the upper floors.

Chapter seven
<u>Selina</u>

Rafael giggled under the towel as Sienna dried his hair, and I couldn't help but smile as I watched them. Seeing my son open up to someone other than me brought a sense of relief. Maybe, after all these years, I had somehow managed to shield him from the darkness of our prison. I winced at the pain in my hand as I finished tying my now-dry hair into a somewhat neat braid. We had all showered, washing away the grime of our journey, and were now in the guest room that Nikolaï Ivanov had assigned to me and my son. Sienna's room was right next door. The rooms were similar—each with a double bed, two nightstands, a large built-in wardrobe concealed by tall sliding mirrors, and an ensuite bathroom. The color scheme of white, grey, and gold was refreshing. A soft knock at the door startled me, and when I turned, I saw Elif's smiling face peeking through the opening. "May I come in?" I nodded, returning her smile, ignoring the wary expression on my sister's face as she pulled Rafael's sweater over his head, her eyes locked on our host. Elif, however, simply nodded approvingly after scanning us from head to toe.

"I'm glad the clothes fit you," she said as she picked up a pair of children's socks from the floor and handed them to Sienna. My sister took them in silence before kneeling to put them on Rafael. To my surprise, Elif looked more amused than offended by Sienna's coldness. "Thank you for the clothes. That was very kind of you," I said, running my hand over the soft white cotton of my wide-legged pants and matching oversized sweater. I shot a pointed look at my sister, who sighed, glanced at her green tracksuit, and muttered through clenched teeth, "thanks." "Yeah! Thank you!" my son suddenly exclaimed, bouncing on the bed. "You're welcome, *kuzum* (sweetheart). I think you're about the same age as my youngest son, Dimitri. These were his clothes. Do you remember him? You met him at the gala. Maybe you two could play together," Elif suggested with a smile. Rafael hesitated, his wide eyes immediately searching mine—not for permission, but for reassurance. He wasn't asking if he could play; he wanted to know if it was safe. The fear in his gaze gripped my heart so tightly I could barely breathe. Without another word, he jumped off the bed and ran to me. I barely managed to lift my injured hand in time before he threw himself onto my lap, curling against me.

I gently rubbed his neck, silently telling him it was okay. He tilted his face up at me, his little lips forming an adorable pout, and I smiled, running my fingers through his hair. Another knock interrupted us, but this time, the person waited for permission before entering. Elif opened the door to reveal Nikolaï. My eyes instinctively followed his tall, broad-shouldered frame as he stepped into the room, his presence nearly filling the doorway. Our gazes locked instantly, and I froze. Every time I met his icy blue eyes, I felt trapped—bewitched. No one had ever looked at me the way he did.

When I saw him at our motel door, I nearly had a heart attack. I was convinced Antonio had found us, that he had sent the Russians to drag us back to him. But as Nikolaï approached, slowly, his expression as reassuring as his sharp features allowed, I knew my fears were misplaced. Still, that didn't mean I trusted him. I didn't think I would ever trust a man again. But in that moment, I had no choice but to follow him when his brother took my sister away without a word. "The doctor is here, and dinner is ready," he said, and as always, his deep voice seeped into my bones. I tore my eyes away, unable to bear his gaze any longer. Grabbing the brush, I focused on fixing Rafael's hair. "Very well, let's—" Elif started but suddenly stopped. A shadow loomed over me, and I looked up slowly, meeting that piercing blue once more. Nikolaï held out his hand, "come, let's take care of your fingers." I glanced down at his outstretched palm—so large, marked by faint scars.

"*Mamma*?" Rafael called softly when I stopped brushing his hair. I placed the brush aside and stroked his neck to reassure him. Then, I stood, carefully avoiding Nikolaï's offered hand, stepping around him as I left the room. Because no matter what my body or my heart might whisper in moments of weakness, I would never let a man get close to me again. I would live for my son. And only for him.

Nikolaï

My gaze followed Selina and Rafael as they disappeared into the hallway, Sienna trailing behind with a scowl she made sure to throw in my direction. Elif patted my back, smiling at me. I wrapped an arm around her shoulders, brushing a kiss against her temple. "Stop giving me that worried look. I'm not that reckless sixteen-year-old anymore." She shook her head, grimacing, "some days, it feels like yesterday. Other times, like a lifetime ago. But

I will never stop worrying about you, your brothers, your sons… and mine. Those little devils. It's a miracle I don't have gray hair yet." I chuckled, pulling her closer against my side, "even with gray hair and wrinkles, you'll be beautiful." I led her toward the staircase as she sighed, shaking her head. "Don't worry about Grigori, Niko. I'll handle him." She cast a glance toward Selina as we entered the living room, her voice dropping in amusement, "you, on the other hand, should focus on her." Selina sat stiffly on the couch, her wary gaze locked on the doctor as he set up his instruments on the coffee table. Sacha and Roman entered from the garden but hesitated to step further when they noticed how tense Selina became at their presence. "Let's begin, shall we ?" said Doctor Semionov in Russian as he sanitized his hands. He leaned toward Selina, reaching for her face but she made a strangled noise, shrinking away.

Before I even realized it, I was by her side. One hand on the doctor's shoulder, I straightened him up, "gently, doctor. Limit physical contact as much as possible." my voice was low, firm. His eyes flicked to Selina, now trembling, her gaze glued to the floor. I clenched my jaw and stepped back, shoving my hands into my pockets. Understanding the unspoken request, Semionov knelt in front of her instead, focusing on her injured hand rather than her face. He carefully examined her swollen, purplish fingers, frowning. Selina whimpered in pain, silent tears slipping down her cheeks. Behind the couch, Elif's worried gaze darted between her and Rafael. "Rafael ? Would you like to see the children's playroom? I bet you'd love it." Rafael shook his head, struggling against my sister's gentle hold. "Rafael, *Pulcino mio*, how about we go together ?" Sienna suggested, standing up. "No ! I want to stay with *Mamma* ! I have to protect her

!" Selina pressed her lips together, her eyes shining with emotion as she looked at her son. I crouched to his level, stilling him. "Let's make a deal, *moy mal'chik* (my boy)" From my pocket, I pulled out my steel lighter, engraved with my name and a bear. I placed it in Rafael's small palm.

"This lighter is very precious to me, just like your mother is to you. I'm entrusting my treasure to you. In return, I will protect yours. What do you say ?" He studied the engraving, then looked up at me, "you'll protect my *mamma* ? The monster won't hurt her anymore ?" I grabbed his right forearm and gently positioned his fingers more or less around mine. "On my honor and my blood, I swear that no one will ever lay a hand on your mother again, Rafael," I vowed, making the *Bratva's* oath—without the cut on our palms meant to seal it in blood. For a few long seconds, he studied me with those scrutinizing green eyes, as if measuring the weight of my words. Then, slowly, he nodded, making the corner of my lips curl in satisfaction. "Good. Now go with your aunt. I won't take my eyes off your mother, don't worry," I assured him. He nodded again, clutching my lighter in his small hand before following his aunt. Elif led the way, and just before stepping out, he turned back, throwing his arms around his mother in a brief embrace.

I straightened up, and as I did, my gaze met my brothers'. They stared at me, surprised—perhaps even shocked—but it wasn't surprising. That lighter was one of the few possessions of my father that I truly valued. The fact that I had entrusted it to a child—one I had just met—was bound to throw them off. But when my eyes found Selina's, I knew without a doubt that it had been worth it. And fuck, everything else faded away. She was looking at me in a way that ignited something deep inside me—something primal, something fierce. It made me want to burn down the entire world if it meant keeping her safe. I wanted to shield her like I did my own sons. I wanted to pull her against me so she'd know—so she'd feel—that nothing, nothing could touch her anymore.

That she was safe.

With me.

I walked Semionov to the door after he finished. He handed me a tube of cream and pulled on his jacket. "Apply this to the bruises on her face. I'll come back in three weeks to check on the condition of her fingers. No water on the cast," he reminded me before stepping outside. I closed the door and rubbed my face, clenching my jaw at the sound of sobs coming from the living room. Her cries, her tears as the doctor treated her—I was ready to go to Rome and rip Rasili's damn head off. "*Moy brat ?*" Sasha's voice echoed behind me, and I turned to see both him and Roman watching me intently. "What ?" I asked, trying to step into the living room, but they didn't move. "What ?" I repeated, glaring at them. Roman glanced at Sasha, who hadn't taken his lynx-like eyes off me. "This is the first time I've seen you like this. What's going on ?" he asked, and all I wanted to do was slam my fist into his stone-cold face. "What the hell are you talking about, *moy brat ?*" I grit out. His eyes scanned mine, then flicked to my clenched jaw, my fists, before returning to my face. "You want to hit me, Niko ?" he asked, raising a brow. Roman stiffened beside us, ready to either break us apart or throw a punch himself—it was hard to tell with him sometimes. I shoved past them, but Sasha grabbed my shoulder. "These women need help, Niko, we agree on that. But Grigori is right too, *moy brat*. We can't afford to get involved in another war with the Italians, not when Minnesota is weakened after Yelsky's death. We could hide them, send them to Florida…" I shook off his grip and slammed him against the wall, my forearm pressing into his throat. "Nikolai," Roman growled from behind me. "They're not going anywhere, Sasha. As long as I haven't seen that woman's fingers heal, she stays here. And if you dare go behind my back and try to send them away, I swear, I'll beat the shit out of you, *moy brat*," I said, my nose nearly touching his.

"Well, well, the last time I had to separate you two was a long time ago. I think I even took a hit," Elif said, stepping toward us. She placed a hand on my arm, giving me the same look she always used when I was younger. I finally released my brother, who didn't move, still scrutinizing me. I pushed past him and entered the living room. Now calmer, thanks to the painkillers, Selina lifted her head from her sister's shoulder and looked at me with red-rimmed eyes. Her small nose sniffled softly, making me smirk. "Let's eat," I said, nodding toward the dining table. "Yes, let's! Before it gets cold," my sister-in-law chimed in, linking arms with my brothers. "Sena! Velma! You can serve the dishes, girls ! Roman, could you go get the kids ?"

My brother kissed her cheek and disappeared down the hallway to fetch our nephews, my sons, and Rafael. I placed the cream in a drawer and pulled out a chair for Selina. She sat without looking at me, I went to take the seat beside her, but Sienna slid into it with a wide grin. "What a gentleman, thank you," she said before turning her attention elsewhere, Elif burst into laughter as she took a seat. I groaned and sat opposite Selina, next to Sasha, who was directly across from Sienna. Sena and Velma entered the room carrying various dishes. "Selina, Sienna, this is Sena and Velma. They've been with us for years," I introduced. "Welcome to the Ivanov household, ladies," Velma said warmly. She was in her sixties and had been hired by my mother. Sena, who was twenty-four and had been hired by Elif a few years ago, simply nodded shyly. "Thank you," Selina replied.

The front door slammed, making both sisters jump, and Grigori strode into the room, only to freeze at the sight before him. "They're still here ?" he asked, his eyes darting between the two sisters. "Grigori, please," Elif pleaded, moving toward him. "No, Elif. I understand they need help, but that help cannot come from us." "We don't need your pity ! We can handle ourselves— just let us go !" Sienna exclaimed, standing from her chair. "Sienna, no," Selina begged, gripping her sister's arm. "No ! We're not abandoned puppies that need saving ! If they hadn't kidnapped us, we'd already be far from here…" "enough. Shut up and sit down," Sasha ordered, his cold gaze locked onto her. "Or what? You'll knock me out again?" she fired back. Sasha pushed to his feet, but before he could act, several voices sounded from the hallway.

"No, Ivan ! Give it back !" Roman yelled as Ivan burst into the room, clutching Roman's phone. My brother followed close behind, with Dimitri clinging to his back like a monkey. Ivan hid behind his father's legs, taunting Roman. Roman yanked Dimitri off his back, holding him up so their faces were level, "what did I say about sneak attacks? They're the best—but not on family.", he set Dimitri down and strode toward Ivan, extending his hand. Ivan pouted but eventually handed the phone back, though not without sticking out his tongue. Roman mimicked the gesture but then froze as he registered the tension in the room. "Well, seems like we're all in great spirits," he joked, "shut up, Roman," Grigori and I said in unison. My twins entered the room, followed by Mikhail and Rafael, who held a sheet of paper. The moment his eyes found his mother, he beamed and ran to her side. "*Mamma* ! Look ! I did a coloring page with math problems. Mikhail showed me how, and Andrei lent me his crayons." "It's beautiful, *Angelo mio*," Selina murmured, kissing his forehead.

"Mom ?" Andrei's voice suddenly rang out from behind Rafael, "did you find me? Because moms never abandon their children?" I clenched my jaw at the hope in his voice and prepared to intervene, but Selina gently took his hand, pulling him closer. "That's true—moms never abandon their children. But I can't be your mama, Andrei. I have to leave." "But why ?! I need a mom! Everyone has one!" my son exclaimed. Selina smiled gently and kissed his cheek. "How about a trade?" she suggested. "A trade ? What kind ?" he asked excitedly. "You can call me Mama if, in return, you promise to eat all your meals. You're much thinner than your twin. Don't you want to grow big and strong like your big brother?" "Really?! I can call you Mama?!" Andrei shouted with joy, throwing himself into her arms. "The table is set for the children in the kitchen," Sena announced as Ivan and Dimitri rushed past her. "I'll eat everything! You'll see, Mama!" Andrei called before joining his cousins. "Are you coming ? Let's eat ?" Mikhail asked Rafael, motioning for him to follow. Rafael glanced at his mother with wide eyes, and Selina simply stroked his neck reassuringly. He grinned before following my son. She watched him go, lips pressed together, clearly hesitating to follow, but ultimately stayed seated. "This is a bad idea. He'll be even more miserable when you leave," Sasha said, unfolding a napkin onto his lap without looking at her. "Maybe. But at least he'll eat—even if only for two days. Something that doesn't seem to matter to you, considering how thin he is," Selina retorted coldly.

A heavy silence settled. My brothers and Elif all looked at me as Selina stiffened before turning toward me, hesitant. "I'm sorry, I didn't mea—" "No, you're right. Lately, Andrei and I have struggled. He won't even let me near him. Maybe you could help, at least while you're here. Until your fingers heal." "What ?!" both sisters exclaimed at the same time, making Roman chuckle. But my focus remained on Grigori, whose dark gaze was locked onto me. "What are you saying, Niko ? These women cannot stay here !" "We have no intention of staying anyway, so don't worry about it !" Sienna shot back, making Sasha growl. "They will stay until I see Selina's fingers healed—" "Nikolai !" my brother cut me off, slamming his fist onto the table, making Selina jump and whimper in pain. I clenched my fists, ready to argue with him, when suddenly, Elif stood up, pointing one finger at me and the other at my brother, her expression downright dangerous. "You two ! Don't even think about fighting under this roof—especially not at this table! Otherwise, you'll both sleep outside, and this time I won't even give you a sleeping bag. I'm hungry, and I want to eat before the food gets cold. So either shut up or take your fight somewhere else!" She sat back down, flipping her hair over her shoulder before signaling to Velma and Sena, who immediately began serving the food.

Grigori shot me one last deadly glare before pulling his chair closer to his wife, speaking to her in a hushed tone—probably trying to calm her down so he wouldn't end up sleeping on the couch. "Could you serve her more, please?" Selina suddenly asked, just as the women finished serving Sienna. "No, it's fine. This is enough, thank you," Sienna replied, sending her sister a pointed look. "You need to eat more, and you know it. Otherwise, you're going to collapse again," Selina insisted. "I've survived on much less, believe me," Sienna muttered. "What do you mean, 'much less'?" Sienna was about to snap back when Sasha suddenly stood up, grabbed the serving dish from Sena's hands, and piled a generous portion onto Sienna's plate. She stared at him in pure shock. "Are you completely insane?! There's no way I can eat all of that!" "You can, and you will, *malen'kaya gadyuka*, or I'll make you," he said as he set the plate down in front of her. "Try it, and I'll make sure you get a second bruise to match the first!" she retorted, her glare burning into his. "And stop this act of kindness. Don't you dare pity me!"

"I wouldn't be proud either if I had strangled a sick woman," Roman said, chewing on his meat. "Shut up, Roman!" Grigori, Sasha, and I all snapped at the same time. "Sienna, please," Selina murmured, squeezing her sister's hand, her eyes pleading. Sienna pressed her lips into a thin line, hesitated, then finally gave in, grabbing her fork. Sasha nodded in satisfaction and sat back down. Sienna, however, stabbed her fork violently into her steak, slicing into it with a little too much force, her eyes never leaving Sasha's. And when I saw my brother lips twitch, I knew. This cohabitation—because there was no doubt that it was happening, no matter who said otherwise—was going to be very entertaining.

Chapter eight
<u>Selina</u>

"Thank you, my dear Selina, you have such a gentle touch !" Mrs. Rossi said, patting my cheek softly with her wrinkled yet delicate hand. "You're very welcome, Mrs. Rossi. If only all my patients were as calm as you when they saw a needle," I replied with a smile, securing the bandage before putting away my supplies. "Come now, child, you're only at the beginning of your journey. How long have you been a nurse? Six months? Seven?" she asked, raising her eyebrows. "Four," I answered in a small voice, pressing my lips together. "Well, my dear, you have a long road ahead. But you'll manage just fine—you are young, and I can always recognize a strong woman when I see one." "Oh, if you only knew," I chuckled, picking up the tray. "I cry at the smallest things—movies, kittens, babies…" "We women have big hearts, my dear. God gave them to us to bring light into this dark world with our emotions, but also so we could fight the monsters that live in it." She smiled at me and laughed when she saw my eyes glistening. I wished her a good evening and stepped out, closing the door behind me. The hospital corridors were quiet as I made my way toward the break room, hoping to catch a few hours of sleep.

But that was before my phone went off, signaling an emergency. "Damn it," I muttered, placing my tray on a cart before hurrying toward the emergency department. I frowned at the sight of numerous men in black suits, their eyes scanning the room with dark, wary expressions. "Selina !" Luca called, sticking his head out from behind a curtain. I rushed to his side under the suspicious gazes of the new arrivals. As I reached him, I saw an unconscious man lying on a stretcher.

"I'll handle this one—he's hemorrhaging. Go check the next bay; it's just some stitches," my supervisor instructed, and I quickly moved to the indicated area. "It's fine, Alia, stop crying. I'm okay, it's just a cut," the man sitting on the bed reassured the young woman beside him, squeezing her hand. He lifted his head as I entered, and our eyes met. Blood trickled from a wound on his cheek where a deep gash had opened. He froze when he saw me, his intense gaze locking onto mine in a way that made me uncomfortable. I quickly turned away, disinfecting my hands.

"Good evening, I'm Selina. I'll be taking care of your wound, Mr....?" "Rasili," he said, smiling as he extended his hand. I hesitated for a moment before finally shaking it, but all I felt was coldness.

I woke up with a start, groaning at the pain shooting up my arm. I looked down at my son, still fast asleep against my side. Leaning down, I kissed his forehead before pulling back the covers and slipping out of bed. A shiver ran down my spine as I felt the cool air against my damp skin—I was soaked in sweat. I made my way to the bathroom, grabbing my painkillers before returning to the bedroom to take them with a glass of water. I groaned again when I saw the empty bottle.

Cazzo.

I sighed, slipping on a thin cardigan over my tank top before heading for the door. I cracked it open and peeked into the dimly lit hallway, the soft glow from the floor-level LED lights casting long shadows. I closed the door quietly behind me and started down the white staircase leading to the ground floor, holding the box of pills close to my chest. The cold marble under my bare feet made me shudder. I moved as silently as possible, my eyes darting around the dimly lit space. In the kitchen, I set the medication on the counter, opened the fridge, and grabbed a bottle of water. I retrieved a glass from the dishwasher and quickly swallowed two pills, bracing myself against the counter with my free hand as I squeezed my eyes shut.

It's okay. It's okay.

I gripped the countertop harder, trying to ignore the pain. Then, I felt it. The hairs on the back of my neck stood on end. I was being watched. It was a skill I had been forced to learn over the last eight years—when I had been prey to a monster. I straightened and slowly turned toward the second doorway leading to the living room, my body locking in place when I saw Nikolai Ivanov standing there. He was still dressed in his black shirt, the sleeves rolled up to reveal his muscular forearms, and his tailored dress pants. His eyes traveled up the length of my bare legs, pausing on my cast, before finally meeting my gaze.

"You felt me watching you," he said, crossing his arms and leaning his shoulder against the doorway. I said nothing, staring instead at his feet clad in black slippers "Elif doesn't like us walking around in our shoes. Once, she hit Roman with a wooden spoon—right on the knee. Very strategic spot." I laughed at the image of Elif chasing Roman through the house, brandishing a wooden spoon. "You have a dimple on your right cheek," Nikolai said suddenly, his deep voice startling me. I lifted my gaze and met his. He straightened and began walking toward me, his movements slow and deliberate. I stepped back without even realizing it, but I didn't get far—trapped against the counter. He stopped in front of me, his towering frame looming over mine, the scent of his cologne—fresh, warm, with a hint of something sharp—filling my lungs.

He raised a hand toward my face, and instinctively, I flinched, closing my eyes and tensing. His fingers brushed against my chin, tracing the line of my jaw, tucking my hair behind my ear. His breath fanned across my forehead, making me shudder as I finally forced myself to look up, meeting his gaze. His fingers traced the bruise on my cheek, then ghosted over the cut on my lip. His eyes lingered there before returning to mine.

"How long ?" he asked, still gently caressing my cheek with his knuckles. My lips trembled as his question forced memories to the surface—memories dark and painful.

I shook my head and tried to pull away, but his hand moved quickly, sliding around the back of my neck, holding me in place. His thumb stroked the side of my throat. "No. Answer me, *Solnyshko* (Sunshine)." I lifted my damp eyes, trying to steady my breath, "eight." I whispered the word, my voice trembling. He took a deep breath, leaning in closer until our noses almost touched. We held each other's gaze for several long seconds before he tilted his head and brushed his lips against my bruised cheek. I closed my eyes, inhaling shakily as my throat tightened. It was such a soft, tender gesture. One I had never received before. He pulled back just enough to reach into a nearby drawer, retrieving a small tube.

"For the bruises on your face," he said, showing it to me. I lifted a hand to take it, but he pulled it away. "Let me."
"I can do it myself," I argued, trying again, but he shook his head and stepped back. "I know you can, and you did Selina. But you don't have to, not anymore." He moved forward again, caging me in against the counter with his hands resting on either side of me. "You're not alone anymore, Selina. You don't have to fight alone." His eyes held mine, steady and certain. And for the first time in a long time, I wanted to believe in something, in him.

Nikolai

Selina looks at me for a few more seconds with those stunning green eyes, hesitant, before finally lowering her hand, abandoning her attempt to take the tube. I nod in satisfaction, uncap the cream, and squeeze a small amount onto the tip of my index finger. "Don't move," I say, as she instinctively pulls her head back the closer my hand gets. She presses her lips together and closes her eyes, staying still. She flinches when the cool cream touches her skin as I apply it to the bruise on her cheekbone. My jaw tightens at the sight of the numerous marks on her face—and on her legs, particularly her calves. Pale scars stand out against her sun-kissed skin. I move to the cut on her cheek, which is already turning a deep purple. She lets out a soft whimper, making me wince. *Blyat'.*

Finally, I reach her lips. Her eyes snap open, and fuck, this is worse than every bullet I've ever taken. I finish applying the balm to her wound, her breath escaping from her slightly parted lips, brushing against my fingers.

"There," I murmur, stepping back to put the tube away and wash my hands. "Thank you," she exhales behind me. I hear her footsteps retreat, but then they stop. I sense her hesitation—and, unfortunately, her fear—before she finally speaks. "For how long ?" she asks softly. "For how long will I not have to fight alone?" My fingers tighten against the marble countertop, my eyes staring blankly ahead. I don't answer. Not when the shadow of the Italians looms over my family. But then I hear it—a quiet sniffle. And retreating footsteps. Before I even realize what I'm doing, I move.

I grab her uninjured arm and turn her around, her body colliding softly against mine, a small gasp escaping her lips. Her tear-streaked cheeks, trembling lips, those watery green eyes—*fuck*. "I'm sorry," she whispers. "I know our presence puts your family in danger. I shouldn't have asked that. I—" she stops when my thumb presses against her lips. "What have you done to me, woman ?" I murmur, frowning, strangely breathless. "You can't even begin to imagine the things I'm willing to do for you and your son." She shakes her head, gripping my arm tightly, fear in her eyes. I shut my eyes, inhaling deeply, then finally release her and take a step back, shoving my clenched fists into my pockets. "Go to bed, *Solnyshko*. To your son."

And I turn away.

There's a brief silence before I hear her hurried footsteps retreating down the hall. I plant my hands on the kitchen island, bending over slightly, trying to steady myself, trying to clear my thoughts—thoughts that have never been this fucking chaotic in thirty-two years. But nothing can erase the image of that green-eyed woman looking at me like I was her last hope.

Chapter nine
<u>Selina</u>

Laughter—no, giggles—suddenly erupted around me, tugging me out of sleep little by little. I tried to regain my senses, but a weight pressed against me, keeping me down. More giggles followed. I frowned, slowly opening my eyes, only to be met with a pair of wide, bright blue ones staring back at me. "Good morning, Mom !" Andrei beamed, perched on my lap. "Good morning, *Mamma!*" Rafael echoed, his head resting on my outstretched arm. I stared at them both, speechless, as Sasha's words echoed in my mind: *This is a bad idea. He'll be even more miserable when you leave.* And he was right. The pure joy in Andrei's eyes was a cruel reminder of how much worse the heartbreak would be when the time came. I sighed, offering them a soft smile. "*Buongiorno, angeli miei,*" I said, adjusting against the headboard. "So, what's so funny ?" I asked, giving them a suspicious look.

The two exchanged glances before proudly holding up markers. "What..." My voice trailed off as I turned toward the mirrored wardrobe doors—only to be met with my own reflection, my face covered in what appeared to be tiny hearts... or at least their attempt at drawing them. My mouth fell open in shock—then amusement—as I slowly turned back to them. "You little rascals... Just wait until I catch you ! I'm going to draw such ridiculous mustaches on your faces that you'll be begging me to stop !" I warned, throwing off the covers. They burst into laughter and bolted off the bed. I chased after them, but just as they reached the door, it swung open, revealing my sister and Elif. "You should've warned us there was an art session happening in here," Elif teased, barely holding back her laughter—unlike my sister. "Selina ! Oh my God, your face !" Sienna burst out laughing, throwing her head back.

"What's so funny ?" a deep voice suddenly interjected. Sasha appeared behind my sister, his eyes immediately locking onto hers. Nikolai followed right behind, dressed in a crisp white shirt, his hands buried in the pockets of his dark pants. His presence filled the room like a protective shadow—not ominous, but rather shielding, watchful. His gaze met mine, his brows furrowing slightly as he took in my appearance. And then… his lips stretched into a smirk. The same lips that had brushed against my face last night. His words echoed in my mind: *You're not alone anymore, Selina. You don't have to fight alone.* Maybe, for now, that was true. For however long I remained here. But after that, I'd have to survive on my own again. Perhaps I should let myself believe him. Just for now. Just until I had to fight again.

"Rafael, Andrei, breakfast is ready. Go wash your faces," Elif instructed, gesturing for them to follow. They obeyed without hesitation, and an unfamiliar warmth bloomed in my chest as I watched Rafael leave without his usual, hesitant glance toward me for permission."You should head downstairs too, if you want to eat before Ivan and Dimitri make everything disappear," Sasha said, walking toward my sister. Sienna leaned against the doorframe, arms crossed, her head held high, "don't worry about me, *Hardman*. I'll manage just fine with what I have." Sasha raised an eyebrow, tilting his head slightly. "*Hardman?*"

"What? You're a crooked lawyer, aren't you ? So is he," she quipped, flipping her hair over her shoulder as she brushed past him. Sasha's jaw tensed as he stared at the spot where she'd stood before following after her, muttering something I didn't catch. But my attention was quickly stolen when Nikolai stepped toward me, his towering frame making me tilt my head back slightly to meet his gaze. "If you'd asked for paper, I would've gladly given you some," he remarked, amusement glinting in his eyes. "If I'd been awake at the time, I would have," I replied with a grimace.

I tensed as he closed the distance between us, forcing me to lift my chin to keep looking at him. His hand lifted slowly, and I watched it with wary eyes—but I didn't move away like I had last night. He gently rubbed his thumb across my forehead before pulling back with a smirk. I couldn't stop my eyes from flicking to his lips as that same unfamiliar heat rose inside me, my palms turning clammy. He held up his thumb, now smudged with black marker. "You're lucky they didn't use permanent ones. A little water and you'll be good as new." I simply nodded, mumbling a quiet thank you before stepping past him toward the bathroom. "Be careful not to get your cast wet," he reminded me before quietly shutting the door behind him—leaving me alone and… lost, again.

Nikolai

I walked into the main hall, unable to shake off my amused expression—or, worse, the visceral urge rising inside me.

The urge to kiss her.

My thumb, tucked into my pocket, still burned with the memory of Selina's soft skin. I clenched my jaw as desire coiled tightly in my chest. I entered the dining room just as Rafael nearly collided with me, his head lowered. I caught him before he could stumble back, "watch where you're going, boy." His wide, startled eyes lifted to mine, a flicker of fear still lingering in them, "sorry... I didn't see you," he murmured. "I was looking for *Mamma* to help me with my shirt." "It's fine, don't worry. What's wrong with your shirt?" I crouched to his level. "I have one button left all alone, and all the others are messed up," he explained, tugging at the fabric. Sure enough, he'd buttoned it all wrong, leaving the last button dangling awkwardly. "Let me see" I unbuttoned and redid the shirt while he stood perfectly still. As I neared the last button, I noticed a small mark just above his navel—a birthmark.

"*Mamma* says it's a trace of love," Rafael said, pressing his fingers to it. "She gave it to me when I was born." A trace of love. I finished buttoning his shirt, grabbed the black sweater he held, and helped him slip it over his head. "There. Not so hard, see?" "Thank you," he said before running off to join the other kids in the kitchen. I approached the dining table, barely suppressing an eye roll when I saw Sasha and Sienna bickering—*again*. "You have to eat more," Sasha insisted, trying to pile food onto her plate. Sienna swatted his hand away, "I swear, if you don't stop, I'll shove this serving spoon so far down your throat you'll need a surgeon, *Hardman*."

"And I swear, if you don't eat every damn thing I put on your plate, I'll tie you down and force-feed you, *gadyuka*,"

Sasha shot back, his jaw tightening. The last time I'd seen him this concerned about someone was with Elif. And even when she was pregnant with Tarik, she hadn't gotten this level of attention from him. Something had changed in him. And I had a feeling Sienna was the reason. The moment shattered when Grigori stormed into the room, phone pressed to his ear. "What do you mean, attacked ? And the shipment ?! Fuck !" He hung up and tossed his phone onto the table, his glare snapping to me, "what happened, *moy brat ?* " I asked, already feeling the weight of my brothers' stares.

"What happened ?" he stepped toward me, his voice sharp. "The fucking Italians attacked our men in Missouri killing almost all of them. They stole the shipment—four million dollars, Nikolaï ! Because that son of a bitch Antonio thinks we kidnapped his wife and son!" I clenched my fists, "she's not his wife," I ground out. Grigori's glare darkened as he grabbed the front of my shirt, yanking us face to face. "Four million, Nikolaï ! Have you lost your fucking mind ?" I shoved his hand off me, "so what? You're blaming me for our men dying? Calling me the monster? As if handing over a woman and child to an abuser would make us saints?" I stepped closer, our chests nearly colliding, "we're all monsters in this world, *moy brat.* The men who died knew the risks—they made their choices. If protecting this woman and her son means becoming something even worse—so be it."

Chapter ten
Selina

The cool grass beneath my feet sent shivers up my spine as I walked between the tall hedges in the Ivanov garden two days after the confrontation. After the heated exchange between Nikolaï and his brother, Elif had fortunately arrived just in time to calm them down. "Mom, look!" Rafael shouted from farther ahead before kicking the soccer ball at his feet. "Bravo, *Angelo mio*," I called out as he disappeared behind Andrei, waving at me with excitement. A different kind of weight settled on my shoulders—less oppressive, but just as heavy. My son looked so happy… But would he be just as happy wherever we went? Would I be able to protect him?

"You're thinking so hard it's giving me a headache," Sienna said, suddenly appearing at my side with a can of *Chinò Neri* in her hand. I blinked in surprise. "Unbelievable, right?" she chuckled. "Just yesterday, I told Elif this was my favorite drink, and today I found it in the fridge. I need to thank her." She took a long sip. She certainly should have thanked someone—but not Elif, because I had seen Sasha putting those cans in the fridge earlier. I didn't know what to make of that man. He was cold and distant, his calculating stare sending shivers down my spine every time it landed on me. But when his eyes settled on my sister, something else flickered behind them. Maybe Roman had been right, maybe he did feel guilty for knocking her unconscious. Not that it mattered. Once we left in three weeks, the Ivanov brothers would be nothing more than a memory. Well… perhaps not three weeks anymore, given the news from two days prior. Nikolaï and his brothers had withdrawn right after breakfast to discuss the attack. Antonio… of course he would do something like this. His obsession with me blinded him to the point of starting a war.

"What do you think they'll do ?" I asked my sister, slipping my arm through hers as we walked toward the pool, its surface shimmering under the sunlight. "I don't know, and honestly, I don't care," she replied, her voice firm, her gaze locked on the water. "Even if they throw us out, I know people here. We'll manage." I frowned, "how do you have contacts here, Sienna ? What have you been doing all these years, *mia sorella ?*" I felt her stiffen under my touch, though her face remained unreadable as she inhaled slowly, "nothing, *mia sorella*. Nothing worth telling" she drained the last of her can and tossed it into a wooden trash bin before quickly walking away to join the children.

I pressed my lips together as my throat tightened. She was lying. She was trying to protect me from the truth, and that terrified me. It terrified me to think about what she must have gone through just to survive. Eight years. She had had to fend for herself for eight years while still just a teenager, and I hadn't been able to do a damn thing. The image of her covered in blood, her hands shaking, her clothes stained, wouldn't leave my mind. The day we had no choice but to succumb to the monsters that surrounded us. "You'll get sick walking around barefoot," a deep voice said behind me, making me jump. My hand flew to my chest as my heart pounded. "Sorry, I didn't mean to startle you," Nikolaï added, keeping a respectful distance. He stood tall and proud, like a Greek statue, his hands tucked into his pockets. My eyes trailed down to his forearms, where his rolled-up sleeves exposed veins that stood out against his skin. The air between us thickened.

I swallowed hard, forcing my gaze back to his face. His sharp blue eyes scanned me before dropping to my bare feet. Without thinking, I crossed them over each other—a nervous habit I could never seem to control. "I... I like feeling the earth under my feet. It soothes me," I replied, embarrassed, looking away. His polished shoes appeared in front of me, and I felt the warmth of his body surrounding me. My breath hitched when he lifted a hand, brushing a stray strand of hair from my cheek. "This dress suits you, Selina. You looked stunning," he murmured, his breath caressing my forehead. I tilted my head up, his fingers grazing my jawline, and for the first time since we met, I realized just how much taller he was than me. I barely reached his shoulders, forcing me to crane my neck even further to meet his gaze. A mistake.

Everything about Nikolaï Ivanov was careful—the way he spoke to me, the way he touched me, the way he looked at me. As if he were afraid I would shatter into a million pieces, that I might disappear. And somehow, that gaze made me feel vulnerable. Weak. Antonio had wanted to break me. His eyes had always been filled with twisted desires and madness, forcing me to be strong, to fight, to survive. But this ? If Nikolaï Ivanov wanted to break me, I felt like he could do it effortlessly. And that terrified me. "Thank you," I murmured, stepping back, crossing my arms. Avoiding his gaze, I turned and resumed walking, feeling him follow. "I'm sorry about what happened to your... products," I said, hesitating over the word. "It's our fault. Your brothers are right, and you know it. We should leave. I'll call Antonio and tell him my departure had nothing to do with you—" I stopped abruptly as I felt a gentle tug on my braid. I glanced over my shoulder, frowning as I saw Nikolaï holding the end of my plait between his thumb and forefinger. "What are you doing?" I asked, more curious than anything.

His gaze darkened slightly, but he didn't let go, "I liked the texture of your hair. And its color," he said, his voice serious. I was caught completely off guard. What was I supposed to say? Thank you? He finally released my braid and tucked his hands back into his pockets, "listen, Selina, as I said before—you're not going anywhere until I see you healed. You, your son, and your sister will stay here, where it's safe. As for the stolen cargo, don't worry. Grigori and Roman are leaving for Missouri tonight to deal with the issue. Sasha and I will stay here to make sure you're safe. Later, we may join them in California." I blinked, trying to process everything. "California?" "Yes. That's where we actually live. Sochi is more of a retreat for us, but I think we're safer here. Not many people know the location of this estate," he said, looking around with a faint smile. It made him look younger. More attractive. *Attractive?*

Oh God, I was really losing my mind. "I think you're mistaken, Mr. Ivanov. I—" "Nikolaï," he interrupted. "Call me by my name." I stared at him for a few seconds, feeling like an idiot, before closing my eyes. *Get a grip, Selina.* "Fine, Nikolaï," I said, lifting my chin. "You're mistaken. We're not helpless victims who need your protection. As my sister pointed out yesterday, we can take care of ourselves. You have no responsibility toward us." He shook his head, stepping into my space. Determined to make my point, I stood my ground, tightening my arms around myself. "You're wrong, Selina. The moment I saw those marks on your arms, I should have done something. But I chose to turn away. And this…" His gaze dropped to my broken fingers. "This is the result." His eyes lifted to mine, unwavering, "so yes, you are my responsibility. And believe me, I won't make the same mistake twice." I stared at him, speechless, unsure of how to respond, how to push him away, how to change his mind. But did I even want him to change his mind ? The thought of someone standing behind me, ready to protect my son and me after eight long years of watching over my shoulder day and night—it was overwhelming.

Terror seized me again as I realized how easily I was granting him my trust. Nothing guaranteed that one morning, I wouldn't wake up to find Antonio at the foot of my bed, exchanging a briefcase full of money with Nikolaï in return for handing us over. The image was so disturbing, so impossible, that it made me nauseous. But the truth was, I didn't know Nikolaï Ivanov. I didn't know him or his brothers. I couldn't let myself be swayed by his words. This wasn't just about my safety—it was about my sister's, and most importantly, my son's. "No matter what you feel, Nikolaï, once my fingers are healed, we will leave. I will never be able to thank you enough for your help, but…" I stopped when I saw his lips curl into a smile. "What… why are you smiling ?" I asked, confused. "I just find it adorable how you try to stand your ground, yet you keep crossing and uncrossing your feet in discomfort." We both lowered our gazes at the same time, and I went crimson when I realized he had caught me doing exactly that. I quickly straightened up, firmly planting my feet on the ground. "Are you making fun of me?" I asked, my mouth slightly open, offended.

He shook his head, still smiling, about to reply when his gaze suddenly shifted behind me. He moved so fast that I didn't even have time to react. In an instant, I found myself pressed against his chest, his left arm wrapped around my waist as he used his other arm to stop the soccer ball hurtling toward us. "Mom ! Mom !" a voice suddenly cried out just as Nikolaï lowered his arm, though he didn't release the one still holding me against him. His gaze, filled with concern, locked onto mine, but I could only stare back, unable to say a word. Andrei and Rafael came running toward us, followed closely by Alexei and Sienna. "Sorry, Mom, we didn't mean to !" Andrei sobbed, wrapping himself around my legs, rubbing his face against me. I knelt down, gently slipping out of Nikolaï's grasp, and caressed Andrei's cheek. "It's okay, I know you didn't mean to, *Angelo mio*," I reassured him softly. "So you're not leaving, right ?" he asked, lifting his teary eyes to mine, and I felt my heart clench at his expression. "No, I… I'm not leaving because of this," I said quietly, holding him against me as he hugged me tightly. Not because of this, but I would have to leave eventually.

"My *mamma* is strong, and she knows how to fight. She even hit the monster. Come on, let's go play !" my son shouted as he ran off, completely unaware of the weight of his words. I rose to my feet, my legs trembling, feeling Nikolaï's presence beside me. He hadn't moved, but before he could say anything, Alexei hesitantly stepped forward. "I… actually, it was me who kicked the ball by accident. I… I'm sorry," he said, lowering his head, his hands clasped behind his back, making me smile. I ruffled his hair, pushing it back from his forehead as he lifted his eyes, so much like his father's, toward me. "It's okay. You're very brave," I told him, and he looked at me, confused. "Brave ? Why ?" he asked, his eyes lost. "Because…" I began, kneeling to zip up his jacket, "admitting a mistake and apologizing takes a lot of courage." He studied me for a few seconds before nodding slowly, as if absorbing my words bit by bit. He cast one last glance at me from beneath his lashes before finally walking away to join his brother and my son.

I stood up, smoothing out my dress, carefully avoiding the gaze of the man beside me. Luckily, my sister came to my rescue, slipping her arm through mine. "Come, there are beautiful flowers over there, just like the ones in *papà's* garden," she said, pulling me away, deeper into the garden, far from the man and his piercing gaze that still burned into my back.

Chapter eleven
Nikolai

Dimitri hugged Andrei one last time before joining his brother in the car. "You're suffocating me, Elif," Sasha grumbled beside me as Elif tightened her arms around his waist. Despite his protests, he held her just as tightly, pressing a kiss to her temple. "I'll really suffocate you if you don't watch how you behave with our guest, idiot," she said, kissing his cheek before stepping back. Then she turned to me and embraced me in turn. I inhaled deeply, taking in her scent, one that always managed to soothe me. "Sorry for putting you in uncomfortable situations, Elif," I murmured, holding her close. She lifted her head, smiling softly as she gently caressed my cheek, just like she used to when I was younger. "Come on, Niko. With idiots like you, I'm in for a long ride. But thankfully, I like you guys enough," she teased. I smiled, squeezing her hand gently, and began to step back, but she stopped me by placing a hand on my back. "Niko, be careful with what you do. Don't act on anything unless you're a hundred percent sure. You Ivanov brothers don't always realize the weight of your actions, and believe me, I know what I'm talking about," she warned.

I grimaced at her words, knowing exactly what she was referring to, the greatest mistake Grigori had ever made. The one that had nearly cost us Elif. I didn't even want to imagine the state we'd be in now if he hadn't managed to fix it. I sighed and nodded. She seemed satisfied, then walked over to Selina and Sienna, who were waiting by the entrance. I tensed slightly as I saw Grigori approach, while Sasha and Roman remained in their usual state, either arguing or caught in one of their heated discussions. It was never quite clear with Roman. "You think they're talking or fighting ?" Grigori asked, reaching my side.

"I'd say they're talking. Sasha hasn't hit him yet," I replied with a smirk. Our younger brother had an exceptional talent for getting under Sasha's skin.

"Niko," Grigori began, turning to face me with his hands buried in his pockets, "I know I come off as harsh, maybe even cruel but all I want is to protect our family, brother." I nodded, squeezing his shoulder. "I know, brother. But understand this, I will never let any harm come to our family. But I also won't turn my back on a woman and her son who need help. That's not who I am, and it's not who you are either, Grigori." He held my gaze for a moment, then sighed and pulled me into a hug, "I hope you know what you're doing, Nikolaï," he murmured before stepping back and heading toward his family, already seated in the car. Roman rolled down the window and leaned out, waving dramatically, "see you later, idiots ! Try not to make more little Ivanovs while we're gone!" the fool shouted. Elif grabbed the back of his shirt, yanking him inside while smacking him just as the car began pulling away.

"I swear, I'll drown him in the pool the next time I see him," Sasha growled, glaring after the disappearing car. "What were you two talking about ?" I asked, casting him a sideways glance. He grimaced, never a good sign. "I'm worried about him," Sasha muttered, "Roman?" I asked, my concern sharpening. Sasha exhaled, running a hand through his hair. "He's completely obsessed with that woman, Nikolaï. No matter what he's doing, fighting, working, even killing, she's always on his mind. He's torturing himself. He just told me he dreamed of her again and that he's thinking of going back to Iraq to find her." A chill ran through my veins. The thought of our little brother returning to that hell was unthinkable. We'd made the mistake of letting him go once, but that wasn't happening again. If only we had found this woman… It wasn't like we hadn't tried. But all we had were dark eyes, dark hair, olive skin. That described thousands of women. "He's not going back there. Ever," I growled through gritted teeth. "I'll break his damn legs if I have to." Sasha nodded, equally resolute. We all carried the regret of having let him go eight years ago. We should've listened to Elif.

Silence settled between us until the sound of approaching footsteps drew our attention. Sienna strode toward us with firm steps, her shoulders squared, her gaze defiant. Selina was nowhere in sight, probably with the boys, which made me a little anxious. Those little devils could easily drive her mad with their pranks. Sienna didn't spare Sasha so much as a glance as she stopped in front of me. "I need to go out. I have an appointment," she announced. Or rather, judging by her tone and posture, she informed me rather than asked. "Not happening," Sasha growled, stepping toward her, Sienna took a deep breath, still ignoring him, her eyes locked on mine. "I don't think that was a request, *moy brat*," I said, smirking. "It wasn't," she confirmed. "I'm just letting you know, and I hope you'll watch over my sister." She stepped back, ready to leave, but Sasha grabbed her arm, pulling her against him, his face mere inches from hers.

"I said no," he growled, his jaw clenched, eyes dark with warning. "And I said it's not up to you. And frankly, I don't even see why you're here. Your brother seems more than competent enough to handle our safety…" "Actually…" I cut in, placing a hand on Sasha's tense shoulder and looking down at her. "I'm only ensuring the safety of your sister and nephew. You, however, are under my brother's watch. No offense, Sienna, but you're a little too much of a pain for my patience and I fear I'd be the one endangering your safety." She blinked at me, clearly offended. *Perfect.* Her eyes darted between Sasha and me before her face shut down entirely. And for the first time since I'd met this woman, I found her truly dangerous. The ability to erase emotion like that wasn't ordinary. Disturbed by the shift, Sasha let her go, his gaze scanning her face. "Sienna…" he began, his voice softer than I'd ever heard it, reserved only for Elif and the children. "I… I think I'll go lie down. I feel tired," she muttered, stepping back again. "I'll have someone bring you food…" Sasha offered, about to follow her, but she shook her head, "no. I just need to rest. I'll be fine," she said weakly, disappearing inside. We both stared at the closed door.

"Shit," Sasha swore, clenching his fists, "you should've stopped me. I handled her wrong. Again." He ran a hand through his hair, looking away, "oh, so now I'm supposed to control you too ?" I arched a brow. He sighed, casting one last glance toward the house, clearly debating whether or not to follow her. "Calm down, Sasha. You didn't hurt her. She's stronger than she looks. And it's not like you've never tortured or killed a woman before, where's all this sudden softness coming from ?" He didn't answer, just stared at the house for another second before turning away and heading toward the gardens, pulling out a cigarette. I sighed. Should I worry about Roman, Sasha, or the Italians?

Yet all I could think about was the face of a woman with dark green eyes, carrying both vulnerability and immeasurable strength.

Selina

"I don't understand any of this !" Mikhail groaned, letting his head fall back, arms flung toward the ceiling, an image that made me smile. "But it's actually quite simple. Once you understand the basics, everything else falls into place," I said, handing another colored pencil to Alexei, who was frowning at his coloring book with fierce concentration. Andrei and Rafael, however, were far less focused, which wasn't surprising considering how much time they spent laughing and bickering.

"What's the point of knowing how many red blood cells are in the human body, seriously ? I don't need that to sell drugs," Mikhail muttered, leaning over his notebook again. I looked up at him, startled. "You... you don't want to have another kind of job ?" I asked cautiously, unsure how to phrase it without offending him. This time, he glanced up, looking equally surprised. "A job ?" he asked, curious. I nodded with a faint smile. "Yes, like your uncle, for example. He's a lawyer, isn't he ?" "Yeah, but he works for the *Bratva*. Same thing. He still manages shipments and all that." I shook my head gently, "that doesn't change the fact that he worked hard to earn his title, or that he has knowledge others don't. He's the one people turn to when they're in trouble with the law, right

? That makes him useful." Mikhail stared at me, clearly thinking, "so I should be a lawyer ?" he asked, genuinely puzzled, and I couldn't help but laugh. "No, of course not. What I'm saying is that you can become whatever you want while still being useful to your family. I don't know... maybe an accountant to manage the finances, or even a doctor, to take care of the people you love when they're hurt." "A doctor ?" he repeated, frowning slightly, scratching his chin as if truly considering the possibility. "I'm gonna be a race car driver so I can win all our races like Uncle Roman!" Andrei suddenly shouted, flinging his colorful hands into the air. "And I'm going to be an engineer to build faster cars so you can win even more easily !" Alexei added, lifting his bright, determined eyes. I smiled even wider.

"Those are amazing goals, boys. I'm sure you'll succeed," I said, gently rubbing Alexei's back. For the second time that day, he gave me a smile that warmed my heart. "And what about you, Rafael ? What do you want to be ?" Andrei asked suddenly, turning his excited gaze to my son. Rafael straightened, glanced at me, then answered with unwavering pride, "I'm going to be the strongest fighter of all time, and I'll protect my mom." My smile faltered. That was his dream, to be strong enough to protect me. No child should ever have to think that way.

"No ! I'm going to be the strongest and protect Mom !" Andrei shouted, and just like that, another argument erupted between them. I sighed, about to rise and separate them when Nikolaï's voice echoed behind me. "There's no need to argue about that. She already has a protector," he said as he approached, hands tucked in his pockets. I hadn't even heard him come in, how long had he been standing there ? What had he heard ? What if he'd taken offense to my suggestion that his son choose a different path ? What if he decided I needed to be punished for that ? A cold sweat broke across my skin. I glanced over my shoulder and gasped when I realized how close he was, my nose nearly brushed his white shirt. When had he gotten so close ?

His scent, fresh and faintly spiced, invaded my senses again. I gripped the table's edge and turned away. "But I'm the one who has to protect her !" Rafael insisted, pushing back his chair and stepping forward. I couldn't help but giggle when I saw the colorful smudges on his serious little face. I felt Nikolaï's eyes on me as I covered my mouth, trying not to let Rafael think I was laughing at him. He stood before us, hands on his hips. Nikolaï narrowed his eyes and mimicked my son's stance, placing his hands on his hips too, his shirt pulling tight across his muscular arms. "I thought we had a deal. Did you forget ?" he asked, his gaze never leaving Rafael. My son's defiant stance vanished as he blinked, clearly remembering their earlier agreement. He was just about to respond when heavy footsteps pounded down the stairs. We all turned toward the doorway. Sasha appeared, his eyes blazing, his jaw clenched tight.

"Where is she ?" he demanded, and the fury in his voice sent a shiver through me. His gaze locked onto mine, cold and sharp. Nikolaï stepped between us, placing a firm hand against his brother's chest. "What's going on, *moy brat ?*" he asked, voice low and dangerous. "What's going on is that Sienna is gone ! And you know where she is !" Sasha snapped, his glare fixed on me. "I don't understand. She told me she was going to inform you before leaving," I said, startled. I remembered her words earlier at the entrance, how she had to meet a contact in the city, how there'd be consequences if she didn't go. I had insisted she refuse, but when I saw the fear in her eyes, I hadn't pushed her further, on the condition she inform Nikolaï. "She did inform us. And we said no," Sasha bit out. "When I went upstairs to check because she wasn't feeling well, she was already gone."

My mouth dropped open in shock. "She pulled a trick on you," I muttered and pressed my lips together, avoiding their eyes. "A trick? What do you mean? I don't get it…" "Shit, she played me," Sasha muttered. "She pretended to be sick so she could run off." He turned away, hands locked behind his neck. The tension radiating from him was palpable. "Do you know where she went? She could be in danger, Selina." his voice was quiet now, but it carried the weight of a real threat. I hesitated… until I met Nikolaï's gaze. It was calm. Grounding. "No. She said she had a meeting with her contact in the city. That's all I know," I said truthfully. Now, I was truly afraid for my sister. Sasha nodded once, then moved toward the door.

"Where are you going?" Nikolaï asked as his brother passed. Sasha paused at the threshold. "To find *malen'kaya gadyuka*," he muttered, then strode out without another word. *Oh, Sienna… What have you done?*

Chapter twelve
Selina

The rain pounded against the large bay windows of the living room as I paced restlessly since Sasha's departure. Night had fallen, and Nikolai and I had already put the children to bed. I sighed, pausing once more in front of the window overlooking the garden. The shadows of the tall bay trees and other foliage danced across the pool's surface. "Don't worry, I'm sure she's fine. Sasha will find her soon," Nikolai said from the kitchen, holding a glass of water in one hand and my painkillers in the other. He handed them to me, and I thanked him as I took the pill, gripping the glass tightly. The pain in my fingers had become secondary with everything going on, and I had completely forgotten to take my medication—but Nikolai hadn't. "What if something happened to her ?" I asked in a small voice, my mind conjuring up the worst scenarios, blood, so much blood, just like eight years ago.

I entered the hotel room, breathing heavily, still dressed in my nurse's uniform. The door clicked softly behind me, signaling it had locked. I glanced down the dim hallway leading to the suite's living room, which lay shrouded in darkness. There was no noise, only the distant hum of cars twenty-six floors below. A strip of light glowed from beneath a door, and my heart clenched as fear gripped me. I stepped forward, my trembling hand pushing the door open. A gasp escaped me. All I could see was red, on the floor, on the bed. Red like blood. The blood of the man lying there, a small pair of scissors embedded in his throat. A faint sniffle caught my attention. Time slowed as I spotted my sister curled against the wall, her clothes soaked in crimson.

"Sienna..." I whispered, rushing to her side, I placed a hand on her knee, and she flinched, lifting wide, tear-filled eyes. She was in shock. "Selina," she breathed, her lips trembling. "I... I didn't mean to, Selina. He... he tried to touch me. I said no, Selina! I swear I said no! But he wouldn't listen. He hit me. He tried to... to..." I pulled her into my arms, running my fingers through her hair. "Shh, shh, you're okay, Sienna. Everything's going to be okay. Calm down," I soothed, though tears burned in my own eyes. She was only sixteen. Oh God. What were we going to do?

"Well, I didn't expect it to end this way. But it's even better than I imagined." I jumped to my feet, shielding my sister, and froze at the sight of Antonio Rasili standing near the door, his hands buried in his pockets, a smirk curling his lips. "I think you're finally ready to negotiate, Selina," he said, stepping closer, his presence cloaking the room in darkness.

"Selina?"

Nikolai's voice pulled me back to the present, tearing me from the depths of that memory. "Are you alright? You've gone pale," he asked, concern in his voice. "I'm calling the doctor. He can prescribe something stronger for the pain." He reached for his phone, but I shook my head quickly, setting the glass down and grabbing his wrist without thinking. "I... No, don't call. I'm fine. I'm just worried about my sister," I murmured. His eyes flicked to my lips just as I wet them with my tongue. "I hate seeing you like this, *Solnychko*," he said softly, gently wrapping his warm hand around my trembling fingers.

There it was again, that tenderness, that comfort. I should have pushed him away, rebuilt the walls I had so carefully constructed. But I didn't. His warmth was a lifeline. I wanted to rest in it, just for a moment. I was so tired of fighting.

That was why I didn't move when his other hand slid to my cheek, when I leaned into his touch. That was why I didn't move when I felt his breath against my skin, his nose brushing my temple, his lips gliding along my cheekbone. "Selina… push me away. Tell me to stop," he whispered, his lips brushing mine. He was right. I should have stopped this. I would be leaving in a few weeks. He wasn't the kind of man I should be with, not after escaping Antonio's grasp. But I couldn't. "I can't," I breathed, gripping his hand as his lips grazed mine. A sudden noise shattered the moment, the front door swung open, followed by loud voices.

I jerked away, breathless, as Nikolai turned sharply, stepping in front of me, his hand reaching behind his back for his weapon. "Go to hell!" a female voice yelled. "Sienna!" I cried, pushing past Nikolai toward the entrance. My sister stood there, drenched from head to toe, slamming the door shut behind her. I immediately pulled her into my arms, "oh God, Sienna, I was so scared," I whispered, stepping back to examine her. All the anger in her face vanished, replaced by guilt and regret, "I'm fine, Selina. I'm so sorry for worrying you," she said, wiping tears from my cheeks, tears I hadn't even noticed were falling. I shook my head, brushing wet strands from her face. "It doesn't matter. You're safe, *mia sorella*. You need to get changed, you're freezing," I said, sniffing. I took her hand to lead her toward the stairs only for us to freeze as the door swung open again.

Sasha stood in the doorway, just as soaked as my sister. This conversation isn't over, *malen'kaya gadyuka*," he growled, his dark gaze locking onto Sienna. She visibly shuddered whether from the cold or fear, I couldn't tell. But Sienna was Sienna. She yanked her hand from mine, squaring her shoulders before him, "I have nothing to say to you! And I swear, if you so much as touch me again, the next thing flying out of your mouth will be your goddamn teeth!" she snapped, her eyes blazing. Sasha took a deep breath, rubbing a hand down his face as if trying to keep himself from losing control. Nikolai noticed too, stepping forward, "Sasha…" he started, but everything happened too fast. Sienna let out a startled yelp as she was suddenly hoisted over Sasha's shoulder, and he stormed down the hallway toward his room.

"Sienna!" I screamed, rushing after them, but Nikolai passed me and grabbed his brother's shoulder, "Sasha, what the hell are you doing?" he asked, his jaw tense as my sister kept fidgeting and swearing into his brother's shoulder. "Don't get involved, Niko. I know what I'm doing. Like you said yourself, take care of yours, and I'll take care of mine," he said as he freed himself from his brother's hold before heading down the hallway. I called my sister again and tried to follow her, but Nikolai stepped in front of me, catching my arm. "Let me go !" I growled, trying to yank my arm free, but he didn't budge. "Calm down, Selina. My brother would never hurt your sister," he said, his eyes steady on mine. "I don't believe you, not after how he just dragged her away," I snapped, anger boiling inside me.

I didn't care that this family had helped us. If they dared hurt my sister, I'd rip their hearts out myself. "Listen to me, Selina. I know my brother. He would never harm an innocent woman. The best thing to do now is to get some dry clothes for your sister, and then we'll check on them together in a few minutes, alright? Let them talk." I glared at him, my lips pressed into a thin line, "I'm trusting you. But if he does anything to her, you'll be the first one I kill," I said before turning and heading up the stairs to get Sienna some clothes.

Nikolai

"…you'll be the first one I kill," she said, her lips forming a determined pout before she turned on her heel and disappeared upstairs. I remained frozen for a few seconds before suddenly chuckling to myself like a madman.

This woman…

Sometimes, I didn't know what to make of her. One moment, she was the most fragile thing in need of protection, and the next, she was a tigress ready to fight for those she loved. My gaze shifted back to the hallway where Sasha had disappeared with Sienna. Since the Floros sisters had arrived, I didn't know what to make of him either. I suddenly heard footsteps echoing on the stairs, and I knew it wasn't Selina, these were lighter than hers. I lifted my gaze and frowned as I saw Rafael coming down, tears streaming down his face. "*Mamma?*" he called weakly, his voice filled with confusion as he descended. I moved toward him, crouching to his level, but he hesitated when he saw me. "What's wrong, little man?" I asked, gently taking his trembling hand. "Where is *Mamma?* Did the monster take her?" he asked, warm tears running down his cheeks. I stared at him, trying to grasp the meaning of his words.

"I... no, your *mamma* is fine Rafael. She's upstairs; she'll be down soon," I reassured him, wrapping an arm around his frail shoulders. He buried his face against my chest, sniffling softly. "He won't use his belt on *Mamma* anymore, right ? She won't scream ?" he suddenly asked, his small voice trembling. Every muscle in my body tensed at his words, "what... belt? What are you talking about?" I asked, my jaw tightening as a slow, seething rage started to consume me. "Rafael?" Selina's soft voice called from the top of the stairs, and we both turned. She stood a few steps above us, holding a set of clothes in her uninjured hand. "*Mamma!* " Rafael cried before racing up the stairs toward her as I straightened slowly, struggling to suppress the violent fury threatening to take over. Images flashed through my mind, images of this delicate, beautiful woman screaming, crying, suffering. I didn't know if I'd be ready to let them go when the time came in a few weeks. But one thing was certain, the next time I crossed paths with Antonio Rasili, I would kill him.

Chapter thirteen
Selina

The cool night air made me sigh in relief as I stepped out of the hospital after a long shift. Several emergencies had come in throughout the night, leaving me with no time to rest. My feet protested with every step, making me groan. I finally reached the parking lot, walking toward my little canary-yellow car, the one my sister never stopped ridiculing. She practically ignored me whenever I picked her up from school, claiming I embarrassed her by showing up in my "rolling chick." That little brat. *I jumped when headlights suddenly flared behind me, casting my shadow long and distorted. My heartbeat skyrocketed as I turned, squinting into the blinding light. The back door of a sleek car swung open, and a man stepped out, approaching with his hands buried in his pockets. As his features became clear, I froze.* Antonio Rasili. *It had been two months since our first meeting, and ever since, he hadn't left me alone. Texts and calls at all hours, insistently asking to see me, I didn't even know how he got my number. The man was insane.*

I didn't like him. He exuded danger, something that sent chills down my spine. He wouldn't stop sending flowers every day, showing up at the hospital unannounced just to see me. I had refused him every time, making up the most ridiculous excuses, but he was like a relentless Doberman, never letting go. By the time he reached me, his usual smug smile was already in place. "Selina, you're as breathtaking as the first time I laid eyes on you," he said, reaching up to touch the end of my braid resting on my shoulder. I pulled back instinctively, avoiding his touch. "What are you doing here?" I asked, my eyes darting around the empty lot, searching for anyone who could help me if things went south. But there wasn't a soul in sight. "You haven't been answering my messages," he said simply, as if that justified his presence. Anger simmered beneath my skin. I clenched my fists, my patience wearing thin.

"Listen, Mr. Rasili, like I told you the first time you asked, I have no interest in seeing you for any reason. If you continue harassing me like this, I will call the police." For a moment, he just stared at me, his eyes gleaming with something sinister. My stomach twisted as dread settled deep inside me. I was about to take a step back when, in an instant, my body slammed against a parked truck. My bag and keys slipped from my hands as his fingers tightened around my throat, cutting off my air. "Ah, Selina... I can't wait to own you," he whispered, his lips brushing from my temple down to my cheek as I struggled against his grip. Black spots danced in my vision as I fought to breathe. "You will belong to me, Cara mia. Your body and your soul. You'll be mine." His lips inched closer to mine.

No.

A scream, one I barely recognized as my own, ripped from my throat as I drove my knee upward, striking him between the legs with every ounce of strength I had left. A groan of pain left him as he staggered back, his hands clutching his groin. I grabbed my things and ran, my breath ragged, my chest burning. The hospital entrance was my only goal. But then, behind me, a chilling laugh echoed in the darkness. And I felt the monster's breath at my nape.

The cold water did nothing to rid me of the filth I felt clinging to my skin. Rafael had finally fallen back asleep after I sang to him, holding him close. I turned off the water, but my son's words replayed in my mind like a haunting melody. "*He won't use his belt on Mamma anymore, right ? She won't scream ?*" A choked sob escaped before I could stop it. I clamped a hand over my mouth, muffling the sound. *My baby.* He had witnessed too much, suffered too much. And I didn't know how to help him forget. I exhaled slowly, reaching for a towel and drying myself quickly before slipping on a pair of underwear, then a loose paire of shorts, and a tank top that belonged to Elif. It was too tight around my chest, but I didn't care. Wiping away the steam on the mirror, I grimaced at my reflection. Red-rimmed eyes, fading bruises, a swollen lip, I was a walking disaster. I sighed, beginning to remove the plastic bag covering my cast, wincing at the slight pain. Then, I picked up my comb, trying to detangle my hair, but my hand wouldn't stop shaking.

My breathing hitched. My chest tightened. The world tilted. I knew this feeling, I had lived through it thousands of times before, curled up in the dark corners of my gilded cage. *A panic attack.* I reached out, pressing my palm against the cool marble wall, willing myself to calm down. But nothing worked. My heart pounded, my lungs constricted, and my vision blurred. Nausea clawed at my throat. I was going to vomit, no, I was going to die. The hundreds of times I had thought those words resurfaced in my mind. Breathing became impossible. Water, I could feel water rushing into my nose, my mouth, my lungs.

I was going to die. I was going to die.

"So, Cara mia, are you going to try escaping again?" Antonio's voice was the last thing I heard before he put my head under the water, in the bathtub filled to the brim. I thrashed, clawing at his grip, kicking, but I couldn't break free. His weight pressed against my back, pinning me down.

My limbs weakened. My vision darkened. And just as my body began to give in, he yanked me back up by my hair. I gasped, coughing violently, my lungs burning as I struggled to suck in air. Water dripped from my face, clogging my throat, making it impossible to breathe. "Answer me when I ask you a question!" he roared, jerking my hair, making me cry out. Choked sobs left me as my son's voice rang out from behind the locked door, calling for me, trying to get in.

I wanted to tell him to run, to hide. But no words came out. Antonio laughed behind me. Cold. Empty. Like a man unhinged. "No" I whisper in a weak voice. "Liar," he murmured against my ear. Then, without hesitation, he shoved me forward, my face plunging back into the water.

I screamed. And then, silence. Only the water swallowing me whole.

I was going to die. I was going to die.

Something warm suddenly wrapped around my hand, prying it away from its grip on the counter. My fingers instinctively clutched onto it, squeezing tightly, my nails digging in. That same warmth coiled around my waist, pulling me against something firm yet comforting. I gasped, struggling to breathe. Antonio's voice slowly faded, replaced by a deeper one with a slight accent, as a scent began to infiltrate my senses, sea salt and pine. "Selina, you're safe. Just breathe," the voice murmured near my ear, piercing through the suffocating fog in my mind. "You're safe. He will never touch you again, Selina. Never again," the man continued, his hold tightening around my waist. "But you need to breathe, *Solnyshko*. Don't let him win. Don't let him break you. Not after you fought so hard to survive all these years.

Come on, breathe," Nikolaï coaxed gently, his lips brushing against my throat where my pulse pounded erratically.

I jolted at the warmth of his touch against my sweat-dampened skin. Blinking rapidly, I focused on the lightbulb above the mirror, inhaling deeply as tremors continued to shake my body. The hand enclosing mine moved it to my stomach, securing me against him as he buried his face deeper into my neck. "That's it, *Solnyshko*. Just breathe. Fight," he whispered. My vision gradually cleared, the chaos in my mind retreating, leaving behind only exhaustion, bone-deep and unbearable. And then, another emotion surfaced. My lips trembled, my eyes burned, and before I could stop it, a sob escaped me. I began to cry. I cried in a way I hadn't in eight years, years spent fighting, surviving, enduring. The weight of my fatigue crushed me. It had been so long. So many nights spent sleeping with one eye open, so many endless days spent hiding in dark corners, hoping he would forget I existed. I sobbed so violently that my entire body shook. My tears fell uncontrollably, and I didn't react when Nikolaï leaned back against the wall, pulling me onto his lap. One of his arms wrapped securely around my shoulders while his other hand slid to the nape of my neck, massaging it gently, *it will be okay*.

My eyes widened, snapping up to his face in astonishment and he offered me a small, knowing smile. "Rafael explained a little about your secret language," he murmured before pressing his lips against my forehead. And somehow, I cried even harder, burying my face against his chest, I clutched at his black T-shirt, the one he must have thrown on to sleep in. He continued to cradle me, his hand never leaving my nape, his lips occasionally brushing against my hair. Slowly, my sobs quieted into soft hiccups and sniffles. I finally lifted my gaze to meet his, embarrassment creeping over me. Oh God. Had I really just broken down like a child in the arms of a Russian mafia mobster ?

Our eyes locked, and I pressed my lips together. His gaze scanned my face, lingering on my puffy eyes, my tear-streaked cheeks, and, oh God, my nose, which was probably red from all the sniffling. His lips curled into a smirk. He brushed his thumb over my damp cheek before lowering his head, his lips grazing the tip of my nose, "you're beautiful, *Solnyshko*," he murmured, pulling back slightly, his fingers combing through my damp hair. "What does that mean ?" I asked hoarsely, struggling not to let my eyes flicker to his lips so dangerously close to mine. His smirk widened as his fingers tangled deeper in my hair, massaging the back of my head. A soft, involuntary moan escaped me, and my eyes fluttered shut. He stilled. Then, he took a deep breath, and I was forced to reopen my eyes, meeting his intense gaze once more.

"It means sunshine, someone who shines like the sun in our lives," he explained. "The first time I saw you in that reception hall, I couldn't take my eyes off you. You were like a radiant sun, impossible to ignore, impossible not to be drawn to." His words sent fresh tears welling in my eyes. "Shh, you've cried enough for tonight, enough for a lifetime," he soothed, pressing his nose against my hair before kissing my temple. At his tender gesture, more tears slipped down my cheeks, and I pouted, which only made him chuckle, a sound that vibrated through me, warming something deep inside my chest.

"Come on, let's get up before you catch a cold," Nikolaï said as he straightened up, helping me to my bare feet. That was when I noticed that he was barefoot too, I didn't know why, but it felt oddly intimate. Keeping one arm around my waist, he reached out with his other hand to grab the high-backed chair against the wall and placed it in front of us, facing the mirror. "Climb up," he said, patting the dark leather of the seat. I frowned, glancing between the chair and him. "Why?" "So I can dry your hair," he replied, as if it were the most natural thing in the world. "I can dry my own hair," I retorted, lifting my chin defiantly and narrowing my eyes at him. One of his eyebrows arched. "I know you can, but let me do it," he said, his gaze filled with quiet determination. And honestly, I was too exhausted to fight this battle.

I sighed in surrender and stepped closer to the chair, turning to hoist myself up, but with only one good hand, it wasn't exactly easy. Before I could struggle, the arm still wrapped around my waist lifted me effortlessly, and suddenly, I was seated, my head just below his chin. Our eyes met in the mirror as he slowly removed his hand from my body, his fingers trailing over my stomach, his thumb grazing just beneath my left breast. A shiver ran down my spine. He stepped back and moved around me, heading toward the counter. Bending down, he opened one of the drawers and retrieved a towel. I couldn't help myself, I glanced lower. His sweatpants sat low on his hips, and his backside was… well, distracting.

I let out a deep sigh and quickly shifted my gaze back up, only to freeze when I caught his reflection in the mirror, his eyes locked onto mine, a knowing smirk tugging at the corner of his lips. I didn't move. I didn't even breathe as he returned to stand behind me, gathering my damp hair at my back, his fingers brushing against my neck, sending a shiver through me. He started drying my hair with slow, careful movements, his touch gentle and deliberate. I closed my eyes, allowing myself to relax, the unexpected sense of trust I felt toward this man lowering my guard in a way I never imagined possible. Listening to his steady breathing, feeling his warmth behind me, I didn't even realize when sleep finally claimed me.

Chapter fourteen
Nikolai

Selina immediately turned toward her son, her hand resting on his stomach after I laid her down on the bed. I gently pulled the covers over them and straightened up. I shoved my fists into my pockets, my jaw clenched, as the image of how I had found her refused to leave my mind. I had only intended to check if the painkillers were working, but when no one answered my knock, I entered the room. She wasn't in bed beside Rafael, and I froze at the sound of a soft whimper coming from the bathroom. When I reached her, my world stopped. She was on her knees, gripping the counter with all her strength, her breath coming in short, sharp gasps. When I pulled her into my arms, she was freezing, her body trembling uncontrollably, her face twisted in pain, tears streaming down her cheeks, tears that unsettled something deep inside me. I exhaled heavily and stepped out of the room, closing the door softly behind me, trying to regain some semblance of control. I made my way to the office where Sasha spent most of his time, handling the paperwork. As Sienna had pointed out when we first met, each of us had a specific role in the organization.

Grigori was the leader, the one who commanded respect and directed our men. Sasha handled the administrative and legal aspects, as well as recruiting new members. Roman was the face of our operations on the ground. I was in charge of strategy, deciding when, where, and how our trades, meetings, and exchanges took place. And as Sienna had also pointed out, Elif was the unseen force, guiding and advising us, her vast network of contacts saving us more times than we could count. I stopped in front of the large bay windows and pulled out my phone, dialing an unregistered number. "Ivanov," the man answered on the first ring, his voice flat and expressionless, tinged with an Italian accent.

"What is he doing?" I asked, Selina's sobs still echoing in my head. "He's completely lost it," Abbiati replied, and I heard the flick of his lighter, probably lighting his thirtieth cigarette of the day. "He tried to get on the first flight to Russia, but his father stopped him. He's on his way to the United States now, likely to meet with your brother." My grip tightened on the phone. "He's obsessed with that woman, Ivanov. His son barely crosses his mind. All he wants is her." "I want him dead, Abbiati," I said through gritted teeth. A dry chuckle reached my ears, laced with obvious disdain. "Trust me, you're neither the first nor the last to wish for that. Unfortunately, that's not an option. He's the sole heir to that pig, Rasili. Killing him would ignite a war that would make the last one look like a children's cartoon. And tell me, who do you think the Italians will turn to as the next heir after his death?"

Rafael.

My entire body tensed at the realization, "no one will touch Rafael or Selina. I'll snap their fucking necks with my bare hands before that happens." A long silence stretched between us, only broken by the faint crackling of his cigarette as he inhaled. Then, in that same dull, infuriating voice, he said, "I see." "What?" I growled, turning away from the window and dropping into the leather chair behind the desk, propping my feet up, taking advantage of my sister-in-law's absence, knowing she wouldn't appear out of nowhere like she usually did. "Are you going to make her yours ?" he suddenly asked and I froze, caught off guard. Make her mine ? Keep her by my side ? Me, a monster, someone who killed and destroyed ? After everything she'd been through to escape exactly that kind of man ?

"I'm not the kind of man she needs," I said, my grip tightening around the phone, my gaze unfocused. "And what if you're exactly the man she does need?" he countered, making my brows furrow. "What do you mean?" A grunt and the sound of shifting leather reached my ears, as if he were standing up from a couch. "I'm saying that an ordinary man wouldn't be able to fight the monster chasing her, Nikolaï," he stated before hanging up, leaving me alone with my thoughts. I sighed and closed my eyes, tilting my head back, a monster to fight a monster, then?

My phone vibrated in my hand, and a smirk tugged at my lips. Her and her damn sixth sense. "You're not sleeping ?" Elif's soft voice came through the line, well, soft when she wasn't yelling at her sons or at us. "And you ? Has the jet lag not knocked you out ?" I countered, smiling when she laughed. "Niko, I've survived sleepless nights handling Roman's meltdowns over losing his dinosaur toys. A little jet lag isn't going to take me down, *aptal*, (idiot)" she teased. I grimaced at the memory. Roman and his tantrums as a kid had been absolute nightmares to deal with. "Does Grigori still want to slit my throat ?" I asked with a sigh, rubbing my forehead as a headache started creeping in. "Oh, come on, Niko, you know he was never really mad at you. He's just worried, like we all are. It's just that his way of dealing with it is a little more…" "Bloody ? Violent ? Murderous ?"

"Excessive," she corrected with a groan. I chuckled. "Very excessive." "Now, tell me what's really on your mind," she said, and I heard the sound of her opening the glass doors to the terrace, the distant crashing of waves making something ache inside me. It reminded me of how much I missed that house. It had been over three months since we'd been back, spending most of our time here or traveling to distract my sons. "It's nothing you need to worry about. I have the situation under control—" "Tu, tu, tu, don't pull that with me, little Niko. Don't make me get on a plane and come back." "Do I need to remind you that we're only three years apart?" I grumbled at the nickname.

She sniffed dismissively. "I'm waiting, Niko." I sighed. "I don't know, Elif. I… I'm afraid of making a mistake," I admitted, frustration lacing my voice. Me, admitting I was afraid ? Afraid of making a mistake ? I would never say that to anyone. But this was Elif, the one who'd seen me at my worst, the one I'd broken down in front of. "Oh, Niko," she murmured. "I still remember the first time you opened up to me, a few weeks after I arrived." Yeah, I remembered that night, too, the night our bond truly formed.

Nikolaï, sixteen years old

Grigori had gone out after getting a call from the guys at the Nevada border about a problem with the Italians. Those bastards had been acting like they owned the place ever since our father was… I clenched my fists, ready to head to the basement gym and blow off some steam after arguing with my brother. Before our father died, I had been part of the trades and sometimes even the meetings, but now, Grigori kept me out of the business. I was sixteen, for fuck's sake. The dim light coming from the living room caught my attention, and as I got closer, I saw a lone figure standing on the terrace.

Elif Ozdemir. My brother's new wife.

I wasn't sure what to think of her at first. I had assumed she was weak, unfit to take on the role left behind by our mother. But that perception shattered when she shot Uncle Anton during dinner last weekend. My gaze flickered to the plaid blanket draped over the armrest, the same one that had belonged to my mother. I glanced back at the woman standing outside, the wind playing with her long hair. I groaned and grabbed the blanket, walking onto the terrace. She lifted her head at the sound of my approach, dark eyes meeting mine. Mother had blue eyes, like me and Sasha. They shone when she smiled or when our father complimented her. Elif's eyes were a deep brown, almost black. And yet, something about them commanded respect.

I draped the blanket over her shoulders, "thank you," she murmured, her voice barely audible over the crashing waves. It was only then that I noticed her tear-streaked cheeks, and for the first time since mother left, I felt something tighten in my chest. I grimace and take a step back, ready to turn away, to leave. I didn't want a new mother, I didn't want to form a bond with this woman, I didn't want to feel the same thing I felt when my mother died. "I don't want to take her place or even impose on your lives," she murmurs, stopping me in my tracks. And suddenly, I understand the reason for her tears, Sasha. I never would have thought that idiot's words could wound her like this. I sigh and drop onto the swing beside her, making it sway slightly. "He's just an idiot, you shouldn't pay attention to what he says," I tell her, my eyes fixed on the horizon where the dark sea and sky blend together. I hear her sniffle, her head lowered, and my brows knit together when I see her scratching the inside of her wrist, leaving marks. Before I even realize it, my hand shoots out, grabbing hers to stop her.

She lifts her face, fresh tears trailing down her cheeks. "I just... I just wanted to help him. I didn't think it would hurt him," she whispers, her lips trembling, making me press mine together tightly. I swear I'm going to break that idiot's neck in the morning. I watch her for a few seconds longer before tugging on my sleeve and wiping her cheeks dry. "When our parents... left, we were like headless chickens, not knowing what to do or where to go. Grigori was overwhelmed by his new role, trying to assert himself, crushed by guilt and unable to take care of us. I was already far from sociable, barely leaving my room except to find food, which I ate alone. Sasha was furious, struggling with the sudden solitude in the absence of our mother, whom he had spent most of his time with. And Roman... he hasn't spoken a word since they died." I lean back, letting the swing rock us gently, watching her legs cross on the seat beside me. My sudden openness surprises even me. Maybe I feel comfortable because we're close in age, or maybe because since she arrived, she's done nothing but try to help us.

"But ever since you've been here, Grigori is doing better. Seeing you take care of us seems to ease him, and the way he acts around you... he looks more alive. When he talks to you, he has this way of looking at you that makes me uncomfortable, even makes me grimace," I add with a smirk. She chuckles softly, sniffling as she does, and I can't help but smile. She's... surprisingly easy to be around. "When you locked my bedroom door that night, I honestly wanted to throw you in the pool. But over time, I realized what you were trying to do. You were trying to bring us

back together, to rebuild our family. But honestly, you didn't have to do it while I was only wearing a damn towel," I grumble, making her snicker. "As for Sasha, even though he's an idiot, he's a good guy deep down. He's just scared. What he feels toward you terrifies him. I know, because I feel it too. We're afraid to get attached again. And like our mother, you…"

I trail off, feeling my damn eyes burn. Blayt'.

Suddenly, cold hands slide against my cheeks, turning my face toward hers. Her dark eyes hold that same determination I've seen countless times before, when she argues with Grigori to impose her ideas or when she forces Sasha to do something he resists. "Listen to me, Niko…" she says, using my nickname for the first time, and it doesn't bother me. "I will never leave. Not as long as you need me. And even after that, I'll still be here, I'm like a damn leech. I'm not going to die, not before I see my grandchildren and your grandchildren. Not before we're back here, on this very swing, watching them try to drown each other. I promise." Her eyes don't leave mine, and before I can think, my body moves on its own. My arms wrap around her waist, my face pressing into her neck as I hold onto her tightly. I feel the tears spill over, hear the quiet sobs breaking free, the ones that have been stuck in my throat since they left us. And Elif holds me, her hand rubbing my back, her lips pressing against the back of my neck.

"Fear isn't a bad thing, Niko, as long as you don't let it control you. Trust yourself. Never doubt what you feel. I will always be behind you, supporting you, even if it means drugging Grigori with sleeping pills for the next few days." I laugh, knowing full well she's capable of doing exactly that. It wouldn't be the first time. "Thanks, Elif. Call me if you need anything." "Don't worry about me, Niko. The only thing I need right now is for you to take your feet off that damn desk."

I freeze.

"How…" "I recognize the sound of the clock I spent three hours picking out, Niko." I glance up at the massive clock behind me and glare at it before begrudgingly lowering my feet. "Good night, Nikolaï." "Good night, Elif."

Chapter fifteen

<u>Selina</u>

"What's all this?" Sienna asked as she entered the living room, stopping beside me as I stared, mouth slightly open, at the three women dashing between piles of clothes. "I have no idea," I murmured. "*Mamma!* Look, I'm Superman!" Rafael suddenly shouted, appearing from behind the armchair with a red scarf tied around his shoulders. "And I'm Batman!" Andrei yelled, running after Rafael with a black pair of underwear on his head. I couldn't help but burst into laughter as I spotted Alexei following behind them, recording everything on his tablet. Sienna chased after them, trying to stop the chaos, while I suddenly felt warm breath against my neck. "Do that sound again, *Solnychko*," Nikolaï whispered, making me shiver. "I want to see how your face lights up."

I turned around and found myself caught in the icy blue of his eyes, as mesmerizing as ever. You know that hidden part of an iceberg, the part submerged beneath the water? When it surfaced, it took on a deep, captivating blue. Well, Nikolaï Ivanov's eyes were exactly that color, deep and entrancing. It had been over two weeks since he helped me through my panic attack, and since then, an unspoken connection had formed between us. Fleeting glances that stole my breath, smiles that warmed my heart, and the occasional touch, his hand brushing against mine when he walked past, his lips barely grazing my cheek or neck as he reached for something on the table, leaning over me. I didn't know what we were doing or where it was leading, but I had never felt so safe, so protected, almost… free. And I had never seen Rafael this happy. He got along so well with Nikolaï's sons, and they never excluded him from any of their activities. Just yesterday, they had gone horseback riding together.

I hadn't even known there was a stable on the estate. I had always loved horses, but seeing one in real life was incredible. I had been frozen in place in front of a stall, unable to tear my eyes away from the magnificent black stallion staring back at me. And, of course, I had later found out it belonged to Nikolaï when he approached me, guiding my hand with his to encourage me to touch the animal.

I had then watched him ride alongside his sons, my eyes welling up when I saw him helping my son stay balanced in the saddle, soothing him when he trembled with fear. I had even discreetly wiped away a tear when his sons came over to encourage Rafael, explaining how to do it properly. His children were truly angels, but I could tell there was some distance between them and their father—something I didn't dare bring up. When he had first suggested going to the stables, they had refused, only agreeing after Rafael got excited and I encouraged them. I suspected it had something to do with the loss of their mother, but I knew it wasn't my place to ask questions. "I don't think I can do it on command," I said with a small smile, trying to hold his gaze. His eyes narrowed slightly, amusement dancing in them before he leaned in, brushing his lips against my cheek as he murmured near my ear, "Then I won't miss it next time." I took a deep breath, his voice igniting something deep inside me, something unknown, something terrifying and thrilling all at once. He pulled back with a smile before taking my hand, leading me toward the chaos in the living room. "Come, they're here for your sister and you," he said.

"For us ?" I asked, confused, as Sienna reappeared with Andrei laughing hysterically over her shoulder, the underwear on his head now gone. My son ran up again, still wearing his "superhero cape," his eyes lighting up the moment he saw Nikolaï. "Niko ! Look, I'm a hero !" he exclaimed, raising his arms in the air, the towering man beside me, who could easily intimidate anyone, bent down and lifted my son onto his shoulders. "Is this better, Rafael the Hero ?" he asked before taking off, running around the table. I smiled, my eyes misting over as my son let out delighted squeals.

From the corner of my eye, I saw Andrei hesitating, taking a small step forward before stopping behind me. I turned and knelt before him. "What are you waiting for ? Go join them," I said, gently taking his hand. With his gaze lowered, he only shrugged, making me press my lips together. I glanced up and spotted a blue shirt lying nearby. Picking it up, I tied it around his shoulders like a cape. "Come on! It's Andrei's turn now. Get down, Rafael," I said as I stood, rubbing Andrei's back while he stared at me wide-eyed. Nikolaï froze, his eyes shifting from his son to me before nodding slightly. He carefully placed my son back on the ground, knelt down, and opened his arms toward Andrei. The boy hesitated, so I gave him a gentle push, smiling at him encouragingly. Nikolaï lifted him effortlessly, hoisting him onto his shoulders just as he had with Rafael. "You holding on tight, son ?" he asked. Andrei nodded, and that was all it took, Nikolaï took off running, and Andrei burst into laughter, making me smile.

Maybe, just maybe, I could do something for them before I left, "Madame Ivanov?" a voice suddenly called from behind me, making me jump. I turned to see one of the women who had been unpacking clothes when I arrived, "I... I'm not..." but my words died in my throat as an arm wrapped around my waist. "Thank you for coming to assist my wife and sister-in-law, Miss Lugovaya," Nikolaï said, making my eyes widen in shock. Sienna stiffened beside me, throwing me a bewildered look. "It's my pleasure, Mr. Ivanov. It's an honor to assist your family. Without Madame Elif, I would never have been able to open my boutiques." She turned and began wheeling a rack full of dresses in every imaginable color, each one more beautiful than the last. I lifted a questioning gaze to the man beside me, whose arm remained firmly around my waist.

He simply smiled before leaning down to murmur, "Better to keep your identity a secret." I frowned, gripping the fabric of his shirt to keep him from pulling away, "so now I'm your wife? Just like that? Sounds like a very forced marriage to me," I quipped. He chuckled near my ear, and God, that voice,"trust me, *Solnychko*, if we ever get married, you won't even have time to think of an answer," he teased, tightening his hold around me. I closed my eyes, my fingers gripping his shirt, my body betraying me. He stepped back, something unreadable flickering in his gaze before he clenched his jaw and finally let me go. I exhaled slowly, realizing only now that I had been holding my breath. What was I doing?

"My dearest brother-in-law, may I ask what all of this is about?" Sienna's voice cut in, filled with skepticism. She picked up a dark-colored dress, inspecting it with narrowed eyes before shifting that same sharp gaze to

Nikolaï. He met her glare with an expression I could only describe as deliberately provocative, a smirk tugging at his lips. "Well, my angelic sister-in-law, I thought you might need clothes in your sizes and tastes, though I would never question Elif's taste, unless I wanted to lose an eye," he responded, turning away to unhook an emerald green gown from the rack. I watched as my sister bristled, her lips pressing into a thin line as she directed her deadliest glare at Nikolaï. "I don't think we need anything. What we have is more than enough... for the weeks ahead," she said, emphasizing the last words. Nikolaï ignored her, striding toward me with the emerald dress in hand, "you should try this one," he said, holding it out to me. I glanced between the dress, him, and my sister, who looked ready to commit murder. I took the dress, mumbling a thank-you, and followed one of the women behind a folding screen. The young woman extended her hand, offering to help me undress, but I instinctively recoiled, my breath catching in my throat. My scars itched, as if desperate to be exposed, but I refused to let them.

"Leave it. I'll help her," my sister muttered in a clipped, tense voice, slipping behind the partition, the woman nodded and stepped away, leaving us alone as Nikolaï began discussing something with Miss Lugovaya, the children resuming their noisy play. Sienna started unbuttoning my dress, her brow furrowed, her jaw clenched, she was clearly furious. "Sienna..." I began hesitantly. "I don't know what game you're playing, Selina, but it has to stop," she murmured so softly I barely heard her. I winced at her words. The truth was, I didn't even know what was happening between Nikolaï and me. She carefully pulled my arm free from my sleeve, mindful of my still-healing fingers. Just yesterday, Dr.

Semionov had finally removed my cast, prescribing a cream to help with the lingering pain. "We need to leave," she continued in the same low tone as she unzipped my dress. I looked up at her in shock. "That's what we're going to do… in a week, *mia sorella*." "No, Selina. We're leaving tonight," she interrupted, pulling the new dress over my head. "What? We can't just up and leave like that without telling anyone—" Sienna gripped my arms tightly, her dark eyes locking onto mine, sending a shiver down my spine. "Wake up, Selina ! We've known these people for barely two weeks. You think we can trust them? Trust me, *mia sorella*, the first chance they get, they'll sell us out, because that's in their nature. I've made that mistake too many times over the years, and it's cost me dearly. I won't let it happen again, not when you and Rafael are part of the equation."

I felt my knees weaken as I caught the fear and suspicion she was trying so hard to mask beneath her hardened gaze. My lips trembled as I reached up to brush my fingers against her cheek, gently caressing her high cheekbone. "What happened to you, *tesoro mio?* " I whispered. She froze under my touch, her walls cracking for just a fleeting second, long enough for me to see that lost, trembling sixteen-year-old girl beneath them. But just as quickly, she pulled away, rebuilding those impenetrable walls, "be ready tonight. I'll come for you," she said, zipping up my dress before leaving. I let out a slow, unsteady breath, my trembling hands pressing against my stomach. So, I was leaving tonight? "Selina? Are you alright in there?" Nikolaï's deep voice suddenly snapped me back to reality, making me jump. I took a deep breath and stepped out, smoothing down the fabric of the dress, so soft, unlike anything I'd ever touched before.

I lifted my gaze and froze as his eyes trailed slowly down my body, lingering at the modest neckline just above my chest before traveling up my throat and finally locking onto mine. I swallowed hard, wetting my lips slightly, and without realizing it, I pressed my thighs together. "You look stunning, Solnychko," he murmured, stepping closer. But I instinctively took a step back. He stopped. What if my sister was right? Two weeks wasn't long enough to trust anyone. These lingering glances, these touches, these words that soothed my mind like a balm, should they terrify me instead? What if all of this was just a way to keep me occupied while he negotiated with Antonio? A sudden thought stole my breath away. If Nikolaï Ivanov asked me to stay at the end of these three weeks... I might actually say yes.

"Selina?" he said, frowning as he stepped toward me again. I shook my head, retreating another step. "I... I feel tired. I think I'll go rest for a bit." He watched me for a long moment, as if trying to read my thoughts, but then nodded, stepping aside to let me pass. I kept my head down as I hurried up the stairs, retreating to the guest room, where I began gathering our things. Sienna was right. Trust had no place in this world, especially not in the mafia.

I paced back and forth across the room while Rafael slept peacefully, unaware of everything. The night was well advanced, it had to be around three in the morning. I froze when the door opened, and my sister slipped inside, dressed entirely in black, quietly closing the door behind her. "Are you ready ?" she asked, approaching me with a black jacket in her hands. "I… Sienna, what if he finds us outside ?" I asked, my voice trembling as she helped me slip into the jacket. "Selina, look at me," she said firmly, I turned to meet her gaze as she zipped up the jacket over my light sweater. "I was the one who got us out of that hotel, wasn't I ? And the rest of my plan was solid until those Ivanov brothers interfered. So don't worry, I know what I'm doing," she said, her expression filled with determination.

I nodded, forcing myself to ignore the crushing fear. Moving toward my son, I gently shook him awake while pointing at our packed bag for Sienna to take. "*Mamma? What's happening?*" he asked, struggling to open his eyes as I helped him into his jacket. "Nothing, *Angelo mio*, we're just playing a little game, okay? We have to be very quiet." "Are we playing hide and seek? Is Niko going to find us?!" My hands trembled at the mere thought. If Nikolaï caught us, I had no idea how he would react. Would he punish me like Antonio? A cold sweat gripped me as I exhaled slowly, trying to calm myself. "Yes, it's hide and seek, but we have to win, so no noise, okay, baby?" I lied. He nodded, smiling.

"I'll carry him," my sister said, handing me my bag along with her backpack and a pair of sneakers, which I quickly slipped on. I went first, cracking the door open just enough to check for any signs of movement. Nothing. Silence. I stepped out, motioning for Sienna to follow. She took the lead down the staircase and headed directly to the living room, where she carefully slid open the large glass door leading to the gardens. A gust of cool air rushed in, the wind sweeping loose strands from my braid and making Sienna's ponytail sway.

She moved swiftly between the tall hedges, slipping into a narrow path I had never noticed before. "How do you know this way?" I whispered, following closely so I wouldn't lose her in the darkness. "What do you think I've been doing for the past two weeks ? I know this house like the back of my hand. Well, almost, I couldn't get into the basement because of *Hardman*," she grumbled, pushing deeper into the garden. We walked for a solid ten minutes, a stark reminder of how vast the estate truly was. Eventually, we reached the base of a tall white wall, the boundary of the property. Sienna frowned, glancing behind us. I followed her gaze but saw nothing. "This way," she whispered, continuing along the wall. I couldn't help but be surprised at how effortlessly she moved, barely out of breath despite carrying my sleeping son. She was graceful, fluid. Meanwhile, I was sweating, panting, and tripping over my own feet, having to brace myself against the wall more than once.

A few meters ahead, she stopped in front of a small door I would have completely missed in the darkness had I been alone. She felt around the wall, then opened a concealed panel, revealing a numeric keypad. She quickly entered a code, and the door unlocked with a soft click. I stared at her in shock. She pushed it open slowly, peering outside before stepping through and gesturing for me to follow. We found ourselves on a dirt path at the edge of the forest and a few meters away, a car idled, its engine running. Sienna exhaled in relief and strode toward it while I hesitated, wrapping my arms around myself as I trembled. From the cold ? From fear ? I didn't know. She opened the back right door, motioning for me to get in. I hesitated, casting one last glance at the grand white manor, now shrouded in darkness, a home I might have lived in under different circumstances. Holding Rafael tightly against my chest, I slid into the car, peeking at the driver. His face was obscured beneath a cap, making him unrecognizable.

Sienna placed our bags in the trunk before opening the other rear door to join us, then suddenly froze. Her grip tightened on the door handle, her gaze fixed in the distance, vacant. "Sienna?" She slowly lifted her eyes, her expression one of shock, turning her head toward the driver, who remained motionless, hands gripping the wheel, shoulders stiff. "You bastard !" she suddenly shouted, making both Rafael and me jump. She straightened, slamming the car door shut as the driver stepped out, also slamming his door, much harder.

My breath caught in my throat as he removed his cap, revealing the sharp profile of Sasha Ivanov, his ice-blue eyes almost as dark as the sky above us. My door suddenly swung open, making me flinch. I slowly lifted my gaze, meeting the intense blue stare towering over me. "Niko ! You won !" my son exclaimed, grinning. Nikolaï's piercing gaze shifted from me to Rafael, his expression softening just enough to force a smile, "of course I won," he said, his deep voice sending a shiver down my spine. He crouched down to pick up Rafael, bringing our faces level, but instinctively, my arm tightened around my son. Those iceberg-blue eyes settled on me again, and my throat tightened as I caught something behind their hardened gaze. Without a word, my arm loosened, releasing my baby, and Nikolaï lifted him effortlessly with one arm. His other hand wrapped around my arm, gently pulling me out of the vehicle. My eyes widened as I suddenly noticed a dozen men moving around us. Had they been there the whole time ?

"Where is he ?!" my sister's voice suddenly rang out through the darkness, and I turned to see her standing face to face with Sasha, who had yet to say a word. He merely glared at her, his expression dark and unreadable. "Where is the man who was supposed to drive us ?" Sienna shouted again, slamming her hands against his chest in a futile attempt to push him, but he didn't budge an inch. I tensed as I saw Sasha's jaw clench, his patience clearly wearing thin. I took a step toward them, but a steel grip around my arm stopped me. I looked up at Nikolaï, but his attention remained locked on his brother and my sister, his expression unreadable. Meanwhile, he rocked my son gently, lulling him back to sleep, completely unaware of the tension crackling around him. "Why so much curiosity ?" Sasha finally spoke, his deep voice matching the weight of his stare. He lowered his head toward Sienna. "Is he your lover?"

My sister didn't answer. She pressed her lips together, but I didn't miss the slight tremble in her jaw, nor did the Ivanov brothers. "I killed him," Sasha finally said, his voice cold. A strangled gasp escaped my sister, her eyes widening in horror, "no." She shook her head violently, and I froze as I saw a single tear slip down her cheek, for the first time in eight years. "No !" she repeated, louder this time, struggling in his grip, "let me go! Let me go! I'll kill you, Sasha Ivanov, do you hear me?!" I flinched at every one of her screams, her voice breaking toward the end as Sasha flipped her around, pinning her against the car. He pressed against her back, holding her still. "Stop him," I whispered, my eyes fixed on my sister's twisted expression of hatred and pain. I grabbed Nikolaï's jacket, shaking him, "please, stop him!" His gaze finally dropped to mine, his jaw clenched, his lips pressed into a thin line as he took in my face, "enough, Sasha," he commanded without looking away from me. "The man is alive."

Sienna stilled, panting and trembling. Her eyes squeezed shut, her forehead pressing against the roof of the car. The relief rolling off her was almost tangible. Sasha, however, didn't move. If anything, his expression darkened further. He turned her around again, gripping her shoulders now, fully blocking my view of her face. "So that was the plan ?" he murmured, his voice quieter but laced with fury. "Running away with your lover?" Sienna lifted her chin, sharpening her claws, "it's better than waiting for you to decide when to sell us to the Italians !" she spat, standing on her toes to get closer to his face, her eyes blazing with anger. Beside me, Nikolaï stiffened, his gaze burning into the side of my face. I didn't dare look at him, "we're going home before Rafael catches a cold," he finally muttered.

He grabbed my hand and pulled me along. But I stopped in front of the car, glancing back at my sister, who still refused to back down from her silent battle with Sasha. "Go. I'll be fine," she said simply, not even looking at me. I turned away, my hands trembling as I followed Nikolaï. But inside, rage built, rage at myself, at my uselessness, at my fears that paralyzed me, at the person I had become. The walk back to the manor was silent, except for the curious glances thrown our way by the guards stationed at the gate, Nikolaï released my hand and pushed open the heavy front door, stepping inside without looking back. He started up the stairs, and I closed the door behind us, following quietly. I frowned when I realized he wasn't stopping at the guest floor, he kept climbing to the third floor, where his room and his sons' rooms were. "Where are you going?" I asked. He didn't respond. We reached the twins' bedroom, and he carefully opened the door, stepping inside. He approached Andrei's bed, pulled back the covers, and laid Rafael beside him. After removing his jacket, he tucked both boys in, watching as they instinctively curled up against each other.

He motioned for me to leave, and after one last glance at the children, I quietly stepped out. Nikolaï closed the door gently, but his shoulders remained tense. I barely had time to react before I was lifted into his arms, my own arms instinctively wrapping around his neck. "What are you doing ?! Put me down !" I protested, squirming. "So you can escape the second I look away ?" he said, still avoiding my eyes. "And stop yelling. You'll wake the kids." I pressed my lips together, unable to argue. He strode into his room and kicked the door shut, placed me gently on the bed, then turned to lock the door. And he didn't move, forehead against the wood, his broad back tense, he just... stood there. Slowly, I got to my feet, my legs trembling.

"Nikolaï... I... I'm sorry. I just wanted to protect my family. And yours, too. The longer we stay here, the more v—" I flinched when he suddenly turned around, his hands sliding up to cup my face, fingers threading into my hair. His eyes pierced into mine, studying every inch of my face as if seeing me for the first time. "Nikolaï ?" I whispered. His gaze locked onto mine. "Do you think like your sister ?" he asked, catching me off guard. I swallowed hard, my eyes lowering, "I... We've only known each other for two weeks, but I've known the mafia for years. Trust doesn't exist. There are only strategies, schemes, blackmail, and betrayals," I murmured, slowly raising my head. "I... I can't, Nikolaï. I don't want to keep living in this dark world, not even for what you offer me. Please, I beg you... let us go. For everyone's sake." My voice trembled. Tears fell despite my efforts to stop them. He looked at me, and I felt like he saw everything, my fears, my regrets, my wounds, my pain. He read me like an open book.

"Don't cry," he breathed, wiping my tears before pulling me against his chest, enveloping me in his warmth. His lips pressed against my forehead as he whispered the words that should have freed me from this world of monsters. But in reality, they wounded me in a way nothing else ever had. Not even Antonio. "All right, *Solnychko*. Whatever you want."

Chapter sixteen
Nikolai

It was almost ten in the morning when I entered the office, a draft of cool air hitting me as I noticed the balcony door open. Sasha was leaning against the railing, smoking. "Is everything ready?" I asked as I sat down behind the desk, where my brother's laptop was already on. "Yeah," Sasha grunted as he stepped inside, shutting the door behind him, then reopening and closing it again. I grimaced at his action, his OCD becoming uncontrollable whenever he was on edge. His dark tone and expression confirmed my thoughts. If there was one person in our family you didn't want to anger, it was Sasha. Not because he was the most violent, Roman held that title despite his excitable demeanor. Nor because he was the most vindictive, that honor belonged to Grigori, our old wolf of a brother. And certainly not because he was the most devious, that was a title I proudly claimed.

Sasha was dangerous because he was unpredictable. Even to us, who had grown up together. He struck where no one expected, and it hurt, badly, as I'd learned from childhood experiences. But I had to admit, last night, I truly thought he was going to snap Sienna Floros's neck, and I wasn't sure I would have stopped him. They had almost escaped. If one of our men hadn't spotted Sienna lurking near the east wall and alerted Sasha, they would have succeeded. When Selina had walked in, looking more breathtaking than ever in the emerald dress I had chosen for her, I thought I was seeing a mirage. Her dark hair contrasted beautifully with the fabric, making her deep green eyes even more striking. But all of it shattered with that one small step she took backward. I didn't know what Sienna had said to her behind that screen, but she had managed to push Selina miles away from me. And when Sasha had told me about Sienna's escape plan, though I had no idea how he found out, I thought I might lose my mind. But I had to wait until nightfall to get my hands on Sienna's accomplice. Sasha had taken it upon himself to handle the interrogation, probably breaking the guy's nose given the force he had used when restraining him.

I glanced down at the screen as an incoming call popped up. Without hesitation, I answered, and Sasha moved to stand beside me. Elif's smiling face appeared, and the tension in my shoulders, built up since last night, eased slightly. "Oh my god, what happened ?" she asked, her expression shifting to concern. Behind her, Grigori and Roman immediately appeared over the back of the couch where she was sitting. I sighed, running a hand through my hair. "Nothing important, we're handling it—" "Nikolaï and Sasha Ivanov, you are going to tell me right now what's going on ! Are you hurt ? Are the kids okay ?!" she nearly shouted, leaning so close to the camera that her forehead almost filled the screen. This woman, seriously. Cursing under my breath, I quickly summarized the events of last night, keeping the details to a minimum.

A heavy silence followed.

"I hope you didn't do anything stupid to those women," Elif finally said, placing the tablet on the coffee table and leaning back into the couch. Grigori massaged her shoulders, his dark gaze fixed on us, while Roman sat down beside her. Sasha scoffed, rolling his eyes. I simply shook my head, closing mine for a brief second. With the way Elif had raised us, that was never even a risk. "Did you manage to get anything out of Sienna's boyfriend ?" Roman asked, his usual playful tone returning as he looked at Sasha. Sasha tensed, his jaw clenching. If Roman had been within arm's reach, he'd be dead by now. "No, he hasn't said a word," Sasha muttered through gritted teeth, knowing full well that he had personally interrogated the man. "But he's definitely Korean. I'll run a facial recognition search—someone with a scar like his can't be that hard to track." "And what about you guys ?" I asked, shifting the conversation. "How did the meeting with the Italians go ?" It was around 10 p.m. there, plenty of time for it to be over.

Elif's expression hardened as she sat up, slipping out of Grigori's hands, "I don't know how Selina endured that man, Niko, but I was this close to pulling out my gun and putting a bullet in his head," she growled. I frowned as Sasha leaned forward, resting his hands on the desk, "what do you mean you were ready to shoot him ? You let her attend a meeting with the Italians?!" Sasha barked at our brothers, and I couldn't blame him. "As if we had a choice, you know her," Roman retorted, rolling his eyes as Grigori nodded, his dark gaze still locked on his wife. "Oh, excuse me ! I'm right here, in case you forgot," Elif said, elbowing Roman in the ribs and waving her hand dramatically over her head toward her husband, "and stop looking at me like that unless you want to spend the night on the couch with your dear brother." Grigori immediately shifted his glare to us, lips pressed into a thin line, while Roman groaned, rubbing his side.

"Of course I had to see that monster with my own eyes and give him my best death glare," Elif continued. "But I made it clear that we would never hand over Selina, Rafael, or Sienna—especially since that psycho seems to want to gut her." Sasha stiffened beside me, straightening up, "she helped her sister and Rafael escape. No surprise he wants her," I muttered, tapping my fingers against the desk. "Still, those bastards were ready to offer us a significant stake in their Illinois operations just to get their hands on the Floros sisters and Rafael," Grigori said. Elif shot him a sharp glare over her shoulder, "whatever they offered, we refused," she said firmly before turning back to me with a soft smile. I nodded, silently thanking her. I knew that, despite his ruthless nature, Grigori would never have made a deal with the Italians. "But I noticed something during the meeting," Elif continued, her fingers tapping her chin as her mind raced like a quantum computer. "What is it ?" I asked, intrigued.

"There's a division within the Rasili family," she said. "Antonio's father doesn't agree with his son. I think when Selina told us she wasn't Antonio's wife, she was telling the truth. I believe his parents never approved a marriage. They're probably looking for a suitable match that will strengthen their influence in the *Cosa Nostra*. To them, Selina was just a pastime for their son." A pastime. A toy to be broken. I closed my eyes, struggling to keep my composure as a shadow of rage crept through me. "These fuckers," Roman muttered, his eyes darkening. "You're right," Grigori added. "If Antonio weren't around, his father would've only negotiated for Rafael." "He won't get either of them," I said, my voice cold but unwavering. "Of course not," Elif agreed. "We need to prepare for possible attacks," Grigori stated. "They know they're under our protection now. I'll reinforce security around the estate until—" "That won't be necessary," I cut him off, gripping the armrests of my chair.

All eyes turned to me. "We'll bring them to you," I said. "We'll stay until Elif finds a safe place where they can live peacefully." "What the hell are you saying, Niko ?" Elif asked, confused. "I thought—" "Grigori is right. For everyone's safety, they have to go," I replied, my throat tightening. Grigori nodded, satisfied. "I knew you'd make the right decision for our family." "Elif, please find a location by next week," I added. She held my gaze for a long moment, lips pressed together. Then she sighed, "fine, whatever you say." "Roman and I will return to escort you," Grigori said. "Okay. Sasha will pick you up," I confirmed. As the call ended, Elif's sorrowful expression darkened my mood even further. I leaned back, exhaling. I could feel Sasha's gaze on me, "what ?" I snapped, getting up. "Are you really going to let them go ?" he asked, his jaw clenched.

I let out a bitter laugh, "wasn't it you who wanted them gone when they arrived ?" I countered, raising an eyebrow. He took a deep breath, shoving his hands in his pockets before stepping closer, "I just hope you won't regret your decision," he said before walking past me and out the door. I hope so too.

Selina

I pressed my lips together as the sports car came to a stop in the manor's driveway and the three Ivanov brothers stepped out of the vehicle. It had been almost two days since we had tried to escape, and since then, Nikolaï and I had been avoiding each other. Thanks to the children, meals remained bearable, if you ignored the dark glares and occasional sharp remarks exchanged between Sienna and Sasha. Ever since Nikolaï had agreed to my request, I had felt lost. Over the past three weeks, I had thought I had found some kind of rhythm, a life where I felt somewhat at ease. But I knew this was the right decision, for my sister, for me, and most importantly, for my son. He deserved to live a normal life like other children, without the constant shadow of fear looming over him. Everything would be fine. Once we were far from all of this, I would find a job as a nurse in a hospital like before, and Sienna could resume her studies where she had left off. Far away from all of this.

A sudden knock on the door startled me, and the door opened gently. Sena entered, offering me a soft smile, "Mr. Nikolaï is waiting for you in his office, miss Selina," she said. I nodded and followed her out of the room so she could lead me to the office, which I had never been to before. I frowned upon seeing my sister already waiting by the door, arms crossed and wearing an expression of displeasure. "They summon us like we're nothing more than stray dogs," she grumbled upon seeing me approach. I simply sighed as Sena knocked on the door, announcing us before stepping aside to let us enter. Sienna walked in first, and I followed closely behind, so closely that I ended up bumping into her when she suddenly stopped. I groaned and moved to the side, only to freeze as well upon seeing the four brothers staring at us intently. They looked much more intimidating without Elif there to soften the atmosphere. Despite myself, my gaze dropped to the floor, and I anxiously clenched my hands against my stomach, unlike my sister, who even took a step in front of me as if to shield me.

"Here they are, our little fugitives !" Roman exclaimed, straightening up from the chair where he had been lounging. I tensed even more, expecting the worst. What if Nikolaï and Sasha had waited for their brothers to punish us ? What if he had lied about letting us go ? "We're simply adapting to the situation," my sister responded, crossing her arms again and raising an eyebrow. I winced at her provocation. *Oh god, this girl*. Roman laughed, the only one who did. His brothers remained expressionless, their gazes dark. "Please, take a seat," Grigori said, gesturing toward the long couch facing the dark wooden desk where he was seated. My eyes briefly met Nikolaï's as he stood behind his brother. His face revealed nothing as I slowly sat on the brown leather couch, rubbing my hands against my jeans. Sienna joined me, placing a hand on my thigh, stopping my leg from trembling, something I hadn't even realized I was doing.

"What's going on ?" she asked, her gaze moving across each of the brothers, except for Sasha, who was perched on the corner of the desk, arms and legs crossed, his eyes fixed solely on her. "We're arranging your departure," Grigori explained. "You'll travel with us to California and then move to a secure location that my wife will find within the next few days." My breath caught in my throat, and my eyes slowly lifted toward Nikolaï, who met my gaze, his jaw clenched. "We don't need you to find us a safe place. Just let us go—" "This situation no longer concerns just you," Sasha cut in with a low growl, shoving his hands into his pockets.

"Sasha is right," Grigori agreed, folding his hands on the desk. "The Italians believe we helped you escape and are currently holding one of our shipments hostage. If you get caught before we can recover it, we'll suffer a significant loss. On top of that, our reputation will take a hit if something happens to women under our protection." So, they were only helping us to maintain their power and influence in this monstrous world. In reality, I couldn't blame them. This was their world, one where they had to survive and protect those they loved. I felt Sienna bristling beside me, ready to argue, but I squeezed her hand, inhaling deeply as I locked eyes with Nikolaï, the only one I could stand to look at. "Fine," I agreed as I felt my sister's gaze on me, but she said nothing. "Good. To ensure everyone's safety, we'll travel in two groups," Grigori continued. "The first group will include the children, Rafael, and Roman. The second group will be you two, Nikolaï, Sasha, and myself."

I was on my feet before I even realized it, all my fear and hesitation evaporating, "there is no way I'm being separated from my son," I said, my brows furrowing at the mere thought of it. "Don't worry, nothing will happen to him with me," Roman said, rising from his seat beside me. My throat tightened as he towered over me, my vision narrowing. I let out a shaky breath, instinctively stepping back and lowering my head. "Sit down, Roman," Nikolaï growled. His brother obeyed instantly, his expression apologetic as he glanced at me. Sienna's hand slipped into mine, gently pulling me back onto the couch as Nikolaï stepped forward, settling into the second armchair. "This is the best decision, Selina," he said. "The Italians are watching our every move. We can't afford for them to capture both of you at the same time. If they get one of you, we still have a chance to get the other back through negotiation. And Roman is right, if there's anyone who can protect Rafael, it's him." "And I don't just say that lightly," Roman added, crossing his arms behind his head, his usual playful tone absent from his gaze. "I've been through training none of my dear brothers would have survived."

Despite their reassurances, the thought of leaving my son, even for a few hours, twisted my stomach, "hey, I'll go with him, okay?" Sienna said, rubbing my back gently. "I'll watch over him. I would give my life to protect him if necessary, Selina," she added, her determined gaze locking onto mine. Out of the corner of my eye, I saw Sasha straighten slightly from where he stood. "Very well, that's how we'll do it then," Grigori said, standing up. "The children, Sienna, and Roman will leave tonight. Night flights are the safest. The rest of us will travel in the morning." He moved toward the door but stopped when Sienna stepped in front of him. I stood as well, tension filling the room. "I want to see the man you captured the night we tried to escape," she stated firmly, lifting her chin. "Absolutely not," Sasha growled, stepping forward. Grigori raised a hand to stop him, lowering his dark gaze to my sister, who didn't flinch. "You have fire in your eyes," he observed with a smirk. "You've seen worse than us, haven't you? That's why we don't scare you."

"I'd be a fool not to be scared," she admitted, inhaling deeply. "But if I had let fear control me, I would have died hundreds of times." *Hundreds of times...* My hand pressed against my chest as if to keep my heart from bursting. The walls of the room seemed to close in around me. "You want to see this man? What are you willing to do?" "Anything," Sienna replied without a moment's hesitation, "I would die for him." I held my breath as they stared each other down. Then Grigori smirked and nodded before glancing at Sasha, "take her to see him before she leaves. Then let him go, he's of no use to us" he said before leaving. Sienna exhaled in relief, and I quickly grasped her hand. Sasha suddenly stormed toward us, fury etched on his face. I instinctively recoiled, stumbling over the carpet. My sister tried to catch me, but I landed on the couch. "Sasha !" Nikolaï's voice cut through the tension, freezing his brother in place as he knelt in front of me, "are you okay ?" he asked gently.

I nodded, unable to look away. "I'm sorry, Selina. I didn't mean to scare you," Sasha said from behind his brother, his shoulders slumped, his gaze avoiding mine. "No, it's me who overreacted. I… it's going to take me some time to get used to being around men again," I murmured, pressing my lips together as I forced myself to look up and meet Sasha's eyes. He studied me for a few seconds, and little by little, his gaze softened. Finally, he nodded and gestured for my sister to follow him. She gave me a concerned look, but I smiled at her reassuringly, and she eventually followed Sasha out of the room. I let out a soft sigh and stood, forcing Nikolaï to step back. "I should go see Rafael and explain what's happening tonight." "Let's go together," Nikolaï said, opening the door for me to pass through, while behind us, Roman hummed what sounded like a love song.

Chapter seventeen

Selina

My eyes settled on the jet, ready for departure on the tarmac, as Roman brought the car to a stop nearby. In the end, Sasha and Roman had decided to switch places, so Sasha had left with Sienna and the children a few hours earlier, despite my sister's protests. My heart clenched at the thought of my son waving goodbye, his eyes glistening with the tears he had tried so hard to hold back as the car took them away from the mansion. In just a few hours, I would hold him in my arms again, and with Sienna, he was safe, I trusted her completely. My hands trembled slightly as I unbuckled my seatbelt while Nikolai opened my door, extending his hand to help me down from the large 4x4. I thanked him, pulling my wool coat tighter around me against the morning chill. Roman climbed the steep steps to the jet with an ease that was almost unsettling, while I watched Grigori approach a few men near the wing, his presence commanding their full attention, their expressions almost reverent. "Let's go," Nikolai said after retrieving two suitcases from the trunk, along with my bag. I tried to take it from him to help, but he simply shook his head and strode ahead at a brisk pace. He climbed the steps just as effortlessly as his brother, despite carrying all the luggage. How was that even possible? I sighed, following much more cautiously, gripping the handrail to keep myself from slipping on the steps, slick with morning dew. I envied my sister's physical endurance, she wouldn't have struggled with something as trivial as this. But being locked up for eight years had robbed me of any physical strength, unless one counted the times I was beaten. I grimaced at my own dark humor. Maybe I really was losing my mind.

Lost in thought, I suddenly looked up as footsteps rushed toward me. I frowned, watching Nikolai descend quickly in my direction. Before I could react, his arm wrapped around my waist, and in the blink of an eye, my feet left the ground. Within seconds, I found myself at the entrance of the jet, blinking in surprise. He looked at me with a small smile. "Thank you," I breathed. He nodded, gesturing for me to step inside with his arm. I cast a hesitant glance at the interior before finally stepping in. My eyes widened at the luxurious cabin. Thick beige leather seats were arranged in sets of four, facing each other. A soft white carpet covered the floor, and the ceiling was lined with more of the same elegant beige leather. I sank into one of the seats by the window, nearly groaning in pleasure as I sank into its plush comfort. Nikolai took the seat beside me, slipping off his light coat and suit jacket. Rolling up his sleeves, he revealed strong forearms before leaning toward me, entering my personal space. I froze, holding my breath as he reached down and buckled my seatbelt, adjusting it snugly around my waist. Then, without a word, he leaned back and fastened his own. I took a deep breath, turning my face toward the window to hide the warmth creeping up my cheeks. His scent and presence overwhelmed my senses.

Grigori entered next, greeting the flight attendant who appeared behind the thick curtain at the front of the plane. She secured the door as the engines hummed to life, making me tense in my seat. "Ladies and gentlemen, I wish you all a pleasant flight and thank you for choosing *Roman Airlines*. I advise you to fasten your seatbelts and inform you that there is one, yes, only one, parachute located at the back of the aircraft for whoever reaches it first in case of an emergency! So, I hope your cardio is up to par!" Roman's voice suddenly crackled through the speakers. I blinked in disbelief, my gaze snapping to Nikolai, who simply rolled his eyes and shook his head.

"My cardio is terrible," I murmured, feeling my stomach drop. Nikolai glanced down at me for a second before bursting into laughter, making me frown even more. "Don't worry, *Solnyshko*," he said between chuckles. "Roman is an excellent pilot. He'll get us there safely. And even if someone had to use that parachute, I'd make sure it was you." "I don't know how to skydive," I blurted out stupidly, my attention fixated on the way his fingers brushed a loose strand of my hair behind my ear. His smile widened as he leaned down to press a soft kiss to my forehead, "I'll teach you on the spot, don't worry," he murmured, his shoulders shaking again with laughter. And despite myself, despite the fear, despite the uncertainty, I felt a smile tug at my lips just as the plane began to move.

Nikolai

I adjusted the blanket over Selina's curled-up body as she slept, having dozed off a few hours earlier after eating. We were nearing San Francisco, our home base in the United States, where we oversaw all our operations. I had received a call about four hours ago from Sasha, informing me that they had landed safely and were en route to the house, much to my relief. I had decided to wait until Selina woke up before telling her, knowing the news would finally ease some of her anxiety after spending the entire flight worrying about her son and sister. I frowned, lifting my eyes from my laptop as the plane suddenly shook. Grigori stirred from where he had been dozing, shooting me a concerned look. Another, far stronger jolt made Selina jolt awake with a startled gasp. "What's happening?" she asked, disoriented and frightened, clutching my arm. I took her hand in mine, squeezing gently, "It's probably just turbulence, don't worry—" But Roman's voice cut through my attempt to reassure her. "Uh, guys… I think we actually need to decide who's getting that parachute," he said, his usual cocky tone laced with hesitation.

Roman, hesitating? That wasn't good. Not good at all. "Don't move," I told Selina before following Grigori toward the cockpit. My brother knocked on the door, and it unlocked quickly, allowing us inside, straight into pure chaos. Several warning lights flashed across the control panel, and the robotic voice of the plane blared out emergency alerts. "What the hell is going on ?" Grigori growled, gripping the co-pilot's seat to steady himself as the plane lurched again. "What's going on is that our engines are about to give out," Roman gritted out through clenched teeth, freezing us all in place. "What do you mean, 'give out' ?" I demanded, leaning over his shoulder as he gestured toward a flashing warning light. "We're out of fuel," he explained. "No fuel, no engines. The amount that was loaded wasn't nearly enough." "How is that possible?" I asked, straightening up as Grigori dropped into the co-pilot's seat, struggling to stay upright against the plane's violent shaking. This had been a routine flight for us; our technicians knew the exact fuel requirements. A mistake like this was impossible. Unless it had been deliberate. "Rasili," I hissed between clenched teeth.

Grigori looked at me, confused. "Why would he do that? If we crash, Selina dies too." "He doesn't want us to crash," Roman interjected, grimacing as another warning light flashed. "He wants us to land, but not in San Francisco. With what's left, we can make an emergency landing at the Fremont airstrip," he continued, "but we don't have enough fuel to go any further." "They've set a trap at the airstrip," I stated, my jaw tightening. Somehow, that bastard had gotten intel on our flight plan—but he wouldn't get his hands on Selina. Not today. Not ever. "What do we do?" Roman asked, glancing at me over his shoulder. I pulled my phone from my pocket and dialed Sasha's number. Nothing. No signal. "We don't have a lot of options," I said, gripping Roman's shoulder. "We land, and we fight." He held my gaze for a few seconds before nodding. "I told you we should've armed the damn plane," he grumbled, flipping switches on the control panel. "Brace for landing in twenty minutes."

Grigori and I quickly returned to the cabin, where Selina looked at me with wide green eyes. She was pale and trembling slightly, "what's happening, Nikolai ?" she asked, standing, but another sudden jolt sent her stumbling. I caught her before she fell, guiding her back into her seat and securing her seatbelt. "We'll be fine, just stay put," I told her. "We're landing in twenty minutes, but there's a good chance we'll have a welcoming committee waiting for us." She stiffened, "he's there, isn't he? He found me? Oh my God, Rafael and Sienna! Did he get them too?" she cried, trying to get up, but her seatbelt held her in place. "Hey, look at me," I said firmly, tilting her chin up so she met my gaze. "I spoke to Sasha a few hours ago while you were sleeping. They arrived safely. They're okay." Her frantic breathing slowed slightly, but she was still tense, still terrified. "And you will be safe too, Selina," I vowed, my tone unwavering, "I won't let him take you. I swear it on my honor."

Chapter eighteen
<u>Selina</u>

I closed my eyes as the plane shook like a cocktail shaker, gripping Nikolai's hand tightly as he tried to reassure me with words. If we survived the landing, which already seemed like a miracle, it would be Antonio who would kill us. I didn't even want to think about everything he would make me endure if he caught me. But at least Rafael was safe, and I knew Sienna would protect him. "We're going in nice and easy," Roman's voice came through the intercom as I watched the runway drawing closer and closer through the window. I said a silent prayer, burying my face against Nikolai's shoulder, and he slid his hand around the nape of my neck, squeezing gently. *It's going to be okay.* The plane finally touched down, smoothly, to my great surprise, and began to slow little by little until it came to a complete stop in the middle of the runway. "It's over, *Solnyshko*. We've landed," Nikolai murmured, and I lifted my eyes to his. His gaze drifted over my face, darkening at the tension he saw there. "Our welcoming committee is here," Roman said as he joined us, loading a gun with quick, practiced movements, as if he had done it a thousand times before.

I glanced outside and froze when I saw several black SUVs pulling up, with a dozen men getting out. There must have been just as many on the other side of the plane, judging by Grigori's grimace as he peered through the opposite window. "There are too many of them," I whispered, watching the men surround the plane, weapons in hand. Panic gripped me tighter and tighter, making it nearly impossible to breathe. I turned to the three brothers, watching them swiftly load multiple weapons and strap on black vests, which I assumed were bulletproof. Nikolai approached me, holding another vest in his hands, "Nikolai, there are too many of them. We'll never make it," I said as he fastened the protective gear around me with firm, efficient hands. I struggled to breathe, my whole body trembling.

I grabbed his wrists, and finally, he stopped. His gaze locked onto mine, "maybe I should… They'll let you go if I surrender…" Every part of me froze as his hands glided up to my neck, his thumbs tilting my face upward. His lips brushed mine, just the faintest touch, not even a kiss, but the impact felt like a shockwave. My eyes widened as my grip on his arms tightened. He pulled back as quickly as he had leaned in, studying me with dark intensity, his thumbs tracing gentle circles on my cheeks. "Look at me, Selina, and take in every word I say," he said, his entire body coiled with tension. "As long as I'm alive, you will never fall back into that monster's hands. I would die a hundred times before letting that happen." His words carried an unshakable force and determination, "do you understand me, *Solnyshko*?"

I nodded slowly, unable to form any words, my lips still tingling from his touch. Satisfied, he straightened, pulling me to my feet as he finished adjusting the vest. "You're staying with Roman. He'll protect you." I grabbed his shirt, frowning, deeply uneasy about being close to any man other than him. "I can't…" "You can, and you will. Unfortunately, this isn't the time to let your weaknesses take over, Selina. If you want to survive, you have to trust him, but more importantly, you have to trust yourself," he gripped my hand gently. I said nothing, just pressed my lips together as he stepped back. His brother approached slowly, hands behind his back, his shoulders slightly hunched, and I realized he was deliberately making himself appear less imposing. He stopped a few steps away from me, leaning in slightly to meet me at eye level, "can I come closer?" he asked gently, and after a few seconds, feeling the weight of Nikolai's gaze, I nodded. Roman closed the remaining distance and extended his hand carefully, as if approaching a frightened animal. I took a deep breath and hesitantly placed my trembling hand in his. He squeezed it lightly before fastening a thin gray bracelet around my wrist. "It's a tracker," he explained, lifting his dark eyes to mine, so different from Nikolai's but filled with just as much emotion. "We'll find you in less than a minute if anything happens. But nothing will happen to you, not while I'm watching over you."

A small, fleeting smile tugged at my lips, despite everything. He turned slightly, positioning my hand near the strap at the back of his vest. "Grab this and don't let go, not until I tell you to. If I tell you to get down, you do it. If I tell you to hide, you do it. If I tell you to run, you run. Understood?" I nodded, my apprehension growing by the second, "you'll be okay," he reassured me, releasing my hand and stepping back. "Think of your family. Tell yourself you have to fight and survive to get back to them." Rafael's face suddenly appeared in my mind, my baby, the reason I had fought so hard to survive. Then, the image of my little sister, who had to fight and survive alone, without me, when she was just a teenager. "I will fight," I said, determined to reunite with my family, Roman nodded and turned away, grabbing two more guns and slinging a larger one over his shoulder. "I'll go first with the grenades," Grigori said, pulling several from a bag Nikolai had brought from the back of the plane. "I'll follow right behind. We'll carve out a path for Roman," Nikolai added, stuffing extra magazines into his pockets. "Let's push toward the front, they'll least expect it," Grigori said, moving toward the door, where the terrified flight attendant stood watching. He told her to stay inside where she'd be safe, then paused at the exit. He glanced at his brothers one last time before gripping the handle, and stopped when gunfire suddenly erupted outside, and I found myself on the floor.

Nikolaï

I shielded Selina with my body as multiple rounds echoed around the aircraft. "What's happening?" Selina asked, frozen beneath me like a statue. I exchanged glances with my brothers, who looked just as confused as I felt. After several long moments, everything stopped. A heavy silence settled in, broken only by Selina's ragged breathing and the soft sobs of the flight attendant. Selina jumped when my phone suddenly started ringing. I answered it, pressing my free hand gently against the back of her neck. *It's going to be okay*. "Are you coming down, or do you need a red carpet, Ivanov?" a monotone voice said, "Abbiati?" I frowned, sitting up and peering through the window. The men who had been ready to kill us now lay on the ground, dead. In their place, several figures dressed in black tactical gear, faces hidden by balaclavas, now stood at attention. One of them stepped forward and removed his mask, revealing the same expressionless face as his voice, Lorenzo Abbiati.

"It's Abbiati," I said, rising to my feet and hanging up. Then, I helped Selina up as my brothers cautiously opened the door. Roman stepped out first, gun raised and ready to fire, followed by Grigori. "Don't look at the ground. Keep your eyes on me," I told Selina, brushing her hair back from her slightly flushed face. She nodded and clutched my hand as we stepped out of the plane. We reached the bottom of the stairs, and Roman moved behind Selina, guarding her back as Lorenzo approached, a cigarette between his lips, hands stuffed into the pockets of his black cargo pants. "Any injuries?" he asked in his cold, flat voice, scanning each of us before his gaze lingered on Selina, which made my muscles tense instinctively. Without thinking, I stepped in front of her. "No. What the hell are you doing here?" I demanded, eyeing the dozen armed men surrounding us. "We got last-minute intel about Antonio Rasili's plan. He acted alone, no one else knew about his attempt to attack you."

"And how exactly did you find out?" Grigori asked, his dark gaze locked on Abbiati, the latter didn't respond, merely returning my brother's stare with his own blank expression. I suddenly felt Selina's cold, clammy hand wrap around my wrist as she buried her face against my back. I glanced down, following her line of sight and spotted the man lying nearby, bleeding out. *Shit.* "Doesn't matter how," I said, pulling Selina closer, wrapping an arm around her shoulders, "we need to move before more of them show up." "You're right," Lorenzo agreed, exhaling a slow drag of smoke as he turned to one of his men. "Once he realizes his men aren't responding, Antonio will come to see what's happening." Roman appeared at my side, his gaze sharp and calculating as he watched the two men speaking a few feet away, "what is it?" I asked, noticing his expression. "I feel like I know that guy," he muttered, nodding toward the younger-looking man gesturing animatedly at Abbiati. Despite the balaclava, his stature was noticeably lean, his body not yet fully developed, his posture, his movements, the rebellious energy about him... it reminded me of Roman when he was a teenager. "From where?"

"No idea. I'm going to check." Roman took a step toward them, but just as he did, Abbiati signaled to his men, who immediately climbed into their vehicles, including the young man Roman had been eyeing. Within seconds, they were gone, leaving us alone with Lorenzo. "Let's go," Abbiati said, heading toward the last remaining SUV. "We'll spend the night in a safe location. Antonio has shut down all the roads leading to San Francisco. You'll return home tomorrow, it'll be safer then." The three of us exchanged glances. Grigori shook his head, while Roman simply shrugged. I looked down at Selina, still pressed against my side, her bright eyes already locked onto my face, silently searching for an answer. I clenched my jaw. With no better option, I followed Lorenzo into the vehicle.

Chapter nineteen
<u>Selina</u>

A shiver ran through me, pulling me from my sleep, one I had fallen into without even realizing it. My eyelids fluttered open, and I rubbed my cheek against the warm, firm cushion beneath me. Warm and firm? I tensed up, holding my breath, forcing my eyes open and lifting my gaze, only to meet dark blue ones. "Finished drooling on my arm?" Nikolaï asked with a slight smile. I sat up at lightning speed, rubbing my chin, and frowned when I realized there was nothing there. "That's not funny," I grumbled, shooting him a glare, which only made his smile widen. It was only then that I realized we were alone in the vehicle. Roman, who had been sitting to my left, had disappeared, along with Grigori and the other man, Lorenzo, if I remembered correctly. "Where are we?" I asked, squinting out the window, but the darkness outside revealed nothing. "The safe house Abbiati mentioned. My brothers went ahead to make sure there's no danger," he replied, his hand still holding mine. He hadn't let go since we had gotten off the plane. "Why? Is this Abbiati our enemy?" I asked, struggling to understand their relationship.

Nikolaï froze, looking at me for a few seconds before shaking his head slightly, "no, he's not *our* enemy. He works with the enemy, but he isn't one of them. He's a very close friend of Elif. Her brother saved his life and his cousin's when they were young. He would never betray Elif, which means he won't betray us either," he explained, his blue eyes scanning the darkness outside the car. "I didn't know Elif had a brother," I said, confused. It hadn't been long since I met her, but she had never mentioned him. Nikolaï's expression darkened, and his grip on my hand tightened. "He died sixteen years ago," he said, his gaze still lost in the shadows outside.

"Oh my God, that must have been horrible for Elif," I whispered, feeling a pang of sorrow for the woman who had welcomed us with open arms, despite the dangers we brought into her family. "More than horrible. Their mother died when Tarik was six. Elif raised him, he was her baby," he said, his now-blackened eyes locking onto mine. I inhaled deeply, trying to push away the tightness in my throat, turning my gaze away in an attempt to hide the moisture forming in my eyes. But his warm palm against my cheek stopped me, his thumb tracing my cheekbone and gliding beneath my eye, "you get dark circles when you're stressed," he murmured. "I've always had dark circles," I replied with a small smile, but he shook his head. "No, they disappeared after you arrived," he countered, and I realized he was right. I hadn't looked this healthy in years.

The sound of a car door opening made me jump, and Roman appeared. "It's clear. The place is secure," he said, gesturing toward the darkness behind him, where I assumed the safe house was located. "But it's small and... primitive," he added, grimacing as he glanced at me hesitantly. "A blanket will be more than enough," I assured him with a small smile, while Nikolaï got out and held out his hand to help me. "I said primitive, not rundown," Roman chuckled, draping a blanket over my shoulders. "It gets chilly in the mountains," he added before disappearing between the trees. I clutched the soft fabric around me, feeling an unfamiliar warmth bloom in my chest at his gesture, he had thought of me, even when I had long since stopped taking care of myself. "He likes you. Despite his childish attitude, he doesn't trust people easily. But you seem to have a knack for drawing people in, Miss Floros," Nikolaï murmured, wrapping his arm around my waist. I smiled softly and followed him into the dark forest, the scent of pine and earth welcoming us, an aroma I hadn't breathed in for years.

After several minutes of walking in the darkness, during which I nearly tripped a dozen times if not for Nikolaï holding me up, we finally arrived at a small cabin, its porch dimly lit. "And here is our hotel for the night," Roman announced, dramatically bowing as he held the door open. I thanked him and stepped inside, closely followed by Nikolaï, so closely that he nearly crashed into me when I suddenly stopped to avoid Grigori, who was carrying an armful of blankets, completely blocking his view. He dropped them onto a large mattress on the floor, and my eyes shifted to the pull-out sofa against the wall beside it. "We're sleeping on the floor?" I asked, tilting my head up to Nikolaï, who scanned the room with a frown. "Stop making that face, *moy brat*. There's a small room next door with a cozy little bed and its own tiny bathroom," Grigori said as he sat on one of the couches, already pulling off his shoes. I wouldn't admit it out loud, but relief flooded through me. Sleeping in the same room with four men wasn't exactly an idea that thrilled me. I felt Nikolaï relax behind me, then gently pushed me forward. I let him, and he opened the door to our right, revealing a modest room with a single bed, a small shower, and a sink built into the space.

"You'll have to make do, *Solnychko*," Nikolaï said, moving toward the only window to ensure it was securely locked before turning back to me. "This is more than enough," I replied, sitting on the edge of the bed and loosening my splint, which had been bothering me since that morning. He knelt before me, helping me remove it, then gently massaged my palm, careful not to touch my still-healing fingers. "Does it hurt?" "It's bearable," I murmured, watching his face, the way his brows knit together in concentration, the way his lips pressed into a tight line as if holding back words that could change everything. "Where are your painkillers?" he asked, lifting his gaze to mine. I froze, just like always. My face warmed, and I opened and closed my mouth like an idiot as his eyes dropped to my lips.

I saw him inhale deeply before his thumb suddenly brushed over them, stealing my breath, "Selina," he murmured, leaning in, "so beautiful and so strong." His nose glided along my cheek, and his lips left a trail of light kisses along my jaw, sending a shiver down my spine. I gripped his shirt, my whole body trembling, "I'm not strong," I whispered, feeling more vulnerable than ever. "I'm scared... so scared." He pulled back, his gaze locking onto mine as he tucked a stray strand of hair behind my ear, "let me tell you something a great woman once said to me," he murmured, studying my face. "Fear isn't a bad thin, as long as it doesn't control you." "Elif ?" I guessed, recognizing her strength in those words. He nodded, and I exhaled shakily before lifting my trembling hand to his face, touching his slightly rough cheek for the first time. He closed his eyes, turning his face to kiss the tips of my fingers, and I bit my lip to keep from making a sound, but the sensation was overwhelming. "Nikolaï," I whispered, my voice unfamiliar, trembling, breathless. He didn't speak. Instead, he gently grasped my wrist, pressing my palm against his cheek, his lips trailing over the inside of my wrist.

"Nikolaï!" Roman's voice suddenly broke the moment, yanking us back to reality. I instantly pulled away, gasping, clutching my hand to my chest, while Nikolaï remained still, eyes closed, fists clenched on either side of my thighs. He rose, shoving his hands into his pockets. "Your painkillers?" he asked again, his voice rougher. "In my purse," I answered, straightening up. He nodded and left, closing the door behind him, leaving me alone with the storm raging inside me.

Nikolaï

I draped an extra blanket over Selina's sleeping form and clenched my fist at the memory of her soft lips against my fingers. Groaning, I scrubbed my face with both hands and stepped out of the room, trying to shake off the flood of images running rampant through my mind. I shrugged off my jacket and made my way toward the mattress on the floor, which I'd be using for the night, since Grigori had already claimed the couch, sprawled out like he owned the place. I frowned when I saw Abbiati already lying on one side of the mattress, eyes closed. "Already asleep?" I asked, kicking off my shoes. "Hmm," he grunted without moving. I glanced around, looking for Roman, "he already left for patrol?" "Yeah. You'll take the shift after Abbiati in four hours, so get some rest," my brother replied, pulling his blanket over himself. I sighed and lay down, trying to relax, but it was impossible with the tension radiating from the statue of a man beside me. "Are you not going to sleep?" I muttered, shooting Abbiati a glare.

He lazily cracked one eye open before closing it again, clearly uninterested. I swear, sometimes I wanted to put a bullet in him just to see if he was capable of showing an actual expression. "Take my advice, fall asleep as fast as you can," I warned, turning my back on him and ignoring his questioning look. But after several minutes, neither of us had fallen asleep, which was about to become a serious problem. And sure enough, the walls and floor began to shake violently as the unmistakable sounds of my brother's snoring filled the room. I felt Abbiati bolt upright behind me. "What the hell…?" "I warned you," I groaned, burying my head under the pillow.

Screw this.

Chapter twenty
Selina

The cool breeze coming through the window swept through my hair as I took a deep breath, inhaling the scent of the forest and the nearby sea, which lay just beyond the tall trees lining the road we were driving on. The landscape was idyllic. "You like it," Nikolaï's deep voice said beside me. When I looked at him, I realized it wasn't a question but an affirmation. Still, I nodded, smiling like a child. He smiled in return, gently took my hand, and I couldn't take my eyes off his lips, suddenly remembering the moment he had kissed me on the plane. Well, "kiss" was a strong word, his lips had barely brushed against mine, but they had stirred emotions I had never felt before. His lips, which would surely haunt me until the end of my days, stretched into a slow smile, pulling me out of my thoughts. When I lifted my gaze to his, I wanted to disappear on the spot because his eyes reflected a desire I had come to recognize all too well in recent weeks.

"We're almost there," Roman announced, making me remember his presence, along with Grigori's. Lorenzo Abbiati had left early that morning, picked up by another SUV. The vehicle turned onto a small path through the forest, and I felt excitement bubble up at the thought of seeing my son, my sister, and even Mikhail, Andrei, and Alexei again. I had missed them all so much. I frowned when I noticed several men patrolling the forest, some accompanied by dogs, bodyguards. Nikolaï squeezed my hand as the trees gradually gave way to high white walls and a tall gate, several meters high. As we approached, it opened, allowing us to enter, and I pulled back from the window when I saw several men approaching the car with devices in hand. "They're checking for any trackers or other devices on the vehicle," Nikolaï explained when he saw me tense up. I simply nodded, watching as one of the men crouched near my door.

After a few minutes, the vehicle moved forward again, and I slowly relaxed, momentarily forgetting my stress when I saw a grand Venetian-style villa emerge at the end of a long white stone driveway. "It's beautiful," I whispered without even realizing it. The car circled a small fountain before stopping at the base of a staircase leading to the entrance, lined with tall columns. I practically threw myself out of the vehicle when the doors burst open and my son ran out, calling my name. "*Angelo mio*," I breathed, rushing up the steps and kneeling to scoop him into my arms, ignoring the tight pull in my almost, healed fingers. I inhaled his baby scent deeply, running my fingers through his soft hair, feeling tears well up in my eyes as he wrapped his little arms around my neck and peppered kisses all over my cheek, making me laugh.

"*Mamma* ! I was in a little plane with lots of toys, and I saw the clouds !" he exclaimed, pulling back, his eyes shining with excitement. "Mom! Mom!" another voice suddenly called out, and Andrei appeared, followed closely by Alexei and Mikhail. Andrei rushed into my arms while Rafael dashed past me, shouting, "Niko!" I held Andrei just as tightly as I did my son, then did the same with Alexei, who hesitated near me. I stood and moved toward Mikhail, who remained in the background, merely observing. I cupped his face in my hands and kissed his forehead. "Hey there, big guy," I said with a smile. After a few seconds of silent contemplation, he leaned in to kiss my cheek before quickly hurrying past me, blushing, to join his father. My smile widened, such a shy boy.

"Selina ! Thank God you're okay !" Sienna exclaimed as she stepped out, Sasha right on her heels. She hugged me tightly, and I relaxed in the familiar presence of my sister. "Sienna, I've missed you," I said, hugging her back and running my fingers through her slightly wavier hair. My eyes met Sasha's over my sister's shoulder, and he gave me a small nod before joining his brothers and nephews near the car. "Are you okay ?" Sienna asked, pulling back and cradling my face in her hands, her light green eyes locked onto mine. "When I found out that bastard attacked you, I nearly lost my mind," she said, the worry still evident in her voice.

I stroked her cheek, nodding, "I'm fine. Everything is okay," I reassured her, kissing her cheek. She studied me for a moment longer before hugging me again. "I want a hug too !" Elif suddenly chimed in, appearing in the doorway, looking effortlessly stunning as always, with a messy bun, minimal makeup, and a flowing white cotton dress. "Elif !" I exclaimed as my sister stepped aside to let her through. She pulled me into a hug just as tight as Sienna's. "I knew he wouldn't let anything happen to you," she murmured, rubbing my back, and I knew she was talking about Nikolaï. "I'm getting jealous here !" Roman suddenly announced, appearing beside us. Despite myself, I flinched slightly at his imposing stature, but he ignored it, scooping Elif into his arms and twirling her around while she cursed at him between bouts of laughter.

"Give me back my wife, idiot," Grigori grumbled, wrapping his arm around Elif's waist and pulling her to him. "I warn you, this house is always noisy," Nikolaï said as he joined me, while the children clung to Roman's legs. "My mother always said a noisy home is a healthy home," I murmured, recalling my mother's scent of lavender, the warmth of her touch on my cheek. I pressed my lips together as a lump formed in my throat, emotion welling up. Nikolaï didn't respond. I doubted he even heard me amid all the chaos, the children's laughter and shouts, Roman's booming voice, Elif and Grigori whispering to each other, and even Sasha and Sienna exchanging biting remarks despite their efforts to be discreet.

But when I felt his hand brush the small of my back and our eyes met, I knew he had heard me. And, more than that, I knew he understood me, just as he had since the very first moment.

Nikolai

I thanked Elif as I took the glass of water she handed me while she sat beside me in the living room. Sena and Velma were expected to arrive the next day, and my sister refused to hire anyone else for security reasons. Until then, Elif took great pleasure in managing the house, something she absolutely loved to do. "Did Abbiati ever say how he found out about the attack?" Sasha asked from the couch across from me, sitting beside Roman, who was immersed in his phone. "No, he protected his source as if it were his own mother," I replied, my eyes fixed on the two figures sitting at the table in the garden. Selina listened intently as Mikhail explained something to her on his laptop. I couldn't help but smile as I watched her frown, clearly struggling to keep up with my son's fast-paced explanations. She was saved by Alexei, who came running barefoot to their side, a large sheet of paper in his hands, quickly joined by Andrei and Rafael, who had been playing soccer on the grass. Selina laughed at something Alexei said, and the faces of all four boys lit up at the sound. I knew mine must have looked exactly the same. I lowered my gaze when Elif placed a hand on my back, my throat tightening at the sight of the emotion in her eyes.

"Your sunrise is here, Niko. Don't let it set. No matter the consequences, we'll face them together, for you, for her, for the family," she whispered, gently rubbing my back. And damn, my eyes stung at her words, I took her hand in mine, squeezing it softly. "Don't worry, Elif. I made my decision on that plane when I thought I was living my last moments. This sun will never set on my life again," I answered, making her smile. "So, I don't need to find a safe place anymore?" she asked. I shook my head, remembering Lorenzo's words.

I had closed the door of the cabin behind me, slipping between the trees into the night for my turn at watch after Lorenzo. He sat on the trunk of a fallen tree, smoking a cigarette. "How can you sleep with that noise?" Lorenzo had grumbled when he heard me approach, and I couldn't help but smirk. "You get used to it after spending twenty years sleeping in the same room," I replied. I sat beside him, pulling out my own cigarette and taking the lighter he handed me to light it, "so, do you see the future now?" I asked, handing the lighter back to him. "Don't waste your time, Ivanov. My source will remain mine," he said, standing up and dusting off his pants. "But I can give you some advice about Rasili's source," he added, making me freeze as I stared at him.

"What?" I demanded. "We don't know how, but he's tracking Selina's every move. Maybe there are traitors in your ranks, or maybe he managed to plant bugs somewhere, but he always knows exactly where she is. The safest place for her and her son is by your side, within your walls. If she leaves, he'll find them in no time."

"No, no one is going anywhere," I said as the pieces of fate fell into place in my mind. Our destinies, mine and Selina's, were now entwined. And I wouldn't let anything separate us. Ever.

Chapter twenty-one
Selina

"And he won the race under the cheers of all his friends and family," I finished reading, closing the book as the children exclaimed in excitement over the character's victory. "I'm going to be like Tommy too!" Rafael exclaimed from his bed, which Nikolaï and Roman had set up in the twins' room after our arrival. "Me too, me too!" Andrei chimed in, bouncing on his knees over his blanket. "I didn't understand why he chose the yellow car when the blue one was faster," Alexei commented from his bed, staring at the ceiling. "But you're silly ! He chose that color because it was his mom's favorite ! Right, Mom?" Andrei asked, his eyes sparkling. That was what I first noticed about Andrei, his emotional intelligence, the way his face showed exactly what he felt. I loved that about him, just as I loved how Alexei questioned everything, even the simplest things. "Yes, you're right, sweetheart. He picked it because it was his mother's favorite color. And it was thanks to her love and encouragement that he won the race," I said, lifting Andrei's blanket so he could snuggle underneath before kissing his cheek. I did the same with Alexei.

I finally kissed my son's forehead, but he stopped me when I tried to move away, "mama?" he whispered softly, gazing at me with his green eyes, and I smiled before whispering back, "Yes, *Angelo mio* ?" "Let's never leave here, okay ? I want this to be our home with Niko, Andi, Alex, and Mika. Please, Mama." My smile faded as he waited for my answer, his eyes pleading, and I didn't know what to say, "I… Rafael…" light knocks on the door interrupted me as it slowly creaked open, and Nikolaï peered inside without stepping in. Dressed in gray sweatpants and a simple white T-shirt, I caught a glimpse of a new, more personal side of him. "Niko !" my son exclaimed, completely forgetting about me, and I took the opportunity to stand up, avoiding a conversation I wasn't ready to handle. "You came to say goodnight ? That's perfect," I said as I walked toward the door, opening it wider to let him in, but he froze in place, staring at me with wide eyes, as if I'd just asked him to catch a shark with his bare hands while jumping off the villa's terrace.

I gave him a questioning look, but he stayed put, unmoving, as an awkward silence filled the room. I could sense that familiar tension between Nikolaï and his sons creeping in, and I knew I had to act. I reached for his hand, locking my gaze with his, offering him a gentle smile before pulling him into the room. He followed without hesitation. I guided him to Andrei's bedside and tried to step back, but he caught my wrist, pulling me close again, shooting me a look over his shoulder with furrowed brows. But I saw it in his eyes, he needed me here for this. So I placed my hand on his back, feeling the stiffness of his muscles as he bent down to kiss Andrei's cheek. The boy remained still, like a statue. "*Spokoynoy nochi, syn moy,*" (Good night, my son) he murmured softly before straightening up, running his fingers through his son's hair. Then he moved to Alexei's bedside, and I followed, keeping my hand on his lower back, "*Spokoynoy nochi, syn moy,*" he repeated after pressing a kiss to Alexei's hair. Unlike his brother, Alexei pulled his blanket over his face, turning his back to us. Nikolaï lingered for a few seconds, watching him, before stepping away. I slowly removed my hand and headed toward the door, expecting him to follow. But he stopped at my son's bedside this time, and I froze as I watched him kiss Rafael's forehead, repeating the same words whose meaning I still didn't understand. My son kissed him on the cheek, his eyes glowing with a light I once thought was reserved only for me. And an overwhelming sense of relief washed over me.

Finally, Nikolaï joined me at the door. And just as we stepped out, Andrei's small voice echoed behind us, "*Spokoynoy nochi, papa.*" Nikolaï stopped in his tracks, his surprised gaze locking with mine as I smiled and gently closed the door behind us, "you did the right thing," I praised as we walked down the hallway. "I'm sure that with a little effort, everything will get better. Maybe you could find a nanny with a background in child psycholo—" I stopped when he took my hand gently, bringing us both to a halt, "thank you. That meant a lot to me, Selina." I stared at him, unsure how to respond, especially when he looked at me like that, like I was something precious. His eyes wandered from my face to my braided hair, which rested over my shoulder. He reached for the end of the braid, twirling it between his fingers, "Nikolaï…" "We need to talk, Selina," he said at the same time, and a silence settled between us. Not an uncomfortable one, but a peaceful, grounding one. I finally nodded and took a step back, gently slipping my braid from his grasp. "But first, I need to check on Mika. I promised him I'd help him with his math homework before he submits it tomorrow," I told him, slowly backing away toward the other end of the hallway without breaking eye contact. He watched me, his blue eyes still locked onto mine, a small, knowing smile playing on his lips.

Nikolai

I watched Selina's beautiful silhouette disappear into Mikhail's room, dressed in cotton pajama bottoms with smiling suns printed on them and a matching T-shirt. I couldn't help but smile even more, remembering her smile and the way she had helped me with my sons. When she pulled her hand away from mine, I had felt incapable of continuing, of facing my sons, of facing my past. I didn't even know why, to be honest. But with her hand on my back, I had been ready to take on the entire world if necessary. "Wow, you even got the bonus question right, and everything is correct!" Selina's voice echoed from inside the room, and I couldn't help but move closer, sneaking a glance inside. Mikhail had given up his desk chair for Selina and pulled up a stool to sit next to her in front of the cluttered desk, covered in books. "It wasn't that hard," my son mumbled, but I could clearly see his cheeks turning red. Selina ruffled his hair with a laugh. "You're way too young to be humble, Mika. Enjoy your youth, this is the time to brag a little." Mikhail looked at her with wide eyes, like he was watching fireworks, and I completely understood why. That sight, along with the moment I had shared with Andrei and Alexei earlier, only confirmed my decision, a decision that would change all our lives. "Maybe your father could take a look too? What do you think?" Selina suggested, and I froze, realizing she was talking about me. I barely stopped myself from grimacing when I saw both of them looking at me now. *Damn it.*

I cleared my throat, stepped inside, and moved toward the desk, stopping behind Mikhail's chair. He watched me without revealing what he was feeling. I leaned over his shoulder to look at his work. "This is really good, Mikhail. You've improved a lot. I'm proud of you, my son," I said, giving his shoulder a gentle squeeze, meaning every word. He looked at me with an expression I couldn't quite decipher, one I hadn't seen in over a year. He nodded, quickly averting his gaze back to his work, and I glanced down at Selina, who gave me a thumbs-up with a bright smile. And for a moment, time stopped, shrinking down to just her and that smile.

"See you tomorrow, sweetheart," Selina said, closing Mikhail's door before joining me near the stairs. She hummed softly, rocking on her feet with her hands clasped behind her back. "So? What do we need to talk about?" she asked as she reached me. "Let's go to my office," I said, taking her hand and leading her up to the third floor, where the offices and armory were located. The lower floors were divided into two wings: east and west. The east wing of the first floor belonged to Sasha and his future family, while the west was Roman's. The second floor's east wing was reserved for Grigori's family, and the west was mine. The guest rooms were on the ground floor. No matter how much we loved each other as a big family, sometimes we needed space to be alone with those closest to us.

I opened my office door and let her step in first. She paused, taking in every corner of the room with wide eyes, "all the rooms are so different from one another," she remarked as I closed the door behind us. I watched her move through the dimly lit room, the only light coming from the lamp I had left on earlier when I went downstairs for dinner. To our surprise, Sienna had cooked and it had been delicious, especially with Elif's dessert. Selina stopped in front of my bookshelf, running her fingers along the spines, "believe me, Elif has left her mark in every single room. She's put her touch on each one," I said, joining her as she pulled out a book on financial strategies in the medical sector. She laughed while flipping through the pages, stopping at a few handwritten notes I had made. "That doesn't surprise me at all," she said, replacing the book and turning to face me. Her large green eyes settled on mine, waiting for me to speak and I couldn't. Not when she looked at me like that. Not when she had that soft smile lighting up her face, "I can't let you go, Selina." The words escaped before I even thought them. An instinct to keep her close, I had to.

Her cheerful expression faded into confusion, and I hated the shift, "I don't understand. You promised, Nikolaï." I shook my head and stepped toward her, but froze when she stepped back, her eyes searching my face. I realized then I could ruin everything. I could shatter the fragile trust she had placed in me since the day we met. "I spoke to Lorenzo before he left. He doesn't know how, but Antonio is tracking you. He's known where you were this whole time. Even if I let you go, he'll find you in no time, Selina. But within these walls, you're safe…", within these walls ?!" she suddenly exclaimed, her eyes widening, her anger palpable.

It was completely understandable. She had just been freed from one cage, why would she want to be locked in another? I shook my head and moved closer again.

She tried to back away but found herself trapped against the bookshelf. "Don't run from me, Selina. Don't push me away, I can't bear it," I murmured, resting my forehead against hers, my eyes closed. She tensed for a few seconds, not moving at all, then she relaxed, and I held my breath as her arms slowly wrapped around me, her face pressing into my chest. "I'm scared, Nikolaï. I'm so scared. I'm afraid of facing that monster again." I tightened my arms around her trembling frame, holding her close, "never. You'll never have to face him again. I swear to you, Selina, never again." I kissed the top of her head, and she lifted her face to meet mine, her eyes shining. Shining with something I had never seen before.

"I want to kiss you," she suddenly breathed, and everything stopped. "I know that kiss on the plane was just an exception to shut me up, but…" her words faded as I slid my hand behind her neck, pressing a feather-light kiss against her lips, then another at the corner of her mouth, and another on the other side before pulling back. "Don't ever ask me to kiss you again, *Solnychko*. It's me who should be begging you." I tilted her face up toward mine. "And every kiss with you will be an exception, Selina. Now open your mouth for me, please." She looked at me with wide eyes, flicking her gaze between my lips and my eyes, her pupils blown with the same hunger I felt. Finally, hesitantly, she parted her lips, granting me permission and I didn't waste a second. I claimed her mouth, and I tasted paradise. My tongue met hers, and I groaned as her cold, trembling fingers traced my jaw, reminding me of her fragility. I wrapped my arm around her waist, lifting her slightly to deepen the kiss, grinning when she stood on my feet to get even closer.

Fuck.

I finally released her when she gently pushed against my chest, gasping for air. And my growing desire surged as I took in her swollen lips, her ragged breaths, and the dazed look in her eyes. It terrified me, the things I wanted to do to her. I groaned as I felt myself harden inside my sweatpants and lowered my head to steal another kiss, swallowing her soft moan. That sound, *fuck.* My legs shook, and I braced my hand against the bookshelf above her head, pulling her flush against me. Against my arousal. And just as I deepened the kiss, she suddenly stiffened beneath me. I stopped immediately, pulling back, and froze when I saw her eyes squeezed shut, her lips trembling. Not in pleasure. But in fear. No, terror.

Chapter twenty-two
Selina

"Selina, look at me," Nikolai said, gently pushing back the strands of hair that had escaped my braid as I struggled to regain control of my trembling body. *Uno, due, tre...* I exhaled softly, opening my eyes and waiting for the black spots to fade before fixing my gaze on his chest, my cheeks beginning to flush. This was the second time I had lost control in front of him. "Selin...", "I'm sorry, Nikolai, I... my body just reacted on its own, I'm sorr..." I froze when he brushed his lips lightly against mine without deepening the contact. He quickly pulled back, cradling my face carefully between his hands. "Never apologize for the scars you carry, *Solnychko*. They are the proof of the war you survived. As for the rest, we'll take it step by step." I nodded slowly, overwhelmed by the tenderness in his voice. He gently took my hand and led me toward the long black leather couch, where he sat beside me.

"I will find a solution, Selina, I promise you. You will be free. No more walls, no more cages to hold you back, Solnychko. But I need time. Will you wait for me within these walls? I promise, it's not the prison it seems to be." He smiled, and I couldn't help but return it, "I will stay, Nikolai. Rafael too. We will stay, not just within these walls, but by your side," I said, watching him inhale deeply at my words, his grip tightening around my hand. "But Sienna... she has a will of her own. She may not want to stay." "In these past few weeks, if there's one thing I've learned about your sister, it's that she would do anything to protect you and Rafael," he reassured me.

I truly hoped he was right, because I couldn't imagine being separated from my sister. If she refused to stay, then I would leave too. "I have something for you," Nikolai said suddenly before standing up and walking over to his desk. He picked up an envelope and returned to me, holding it out. "This is for you." I frowned as I took out a bank card and a document. "You opened a bank account in my name?" I asked, confused, scanning my personal information alongside an account number. "For what? I don't earn any money to put in it," I added, looking up at him as he handed me another, slightly thicker envelope. "Now you do. Elif deposited your salary for last month. Your employment contract is inside."

"Con...tract?" I pulled out a neatly typed set of papers and began scanning the paragraphs. "A nanny?" I asked, lost, and he nodded, shoving his hands into his pockets. "You've done so much to help my sons over the past month, and I hope you'll continue to help them while you're here." "Of course I'll help them, Nikolai, but not for money!" I exclaimed, standing up, feeling offended. "I didn't do this for money or for anything else!" "Of course not, and I know that," he said, catching my hand. "But I can't let you take on this responsibility without something in return. Accept it for me, or I'll feel like I'm taking advantage of you. You don't want me to live with that guilt for the rest of my life, do you?"

I pressed my lips together, staring at him. I didn't want to accept it, but once I was free, I would need money, to rent a home, to pay for Rafael's school, and so many other things. I looked at the bank card, hesitating, and then an image of Rafael on a new bicycle, his eyes shining with joy, flashed through my mind. I sighed and finally nodded. "Alright." He smiled, making his blue eyes gleam, and dear God, his charm was going to be the death of me. I cleared my throat and stepped back toward the door. "I should go to bed. It's been a long day. Good night," I said, turning to open the door, but suddenly, his hand appeared above my head, holding the door shut.

I turned to ask what he was doing, but the words died on my lips when he gently but firmly tilted my chin upward before kissing me. He deepened the kiss slightly before pulling away, murmuring, "Good night, Solnychko," against my lips. And then, just like that, he stepped back and opened the door for me, stunned, I found myself standing in the hallway as he closed the door in my face, as if nothing had happened. I stared at the wooden door for a few seconds longer before heading to my room, my mind foggy and already anticipating dreams I would have never dared to indulge in just a few weeks ago.

Nikolai

The next morning, I sat at the breakfast table, still tasting Selina on my lips. Even if it had been just a small step, it was a step nonetheless, one I never would have imagined taking just days ago. I nodded my thanks to Elif as she handed me the bread basket while she debated with Roman about the best way to eat crepes. It was either sugar or chocolate spread, I thought. Food and Roman? That was an entirely different level of attachment. Grigori had left early that morning for a meeting.

Normally, I would have gone with him, but he had allowed me to stay this time.

"Would you stop that?!" Sienna suddenly exclaimed from the other end of the table. She was sitting next to Sasha, who was dressed in a perfectly tailored suit. Looked like he was back to work today, "I have no idea what you're talking about," my brother replied as he calmly cut his eggs into pieces. "Oh, you know exactly what I'm talking about ! Stop adding food to my plate when I'm not looking !" she snapped, throwing him a glare. "I have no idea what you mean," Sasha repeated, sipping his orange juice with infuriating composure. Predictably, that only fueled Sienna's frustration. She muttered insults under her breath while pointing her knife at him before attacking the extra food he'd snuck onto her plate. I really needed to talk to my brother about this situation, especially since Sienna would be sticking around for a while. The last thing I wanted was for her to find a way to escape and take Selina and Rafael with her because of Sasha. "Good morning, everyone," Selina said as she entered the room with the boys. And, like every time I saw her, the rest of the world faded away. My eyes first landed on her lips, the ones I had tasted and would soon claim again. Then, my gaze traveled lower to her brown dress, which left little to the imagination, hugging every curve perfectly. A whistle suddenly pierced the air, and I shot a deadly glare at Roman, who only smirked and winked at me, the little bastard.

"Oh my God ! That dress fits you like a glove, darling!" Elif exclaimed, nudging me playfully. "See? I have a great eye for clothes!" All I could do was nod, struggling to find words, "you look just like Mom," Selina froze and turned toward her sister, who watched her with a soft smile, "not just in appearance, but in character too, gentle and brave." "Oh, Sienna, we both take after her," Selina replied, moving to kiss her sister's cheek. But Sienna's smile faded instantly, replaced by a distant expression. "I only have a few physical traits left," she murmured, her voice devoid of emotion.

I barely caught her words, but Sasha did too, because he stiffened beside her. Sienna quickly excused herself, reassuring Selina that she had calls to make. On her way out, she ruffled Andrei and Rafael's hair, making them laugh, "I want crepes too !" Andrei exclaimed, climbing into his chair next to Dimitri, who was already on his third one. Elif smiled as she pushed her chair back, "of course, my little duck. I put yours in the oven to keep them warm. I'll go get…" "I'll do it," Selina interrupted, smiling warmly. "I'm already up anyway," I cleared my throat and stood up, ignoring Elif's amused expression and the stupid smirk on Roman's face. "Where are you going, *moy brat* ?" he asked, raising an eyebrow. *Great.* Now the kids were looking at me too, "I'm getting some water, *moy brat*," I replied through gritted teeth. "But there's water right here, Uncle Niko!" Ivan piped up, pointing at the pitcher on the table. At just eight years old, this kid was already too damn smart. Roman laughed while Elif's smile widened.

"I want sparkling water, little man. Keep eating," I said before making my escape to the kitchen, I stopped near the kitchen island, watching Selina as she moved around the counter, completely unaware of my presence. My gaze inevitably drifted down her back, settling on the perfect curves highlighted by that dress. I closed my eyes, silently thanking God for this creation, before stepping forward and wrapping my arms around her waist. She gasped but relaxed almost immediately, "good morning," I murmured, rubbing my cheek against hers, making her laugh softly. "Good morning, you," she answered, glancing at me over her shoulder and desire took over, as it always did with her. I leaned down to kiss her, cupping her cheek as she dropped the spoon she was holding to grasp my wrist, "now, this is going to be a good day," I said after pulling away, grinning as she stared at me, cheeks flushed and lips slightly swollen. "Yes," she simply agreed, making my smile grow.

"Let's go before Andrei steals Ivan's crepes and Ivan tries to get revenge," I said, grabbing the steaming plate of crepes while she picked up her freshly brewed coffee. She walked ahead of me, back into the dining room. And may God forgive me, but my gaze once again drifted to a certain spot.

"Yes, we'll be there in an hour," I told Grigori before hanging up. I had completely forgotten about today's meeting of the Seven, the monthly gathering of the heads of the main families in the *Bratva*. There were two meetings happening at the same time. One for the family heads, led by Grigori, where we discussed business, security, and trade routes. The other, run by Elif, was for the wives, sisters, and daughters of these men, where they negotiated damage control and brokered peace when necessary. If we had managed to avoid most wars so far, it was because of them.

I pushed back my chair to stand, but the door suddenly swung open, and Sienna Floros strode in, her expression dark. She shut the door behind her and approached my desk with confident steps, "I assume your sister already spoke to you," I said, shoving my hands into my sweatpants pockets. "We're not staying. I don't know how you manipulated my sister, but we are not staying," she repeated, lifting her chin to hold my gaze as I moved closer. "Manipulated ? Is that what you think of me? That I'm some scheming bastard taking advantage of a woman in distress?" Sienna scoffed, shaking her head, "you're all manipulators in the dark world you live in. I won't let my sister fall into another trap." Before I even registered my own movement, my hand gripped her jaw. But to my surprise, she didn't flinch, didn't even blink. "Never compare me to that son of a bitch again," I growled through clenched teeth.

"Then leave her alone," she fired back, gripping my wrist in a sharp movement that forced me to let go. She stepped back immediately, creating space between us. "Where did you learn that?" I asked, rubbing my wrist. She didn't answer. Just stared at me, arms crossed. I sighed and motioned for her to sit, and unexpectedly, she did. "Antonio has a way of tracking Selina," I explained, watching her frown. "That's how he knew about the plane. If you leave now, he'll find you."

"How?"

"We don't know. But I'll find out…", "Will you ? Or do you just not want to find out so you can keep her here ?" she accused, her eyes blazing with defiance. She had been through hell. That much was clear. I stood up again, moving around the desk to join her. She didn't move as I knelt in front of her, taking her hands, too cold, much too cold, into mine. "I know a promise from a man like me doesn't mean much to you, but I swear, Sienna, I will do everything in my power to make sure Selina and Rafael are free. But I won't lie to you, I won't just let her leave without trying to convince her to stay by my side. I will fight for her every second I have, because she's worth it. And even if, in the end, she chooses to leave despite my efforts, I will respect her decision. I swear this to you, on my honor and my blood. But until that moment comes, you both need to stay. Please." I would have thought that begging someone outside of my family would be humiliating. But when I saw Sienna's wide eyes, I felt something entirely different. Maybe it wasn't too late. Maybe one day, her eyes would shine again, when she finally learned to trust. She nodded at last, and I almost let out a sigh of relief. Almost. But it got stuck in my throat when she added, "but I have conditions."

Of course.

I groaned, straightening up and letting myself fall onto the couch opposite hers, "I'm listening." "Maybe Selina has to stay behind these walls, but I don't. I have a job, and I won't let you stop me from doing it. I'm not asking for anything more, I just want the freedom to come and go as I please. I have a car that will pick me up and drop me off." I scratched my jaw, considering her words. "I assume your driver is the same man who was going to help you escape in Russia ?"

She simply shrugged. "There's no point in digging into him, you won't find anything," she said, crossing her arms. "Just like we found nothing on you ?" I countered.

"The last official record of you is that you were studying to become a computer engineer at a small high school in Italy. Then nothing. You vanished the same year your sister fell into that bastard's hands." I leaned forward, resting my chin on my clasped hands. "Tell me, Sienna, what exactly is your job?" She met my gaze without flinching, then shrugged again. I sighed and stood, walking toward the large windows overlooking the ocean. "I can't let just anyone through these gates. I need to know who he is."

"His name is Kenji," she replied, stepping beside me. "And he would never do anything to harm the people I care about. I promise you can trust him. Please." There was something in her eyes when she said those last words, something reluctant, something that cost her. Maybe we weren't so different after all. "Fine," I said after a moment, "but he doesn't come inside. He picks you up and drops you off, nothing more. And if he makes one wrong move, he's dead." My voice was calm, firm, unquestionable. She nodded, "thank you." She turned to leave but paused just before reaching the door, "I know that Grigori, Roman, and you will respect our arrangement, but…", "I'll handle Sasha," I cut in. "As long as you don't provoke him…", "provoke him? Me?" She scoffed, but when I raised an eyebrow, she pressed her lips together. "Fine," she muttered. "I'll try to be… less reactive." Then she exited the room, leaving me with a smirk.

Sasha wouldn't get off easy with this one.

Chapter twenty-three
Selina

Nikolai waved at me, and I returned the gesture as he climbed into the car with Sasha to meet Grigori, who had called them about a problem. The vehicle disappeared behind the heavy gates as they closed. I brushed my fingers over my lips, still warm from the kiss he had given me in front of Sasha before leaving. His brother hadn't said a word or let anything show on his face about our sudden closeness. Then again, even I didn't know where this would lead, but one thing I did know, I hadn't felt this good in years. I headed back inside, closed the door behind me, and barely managed to catch Andrei as he ran toward me, "slow down, sweetheart," I said as he looked up at me with those bright blue eyes, so much like his father's. "Look, Mama ! I drew you !" he exclaimed, holding up a sheet of paper. I couldn't help but laugh at the sight of a stick figure holding what seemed to be flowers. "Wow ! I love your flowers," I praised him, kissing his cheek just as Rafael, Alexei, Mikhail, Ivan, and Dimitri joined us, abandoning their board game on the garden table.

"But Mama, you've never had flowers," Rafael pointed out as he looked at the drawing, leaving me momentarily speechless. Of course, Antonio had never been the type to hand me a bouquet between his blows. "My dad buys flowers for my mom all the time," Ivan said with a smile, "yeah! Uncle Grigori gets Aunt Elif flowers every week," Alexei added, nodding in agreement. "That's completely normal," I explained, wrapping an arm around Mikhail's shoulders. "When you love someone, you give them gifts to make them happy. It's an act of love." "Then why has no one ever given you flowers, Mama? Doesn't anyone love you?" Andrei asked, his innocent words tightening my throat. I knew I was being ridiculous for letting a child's question affect me, but the absence of love in my life had weighed on me for so long. The absence of someone who would love me without expecting anything in return. I felt Mikhail tense under my arm, throwing a sharp glare at his little brother, ready to step toward him, but I stopped him just as Elif came down the stairs, drawing everyone's attention.

"Well! What a welcoming committee for my departure," she laughed, joining us in the hall. She was dressed in a long, fitted red dress that perfectly matched her lipstick. Her long hair, usually wavy, was now sleek and straight, cascading over her shoulders as she stopped beside me. Her smile faded slightly when she saw my expression, but she said nothing. Instead, she simply took my hand and gave it a squeeze, a gesture that meant more than any words could.

"What good deeds have we poor Ivanov brothers done to deserve such divine women?" Roman suddenly exclaimed as he came down the stairs, now dressed in a black shirt and tailored trousers, looking nothing like the carefree, joy-filled young man he had once been. "Idiot. Start the car and get my sons settled in. We're going to be late," Elif ordered, pushing him toward the door as he tried to kiss her cheek. He chuckled, blowing me a kiss before grabbing Ivan and Dimitri around their waists and carrying them outside as they giggled. "We'll be back in two hours. I really hate leaving you alone on your first day here, but I have to attend this meeting with the wives of Grigori's subordinates. Otherwise, they'll find a way to start an internal war before the Italians even get the chance to come after us."

"No, it's not up to you to adjust to us; it's up to us to adapt to your life. Don't change your routines for us..." "You're not adapting to our life, Selina," she cut me off, locking her deep brown eyes onto mine. "Don't adapt to anything. Just live your own life." She pulled me into a tight hug, and despite myself, tears slipped from my eyes. Her embrace took me back to years ago, when I was just a little girl in my mother's arms. "Everything will be alright, Selina. I promise you," she whispered before stepping back to wipe my tears. "And I've never broken a promise." I nodded, sniffling like a child as she smiled gently at me.

"The kids are going to be late for their classes, Mommy!" Roman called from the SUV's driver's seat. "Good luck with the Ivanov Brotherhood, Version 2," Elif said, casting a glance over my shoulder before heading toward the car. I grimaced and turned to see the boys huddled around the garden table, whispering. Yeah, they were definitely up to something.

I smiled once again as I read one of the many notes Nikolai had scribbled in another book I had taken from the library. Only a fool would let himself be swayed, he had written. I glanced toward the garden, where the boys were still huddled together, deep in discussion for over an hour. When I had tried to find out what they were up to, they had practically kicked me out of their little meeting. Rafael had even slammed the door in my face, making Velma and Sena, burst into laughter.

Sienna suddenly appeared at the entrance to the living room, dressed in slim black pants, a white tank top, a black leather jacket, and high-heeled boots. Her hair was pulled back into a high ponytail, a style I had never seen her wear before. "Sienna?" I stood and moved toward her. "Where are you going?" I asked, grabbing her hand. "I'm going out, and before you remind me of our hosts' rules, I already spoke with Nikolai. We came to an agreement." I stared at her, wide-eyed, "you and Nikolai ? You actually reached an agreement without fighting ?"

"You really think I'm some kind of wild animal, huh?" she sighed, rolling her eyes. She kissed my cheek and headed outside, I followed her, calling her name, and asked Velma to keep an eye on the boys. Sienna got into a sleek sports car, and I immediately recognized the man holding the door for her. It was the same man who had helped us in Italy, the Asian man. He closed the door, then looked up and locked eyes with mine. Summoning my courage, I descended the steps and stopped a few feet away from him. He stood motionless, his hands clasped behind his back. It was the first time I truly got a good look at him. He was tall, not as imposing as the Ivanov brothers, but still muscular and athletic. His dark, narrow eyes were unreadable, and I couldn't help but notice the scar that ran from his left cheekbone to his temple, narrowly missing his eye.

"I... I just wanted to properly thank you," I said, trying to keep my voice steady. "Especially for my son. If you hadn't helped us..." I trailed off as he took a step toward me before halting. "You don't owe your freedom to anyone but your sister," he said in a deep, firm voice. "You can't even begin to imagine what she's done for you, what she's survived to get you out of there. And yet, she still can't let go of the guilt she's carried for the past eight years…", "you know ?" I whispered, stunned by his words. "I know everything about Sienna, and she knows everything about me. She and I are one and the same. And that guilt, which keeps growing with everything that's happened, will end up consuming her. And there's nothing I can do to stop it." He stepped back just as my sister opened the car door.

"You're quite talkative today, Kenji. What kind of grim story are you telling my poor sister ?" Kenji merely grunted before walking around to the driver's seat, while my sister approached me with a questioning look. But I said nothing. Instead, with tears in my eyes, I pulled her into a tight embrace, holding her as if I never wanted to let go. "Thank you. Thank you, my sister, thank you. I love you, Sienna, and nothing will ever change that, not what happened, not what will happen. We're still Amelia and Franco's daughters, the same little girls who used to sleep in the same bed."

I stepped back to look at her, seeing her own tears, "Selina… you don't know… you know nothing," she murmured, shaking her head. But I stopped her, cupping her face between my hands. "I don't give a damn, Sienna. I don't care what you've done. All that matters to me is that you're alive, that you survived." She sniffled loudly and punched my shoulder, "don't swear! It doesn't suit you."

"Idiot. Now go before all your makeup runs," I said, giving her a playful shove, making her laugh as she climbed into the car. The vehicle disappeared through the gates, and as my smile faded, Kenji's words echoed in my mind. I sighed, turned, and started back up the steps, only to stop as the gates reopened, allowing a black sedan to enter. An SUV pulled up in front of the entrance. I tried to make out the passengers, but it was impossible. "Miss Selina?" Velma's voice startled me. "Who is it?" I asked as she stepped down, her expression harder than I had ever seen it. "Trouble," she muttered through gritted teeth as the car came to a halt at the stairs. A man stepped out and opened the back door, helping two women out in turn. The first was a little younger than me, petite, with a lightly tanned complexion and long, curly brown hair. That bastard Antonio would have insulted her, called her fat, but she simply had fuller curves than the norm, and I found her stunning. She wore a long black dress with three-quarter sleeves, perfectly fitted, paired with low heels, she was the very definition of elegance. The second woman was much older, her white hair gathered into a low bun. She wore a pencil skirt that fell below her knees, a loose white blouse, and a black shawl so soft-looking I suddenly had the urge to bury my face in it.

"Madame Agata, we weren't informed you would be coming," Velma said, descending the steps to greet them. "Do I need permission to visit my grandsons?" Madame Agata scoffed, ignoring Velma as she started up the stairs. *Grandsons?*

She stopped in front of me, and I didn't know how to react to this stranger who was clearly sizing me up with dark eyes that felt eerily familiar, "so, you're the Italian leech Nikolai brought in?" "Grandmother !" the younger woman exclaimed, tugging at Agata's arm, but she pushed her aside without breaking eye contact with me. "Stay out of this, Nina. I won't let some Italian trash pollute my boys' environment!" she spat, and my breath caught as I finally recognized those eyes, Mikhail's. He had the same eyes as Agata and Nina. "Madame Agata, Madame Elif is not here, nor are the Ivanov brothers," Velma interjected, stepping between us. "I don't need anyone's permission to see my boys," Agata declared, shoving Velma aside and striding inside, followed by her granddaughter, who cast me an apologetic glance. "Let's stay calm until Elif and the Ivanov brothers return. They're unreachable during their meetings, phones are banned, and that viper knows it very well," Velma muttered, glaring at Agata's back. "How does she even know that?"

"Because she's supposed to be there," Velma replied through gritted teeth, then pulled me inside. "So? Where are my grandsons?" Agata demanded as she sat on the couch like she owned the place. "Miss Selina is the boys' nanny, Madame Agata. She is the one who decides what concerns them," Velma stated, and I could feel the tension rise in the room. Agata stood far too quickly for someone her age and advanced toward us with a threatening air. "How dare you stand between me and my boys!" she shouted, stopping right in front of Velma, and for a moment, I truly thought she might pull a gun and shoot her. "No, no, please. Of course you can see your grandsons. Velma, could you please go get them? They're in the garden," I asked, pleading with my eyes to defuse the situation. She watched me for a moment before sighing and heading outside to fetch the children, "please, Madame Agata, have a seat. Would you like something to drink?" "Why ? Are you going to serve us some Italian specialty from our enemies' homeland ?"

she sneered, still scrutinizing me, while Nina tried once again to calm her. "I didn't mean to insult you…"

"Selina !" Velma's voice suddenly rang out as she rushed back inside, breathless and pale. "What is it ?" "The boys… they're gone. I can't find them anywhere !" "Gone ?! What do you mean ?! Where are my grandsons ?!" Agata exclaimed, her eyes blazing with fury. "They were playing in the garden, but they're gone now. I searched everywhere, the garden, the terrace, and I didn't see them go up to their rooms," Velma replied. Nausea churned in my stomach as panic began to rise, I stepped into the garden on trembling legs, but the table where they had been only moments ago was now empty. "Andrei ?! Rafael ?!" I called out, but there was no answer, "Alexei?! Mikhail?!" I shouted louder this time, but still nothing. A shiver ran down my spine as the sky began to darken above me, "Miss Selina, I'm going to alert the guards. They'll start searching immediately. I already called Marcus, the guard accompanying Nikolai. He'll request a meeting interruption," Velma said. But the buzzing in my ears drowned out her words, I couldn't think, couldn't comprehend.

"You filthy Italian whore !" A voice screamed just before a sharp pull on my arm sent me stumbling, followed by a sensation all too familiar—a searing heat across my cheek, a bitter, metallic taste flooding my mouth as I fell to the ground. "Grandmother !" another voice cried out, but I couldn't focus, my heart clenched, black spots danced before my eyes, a panic attack. "That bastard Nikolai killed my daughter, and now you're going to kill my grandsons !" The voice kept screaming, but I couldn't process the words. Only four names echoed in my mind.

Andrei, Alexei, Rafael, Mikhail…

I tried to rise, but another shove sent me down again. From the corner of my eye, I saw a hand lift once more. *Antonio* ? "Selina !" Someone gently grasped my shoulders, helping me sit up. Tears filled my eyes as I met Sena's concerned gaze. She took my hands, squeezing them tightly, "breathe, Selina. It's going to be okay," she said softly, inhaling deeply through her nose and exhaling through her mouth. I mimicked her movements. I had to calm down, for them.

Andrei, Alexei, Rafael, Mikhail…

"Step aside, Velma!" Agata's sharp voice rang out again. I saw her trying to reach me, her eyes black as coal, but Velma blocked her path, standing firm. "You will either go inside and wait calmly or leave !" Velma ordered, her voice unwavering. Agata's glare shifted between us, "who do you think you are ?" she asked haughtily, Velma didn't flinch. "I am no one, Madame Agata, just an insignificant maid. But I follow the orders of my mistress," she said, taking a deliberate step forward. Agata instinctively stepped back, "and Madame Ivanov told me to eliminate any threat to this household."

"Grandmother, let's wait inside," Nina urged, tugging on her arm and this time, Agata obeyed. "Miss Selina ! Are you alright ?" Velma asked, cupping my face in her hands, I couldn't suppress a grimace. "Sena, get some ice. I'll grab the cream," Velma instructed, pulling out a chair before hurrying inside with Sena. I exhaled shakily, rubbing my hands against my thighs, but it was useless. Tears streamed down my face as sobs wracked my body.

Andrei, Alexei, Rafael, Mikhail...

"Miss Selina?" A deep male voice startled me, and I looked up to see David, one of the family's trusted bodyguards. "Have you found them?" I asked, rising to my feet without moving too close, "no, unfortunately not. But the gate leading to the forest was left slightly open. They must have gone through there. We're heading in that direction," he said, nodding before disappearing into the rain, I turned toward the towering trees lining the estate, so massive, so dark. Too terrifying for four small boys. My gaze shifted to another gate behind the hedges, leading north into the forest. Quickly, I rushed toward it and tried the handle, it was locked. Frantically, I felt along the wall, searching for a mechanism like the one in Russia. At last, I found a small panel hidden inside a hatch, "a code ? What was it ? What was it ?"

I closed my eyes, trying to recall the sequence Sienna had once entered. I tried several combinations, my vision blurring with tears, my breath ragged. I cursed aloud at least a dozen times until the door finally clicked open. Without wasting another second, I shoved the gate wide and plunged into the depths of the forest as the rain poured harder and the cold closed in around me.

<u>Nikolai</u>

I leaped out of the car before it had even come to a complete stop, taking the front steps two at a time as the rain poured unnaturally hard for a spring afternoon. The front door swung open to reveal Velma, pale as a ghost.

"Mr. Nikolai ! It's terrible…" "don't worry, we'll find the boys…" "it's not just the boys," she interrupted. I froze, her words slowly sinking into my muddled brain. Turning slowly to face her, I noticed how she avoided my gaze, "what are you talking about ?" I asked, my voice dangerously low as I stepped toward her. "She was in the garden when I went to get a cream for her face, and when I came back out… she was gone." "A cream for her face ? What the hell are you talking about, Velma ?!"

"Nikolai ! There you are at last !" A voice rang out from the living room. I closed my eyes, feeling the last shred of my control slipping away. "Agata ? What are you doing here?" I asked, turning to see her approaching, followed closely by poor Nina, whom she dragged everywhere. "I came to see my grandsons, but that treacherous Italian made them disappear !" she spat venomously. Her hatred was nothing compared to mine, "be careful with what you say, Agata," I warned through clenched teeth, taking a step toward her. Her eyes widened as she instinctively stepped back. "Nikolai, please. We need to find the children and Selina," Nina pleaded softly, stepping between her grandmother and me, her dark eyes begging for reason. I clenched my fists, then turned back to Velma, now standing beside Sena. "What happened?" I demanded.

The fear I had felt when Marcus burst into the meeting room, an act strictly forbidden, and interrupted the session in my name only intensified. "The children were playing in the garden while Miss Selina watched from the living room. I took over for a moment when she went outside with Miss Sienna. But when I saw Madame Agata's car arrive, I went to find Miss Selina so she wouldn't be alone. By the time we came back, they were gone. David said the gate leading to the woods was open, and the men have started searching the area. Miss Selina left through the north gate, I don't know how she got it open…" "The code is the same as the one in Russia. That's how," I muttered, rubbing my face, cursing myself for not thinking ahead. I should have asked Sasha to change the security codes here too. "When the others arrive, send them after me," I instructed, stripping off my suit jacket and tossing it over a chair before heading out through the glass doors leading to the garden, towards the forest.

Ten minutes had passed since I entered the woods when I spotted two of our men standing near a tree. My brows furrowed when I noticed a silhouette crouched at its base and my heart stopped when I recognized the brown dress. I ran toward them, pushing aside Samy and Yuri, two young bodyguards assigned to the northern perimeter, "Selina," I breathed, crouching beside her. She was hugging her knees to her chest, her face buried against them, sobbing, "Selina, look at me, *Solnychko*," I murmured, gently touching her shoulder. Slowly, she lifted her face, her red-rimmed eyes meeting mine. Her damp hair clung to her cheeks, her expression wrecked with distress, "Nikolai, the boys…" she hiccuped, her green eyes filled with such vulnerability that my heart clenched.

I pulled her into my arms, holding her tightly as she trembled, "we'll find them, Selina, I promise," I vowed, cupping her face and brushing her hair aside. But as my fear morphed into something far more dangerous, I noticed the bruise on her cheek and the split at the corner of her lip. The image of her, three months ago, the day I found her in that motel, flashed before my eyes. "Who, Selina ? Who touched you ?" I demanded, my voice unrecognizable. She hesitated, opening and closing her mouth before shaking her head, "I just want to find the boys, Nikolai. Please," she whispered, clutching at my shirt. I shut my eyes, forcing myself to regain control, for the boys, for her.

"Nikolai !" I looked up, feeling a hint of relief as my brothers ran toward us. Helping Selina to her feet, I watched as they approached, still dressed in their suits, soaked from the rain. "Give me your jacket, Roman." Without hesitation, he shrugged it off and handed it to me and I draped it over Selina's shoulders, "go back to the house with Roman. I will bring the boys back to you, Selina. I promise." She gazed up at me with her large, expressive eyes before nodding slowly. Turning, she hesitated for only a second before accepting Roman's offered hand. He helped her step over a fallen tree trunk, but then he froze, his eyes locking onto her face, "who hit you ?" he asked, his brows furrowing, Grigori and Sasha, now closer, leaned in to get a better look at her injuries. I watched her stiffen. "Not now. Roman, get her inside before she catches cold," I ordered. Roman nodded, gently guiding her away and before disappearing into the woods, she cast me one last glance over her shoulder.

"What the hell is going on, Nikolai ?" Grigori asked, running a frustrated hand through his wet hair. "I don't know, *moy brat*. But I will find out, once we get the boys back," I replied, stepping deeper into the darkness of the forest.

Chapter twenty-four
<u>Selina</u>

"Here, drink while it's still hot, my dear," said Elif as she joined me by the bay window leading to the garden, where I was sitting. Roman had left to join his brothers after dropping me off, while Elif had been waiting for me at the house, insisting that I change as soon as I arrived. I thanked her as I took the cup of hot tea, and she sat beside me. The rain hadn't stopped falling, and night had descended, yet still no news. For the thousandth time, a sob escaped me. "It'll be okay, Selina. They'll find them," Elif reassured me, rubbing my back. I shook my head, sniffing. Andrei and Rafael were afraid of the dark, Alexei hated being wet, and Mikhail already seemed to be coming down with something, he was going to get sick. I was a terrible mother and a horrible nanny.

"Selina ?" Sienna's voice suddenly came from behind me as I heard her footsteps approaching quickly. "Selina, what's going on?" she asked, kneeling beside me. Her eyes darkened when she saw my cheek beginning to bruise, "I knew it. I knew he was no different," she muttered through clenched teeth as she stood up. Just as I was about to correct her, Elif rose so abruptly that it startled me, she grabbed Sienna's arm and pulled her sharply towards her, and I froze at the expression on her face. "I like you, Sienna," Elif said, her voice dangerously calm, "you're brave, fearless, and I could never claim to understand what you've been through, because I know it must have been horrific. But never, ever insult my brothers or my husband like that again. They would never hurt a woman. They would never harm you. But me ? You have no idea what I'm capable of. Believe me, Sienna, I could easily be one of your worst nightmares. Don't make me become one."

For the first time, Sienna, who had stood her ground against the Ivanov brothers without flinching, looked away and simply nodded. Elif sighed, shaking her head before pulling Sienna into a side hug, "don't worry. I threw out the one responsible for that," she said, glancing at my bruised face, "and Nikolai won't let this slide either."

I sniffled and turned my gaze back to the forest, setting my untouched tea beside me, waiting, waiting for my boys to appear.

I woke up with a start when I felt a weight on my shoulders. "Selina, come wait inside the living room," Sienna said as she placed another blanket over me. "No," I replied weakly, my voice barely audible through my tight throat. Seeing my determined expression, she sighed and went back inside. I closed my eyes, burying my face in my arms, crossed over my knees. And just when I thought I had no tears left, new ones streamed down my cheeks. It was nighttime now. The rain had stopped, but it was cold, and the darkness stretched endlessly. "Please, my God, please…" I repeated over and over, rocking slightly. And when I opened my eyes again, I saw three pairs of muddy sneakers standing in front of me. I froze and slowly lifted my head, a sob burst from me at the sight of Andrei, Rafael, and Alexei standing right in front of me, their faces smudged with dirt and grime. My eyes immediately searched for any injuries, but I couldn't see much under the oversized jackets they were wearing.

"Here, *mamma*," Rafael said, holding out a small bouquet of mismatched flowers. "No, mom ! Take mine !" Andrei exclaimed, thrusting his own bundle of flowers toward me. Alexei, silent as always, also extended his bouquet. I lifted my gaze, searching for Mikhail, and another sob of relief escaped when I saw him a few steps behind them, standing with his father and uncles, just as soaked and filthy as the boys. His wide eyes locked onto mine.

I tried to stand, but my legs wouldn't cooperate, leaving me on my knees, shaking with sobs. The boys hesitated before I pulled all three of them into my arms, clutching them and kissing their faces over and over. "Thank God !" Elif's voice rang out behind me, joined by Sienna's.

"*Mamma*, why are you crying ?" Rafael asked, pressing his little hand to my wet cheek. I thanked the heavens that it was dark enough to hide my bruises from him. I couldn't speak, couldn't stop sobbing. "Selina," Nikolai's voice came softly as he approached, Mikhail right beside him, frowning in concern. "Come, *Solnychko*," Nikolai said gently. "Boys, go take a shower and change. We'll join you soon." The boys hesitated for a moment, looking back at me, but they eventually obeyed. Mikhail lingered. I couldn't help but pull him into my arms, hugging him tightly. After a few seconds of stillness, he hugged me back.

"Go on, Mikhail. Catch up with your brothers," his father said. Mikhail followed them inside, with Elif at their side. I sniffled, watching them disappear, "I should go help them," I murmured, attempting to follow, but before I could take a step, I found myself lifted into Nikolai's arms. I gasped, clutching onto his neck, staring at him with wide eyes as my already damp clothes absorbed more of the moisture from his. Under the watchful gazes of his brothers and my sister, Nikolai carried me inside. "What are you doing, Nikolai ?" I asked softly as he tightened his hold while climbing the stairs. He didn't answer, continuing up until we reached his floor. But instead of turning towards the children's rooms, he went the opposite way, towards his own bedroom.

I craned my neck, trying to catch a glimpse of the boys, but I couldn't. Still, I felt reassured hearing Elif's voice with them. Nikolai entered his room and closed the door behind us with his foot before placing me on his bed. "Did you eat ?" he asked, kneeling in front of me, tucking my damp hair behind my ears before gently brushing his fingers over my bruised cheek. I flinched slightly despite myself. "Elif put some cream on it," I said, grasping his wrist as he shut his eyes, his jaw clenched. "And Velma made me a sandwich."

"But you didn't eat it?" He reopened his eyes, locking his gaze onto mine. I pressed my lips together, saying nothing, because he was right. He sighed, shaking his head before kissing my forehead and stepping away. As he moved toward the bathroom, he plucked a small leaf from my hair and held it up with a smirk, making me blush. I heard the sound of running water. He was probably taking a shower. I decided to wait before going to check on the boys, I felt like I might start sobbing like a child again. Lying back on the bed, I closed my eyes just for a moment.

I sighed softly as I felt a gentle touch on my neck, then on my cheek. I blinked awake and smiled when I saw Nikolai, still dressed in his dirty, rain-soaked clothes. "Did I fall asleep?" I asked, sitting up slowly. "More like a short nap, about ten minutes," he said, helping me up before leading me towards the bathroom. "You go first, I'll go after," he told me, gesturing toward the bathtub.

But I froze. The tub was filled to the brim. Memories crashed into me all at once, screaming, blood, air, suffocation. Nikolai had his back turned, reaching for fresh towels. I tried to call out, but no sound came. I tried to move, but my body felt impossibly heavy. "I'll leave your towel here. I'll ask Sienna to bring you some...Selina?" His hand touched my cheek, and a jolt shot through me, bringing my body back to life, but too fast, too suddenly. I gasped, stumbling backward so quickly that I lost my balance. Nikolai tried to catch me, but I collapsed onto the floor. "Selina!" He stepped toward me but froze when I shook my head, raising a trembling hand to stop him.

"I can't. Please, please. I'm going to die. I'm going to die," I whispered, pressing myself against the wall. "Please, don't make me go in there," I begged, my eyes pleading. He looked lost. Slowly, he raised his hands in a calming gesture and knelt before me, "you're safe, Selina," he murmured. "No, no, no. I'll drown. I'll die."

"Selina, look at me. Look at me, *Solnychko*."

Solnychko.

I lifted my eyes, meeting his blue ones, not brown. Blue. "Nikolai," I breathed, my lips trembling. For the first time, I saw his eyes shine with unshed tears. He pulled me into his arms, holding me so tightly it was almost painful. But I didn't complain, I burrowed deeper into him. "I'm sorry, Selina. I'm sorry I didn't come sooner. I'm sorry I left you behind that night. I'm sorry, *Solnychko*," he whispered, kissing my head over and over as I cried every last tear left inside me. The seconds passed, maybe minutes, maybe hours, I didn't know. But Nikolai never let me go, not for a single second. His grip never loosened, holding me against him as he whispered, again and again, that he was sorry.

"Rafael was four years old," I said at last, once I had finally calmed down, my voice hoarse. "I... I couldn't hold on anymore. I had to protect my son. I had to save him. That was my job as a mother." I sniffled as he kissed my forehead again. "I tried to escape. I hid in one of the garbage containers with Rafael on the day they were scheduled to be emptied by the city truck. I waited for hours inside that box, surrounded by waste, with my son. Antonio knew I was in there, and he took pleasure in leaving me there, in letting me hope." The memories of that day rushed back, the stench, the darkness, Rafael asking for food, for water.

I felt Nikolai inhale deeply against me, "after hours of waiting, I decided to peek outside, and he was there, sitting on a lounge chair, drinking. When he saw me, he said I had taken too long. It was so humiliating. He smiled at me and then ordered one of his men to take Rafael inside. And then everything happened so fast... before I could even process it, we were in the bathroom. He started filling the bathtub, and... and..." I tried to breathe, but the air wouldn't come. It felt like my lungs were filling with water. "Breathe, Selina. Breathe. I'm here," Nikolai said, his voice calm but firm. I clutched his shirt in my fists, struggling to regain control, to return to the present. "You don't have to say it..." he began, but I shook my head. I had to. I had to let it out.

"Water... there was so much water. He... he held my head under, over and over, asking if I was going to run away again. I could hear Rafael's voice behind the door, calling for me... *'Mamma, Mamma, Mamma...'*" I spoke too fast, too softly. I wasn't even sure he could hear me. "I kept telling him no, that I wouldn't try again. But he didn't stop. He never stopped..." I sobbed. My entire body ached, my thoughts, my memories, everything hurt, except the arms holding me. Everything hurt except the lips brushing my forehead. Everything hurt except this man, showing me a tenderness I had never known. I lifted my face, and my lips trembled at the sight of the tears on his cheeks.

Nikolai Ivanov was crying. Nikolai Ivanov was crying for me. He was doing what no man had ever done for me.

"But I didn't give up, Niko," I whispered. "I kept fighting. I tried to escape again and again. I never gave up." He cupped my face in his hands, wiping away my tears. "No, you never gave up, *Solnychko*. You survived. You saved your son. You saved yourself. And a lifetime wouldn't be enough for me to thank you for that. For giving me time to find you. Thank you, thank you, Selina, thank you..." He repeated the words over and over, pressing his lips against mine as I closed my eyes, letting myself sink into his warmth, his touch, searching for something missing, something lost.

Myself.

"Do you trust me, *Solnychko* ?" he asked suddenly. I opened my eyes and nodded without hesitation. He nodded in return, helping me to my feet. Then he stepped back and began unbuttoning his soaked shirt, I froze. "What are you doing ?" I asked, carefully keeping my gaze locked on his. He didn't answer. His shirt fell to the floor. Then he reached for his belt. Panic rose in me, and I spun around, covering my eyes, "I... I don't know what you're trying to do. Maybe I should go to my room..." my words vanished when I felt his warmth behind me. His hands gently wrapped around my wrists, lowering them from my face. Our eyes met in the mirror. I swallowed hard as my gaze dropped to his body. Muscles. Muscles. More muscles. I felt like a twig compared to him. Thank God, he was still wearing his boxer briefs.

"Selina." My eyes snapped back to his, "don't be afraid, Selina," he murmured, pressing a soft kiss to the curve of my neck, making me shiver. He lowered my wrists and grabbed the hem of my sweatshirt. His eyes never left mine as he began to lift it. I didn't move. I didn't stop him. I watched him. I let him. He pulled the sweatshirt over my head and let it fall beside his own clothes, leaving me in my tank top. Slowly, he stepped around me until he was facing me again, still holding my gaze as he knelt before me, "Nikolai..." "shhh," he hushed gently. He carefully slid my pajama bottoms down as my breathing grew uneven. I stepped back slightly so he could remove them completely, leaving me in just my tank top and underwear.

As he began to rise, he suddenly stopped. His fingers brushed against my right calf, and his brows knit together. He leaned in, looking closer, and I held my breath. His dark gaze lifted to mine, filled with silent questions, but he didn't speak. He didn't ask. Instead, he stood slowly, his hand never leaving my skin, tracing from the back of my knee to my thigh, to my hip. I closed my eyes at the gentle touch. "Come, Selina." I opened my eyes to see his outstretched hand. I glanced from his hand to the bathtub, then back to his eyes. I swallowed hard. Then, hesitantly, I slipped my fingers into his. He gripped them firmly, gently pulling me forward—toward the nightmare that had haunted me for years.

Chapter twenty-five
Selina

He entered first and sat down before pulling me in after him. I took a deep breath before stepping in—the hot water made me moan in relief after the freezing night. I slowly lowered myself, and he pulled me against him. I tried to focus on his presence, to ignore the water, to block out the memories. I wouldn't let Antonio ruin my life any longer. I wanted to be Selina again—the girl who had dreamed of becoming a nurse, of living in a small country house with her sister, of tending a vegetable garden on weekends. "You're handling this like a champion, *Solnychko*. I'm proud of you," he said, gathering my hair over one shoulder before kissing my neck. "I don't want to be afraid anymore, Niko," I whispered, gripping the edges of the bathtub, his lips glided from my neck to my cheek as his arm tightened around my waist. "She's going to pay, Selina. I swear, I'll make her regret it," he said, his gaze lingering on the bruise Agata had left on my face.

"She was just as panicked as we were, Nikolai. It's not—" "don't you dare say it's nothing. I promised you nothing would happen to you within these walls, Selina. I didn't keep my pro—" I turned my face toward him and kissed him. At first, he didn't move, letting me take the lead, but when I gently tugged on his lower lip, he cupped my cheek, sliding his tongue into my mouth. He kissed me slowly, carefully, as if he were afraid of hurting me, of breaking me. His hand slipped under my tank top, and despite the warmth of the water, I shivered. He pulled back when I pressed my hand gently against his solid, heated chest to catch my breath.

"*Ty moy ray, ty moyo nebo, ty moye solntse*" he murmured, kissing my cheek. "What does that mean ?" I asked, breathless and his gaze locked onto mine. "You are my paradise. You are my sky. You are my sun," he said, smiling softly as he rubbed his nose against my temple. I felt tears rising.

"Don't cry, *Solnychko*." I sniffled, tilting my head up to stop the tears from falling, but his face appeared in my vision again as he leaned over me, "so ? How was your first day as a nanny ?" I groaned, burying my face in my hands as I felt him laugh against my back, "you should fire me—I'm a terrible nanny," I mumbled, shaking my head. He wrapped his arms around me, holding me tight against him and pressing his face against my neck. "Never. I will never want you to leave," he murmured, kissing my skin, making me close my eyes.

"Selina ?" I jumped at the sound of my sister's voice, though thankfully, it came from behind the bedroom door. Nikolai stood, carefully releasing me, then stepped out of the water, grabbing a towel. He dried himself quickly before wrapping it around his waist over his boxer briefs. "Relax, I'll take a shower in the next room after asking your sister to bring you some clean clothes," he said, kissing my forehead before leaving. I sighed, resting my head against the edge of the tub and closing my eyes, but despite the warmth of the water, the coldness Nikolai had left behind lingered. I heard him talking to Sienna before footsteps approached.

"Selina ?" I opened my eyes and turned slightly, smiling softly at my sister. "Sienna" she stepped closer and knelt beside me. "Are you okay, Selina ?" she asked, her eyes scanning me from head to toe. I didn't know how to get her to stop seeing danger in everyone, to stop searching for the worst in every situation. Maybe it was impossible. "Of course I'm okay, Sienna," I reassured her, taking her hand gripping the edge of the bathtub. "The boys ?" I asked, sitting up as she stood and perched on the edge of the tub. "They're fine. Elif and Sena are helping them clean up. I wanted to check on you, it's been a tough day for you," she said, leaning slightly to get a better look at my bruised cheek. Her jaw tightened, "if only I had arrived thirty minutes earlier, before Elif kicked her out—" I laughed, cutting her off. "Sienna, that woman is almost eighty years old. What would you have done ? Punched her ?" She looked at me, her expression just as stern and closed off as ever, "oh my God ! You would have !" I exclaimed, my eyes wide, mouth agape. She simply raised an eyebrow and I burst into laughter. *Unbelievable.* She smiled as she watched me, "Rafael laughs like that too. He seemed to have a great time with the boys. They told me a little about their adventure," she said. "They went to pick flowers for you in the forest, but they couldn't find any. So Mikhail had the brilliant idea to go to the family cemetery and take flowers from their grandmother's grave, Nikolai's mother."

"Oh my God !" I gasped, covering my mouth. "Calm down. According to them, they asked Elena, their grandmother, for permission, and she said yes," Sienna added, smirking. I grimaced, shaking my head, they had desecrated a grave. Not just any grave, the grave of Nikolai's, Grigori's, Sasha's, and Roman's mother. "But they got lost on the way back, and Mikhail's phone died. The men who went out searching earlier found them over thirty minutes from the house," she continued. My heart clenched at the thought of them wandering in the dark, in the rain, surrounded by towering trees. "It's over, Selina. They're safe," she reassured me, squeezing my hand, now fully healed. "They're safe, but I think they're going to get sick. They kept sneezing," she sighed. Just as I opened my mouth to ask if they had fevers, I sneezed. A shiver ran down my spine as Sienna raised an eyebrow, "and I have a feeling they won't be the only ones," she said, standing up. "Come on, I'll help you."

<u>Nikolai</u>

I pulled on my sweatshirt after my shower just as there was a knock at the door. It opened to reveal Sasha, who had also showered and changed. "So, should I get the cars ready ? Are we paying our dear Agata a visit ?" "By car ? You meant by tank," Roman added, suddenly appearing behind our younger brother, also fresh and changed. "We don't need to go anywhere to make her suffer," I said, grabbing my phone before stepping out of the room, my brothers following closely behind. We headed up to the top floor and entered Grigori's office. He was sitting behind his desk, with Elif perched on the armrest of his chair.

"The boys ?" I asked, settling onto one of the couches. "In bed with Selina in their room. While we had the scare of our lives, they had the adventure of theirs," she said with a small smile, though it faded quickly. "We could have laughed about this day if it weren't for that stain called Agata," she muttered, rolling her eyes. I tried not to dwell on that viper's actions, otherwise, I'd find myself in her bedroom with my *9mm* shoved down her throat. "Did you do what I asked ?" I questioned Elif. She nodded. "No Ignatiev will attend the meetings for the next three months." I nodded, turning to Grigori with an expectant look, "they won't have any hand in our business for the next two months. That's about six million dollars in losses for them. Gleb tried to negotiate, but he got nothing," he said, resting his hand on his wife's thigh.

"Good. I don't want that woman coming anywhere near here," I said, leaning back into the chair and gripping the armrests, the image of Selina flashing through my mind. "Don't worry, she won't even get close to the property," Elif reassured me. "She can try if she wants a hole in the middle of her forehead," Roman added, sitting on the edge of the table, Elif smacked the back of his head, rolling her eyes.

"Let's get some sleep, *askim*," Grigori said, standing and pulling Elif with him. She waved at us before closing the door behind them. "I don't know about you guys, but this day gave me a boost. I'm going to check out tonight's race, who's coming with me ?" Roman asked, grinning. Sasha just shook his head, eyes glued to his phone. "Like you need us. Your pack would gather anywhere and anytime for you," I remarked, watching him. His grin widened, that dangerous glint appearing in his eyes, the same one he always had when talking about his brothers-in-arms.

"They're not around right now. Just a little race to handle," he said, getting up. "A little race ? Where ? Iraq ? Afghanistan ? North Korea ?" Sasha asked, finally looking up from his phone. "That, *moy brat*, is a little secret," Roman smirked, stopping behind me. He squeezed my shoulder. "I'm glad the boys are okay, *moy brat*." I nodded, silently thanking him. "As for you, Shasha…" Roman teased, calling Sasha by the nickname he despised. Our brother scowled, waiting for the rest of the sentence, but it never came. Instead, Roman snatched the cushion from behind my back and hurled it at Sasha's face. Sasha caught it mid-air, but his phone fell to the floor. By the time he stood up, Roman was already gone. I chuckled at the expression on his face, it was the same one he used to have as a kid whenever he got mad. "I'm going to make him eat this damn cushion," he growled, squeezing it in his hands.

But my amusement faded when I glimpsed the image on his phone screen, Sienna with a man. Sasha quickly bent to pick it up, but it was too late. "*Moy brat*," I said, inhaling deeply. "It's time we talked." Sasha clenched his jaw, staring at me, then finally placed his phone on the desk and leaned back in his chair, shifting into business mode. "I'm listening, *moy brat*," he said, his sharp blue eyes locking onto mine. "I convinced Selina and her sister to stay until we deal with Antonio. Of course, Sienna was harder to persuade—I had to negotiate. She agreed on the condition that she could leave the property whenever she wanted and that Kenji would pick her up at the—" "Kenji ?" Sasha cut in, suddenly straightening.

Little shit.

"He's the guy who was supposed to help them escape in Russia—" Sasha suddenly stood, shoving his hands into the pockets of his sweatpants.

Fucking fuck.

"Sasha, what the hell is your problem ? What do you even want?" "I don't fucking know !" he shouted, spinning to face me, hands thrown up in frustration, his gaze dark. "I want her to disappear ! I want her to stay close to me! Sometimes I want to strangle her just to shut her up, and sometimes I want to…" he stopped abruptly, shutting his eyes before turning away, rubbing his face. I sighed and stood up. Sasha began adjusting a chair around the meeting table, moving it, replacing it, over and over again. "Sasha." I grabbed his shoulder to pull him back, but he shoved me off, throwing me a glare. And my patience wore thin. I loved my brother, I tried to understand him, but his behavior, his attitude, it was jeopardizing everything I was trying to build. Everything I wanted for myself. For Selina. For Rafael. For my sons. I grabbed the collar of his shirt and slammed him against the glass window, "for the first time in my life, I'm trying to build something for myself, Sasha. For the first time," I grit out, jaw tight, as he stood there, unmoving. "I won't let you destroy it. Not when everything is already so damn complicated, *moy brat*." I released him and stepped back, cursing under my breath.

Calm down, Nikolai. Calm.

"Nikolai," Sasha called, but I didn't look at him. I sat back down, eyes on the floor, but I caught him approaching from the corner of my eye. "I'll be careful, *moy brat*," he said, grabbing his phone from the desk, he exhaled, glancing at the door. "It's time for you to think about your happiness too." And with that, he walked out of the room.

Blayt.

The next morning, I pushed the door open with my elbow, trying not to spill the soup on the tray, and stepped into the boys' bedroom. I couldn't help but smile at the sight before me—all my world sprawled across the beds, which had been pushed together to create one big sleeping space. Selina was lying in the middle, with Andrei and Rafael to her right, Alexei and Mikhail to her left. All of them were sick, their noses red, dark circles under their eyes, yet they were laughing and chatting as if nothing were wrong. "What's so funny?" I asked, closing the door with my foot as they all turned to look at me. In that moment, the regret I'd felt over my altercation with Sasha lightened just a bit. I would have fought the entire world if it meant I could have that view every day—minus the illness, of course.

"Andrei almost got his pee-pee bitten by a mosquito while peeing in the forest!" Rafael exclaimed, laughing before bursting into a coughing fit. "Easy, *Angelo mio*," Selina soothed, rubbing his back. Thank God she wasn't as sick as the kids, so she could still manage their whims. I set the tray down on the dresser and grabbed the bag of medicine the doctor had prescribed an hour earlier. When Rafael and Alexei had started vomiting during the night, we'd known this illness was inevitable. I pulled up the desk chair near the bed and handed the tray to Selina, who set it on her lap before picking up one of the bowls. Since the kids were still feeling nauseous, we were keeping their meals light. I started feeding Rafael and Andrei while Selina handed a bowl to Mikhail, who quietly started his soup, then helped Alexei.

"I don't like soup. I want a burger, Dad," Andrei pouted. Ever since Selina had entered our lives, my relationship with my sons had been improving. Things were still a bit complicated with Mikhail, but now, more than ever, I had hope. "Sorry, buddy. You'll get your burger once you're better," I said, ruffling his hair. He sighed before opening his mouth for another spoonful. "Can we play a card game later?" Alexei asked, looking at Selina. She glanced at me with a teasing smile. "Only if your father agrees to play," she said, full of challenge. I couldn't help but laugh. "Don't come crying later, *Solnychko*," I warned, feeding another spoonful to Rafael. "Are you underestimating me, Mr. Ivanov?" she grinned, and it was the most beautiful thing I'd ever seen. "Never. How could I dare, Miss Floros?" She laughed, and the boys watched our exchange with fascination. "We want to play too!" Andrei crossed his arms, while Rafael nodded eagerly, making us laugh even more.

Later, I headed downstairs, still smiling at the way Selina had shrieked when she'd won the last round. At first, I'd let her win a few hands, but once she realized I was doing it on purpose, she threatened to ban me from the room. So I gave it my all in the last three rounds, only to be completely defeated in the final hand. I stopped at the entrance to the living room when I saw Elif pacing restlessly while Grigori sat on the couch, phone pressed to his ear. Sasha had left early that morning, so I hadn't seen him—he'd had an early meeting. "Is something wrong ?" I asked, stepping closer. "Roman hasn't come back yet," my sister-in-law said, still pacing. "You know Roman, Elif. He probably crashed at a friend's place, drinking and playing video games," I said, taking her hands, but she shook her head.

"I don't know, Niko. I feel like I can't breathe, I can't sit still. I have a bad feeling." The distress in her eyes was clear. "Have you tried calling him ?" I asked, glancing at Grigori. "That's what I've been doing for the past hour, but nothing," he replied. Roman could be forgetful, but he always answered his phone—especially after the time he'd made Elif cry with worry five years ago. "I'll call Anton. He'll know where he is," I said, referring to my brother's best friend. As I pulled out my phone, I heard a car pulling into the driveway. "That must be him," I said, and Elif rushed outside, with Grigori and me close behind. But as soon as I saw Sasha's car pulling up instead, my stomach dropped. And when I saw the look on his face, I knew.

He stopped at the foot of the stairs and looked at Elif, "what happened to him, Sasha ? Tell me !" she demanded, her fists clenching as she paled. Sasha climbed the steps toward her, glancing between Grigori and me. "There was an attack last night during the race," he said, rubbing the back of his neck. "It was the Italians. They took Roman." The words hit us like a punch. We tried to process it—or at least, we tried. Elif swayed, and the three of us moved to steady her, but she lifted a hand, stopping us. "What do they want ?" she asked, her voice flat. This time, Sasha looked directly at me, and I knew immediately. "It's Antonio. He wants Selina and Rafael in exchange for Roman." A sudden crashing noise shattered the silence behind us. I turned, my stomach twisting, and froze at the sight of Selina standing near the doorway, the tray of soup bowls she'd been carrying now shattered on the floor.

Blayt.

Chapter twenty-six
Selina

I pulled the blanket up over the boys, who had all fallen asleep except for Mikhail, who had gone to take a shower. I stepped out of the room, carefully closing the door behind me and making sure to leave the nightlight on—Rafael and Andrei were afraid of the dark. As I headed toward the stairs, I paused when I saw Mikhail returning, freshly washed and changed. "Do you feel better, sweetheart ?" I asked, placing my hand against his forehead to check his temperature. "You still have a little fever, but it's much lower than last night." I smiled slightly, and just as I was about to remove my hand, he stopped me, gripping it gently. He stayed silent, eyes cast down. "Is everything okay, Mikhail ?" I asked.

He remained quiet for a few seconds before finally lifting his gaze to meet mine. "I… I'm sorry. I didn't think we would get lost. We just wanted to make you happy, not make you sad," he said softly. I couldn't help but pull him into my arms, kissing the top of his head. "That bouquet made me so happy, Mikhail. Thank you." My thoughts drifted to the large bouquet resting on the dresser in my room. "But next time, don't go so far without telling me first, okay ?" I cupped his face gently in my hands. He nodded and kissed my cheek before heading off to join his brothers in their room. That small moment of warmth almost made me forget the chaos unfolding in the house. I made my way downstairs in search of Nikolai, but I didn't find anyone. Just as I turned to head back upstairs to check the office, I stopped in my tracks when I saw Elif sitting on the swing on the terrace, night already having fallen.

I hesitated before stepping toward her, stopping a few feet away. She was staring at something in her hands—a wolf figurine. I remembered seeing it in the office that Nikolai and Roman shared, sitting on one of the shelves. "Come, sit, Selina," she suddenly said without looking at me, making me jump slightly. "I didn't want to disturb you…" I said hesitantly. "You're not. Come," she repeated, and this time, I took a seat.

"I was looking for Nikolai," I said, feeling the need to justify myself, as if I no longer had the right to move freely around the house, as if I were the one responsible for Roman's disappearance. "They're upstairs with Grigori, trying to negotiate with the Italians. We have good relations with Capo Conti—he might be able to help us," she said, taking a deep breath. "When I married Grigori, I didn't know he had such young brothers, that they would need to be raised, educated. Everyone thought I would struggle the most with Sasha because of his cold, distant nature, and especially his illness, but they were wrong. The hardest one to deal with was Roman. Nikolai and Sasha had known their mother, they were grieving her. But Roman was too young. He hadn't really known his mother—he probably didn't even remember her. He needed a mother, and I was not one," she said, lifting her gaze to the sea.

"When I arrived, he wouldn't talk to me. He avoided me. While Sasha resented me because he feared I would replace his mother, Roman was simply afraid of me. And I didn't know how to reach him, how to get close to him. Until that fateful day," she grimaced, tightening her grip on the figurine. "Grigori was shot. Three bullets. The doctors said his condition was critical, that there was a strong chance he wouldn't survive." I couldn't even imagine the terror she must have felt in that moment. I saw every day how much they loved each other—it must have shattered her. "His uncles arrived even before the doctors could give a proper diagnosis, like vultures, ready to claim their share of my husband's downfall. That's when I heard her—Filippa Ivanov, the wife of Grigori's great-uncle. She had cornered Roman, my baby, barely five years old, in a hallway. Do you know what she was saying to him ?"

I didn't answer, feeling only a rising anger at the thought of a little Roman being mistreated by an adult. "She told him his turn would come after his brothers. That we would all die one by one. I saw him trembling, his big brown eyes wide with fear, his tiny fists clenched. I was on that bitch before I even realized what I was doing. I remember shoving her into Roman's room, locking the door behind me, leaving a terrified Roman outside with Velma. This," she held up the figurine, "was sitting on Roman's dresser. A gift from his mother." Her voice dropped lower, almost a whisper. "I hit her. Over and over. I hit her until she stopped moving, stopped pleading, stopped screaming. Until she stopped breathing. I beat her to death."

Her cold, dark eyes locked onto mine, and despite myself, I shivered. "What do you call a person who is willing to kill for their child ?" she murmured over the sound of the waves crashing against the cliffs below. I responded with the only answer that made sense. "A mother." "A mother," she repeated, swallowing hard, her eyes glistening. "You must be wondering why I kept this. You probably think I'm some kind of psychopath," she said with a small smile, and I couldn't help but smile back. "Believe it or not, I actually told Velma to throw it away. And I thought she had, for twelve years. Until the day I made a mistake. A mistake that almost cost Sasha and Roman their lives. I was at my lowest. I felt so guilty that I started having dark thoughts," she said, pulling her knees up to her chest and wrapping her arms around them. Seeing Elif—normally so confident, so powerful—curled up like this broke my heart.

"I can't afford to make mistakes, Selina, do you understand? Hundreds of lives depend on the decisions made in this house. But most of all, our lives depend on them. I can't afford to make mistakes," she repeated, and for the first time, I truly grasped the weight she carried. A weight I could never imagine bearing—and she had done so since she was just a young woman. "At my lowest point, Roman came to this very terrace with a box. He handed it to me, and when I opened it, this figurine was inside. He had retrieved it from the trash after Velma threw it away. Can you believe that? He was only five years old, Selina." And that's when the first tear fell. The first tear I had ever seen Elif Ivanov shed. "He told me he kept it so he wouldn't forget. So he wouldn't forget what a mother was. So he wouldn't forget who his mother was," her voice broke as a sob escaped her. "Oh, Elif," I whispered, pulling her into my arms as she sobbed harder.

"I can't do this, Selina. I can't live if something happens to him." "Nothing will happen to him, Elif. If there's one thing I've learned from living with you all, it's that nothing can happen to you as long as you stand together. His brothers will find him, Elif. I know they will. But for that, you have to stand up. You are the reason they are so strong. You are their pillar." "She's right," a voice suddenly said behind us. When I turned, I saw a woman about Elif's age. Despite her hastily thrown-on clothes, she was stunning, her blonde hair tied back in a ponytail. Her blue eyes scanned me briefly before landing on Elif. "Oh, *moya sestra*, (my sister)" the woman said, stepping forward as Elif began sobbing harder. "Maria," she choked out. They embraced tightly, and just from looking at them, I knew they had known each other for a long time.

"I'll go get you some water," I said, heading inside, where I ran into Velma, ."who is that woman ?" I asked. "That's Maria Vasilkova—Elif's confidante, best friend, practically her sister," Velma replied. "They've fought through every battle at this table of wolves for almost seventeen years." A friendship spanning over a decade. "I was the one who called her. Madam needs her now more than ever," Velma added before walking away. I watched the two women crying in each other's arms, and the guilt that had been suffocating me since I heard the news tightened its grip. I had to do something.

<u>Nikolai</u>

I groaned as I hung up with one of my contacts infiltrated in the Italian mafia—still no news on Roman. It had been almost three days since those damn Italians took my brother, and nothing. Not a single damn update. "Any news from Sasha?" I asked Grigori as he entered the office from the terrace, where he'd been on the phone with one of his own contacts. Two hours ago,

Sasha had left to meet Lorenzo, who had traveled from New York to California for a discussion. "No, still nothing," he said, pacing back and forth, nearly tearing his hair out. "They've never had us pinned like this before, those sons of bitches, Niko. They've got us by the throat," he spat, stopping right in front of me, his gaze locked onto mine. And I knew what he wanted to say. I knew he'd be willing to do anything for our family. "Nikolai—" "Don't even think about it, *moy brat*," I said, standing up from the chair to face him directly. "We're going to save Roman. I'll find a way," I added, and he just stared at me, jaw clenched, holding back something—something that could lead us into a fight.

He finally stormed out of the room, slamming the door behind him. I sighed, rubbing my face. *Blayt*. I would never hand Selina and Rafael over to that son of a bitch, but Roman—were they torturing him? Was he even still alive? "*Blayt!*" I shouted, kicking a chair hard enough to knock it over. "Niko?" a small voice suddenly called from behind me. When I turned around, I saw Rafael standing at the doorway, his eyes shifting between the chair and me. *Shit*. "Rafael, come in, buddy. There was a bug on the chair—I was trying to squash it," I said, quickly setting the chair back up. He stepped forward, scanning the chair, looking for the supposed bug. "Did you want to ask me something, buddy?"

He hesitated for a moment before slowly looking up, pressing his lips together. "Is Roman coming back?" he asked. "I saw Elif crying, and Mom too. Will he come back if we leave with Mom…?" "Rafael," I cut him off, kneeling in front of him, my brows furrowed. "Why are you saying that?" He lowered his gaze, his lips beginning to tremble. "I heard some guards saying that… that it was him who took Roman. He wants Mom and me. But Mom can stay—I'll go alone so he'll let Roman go," he said, his chin shaking, his small body tense as he tried not to cry. His green eyes, filled with fear but also determination, stared at me. Determined to sacrifice himself to save my brother. To sacrifice himself, at eight years old. I pulled him into me, holding him tightly.

Antonio Rasili was going to die. And it would be a slow, excruciating death—but not before he experienced every horror he'd inflicted on Selina and Rafael. "Roman will come back, Rafael. And you're not going anywhere. I will never give my son to the enemy," I said, and he stiffened against me, pulling back slowly. "Son?" he whispered, his eyes wide as I nodded, smiling softly. "There's no difference to me between you, Andrei, Alexei, or Mikhail," I told him. And this time, the tears spilled over, and he started crying, burying his face in my chest as I kissed the top of his head. Yes, Antonio would die in the most agonizing way possible. Later that evening, after yet another failed call with one of my contacts within the Italians, I headed downstairs to find Elif. For the past three days, she hadn't been herself—her gaze lost in the void, speaking little. She was just a shadow of herself. Roman had to come home. My brother had to return. If he didn't, my brothers and I would be shattered, but we'd rise again—to take revenge, to set every damn state in this country on fire.

But Elif—she wouldn't survive it. She wouldn't get back up. And if Elif didn't get up, it would be the end of the Ivanovs as we knew them. We'd become nothing more than bloodthirsty killers. I stepped into the living room, but it was empty. Following the faint sounds coming from the kitchen, I frowned when I heard Elif, Grigori, and Selina whispering. "Are you sure this dose isn't dangerous?" Grigori asked Selina. "She's a nurse, Grigori. She knows what she's doing," Elif responded weakly, leaning against him, wrapped in a thick cardigan—the same one she only wore during her period, when it was best to keep a three-meter distance from her. "I'm sure. I would never hurt him…" "Nikolai ?" Grigori suddenly called out, making both women jump. Shit. Still as sharp as he was twenty years ago, the wolf.

I stepped into the room, and the first thing I noticed was how pale Selina looked, avoiding my gaze, while Elif tensed up. Yeah, they were definitely hiding something. "What could be dangerous? And for whom?" I asked, moving closer to Selina. "I think Dimitri is getting sick too, and since he doesn't weigh as much as your boys, I was asking Selina if we could use the same medication," Elif said, straightening up, her dark, exhausted eyes meeting mine. And I held back my questions—for now. "I… I'm going to check on the boys," Selina said, quickly slipping past me to leave the room, without even looking at me. I followed her without hesitation and caught her at the foot of the stairs, gently grabbing her arm and turning her toward me.

"Selina ? Is everything okay ?" I asked. She nodded, still avoiding my gaze. "Selina, look at me," I said softly, lifting her chin with my finger, finally catching her stunning green eyes. "Is there a problem?" She hesitated at first, then finally sighed, "Nikolai, maybe if I talked to him, maybe he'd release Roman. As much as it disgusts me, I know him inside out, I know—" I silenced her with a kiss, unable to bear the thought of her knowing anything about him, unable to imagine even for a second that she'd have to face that bastard. I pulled away as she slowly opened her eyes. "Forget it, Selina. Forget everything you know about him. And don't worry about Roman—I'll find a solution," I said, kissing her forehead before pulling her into my arms.

My plan was beginning to form in my mind. Rafael was right—a sacrifice was necessary to save my brother. But it wouldn't be Selina. It wouldn't be Rafael. It would be an Ivanov for another.

The next morning, sitting behind my desk after a sleepless night, I stared at the number on my phone screen—Antonio Rasili's number. I was ready to propose a trade. But not the one he wanted. I quickly shut off my phone when a knock sounded at the door, and Selina walked in with my sons. "Is there a problem?" I asked, immediately standing, already on edge, expecting some new threat or complication. "I need to get a shot," Rafael said, glancing at his mother, who smiled at him. "A shot?" I repeated, looking at Selina, who gave me a soft smile.

"He means his vaccine. We haven't done it yet for his eighth birthday. I would've taken him, but Elif said it could be dangerous," she said. "I know it's not the best time…" I shook my head and stepped closer to them, "no, let's go. It's important," I said, ruffling Rafael's hair. "Will it hurt him too much?" Andrei asked, giving me a worried look. "No, he won't feel a thing. And I'll be there the whole time, don't worry," I said, glancing at

Rafael. But he wouldn't meet my gaze, instead stealing quick looks at Selina and I frowned. I'd never seen him this... anxious before. Probably just nerves about the shot.

"I'll go grab his jacket," Selina said, kissing Rafael's hair before leaving the room.

As we waited downstairs, the closer we got to the exit, the stronger the feeling grew—something wasn't right. Elif and Grigori joined us by the door. Elif's pale complexion didn't surprise me, given everything happening, but Grigori's expression—something about it was off. "Is there a problem ?" I asked my brother softly. When his eyes met mine, I knew something was really wrong. But Grigori shook his head, and I couldn't press further because Selina arrived, carrying Rafael's jacket—and mine. She helped me put it on with a small smile, "come on, boys, let's see what the girls are cooking for dinner," Elif said, leading Andrei, Alexei, and Mikhail toward the kitchen. Grigori followed, but not before lingering on Rafael a moment too long.

"Don't worry, everything will be fine. You're so brave, *Angelo mio*, I'm so proud of you," Selina said, zipping up Rafael's jacket. She pulled him into a tight hug, kissing him multiple times, her eyes shining. And I told myself she must be like this because it was only their second time apart. "Don't worry, Mama. I'm a big boy now. I'll see you soon, I promise !" Rafael said, kissing his mother before heading outside to climb into the car. I smiled, watching him refuse David's help as he scrambled into the massive SUV on his own. "Don't worry, Selina. I'll bring him ba—" I started to say, turning back to her. But I didn't get to finish—because she suddenly wrapped her arms around my neck and kissed me. And damn, I didn't even remember what I was about to say. I wrapped an arm around her waist, my hand trailing up her cheek, then her neck, deepening the kiss. Her hands slid down from my shoulders to my chest. Then she slowly pushed me away. "I... I'm sorry," she whispered, I kissed her again to silence her, feeling her fists tighten against my jacket. "Never apologize for kissing me," I said softly, smiling. But she closed her eyes, shaking her head, her lips pressed together.

Something was fucking wrong.

"Selina ? What's going on ?" I asked, brushing her hair back and cupping her face. She took my hands, pulling them away from her face and pressing them against her chest, looking up at me with those huge green eyes and sighing softly. "Nikolai, everything will be okay. Your brother will come home and... and..." she stopped, closing her eyes again and lowering her head as I frowned, trying to understand her behavior. Her hands—ice cold, I only noticed it now, too distracted by that unexpected kiss. "Selina, look at me. Look at me, *Solnychko*," I repeated, lowering my face toward hers, feeling an unfamiliar panic creeping into my chest. Something was wrong. Selina was scared. She was stressed and trying to hide it from me. She finally shook her head, stepping back and releasing my hands. "We... we'll talk when you get back," she said, straightening, clasping her hands behind her back, forcing a small smile. But I shook my head, stepping toward her. Then the sudden sound of honking echoed loudly. It was Rafael, waving at me to hurry up. "Be careful," Selina whispered before heading toward the kitchen to join the rest of the family, leaving me standing in the hall—lost.

"We're going to get you that console you wanted. You were very brave, Rafael," I told him as I helped him buckle his seatbelt. He didn't say anything, just nodded, staring into space, his brows furrowed. "Hey, buddy, everything okay?" I asked, ruffling his hair. He lifted his eyes—eyes identical to his mother's—to meet mine. "Everything's fine. It just itches a little," he said, touching the back of his arm where he'd gotten his vaccine.

"In a few days, you won't feel a thing. Don't worry, big guy," I said, giving him a reassuring smile before gently closing the door. I moved to the driver's side, about to slide behind the wheel, when my phone rang. Grigori. Hopefully good news about Roman. "Meet me at Dock 36 North. Now," he said. "I'll drop off Raf—" "Now," he repeated before hanging up, making me curse. I sighed and started the engine, heading toward the docks. It couldn't have been anything dangerous if he was fine with me bringing Rafael along.

"We're making a quick stop before heading home, son," I told him. Rafael watched me for a moment, then nodded. Too silent. Whatever problem was unfolding right in front of me, Rafael already knew about it. "Is something wrong, Rafael? Is everything okay with your mom?" I hated questioning him like that, trying to pull information from a kid. "No, everything's fine," he said with a smile through the rearview mirror. And that was when the hairs on the back of my neck stood up—like I was looking into the eyes of one of the most dangerous men in the world. I was completely on edge. My instincts were all over the place. Forty minutes later, I pulled up in front of one of our warehouses where we stored shipments. "I'll be right back, buddy," I said, glancing over my shoulder at Rafael. He nodded, showing me the book he was reading. I stepped out and quickly joined Grigori and Sasha at the base of a shipping container.

They were tense, shoulders stiff, eyes dark. I clenched my fists, shoving them deep into my pockets. Something was wrong. Something had been wrong since that morning. And it felt like everyone knew—except me. The only thought running through my head was that something had happened to Roman. That this was the end. "What the hell is going on ?" I snapped, jaw clenched, boiling with—what ? Dread ? Fury ? "We found a deal with the Italians to get Roman back," Grigori said, watching one of our boats disappear into the horizon. "A deal ? How ?" I demanded.

Before I could get an answer, two cars suddenly pulled into the dock, stopping just a few meters from us. The three of us immediately drew our guns, aiming at the newcomers. Three men stepped out. Two were unfamiliar. The third... Abbiati ? I opened my mouth to ask what the hell he was doing there when a fourth man stepped out. And there was no mistaking that son of a bitch's face. Antonio Rasili. "The Ivanov brothers, almost all present," he said with a smirk, nodding to Abbiati. Abbiati walked around one of the cars, opened the trunk, and dragged something—no, someone—out. My brother. And I barely recognized him through the blood covering his face and body. Every muscle in my body tensed. Sasha cursed beside me. "Alright, here's my part of the deal. Where's yours ?" Antonio asked, crossing his arms. *Our part ?* I glanced at my brothers, but they remained locked on Antonio and his men, unflinching.

"If you give this son of a bitch anything, I swear I'll disown all three of you," Roman suddenly rasped, coughing, making me grimace. "I'll take Elif and disappear to some island far away from you all," he chuckled, voice wrecked. "Oh, shut up, mutt," Antonio sneered, kicking my brother in the stomach. "Antonio," Grigori growled, stepping forward—But stopped when one of Antonio's men pressed a gun to Roman's head. "Where. Is. Your. Part ?" Antonio bellowed, saliva nearly foaming from his mouth like a rabid dog. I was about to tell him there was no deal— When the sound of footsteps echoed through the stacks of shipping containers. And then, right in the middle of us and Antonio— A small silhouette appeared. And my world collapsed. "Rafael !" I roared, moving to grab him— But suddenly, I was on the ground. *What—?*

"I'm sorry, *moy brat*. Everything will be alright," Sasha murmured—before jamming a syringe into my neck. I snarled and slammed my elbow into his temple. I shoved him off and pushed myself up, staggering toward my son Then Grigori tackled me.

"What the fuck are you doing ?!" Roman yelled from across the dock. "Don't let him take Rafael ! He's a fucking psychopath !" he kept screaming. I punched Grigori square in the face, but he didn't move—just pinned me down, holding me in place. And my movements—slowed.

My limbs—heavy. *Fuck*—what had they injected me with ? "I'm going to kill you, Grigori. I'm going to kill you, do you hear me ?" I snarled, my voice growing weaker as my vision blurred. "The family, *moy brat*… always for the family," he murmured, pressing his forehead against mine, eyes closed. "Abbiati !" Antonio barked, further and further away— *Rafael*. I fought against the darkness trying to drag me under. I forced it back and slammed my forehead into Grigori's nose. He stumbled away, blood streaming between his fingers as I pushed myself onto my knees, trying to stand—

Lorenzo dragged my brother just a few steps away and then picked up my son. And started walking away. "Rafael !" I shouted, but I hit the ground again. "Stop, *moy brat*. Stop," Sasha gritted out, pinning me with his knee on my back. I lifted my head— And watched Rafael disappear. "With our son by my side, Selina won't take long to come to me," Antonio laughed. "I'm going to kill you. I'm going to kill all of you," I kept repeating. To my brothers. To Antonio. To Abbiati. To everyone. And just before everything faded to black—I saw my son. Waving at me over Lorenzo's shoulder, "see you later, Dad," Rafael said. And then—nothing.

Something was shaking—the bed I was lying on ? The building I was in ? Or was it an earthquake ? I forced my eyes open and groaned as the light blinded me. What the hell ? Why had I drunk so much ? Another one of Roman's stupid ideas…

Roman. Roman. Rafael. Rafael !

"Rafael !" With a loud crash, I hit the ground, my head spinning, my body trembling, drenched in sweat. What the fuck had those bastards injected me with ?! I braced myself against the mattress to get up, and before leaving the room, I grabbed my gun from the drawer. I stumbled into the hallway, my steps unsteady, and headed toward the office. The sun was already high—how much time had passed ? The sun had been setting when they took Rafael. They could have been anywhere by now. I pushed open the office door into a deathly silence. A death that felt closer than ever.

He was there. Standing in front of the bay window, still wearing the same clothes from the night before, his gaze fixed outside. There was no hesitation when I raised my gun, aiming at the back of his head. No hesitation when I released the safety. But my finger wouldn't move. The trigger was right there—just a little pressure. "If you draw your weapon, it's to shoot, *moy brat*," Grigori said without turning around. "You know hesitation kills." My hand trembled, just like the rest of me. My breath was short. Whatever they had injected me with, it was still in my system. "You betrayed me," I gritted out, taking a step toward him. "You betrayed me !" I shouted again, louder.

He turned, hands still buried in his pockets, not making a single move to disarm me. "For the family…" "He's my son now. My family. Your family !" He said nothing, just looked at me with those dark eyes. The same eyes that had watched me grow up. The same eyes that had watched my sons grow up. "Nikolai," a voice suddenly murmured behind me. But I shook my head. "Get out of here, Elif. You don't need to see this." "Nikolai, your brother—" "My brother betrayed me ! He betrayed our family ! And he's going to pay !" I shouted, my throat tight, my voice strangled by the weight of my rage. My brother had betrayed me. My own blood.

"Then you'll have to kill me too," Elif said, stepping between me and Grigori. Between my gun and him. "Elif, he's not in his right mind. Move," Grigori tried to pull her back, but she shook off his grip. "I knew, Nikolai. I knew about the deal," she said, her eyes locked onto mine. Grigori's betrayal had been painful. But this—Elif—It felt like a bullet between the eyes. No— A knife in the back. "What ?" I whispered, nausea rising in my gut. "I knew, Nikolai," she repeated, closing her eyes. "You knew," I echoed. "You knew. And you let him do it. You let him hand over an eight-year-old child to a fucking psychopath !" "Nikolai, watch where you're pointing that fucking gun," Grigori growled, trying to push Elif aside, but she didn't move. "I trusted you. She trusted you, Elif ! How could you betray Selina ?!"

"She didn't betray me, Nikolai." Selina's soft voice cut through the tension behind me. Automatically, my gun dropped as I turned slowly, afraid to look at her face. Afraid of what I would see there. Afraid of how to tell her— That I had failed to protect her son. "Nikolai, look at me," she said again, stepping closer. But I stepped back—so suddenly that I stumbled. Grigori caught me before I fell. "Nikolai ! You shouldn't be standing ! You weren't supposed to wake up for another two hours," Selina said, pressing her fingers against my throat to check my pulse. And her words began to sink into my thick skull. "You knew," I said, my eyes locking onto hers. And I knew—I knew I was right.

She had known.

"I didn't know about the deal," she murmured. And then— "I was the one who came up with the idea." And every betrayal I had suffered until now— Every single one— Became insignificant. Nothing compared to this.

Chapter twenty-seven
Selina

My heart tightened as I watched the car disappear from the living room window. *Forgive me, Nikolai.* I heard approaching footsteps and quickly wiped away the tears that had escaped. "Selina, we can still stop all of this. I'll call Nikolai…" "No, we're not stopping. We have to save Roman, Elif. Antonio will kill him," I said, turning to look at her—only to freeze when I saw her own tears. "Elif…" "I don't know how to thank you, Selina. I don't know what to say. I'm so sorry, Selina. So, so sorry."

I shook my head and pulled her into an embrace as my tears returned. "No, Elif, I'm the one who brought Antonio to your doorstep. This is my fault," I whispered, but she shook her head. She pulled back and took my face in her hands, "nothing, nothing that has happened or could happen will ever be your fault, Selina. It will always be the fault of that psychopath, that son of a bitch. And he will pay, Selina. Believe me, he will." I nodded, sniffling. Yes, Antonio would pay. He would pay for everything he had done to us, to my son, and to me. "For now, let's focus on getting your baby back, okay?" My baby would be with that monster, all alone. But I knew he'd be okay. He was strong, and he knew I was coming. I had promised him.

Twelve Hours Earlier...

I followed Velma into the kitchen, leaving Elif and Maria on the terrace. Sena was peeling vegetables at the sink. "Here, I found your knife," she said without turning, then casually threw a knife in our direction—threw a knife! I gasped and ducked to avoid it, but Velma caught it midair—midair! "Oh my God, Miss Selina! I didn't see you there! I'm so sorry!" Sena exclaimed, rushing over to help me up while I stared at both women, mouth slightly open.

"How...?" "Mama!" Rafael suddenly called, bursting into the kitchen. "We have to help Roman!" he said, grabbing my hand and pulling me out of the room, though I couldn't stop glancing back at the two women now deliberately avoiding my gaze. "What's going on, Rafael?" I asked as he practically dragged me into our bedroom and shut the door behind us. "Mama, we have to help Nikolai find Roman," he said, climbing onto the bed to be at my eye level. Since we had moved in with the Ivanovs and he had started spending time with the twins, Mikhail, and Grigori and Elif's sons, he had gained a confidence I never thought possible. I was so happy and proud of him. "Rafael..." "It's the monster who took him, Mama, and the monster wants you! We'll lie to him! We'll say you're coming, so he'll give Roman back!" he said, bouncing excitedly on the bed as I stared at him.

His idea was childish, but the truth underneath it was undeniable. Antonio was obsessed—an obsession we could use to our advantage. But how could I manipulate him? How could I convince him to release Roman before I actually showed up? "I'll go to the monster, Mama! Since you love me, he'll think you'll come for me. But Niko will come save me!" I froze. "What...? No! What are you saying, Rafael? I would never hand you over to that monster!" I said, gripping his shoulders, my brows furrowed. "How could you even think such a thing, Angelo mio?"

"I know you wouldn't give me to the monster, Mama, but this is to save Roman! I'm a big boy! I'll wait for Niko to come save me!" he said, shaking his head while I stared at him, mouth agape. How could my little boy come up with such an idea—so ingenious yet so dangerous? "Rafael…" "I don't want Roman to die, Mama! We can help him!" And again, I froze. I remembered Roman's warm smile, the way he had welcomed us, the way he had protected us. "Everything will be okay, Mama. We're not alone anymore," Rafael said, hugging me as my lips trembled. We're not alone anymore…

And that was how we ended up in my room again, this time with Elif and Grigori, as my eight-year-old son explained his plan to the head of the Bratva. "Selina, we are not going through with this plan, as ingenious as it is," Elif said, sitting beside me on the bed while Grigori questioned my son. "I will never allow anyone to put Rafael's life in danger," she added, taking my hand. I pressed my lips together, staring at my son, remembering Nikolai's exhaustion since Roman had been taken, and Elif's tears on the terrace. "But what if we can make this plan work?" I asked softly, and Elif stiffened beside me, tightening her grip on my hand. "Selina…" I turned to her, grasping both of her hands. "Roman is your son, Elif. We can't sit around and wait for him to be killed. Because that's exactly what will happen—Antonio will kill him, Elif. I know him. He will kill him."

Elif closed her eyes and sighed deeply, "I won't use an eight-year-old boy to save him, Selina. Roman wouldn't want that…" "Roman won't be able to want anything anymore if we don't do something, Elif," I countered. She stared at me, her expression unreadable, then looked at my son, "Grigori, call Sasha before he leaves Lorenzo. We're going to need him," Elif said softly. Grigori studied me for a moment, and I simply nodded. We had to save Roman. And nothing would take Rafael from me.

Present

"Lorenzo will take care of him until we get him back," Elif said as I followed her into the kitchen. "Sasha will go with you to pick him up, along with Velma and Sena," she added. I froze when I saw the two women waiting inside—and on the counter, where they usually prepared food, lay an arsenal fit for an army. "What the...?" I looked at Velma and Sena, as if truly seeing them for the first time. They were dressed in all black, calmly selecting knives and guns as if choosing vegetables at the market. "I don't understand..." I whispered as Elif picked up a pistol, checked the magazine, and then set it back down. "Velma and Sena have... particular skills. Velma was here long before me. She served Grigori's mother, Elena Ivanov, and Velma taught everything she knew to Sena," Elif explained.

"How do I look ? Is this discreet enough to infiltrate the hotel ?" my sister asked, walking into the room dressed in black cargo pants and a sweatshirt. I had told her the plan last night. At first, she had refused, but once she realized we had no choice, she stopped arguing. "Sienna, you're not coming with us !" I said, stepping toward her, but she raised a hand. "Tut, tut, little sister. You're not going anywhere without me," she said, wagging her finger. I said nothing as she walked to the counter and picked up a gun, checking the magazine before sliding it into the holster at her back. Then she took two knives, tucking them into her boots. Then she picked up another pistol—a smaller one—before handing it to me. "Here. It's a Glock. Smaller, but just as deadly. You release the safety like this before using it," she said, demonstrating before pressing it into my hand.

It was heavy. Cold. And it made me uneasy. I tucked it into my waistband like my sister and shuddered when the metal touched my skin. I sighed and sat on one of the high stools.

"Selina," Elif whispered, placing a hand on my shoulder. "You know this was the right decision. If Antonio had taken you instead, he might have taken you far away. He's obsessed with you, Selina. Rafael doesn't hold the same value to him." She kissed my temple before pulling me into a hug.

Five hours later, several cars stopped in front of the entrance, and we practically rushed outside. "Roman!" Elif cried out, her voice filled with relief and anguish as I choked back a sob at the sight of him—he was almost unrecognizable. So much blood. Sasha carried him inside, followed closely by Elif and Velma, while Grigori approached with Nikolai—unconscious—slung over his back. And Rafael wasn't there. He was with him. With the monster. I followed Grigori as he carried Nikolai upstairs to his room. Once he laid him on the bed, I checked his pulse—steady. The tranquilizer would last another ten hours. "Did he... did he cry?" I asked softly, my voice barely more than a whisper. "No. Not a single tear. On the contrary, he waved at Nikolai and said they'd see each other soon. And he called him 'Dad' before leaving," Grigori said.

I closed my eyes, resting my forehead against the edge of the bed where the man who had won my son's heart—and my own—now lay. "The doctor is here, Grigori," Sasha called from the hallway, and I heard Grigori step out to join his wife at Roman's side. "I'm going to check on Roman," Sienna said, squeezing my shoulder before leaving and quietly closing the door behind her. Alone now, I slowly lay down beside Nikolai, facing him, pressing my face against his arm as I began to cry. "I'm sorry. I'm so sorry, Nikolai. Forgive me," I sobbed, clinging to his arm, trembling, lost, terrified. I held on to him—the one person who had reached for me despite the darkness I was trapped in, despite my resistance and fears, despite my wounds and scars. He had never let go. Not once. He had held me in his arms. And in his heart.

I knew what he felt for me because I felt the same. And I also knew he hadn't said it yet because he was afraid—afraid that his love might scare me away. But right now, it wasn't his love that terrified me—it was the hatred he would feel when he realized what I had done.

As night fell, I gently knocked on Roman's door before entering. Elif was sitting on the edge of the bed, holding a bowl of soup. "Roman," I said softly as I saw him propped against the headboard, covered in bandages, stitches, and bruises. "Hey, beautiful," he greeted me with a smirk—but immediately grimaced in pain. I hesitated before stepping closer… and suddenly, I didn't know what to do. He was in this state because of me. Antonio had tortured him because of me. My thoughts scattered when he reached out his hand. I took it carefully, mindful of his injuries. "I'm so sorry, Rom…"

"No, Selina. I'm the one who's sorry. I'm sorry that you had to live—no, survive—that bastard for all those years," he rasped, his voice hoarse. "I don't know how you did it, Selina. I don't know how you raised Rafael under the same roof as that monster. But if there's one thing I do know, it's that you have nothing to be sorry for." My lips trembled as I fought back my emotions. "And don't worry about me. I've been through worse. A few broken ribs and some cuts won't put me down," he said, lifting my hand to his lips and kissing it. A tear slipped down my cheek, and I quickly wiped it away. He gently pulled me closer, guiding me to sit beside him on the bed next to Elif. "Two beautiful women in my bed," he teased with a weak chuckle. Elif punched his knee, making him groan. "They should've hit you in the mouth instead," she grumbled, shoving another spoonful of soup into his mouth. Roman writhed dramatically.

"It's hot! It's hot!" he whined after swallowing. "I don't need enemies when I have you," he muttered, gulping down some water. I smiled at their bickering, feeling warmth bloom in my chest. Elif looked like she had found her soul again. And soon, I would find mine too.

Chapter twenty-eight
<u>Selina</u>

I climbed into the back of the SUV with Sena and Velma while Sasha and Sienna continued arguing outside the vehicle. "You have no business being there !" Sasha exclaimed as my sister tried to dodge around him to get into the car, but he held her back. "And what if you have a seizure over there, huh ? You'll ruin everything !" "Go fuck yourself, Ivanov ! I survived just fine on my own for over twenty years—I don't need some arrogant asshole telling me what to do !" my sister snapped, shoving him hard before climbing into the front seat.

Sasha stood still for a few seconds in front of the car, probably cursing under his breath, then punched the hood before getting behind the wheel. He started the engine in silence, his knuckles white from gripping the steering wheel too tightly. "Lorenzo will be waiting for us outside ?" I asked, trying to adjust the gun in my waistband. How did they carry these things all day ? "Yeah, he'll sneak us in through the back. Velma and I will wait in the hallway while you two get Rafael," Sasha said, stealing what he thought were discreet glances at my sister, who was staring out the window in silence. I sighed, rubbing my trembling hands against my thighs. My baby was alone. Was he scared ? I jumped when my sister suddenly turned in her seat and placed a hand on my knee. "Everything will be fine, Selina. Just breathe," she murmured, locking eyes with me.

From the corner of my eye, I saw Sasha shift slightly forward—almost imperceptibly—before taking a deep breath. A breath of Sienna's scent. Oh my God, he was completely gone for her. An hour later, we arrived in front of a five-star hotel in the city center, and my heart pounded violently in my chest. My baby was here. Just a few meters away.

Sasha parked in an alley behind the hotel. As soon as we stepped out, the back door of the building opened, revealing Lorenzo Abbiati. He signaled for us to enter quickly, leading us into the hotel's boiler room. I glanced at my sister, and I knew we were thinking the same thing—the day we escaped Rome. The day she saved me. "In three minutes, all the cameras will be down for exactly six minutes and twenty-eight seconds—that's all the time you have to grab the kid and get out," Lorenzo said, his eyes fixed on his phone. "He's on the sixth floor, room 627. He's with Antonio's cousin…" "A… Alia?" I whispered, my hands clenching into fists. "Alia, as in the bitch who did nothing while that bastard beat you?" Sienna asked, her voice dark, and I didn't answer.

"You'll need to take care of her. Quietly. Rasili's in the room next door." "Don't worry, pretty boy," Sienna interjected, pulling a knife from her boot. "She won't even have time to say hello." "What the fuck are you doing with that?!" Sasha growled at her. "Oh, nothing. I was just wondering if Rasili prefers bananas or apples. You know, since I'm preparing him a fruit plate," she smirked exaggeratedly. "She's going to drive me insane. Insane, I swear," Sasha muttered, rubbing his face. "You already are. You don't need me for that," my sister shrugged. I jabbed her in the ribs with my elbow to shut her up. "We go in thirty seconds," Lorenzo cut in, tucking his phone away and glancing at his watch. "Who's handling the cameras?" Sasha asked, his eyes narrowing as they locked onto Lorenzo's profile. But Lorenzo didn't answer—just watched the seconds tick down.

Just like last time, when he helped us escape the ambush at the airstrip, he wouldn't reveal his source. Someone was helping him. No, helping us. But who ? And why ? "Let's go," Lorenzo finally said, pushing the door open. He stepped into the long corridor first, and we followed him to the elevator. Before we could even press the button, the doors slid open—as if someone was already expecting us. Lorenzo held the doors while we stepped inside. "Use the fire escape on your way out. You have six minutes left," he said before stepping back. The doors closed on his somber expression.

I rubbed my sweaty hands against my pants. I'm coming, my baby. I'm here. A few seconds later, the doors opened, and Sasha stepped out first, signaling for us to wait. A few moments later, he waved us forward. The hallway was empty—no guards. We quickly reached room 627, and we all froze. We didn't have a key card. How were we supposed to— Suddenly, the red light on the door lock turned green, and we heard it unlock. We glanced at each other before Sienna quietly pushed the door open and slipped inside, followed by Sena and then me, while Sasha and Velma remained outside. The room was dark. We stepped into a small sitting area. Sienna turned on her phone's flashlight, keeping her knife at the ready, and moved toward the two doors leading to the bedrooms. A fifty-fifty chance.

She looked at me questioningly, and without thinking, I pointed to the right door. She pushed it open gently and lowered her head, checking inside. I followed closely as she entered. The room was still dark. My baby was afraid of the dark. How could they leave him alone like this ? I approached the bed but frowned when I saw it was empty. Then, I noticed the light shining from under the bathroom door.

Oh, my angel...

I rushed toward the door, ignoring Sienna's attempt to stop me and pushed it open—and my heart shattered. My baby was there, curled up in the bathtub, still wearing the clothes we picked out that morning, a pillow tucked under his head. I knelt beside the tub and gently ran my fingers through his dark hair, "*Angelo mio,*" I whispered. He frowned and buried his face deeper into the pillow, making me smile, "wake up, Rafael," I murmured again, leaning over to press a kiss to his forehead.

Finally, he blinked awake, his green eyes—so much like mine—meeting mine. "Mama !" he exclaimed, throwing himself into my arms. I clutched him tightly, tears spilling down my cheeks despite myself, "I'm here, *Angelo mio*. Just like I promised—I came to get you," I whispered, kissing him as he nuzzled his nose against my neck. "I love you," he whispered.

"Oh, Rafael, I love you too," I breathed, hugging him even tighter. "Are you okay, *Pulcino mio*?" my sister asked, kneeling to ruffle his hair. He nodded and hugged her, and I saw her eyes widen in shock. She wasn't used to being shown affection so openly. "We have three minutes left," Sena reminded us from the doorway. She was right—time was running out. I stood and lifted my son into my arms, heading toward the exit with my sister and Sena following. But just as we passed the doors leading to the bedrooms, the other door swung open—and Alia stepped out in a silk nightgown.

She froze. Her gaze jumped between the four of us, and I saw it click in her brain. She opened her mouth— probably to scream for her dear cousin— But Sienna pounced on her, knife against her throat. "Make a single sound, and it'll be your last, you filthy bitch," she hissed, her voice dripping with hatred. Alia's face filled with horror, and she slowly nodded. "Turn around. Face the wall. We're leaving. *Capisce*?" Alia nodded again, and as soon as she turned— Sienna grabbed her by the hair and slammed her face against the wall with a sickening crack. Alia collapsed, unconscious, a massive bump already forming on her forehead. "Eat the wall. A change from all the dicks, bitch," Sienna spat before joining us.

Oh. My. God.

"Let's go," Sienna said, pushing open the door just as Sasha was about to enter, probably to come check on us. She crashed into him, and he instinctively grabbed her by the waist, stopping her from falling backward. For a brief moment, he held her there, eyes locked onto hers. Then, he glanced over his shoulder at Alia's unconscious body sprawled across the floor. His gaze snapped back to my sister, questioning. Sienna shrugged nonchalantly. "She was hungry," she said before shoving past him to exit the room. Sasha watched her go, then closed his eyes and exhaled sharply, as if he had mustered all his patience to stop himself from doing something reckless. "Fire escape is at the end of the hall, left side," he muttered through clenched teeth, his gaze never leaving my sister.

We followed his directions, rushing down the dimly lit hallway until we reached a red emergency door. "Eighteen seconds," Sena reminded us as we pushed through and descended the metal staircase, Sasha took Rafael from my arms so we could move faster, and a cold shiver ran down my spine as we stepped into the night air. We reached the SUV, and Sasha didn't waste a single second before speeding off, putting as much distance as possible between us and the monster who, by now, must be losing his mind. I clutched my son against me, breathing in his scent, feeling his little body relax against mine. He was safe. He was home.

Present

I wilted under Nikolai's gaze, his eyes brimming with hurt. I had hurt him. But it had to be done—because if he had known, he would have stopped us. "Dad ?" Rafael's voice echoed in the room, and Nikolai's gun slipped from his hand, clattering to the floor. He lunged forward, grabbing Rafael and holding him so tightly it was as if he was afraid to ever let go again. "Dad..." And Nikolai embraced him like one. His head bowed, his face pressed into Rafael's small shoulder, breathing him in, as if trying to convince himself that he was real, that he was here. Tears burned in my eyes as Elif stepped up beside me, her hand gentle on my shoulder.

"Are you okay ? Did he hurt you ?" Nikolai asked, pulling back slightly to study Rafael, his large hands checking him over for any injuries. Rafael shook his head vigorously. "No ! I wasn't even scared, Dad ! I knew Mama was coming—she promised !" He grinned brightly, throwing his arms around Nikolai's neck again. "And Aunt Sienna smashed the witch's head against the wall—it went BOOM !" His voice bubbled with excitement, retelling his adventure. But I saw it. I saw the way Nikolai's body stiffened with every word. With every detail that proved he had been kept in the dark. With every reminder that Sienna had known—when he hadn't. Then, with a smooth motion, he stood, lifting Rafael with him and without a single glance in my direction, he walked out of the room.

Leaving me standing there, my lips trembling as Elif pulled me into a hug, holding me tight. "Oh, Selina... Don't worry. He's just angry—it'll be okay." I nodded. But I didn't believe her. Men like him—men who live in control, who build their world on trust and power—they don't handle betrayal well. I had hurt him. I had hurt his pride. I had hurt his trust in me. And without trust, there is nothing.

Nikolai

"If you're going to keep sulking, get out. Your bad energy is slowing down my recovery," Roman muttered, struggling to sit up against the headboard, his focus glued to the screen where he and Rafael were engrossed in their game. My son gripped his controller tighter, his avatar sprinting toward the goal, ready to score. Roman, too distracted by his discomfort, didn't even see it coming. "Yeah !" Rafael shouted triumphantly as the ball hit the net, his face lighting up with a grin.

My son. Because that's what he is. Even if his own mother had refused to acknowledge it. Yet. I pushed myself up from the chair beside the bed, ruffling Rafael's hair before leaning in to adjust the pillows behind my brother. Roman grunted in appreciation, then grimaced when he saw the updated score flashing on the screen. "Be nice to your uncle, son. He's fragile right now," I said as I sat back down as Roman shot me a glare, but I didn't have the energy to smirk back. Maybe it was still the sedative wearing off—the one arranged by the woman I loved. Yes, loved.

Because no matter the secrets, the lies, or the betrayals Selina threw my way, she was and always would be the only woman I had ever fallen for, the only woman I ever would. Before Roman could retaliate with a sarcastic remark, a knock on the door interrupted. "Rafi ?" Mikhail's voice called from the hallway before the door opened slightly. "We're watching a movie downstairs. Wanna come ?" He stood there, hands stuffed into the pockets of his joggers, his posture carefully nonchalant. And I smirked slightly. Since Selina had entered our lives, my relationship with my sons had steadily improved. It was still complicated, especially with Mikhail, but I saw it—the small ways they changed around me.

Like how Mikhail straightened his back, kept his expressions neutral, chose his words more carefully, like a man trying to hold his own. "Yeah ! With popcorn !" Rafael exclaimed, abandoning his controller, his game, and Roman, who groaned in protest behind him. But my son was already out the door, following Mikhail, who glanced back at me briefly before closing the door behind them. Roman kept muttering under his breath, dissatisfied with his loss, so I picked up the controller Rafael had left behind and continued the game in his place. We played in comfortable silence until Roman spoke—and his words made me freeze. "He was going to kill me." He didn't stop playing, his voice eerily calm, as if commenting on the weather. "I'm young, but I've seen a lot of shit in my life, Niko. I've fought in wars. I've spent weeks in hellholes, barely surviving. I've met demons so twisted even hell wouldn't take them. But through all of that, I always knew I'd make it. I always knew I'd come home." His words tightened something in my chest. Guilt. Because I had let him go. I had let him fight those wars alone. "But this time was different, Niko." His voice was low, grim. "I knew the moment I looked into Antonio Rasili's eyes that I wasn't walking out of there alive." I gripped the controller tightly, my teeth clenching, "he's not sane, Niko. Not in the head. He's willing to do anything to get Selina back. When he talks about her, he shakes—like a junkie deprived of his fix. He was going to kill me. If Selina hadn't done what she did, I'd be dead."

I realized what he was doing. I dropped the controller and turned to face him. But he didn't meet my eyes. Not until he scored the winning goal. Finally, he set the controller down and looked at me. "If she had told you, you would've stopped her. And I'd already be dead by the time you figured out a solution, *moy brat*." I closed my eyes, exhaling harshly. "When Sasha called to make the deal, Antonio had a gun pressed to my head. But… I won't lie—I had a great time describing your perfect little family to him. Especially the sounds you and Selina make at night." And the bastard laughed. I buried my face in my hands, groaning. Just the thought of Roman dead— I shook my head.

No.

When I looked back up, Roman was already staring at me, his bruised, swollen eyes unwavering. Antonio Rasili was going to die. Not before he suffered every ounce of pain he'd inflicted on the people I loved. Roman saw it and he smirked. A cold, merciless smirk. "I know that look, *moy brat*. But wait until I'm back on my feet. I've got a few scores to settle myself." his smile was ruthless, filled with the promise of retribution. I nodded. "And another thing…" he met my gaze head-on, "Selina isn't going anywhere," I narrowed my eyes. "Not until we find out how Antonio keeps tracking her, not until we kill him and free her for good. And even after that, she will stay. You know how I know that?"

I said nothing, "because she willingly walked back into hell for you, Nikolai." His words hit me like a punch to the gut. "She risked everything. Not just for me— because sure, maybe she likes me. Maybe she wanted to save my sorry ass. But deep down, it was for you, so you wouldn't have to bury your idiot little brother." He gripped my shoulder tightly, his jaw tensing, his gaze lost in the distance. I reached out, gripping his forearm in return, my other hand clasping his shoulder, "I'm glad you're home, *moy brat*." Roman grinned, "me too, *moy brat*. Me too."

I nodded. Then I stood up, stretching my legs. The lingering numbness in my body was completely gone now. Good. I would need all my strength for what was coming. For Selina. Because behind her silence, behind her calm façade, a storm was brewing. And I intended to chase it down—relentlessly, ruthlessly. To consume it. To consume her.

Chapter twenty-nine
<u>Selina</u>

"But... but have you actually killed before ?" I asked, grimacing despite myself, then quickly pressed a hand to my forehead. "I'm sorry, I didn't mean to disrespect your... your profession," I added hastily, not even knowing how to categorize their work. Bodyguards disguised as household staff. Assassin housemaids? The two women working behind the stove, preparing dinner, burst out laughing while Elif smiled and shook her head beside me as we peeled apples for dessert. "Rest assured, Miss Selina, we have never harmed an innocent," Velma said, chopping a carrot so quickly and finely that I struggled to follow her movements with my eyes. "We only protect," Sena added softly, glancing at me hesitantly, as if gauging my reaction. And I should probably have felt scared—uncomfortable, even—living under the same roof as two assassins in addition to the mafia men around me. But instead—and quite comically—I felt reassured. Reassured to know there was yet another layer of protection for the children, another barrier between danger and the boys.

"I see," I said, returning Sena's smile before reaching for another apple from the basket. But before I could peel it, a hand wrapped around my wrist, lifting it gently above my head, and my eyes widened as I watched Nikolai sink his teeth into it, his gaze locked onto mine. My mouth went dry, and I held my breath. It felt like everything had frozen around us—or maybe it truly had. I no longer heard Velma's knife against the cutting board or Elif peeling apples. "What are you doing ?" I whispered without realizing, my breath shallow. He looked at me, raising an eyebrow, "trying to regain my strength—you know, the strength I lost after the sedative you injected me with." His voice was dark, meant to intimidate me, but instead, it did the complete opposite. I think... I think I squeezed my thighs together. Oh my God. But his words, fortunately or unfortunately, extinguished the dark desire starting to burn inside me.

"A... a sedative can indeed have side effects such as confusion or disorientation, paradoxical effects in some cases, where the person becomes agitated or anxious instead of calm, drowsiness, slowing of motor and cognitive functions, decreased alertness..." I gasped when he wrapped an arm around my waist, lifting me from my seat and setting me on my feet. He grabbed my peeler and tossed it toward Sena, who caught it effortlessly without taking her eyes off us, a small smile playing on her lips. Nikolai took my hand, pulling me with him toward the stairs. "Don't wait for us for dinner. We'll eat later," he said, and I followed him like a lost chick, too stunned to resist or understand his purpose. I had expected to be ignored, pushed away, maybe even despised—but this? I followed him to his bedroom, trying to make sense of his intentions. And I couldn't help but feel a creeping doubt, a doubt fueled by eight years of hell. No. Nikolai would never hurt me. Never.

He closed the door behind him and turned to face me as I stood in the middle of the room, my hands clenched against my stomach. "I know you're angry, and you have every right to be, Nikolai. But I wanted to help, I..." My words trailed off as he slowly approached, measured and deliberate. And I couldn't help but step back.

"Nikolai…" I tried to call his name, but he ignored me. And once again, instead of feeling fear, I felt something else entirely. My breathing turned shallow, my heart pounded against my ribs. "Angry?" he suddenly asked in a dark voice, making me nearly jump. "Furious, then?" I asked in a small voice, and I couldn't stop the shiver that ran through me when his lips curved into a slow smile. "Ah, Selina. My sweet Selina, who is actually so strong and courageous." My legs went weak at his words. Me? Strong? Courageous? No, I never was. Never had been. I was—and still am—the girl who was locked in a cage by a monster. The girl he destroyed, leaving only a shell behind. And a shell was not what Nikolai deserved. His hand suddenly reached out, gripping my forearm when I stumbled, my feet catching on the Turkish rug. I pressed my lips together as tears burned my eyes.

"That's not true," I whispered, lowering my face as his arm wrapped around my waist, pulling me against him. "I was never strong or courageous. Especially not when he locked me up. I cried, I begged him every night. Sometimes, I even… even wet myself," I confessed, my throat tightening, and Nikolai's arm tensed against me. But he didn't speak—he just let me continue. "And when I found out I was pregnant with Rafael, I was so weak that I thought about… ending it all." A sob escaped me, "I was pregnant with… my rapist's child. I didn't want to carry this thing he had inflicted on me. But I couldn't, Nikolai. It was a baby. A baby who hadn't asked for any of this. And he was my baby." I pressed my forehead against his shoulder as my tears finally fell. His hand moved from my arm to my neck, massaging gently, giving me the strength to keep going.

"When he was born, when I held him for the first time, I hated myself. I hated that I had ever thought Rafael was…" My breath caught. I gripped his sweater as he squeezed my neck twice, telling me it was okay. His lips pressed against my temple, his warm breath sweeping away my hair, "that's when I started pretending. Pretending to be strong, pretending to be brave. It was the only way to protect my son. He was the only thing keeping me alive, the only thing that helped me survive until today, Nikolai. Without him, I… I would have…" I fell silent when his hand moved from my neck to my jaw, tilting my face up to his. "Forgive me," he said suddenly, his blue eyes locked onto mine. "Forgive me for not coming sooner. Forgive me. Forgive me, *Solnychko*."

He repeated it again and again, making my sobs grow louder. He kissed my forehead, my temples, my cheeks—everywhere I had scars, everywhere that had once hurt so much I couldn't bear to touch it for days. I shook my head. "You couldn't have known…", "the moment I saw you, I knew, Selina. I knew what was happening. I knew who you were." His lips hovered over mine, his scent overwhelming me, "who am I, Nikolai?" I asked, my gaze flicking between his eyes and his lips, the desire I had been trying to suppress now burning, consuming me. "*Solnychko*. You are my *Solnychko*, Selina. As bright and radiant as the sun, as warm and dazzling as it is, as joyful and light as it is," he whispered, his thumb grazing my lower lip. "I was lost in darkness for so long, Selina."

He shook his head, pressing his forehead against mine, "I lied, Selina. I can't. I can't let you go. I can't live without you, Selina." His voice was rough, and I trembled, inhaling deeply. "I'm sorry, Selina, I can't—" his words faded against my lips as I kissed him, rising onto the tips of my toes, my hand sliding against his nape. He didn't move—he stayed frozen. I pulled back slightly and looked at his face, so perfect, so beautiful. His eyes remained closed, his breath coming in rapid bursts from his parted lips. With trembling fingers, I traced the bridge of his nose, his cheekbones, his beard, and his jawline, then the outline of his lips. "Don't be sorry, *amore mio*," I whispered, and his eyes snapped open, widening at the endearment.

"I don't want to go anywhere, Nikolai. Not today, not ever. I... I shouldn't be able to—no, I shouldn't even be capable of trusting a man after... after him." My hand slid against his cheek, and he leaned into my palm slightly, "but you, Mr. Ivanov, you have your own way of breaking down my walls," I said with a soft smile. But he didn't smile. On the contrary, his face was so serious, his eyes shining with a determination that stole my breath. "So strong and courageous," he repeated, cupping my face between his hands. "So strong and courageous... and mine." Then he kissed me—slow and deep—so tender that my tears returned, and I closed my eyes to hold them back. I clung to his shoulder, my hand slipping from his cheek to the back of his neck. He bit down gently on my lower lip, and I gasped, giving him the opportunity to slide his tongue between my lips, meeting mine, deepening the kiss. Despite my lack of experience, I tried to kiss him back. A small moan escaped me, and I felt him freeze before pulling back.

I slowly opened my eyes, my breath ragged, my cheeks burning. His gaze trailed down my face, stopping at my lips—probably swollen—before rising back to my eyes.

"*Blyat*," he muttered in a husky voice. I yelped as he suddenly lifted me, one arm around my waist, and set me on the small desk against the wall. I grasped his shoulders as he stepped between my thighs, tightening his arm around me. "One word, Selina. Just one, and I'll stop everything," he said, his voice so unrecognizable, so dark… and I liked it. I shook my head, instinctively—or deliberately, I had no idea—tightening my legs around him. He closed his eyes, inhaling deeply, "I don't want you to stop, Niko. Not ever." I pulled him to me, kissing him again. A low groan rumbled in his throat—a sound I had never heard before—and my thighs pressed even closer around him. His free hand encircled my ankle, making me shudder against him. I trembled as he slowly traced his fingers up my calf beneath my long skirt. I moaned again when his touch glided over the back of my knee, and he tilted his head, deepening our kiss.

I clutched his hair—pulling him closer. At my grip, he firmly grabbed my thigh, suddenly dragging me closer to the edge of the desk, and my eyes widened when I felt his arousal pressing against me. "Nikolai !" I exclaimed, surprised and he froze, locking eyes with mine. "Stop ?" he asked out of breath. And my heart clenched at his consideration, at his restraint despite his… evident desire. But no matter how deep I searched within myself, I found no fear. So I shook my head, guiding his hand higher up my thigh. "Don't stop, *amore mio*."

Nikolai

My lips found hers again before my pathetic brain could even process her words. *Amore mio.* My damn heart pounded against my temples, my thoughts, my ideas—all blending together, and damn, I loved it. My fingers slid down to the edges of her panties, and a tingling sensation spread through them. I traced the seam slowly, ready to stop at any moment, waiting for the slightest sign from Selina to put an end to it. But instead, her hand, buried in my hair, pulled me even closer to her. *Blyat.*

I reached her core—hot, wet, for me. She moaned when my fingers pressed gently, and she leaned back slightly, her head tilting, eyes closed, breath erratic. May God have mercy on me—I would have given my arm to witness that vision every day of my miserable life. Her long neck was exposed, and I took full advantage, running my nose along her throat, leaving soft kisses in my way before trailing up to her ear. I stopped the slow circles I had been tracing between her thighs, and her plaintive whimper made me smirk. "Selina," I murmured against her ear as she gripped my wrist, urging me to continue, but I remained still.

"Nikolai, please," she begged, breathless, and despite every primal instinct in me screaming to make her come so hard neither of us would ever forget the sound of her cry, I held back. "Promise me, Selina. Promise me you'll never pull a stunt like that behind my back again. Swear it to me." I hesitated when I felt her tense against me. I shouldn't have brought this up now—not during our first real touch. "Nikolai Ivanov, if you don't make me come in the next few seconds, I swear I'll strangle you," she said, still breathless but firm. For a moment, I was stunned into silence. Then a low chuckle escaped me. How stupid I had been to think, even for a second, that Selina Floros was fragile and weak. "Promise me, *Solnychko*," I repeated, giving her a playful slap against her core that made her jolt and gasp. "Nikolai !" "Promise me," I said again, rubbing my nose behind her ear—a gesture that carried weight, a meaning I knew she understood when she tried to pull back and look at me. But I held her firmly against me. "I can't live without you, Selina. Not anymore. Never again will you put yourself in danger like that. Swear it to me."

I nipped at her throat, and she shivered as I resumed my slow, teasing circles between her thighs. "Nikolai, I… I promise I won't do anything dangerous without telling you," she finally ground out through clenched teeth, and I chuckled again. A half-promise. I'd take it—for now. My fingers picked up their pace, and Selina began to tremble, her arms wrapping around my neck, pulling me flush against her as I softly sucked the spot where her pulse pounded wildly. "Nikolai !" "That's it, *Solnychko*, come for me," I whispered—and she did. A sob escaped her lips as the orgasm crashed over her, forcing my name from her mouth again, and it was the most beautiful sound I had ever heard. "*Khoroshaya devochka* (good girl)."

Chapter thirty
<u>Selina</u>

The boys' laughter woke me up. I barely opened my eyes, wincing as the bright sunlight streaming through the window blinded me. A deep chuckle near my ear made me jolt, just as the strong arms wrapped around my waist and chest tightened, pulling me closer against Nikolai's warm body. "Good morning, my sweet *Solnychko*," he murmured, his nose gliding from my neck to my shoulder, where he gently nibbled, sending shivers down my spine. "Good morning, *amore mio*," I replied, turning my face toward his to place a kiss on his cheek. He smiled before his lips captured mine in a slow, lingering kiss, and I let out a small sigh as the memories of last night flooded my mind. Ever since that first time on his desk, there had been many more. And when we finally became one, I had never felt so alive. He had been gentle, patient, listening to my every need, putting me first in ways I had never thought possible.

It had been perfect. Everything was perfect. Every night had been a new discovery, a new lesson in pleasure, each moment more intense than the last. He never rushed, never took without giving, always making sure I felt safe, treasured… loved. Tears welled up in my eyes just thinking about it. "Hey… what's wrong ?" Nikolai asked, his voice low with concern. His hand, which had been resting over my heart, moved up to cup my cheek, his thumb tracing slow circles on my skin. I shook my head and turned in his arms, pressing my palms against the warmth of his chest. "I'm just… happy," I said with a soft smile. But the crease between his brows only deepened, worry still etched on his face. I lifted my fingers to smooth it away. "Stop looking at me like that. I promise, I'm okay," I insisted. "Everything is just so perfect. After so long... I never thought I'd feel happiness like this. Thank you, *amore mio*," I whispered, pressing my lips to his jaw.

"No, *Solnychko*. Thank you," he murmured. "For stepping into my life, for bringing your warmth into my cold, empty world. Before you, everything was dark, meaningless. And my relationship with the boys..." He exhaled sharply, as if remembering something painful, before holding me even closer, as if afraid I might slip away. "For nearly a year, they barely spoke to me, they avoided me. But since you arrived, since you stayed... everything changed, Selina. Everything." I bit my lip, debating whether to ask the question that had been haunting me since I first met them. But I didn't want there to be any secrets between us. No doubts, no unspoken words. I needed to understand. So I took a deep breath and finally asked, "Why ? Why were they avoiding you, Nikolai ?" His jaw tightened instantly, and regret gripped me like a vice. "I... Forget it. I shouldn't have—"

He cut me off by pressing his thumb against my lips, silencing me with a gentle touch. "No, Selina," he said firmly. "You have every right to ask. You can ask me anything. I want us to build something real, something strong and unshakable." I nodded slowly, my heart pounding. "I was married thirteen years ago," he began, his voice steady, but his gaze locked onto mine. "An arranged marriage." My stomach twisted as he continued, "we married to strengthen the alliance between our families. Her name was Irina. She was quiet, reserved... No, more than that. She was completely closed off. She struggled to connect with people—even with Elif and my brothers—despite living under the same roof. At first, I thought it was normal—she barely knew us, and we're not exactly easy to approach. And we were still young." He paused, his expression darkening, "but when Mikhail was born, during our second year of marriage... nothing changed. It got worse. She refused to nurse him, refused to even see him—not even after giving birth. I was the first to hold him in my arms. He was... he was perfect."

My heart clenched at the tenderness in his voice, but at the same time, I wanted to scream. My poor Mikhail... he had never even felt his mother's warmth after birth. He had been abandoned before he even had a chance. "Elif tried to reassure me. She said some women struggle after childbirth, that I needed to give it time, that Irina would come around... but she never did. She refused to acknowledge him, refused to speak to him, for an entire year." I gasped. A whole year ? I couldn't imagine going even a single day without holding Rafael when he was a baby. "And even after that, she remained distant. Cold. But it wasn't out of cruelty, Selina. Something inside her was already broken. And I know her mother, Agata, had something to do with it." "Her own mother ?" I asked, shocked. He nodded grimly.

"But the woman who was with her the other day... Nina? That's her granddaughter, isn't she ? She seemed... normal ?" "Nina ?" He sighed. "Yes. She's Irina's niece. But she's different. She's shy, introverted... but not broken. Not like Irina. But sometimes, when I look into her eyes, I see cracks forming. Like she's barely holding on." A chill ran down my spine. I thought of the young woman with her delicate features, the way she had tried to calm her mother, the exhaustion in her voice. She was on the verge of breaking. Like so many women before her. Like me. Like I almost had—before Rafael. "We have to help her, Nikolai," I said suddenly, sitting up so fast I almost fell off the bed. "We can—we can take her away. She can hide here. Or we can grab her grandmother and make her stop—" I barely had time to react before I found myself pinned to the bed beneath him, his lips hovering just above mine. "Oh, my sweet Selina," he murmured, brushing a kiss against the tip of my nose. "I should have known... You've spent too much time around us. You're starting to think like us." I scowled and shoved at his chest. "I'm serious, Nikolai! We can't leave Nina to suffer!"

He sighed, sitting up at the edge of the bed. And for a moment, I let myself get distracted by his nearly bare body, clad only in his boxer briefs. Focus, Selina. Focus. "I know, *Solnychko*. We've tried. Elif spoke to her, but Nina refused to leave. I thought she was scared, that her parents were threatening her. So I went with Grigori... but she still refused. She chose to stay." He gave me a helpless look, and my heart sank. I knew there were other ways to keep someone trapped. I knew that better than anyone. I swallowed thickly, resting my head against his shoulder and he lifted my hand to his lips, pressing a kiss to my fingers—the same fingers that had been broken not so long ago. "And Irina?" I asked softly, and he shook his head. "She was already broken when we got married, Selina. We tried to bring her back—I tried—but it was impossible. She was already lost." His voice was heavy, filled with something deeper than regret. He took my palm and began tracing slow circles on it, grounding himself in the touch. I let out a small sigh, turning my face into his shoulder, inhaling his scent, needing his warmth as much as he needed mine. He pressed a lingering kiss to my forehead, his nose gliding into my hair.

"The more time passed, the worse it got. She did things—things that nearly tore our family apart. But every time, we forgave her. For Mikhail. For the twins, who were born three years later. And then… then the worst happened," he said, suddenly standing up, as if just speaking about it made it unbearable to sit still. The loss of his body heat made me shiver as I watched him walked toward the window, his broad shoulders slightly hunched, his arms hanging at his sides, restless. And I hated seeing him like this—exposed, vulnerable to the ghosts of his past. "We were at a business dinner," he said finally, his voice barely above a whisper. "My brothers, Elif, and I. As usual, Irina didn't want to come, so she stayed home. Back then, when I saw how hard it was for her to live with my family, I bought her a small house a few minutes from here. Mikhail was barely three years old. The twins were two months old, Selina. Two months." His voice was so low I could barely hear him. He leaned his elbows against the window frame, lowering his head. My lips trembled. I stood up and walked over to him, gently placing my hand on his back—only to freeze when I felt the cold sweat dampening his skin. "Nikolai…"

"There was so much screaming, Selina," he murmured, his breath shaky. "Mikhail crying for his mother, crying for me. The twins wailing. Irina's screams." His body trembled against mine. I knew what it was like to be haunted. To have memories that refused to fade, that held you hostage in the past. This time, it was my forehead that pressed between his shoulder blades as my arms wrapped around him, holding him tight. "The smell of gasoline, Selina" his voice was distant, hollow. "It was everywhere. On the floor, the furniture, the walls. On her. And… on the children, Selina. On the children. On Mikhail, who was only three years old. On the twins, still babies."

My entire body locked up. *Oh my God.* Tears rushed to my eyes too fast for me to stop them. "When I walked into the living room, she was standing in the middle of the room… with a lighter, Selina. She was going to burn it all down." A broken gasp escaped me. "I told her I would give her anything she wanted, that I would do anything. But she wasn't even listening, Selina. She was going to burn them alive. My sons, Selina. I had no choice." A sob built in my throat, threatening to choke me. "She was about to light it. The lighter—she was about to flick it and set everything on fire. So I… I shot her" his breath hitched. "A bullet straight to the heart. The mother of my children." "Oh, Nikolai." Tears spilled down my face as I slipped under his arm, positioning myself in front of him. I cupped his face, my thumbs brushing against his cheeks. Tears gathered in his gaze, shimmering, threatening to fall.

"Nikolai…" "The boys found out I killed their mother a year ago," he said, his voice raw. "I'm sure it was Agata who told them. I bet she enjoyed every second of it." He let out a bitter laugh, shaking his head. And if I could get my hands on Agata right now, I would make her pay for what she did to Nikolai, to Nina, and to Irina. Yes, Irina, too. Because despite everything, she had been just another victim. A victim of her mother's twisted ambitions. "I should have given her more attention," he murmured, his voice cracking. "Tried harder to love her. Maybe if I had—" "Nikolai. No." I stopped him immediately, sliding my hands to his jaw, forcing him to meet my gaze. His stormy blue eyes finally locked onto mine. And for a moment, it felt like he was here again. Like he truly saw me.

"Listen to me, Nikolai Ivanov, because I will not repeat myself." I inhaled sharply. "What happened to Irina is not your fault. The choices she made were not your fault. And what you did to save your sons ? Nikolai, you did what any parent who loves their child would have done. I would have done the same." I pressed my forehead against his, my breath shaky. "Nikolai…" I hiccuped, trying to pull him back, trying to anchor him to us, to now, to me. And finally, he came back to me. To us. His hands left the window frame, sliding up to my cheeks, pushing my hair back. His palms were warm, grounding. "Nikolai, don't do this. Don't do this to yourself. I can't stand seeing you like this," I whispered, sniffling in the most inelegant way possible—but I didn't care. I just wanted him to stop hurting. His eyes roamed my face, tracing every feature—my eyes, my nose, my lips, my tear-streaked cheeks—before locking onto mine once more. And then—

"Marry me, Selina." My breath caught, "what ?" My eyes widened so much I must have looked like I was about to pop them out of their sockets. "You ask me not to do this, Selina. But this is what I've lived with every single day. I never slept without nightmares. Never spent a moment without hearing the screams echoing in my head. Everything was dark. Cold. Nothing had taste, nothing had meaning. My sons wouldn't even look at me, Selina. They avoided me. Ignored me. Nothing made sense anymore. Until you, *Solnychko*. Until you" his voice trembled. His nose skimmed along my temple, his breath warm, grounding, "I can't, Selina. I can't imagine my life without you. Not now. Not ever." His lips hovered over mine, his breath fanning against them as my heart pounded so hard it felt like it was about to shatter my ribs. "Nikolai..." I whispered. And I didn't even know what I wanted to say. Stop ? Go on ? "Marry me, Selina."

Nikolai

Andrei and Alexei were showing Selina their English homework while Mikhail tried to explain an addition problem to Rafael on the other couch. Ever since the boys interrupted us this morning—right after I asked Selina the most important question of my life—I had been trying to corner her for an answer, but in vain. The more I chased her, the more she fled. And I loved it. I loved everything about her. The way she spoke, the way she laughed, the way she looked at our boys, the way she looked at me. The way her eyes narrowed when something didn't sit right with her, or when she suspected the boys and I were trying to mess with her with our stupid jokes. The way she responded to my kisses, to every single one of my advances. The way her body molded perfectly to mine. Selina was made for me—her body meant for mine, her heart beating in sync with mine, her soul healing mine, her laughter filling the deafening silence in my head. She was made for me. Only me. That same laugh—the one that made my whole body tremble every time I heard it—pulled me out of my thoughts. "No, Alexei ! You can't say that !"

She burst into laughter, her head tilting to the side, her braid swinging over her shoulder, the soft waves of her hair brushing against the high points of her cheeks—cheeks I had spent every night for the past two weeks kissing, worshipping, loving. "It's sheet, not shit," she corrected, pressing a quick kiss to Alexei's cheek, making the boy turn slightly red. I smirked. "This is Roman's doing, isn't it ?" I asked, stepping into the living room, my hands shoved into my pockets. All heads in my little family turned toward me. I sat down next to Selina and glanced at Alexei's worksheet. The exercise was to translate the word лист (sheet) from Russian to English. He had written: *shit*.

I chuckled, reaching for his eraser to correct it before motioning for him to try again. He frowned in concentration, leaning forward to rewrite the word. "With two 'e's, *mio piccolo genio,*(my little genius) " my *Solnychko* told him, placing a hand on my thigh for support as she leaned toward Alexei. A simple gesture. A natural gesture. A gesture she didn't even realize she was making. And yet, it made me absurdly happy. It was just a small touch, wasn't it? But at the same time, it wasn't. Not after everything she'd been through. To willingly lean into a man's presence, to touch a man, to let a man touch her—it wasn't just a simple gesture. I wrapped an arm around her waist, pulling her closer until our thighs were flush against each other. She glanced up at me with a small, knowing smile, but she didn't pull away. If anything, she relaxed against my chest. Mikhail threw us a quick glance before turning back to Rafael. It was time for a conversation. The twins and Rafael were still too young, but Mikhail was old enough to have his own thoughts and opinions. And I wanted to know what he thought about my marriage to Selina. Because it was happening. Selina would say yes. Because 'no' was not an answer I was willing to accept.

Chapter thirty-one
Selina

"You have to tilt it more ! How can you be this useless ?" Roman exclaimed, trying to guide Nikolai and Sasha as they carried the last mattress into the twins' and Rafael's room. Elif and I were stretching the sheets over the mattresses while Dimitri, Ivan, and Rafael bounced excitedly on them, with Roman tossing pillows their way as he carried them in. He'd healed at an impressive speed. In fact, aside from a few lingering marks on his face and the occasional limp from two ribs that hadn't fully mended, he was back to normal—thank God. We'd decided to have a movie night with the kids to help them forget the intense emotions of the past few days, especially Rafael. So Sasha set up a projector, and the guys arranged mattresses to make enough space for all of us. "The popcorn is here !" Sienna exclaimed, carrying large buckets filled to the brim. Since she'd gotten back earlier today, she'd been glowing with happiness. She hadn't argued once with Sasha, to everyone's surprise—especially Sasha's. "Is it sweet, Auntie Sienna ?" Andrei asked, rushing toward her, followed by the others. "Yes, it's sweet, but be careful, or you'll spill everything, okay ? Now sit down, and I'll hand out the buckets, understood ?" she told them in a calm yet firm voice. The boys obeyed without a sound.

The kids settled onto the mattresses we laid out on the floor, while we, the adults, climbed onto the beds we'd pushed against the wall. Nikolai immediately pulled me into him, positioning me between his legs as I rested my head against his shoulder, sighing in comfort. Roman jumped over the kids, landing beside us with a groan of pain. "You're such an idiot," Elif grumbled from the other side of the bed, lying against Grigori. "I'm fine, I'm fine," Roman muttered, sitting properly between us and the projector placed on the bed. Sasha joined us on the other side of the projector, and I froze when I heard the bed creak. "Don't worry, *Solnychko*, it's solid. We had no choice with the wildlings we're raising," Nikolai murmured against my ear, chuckling. I relaxed at his reassurance. Sienna started the animated movie on the laptop connected to the projector and sat on the floor with the kids—right in front of Sasha. And something told me she'd done that entirely on purpose. As the movie began, Mikhail walked into the room carrying two more buckets of popcorn.

"Sena and Velma said they'd rather have coffee in the kitchen," he said, closing the door behind him before handing one bucket to Elif and another to me. Despite the bodyguards posted outside the villa, Velma and Sena preferred to keep watch from the inside. "Come here, Mika, I saved a spot for you," Sienna called, motioning him over. Mikhail joined her, slipping under her arm. And we had an amazing night filled with the children's laughter, Sienna's jokes that made them giggle even more, Roman and Sasha's bickering, and Elif's complaints as Grigori kept distracting her from the movie—more interested in teasing her than watching the film. But most of all, there were Nikolai's soft whispers in my ear throughout the movie, his hand caressing my thigh, his lips pressing gentle kisses along my neck. "Can we all sleep here tonight, please, Mom ?" Ivan asked Elif as we began tidying up. Sienna vacuumed while I straightened the sheets, brushing away the fallen popcorn.

"It's getting late, boys. You need to sleep," Elif said, turning off the laptop while Sasha and Nikolai unplugged the projector. "No, we'll sleep, we promise, Mom !" Dimitri insisted, making me smile. These kids and their angelic faces—seriously. Just as Elif was about to refuse again, Sienna stepped in after turning off the vacuum. "I'll stay with them tonight. I'll make sure they go to sleep quickly," she reassured, ruffling Ivan's hair. He looked up again at his mother with puppy-dog eyes and Elif sighed, finally nodding, making all the boys cheer in excitement. "But you have to listen to Auntie Sienna, promise ?" They all nodded eagerly before rushing off to change and brush their teeth.

"If they become too much to handle, don't hesitate to wake me—" "Don't worry, I can handle six boys," Sienna interrupted with a confident smile before stepping out to put away the vacuum. Ironically, Sasha followed right after her. "Don't worry, Selina, the Ivanov brothers may be idiots, but they would never hurt a woman," Elif whispered, slipping her arm through mine, catching the way I looked at Sasha. I smiled at her words, though my concern remained. "It's not my sister I'm worried about," I replied, making her laugh. "You're not wrong," she chuckled.

I tried to catch my breath between fits of laughter, pleading with Nikolai to stop tickling me. Finally, he relented, and tears of joy streamed from my eyes. He hovered above me, his gaze never leaving my face. The soft glow of the moon filtered through our bedroom window, gently outlining his features. I reached up and traced the contours of his jawline with my fingertips. Our bedroom. Our home. Our children. Our family.

"Yes," I whispered, my fingers brushing lightly against his lips. He frowned, not understanding, and I smiled at the confusion on his face. "Yes, I would marry you a thousand times over, Nikolai Ivanov." His eyes widened in surprise, "yes ?" he repeated. "Yes," I said again, giggling. A second later, we were out of bed and I was in his arms as he spun me around, making me yelp with laughter while he burst into joyous laughter of his own. "Shh, Nikolai ! You'll wake everyone up !" I laughed, playfully smacking his shoulder. He finally stopped, setting me down with care, his hands framing my face as he kissed me—deep and tender.

"*Ya lyublyu tebya, moy solnychko. Moye serdtse i moya dusha, ya lyublyu tebya*, ("I love you, my sunshine. My heart and my soul, I love you,)" he murmured against my lips, his words filling my eyes with emotion. "I love you too, my love. With all my heart and all my soul," I whispered in Italian, "*Ti amo anch'io, amore mio. Con tutto il cuore e tutta l'anima*, (I love you too, my love. With all my heart and soul.)" kissing him again as his arms wrapped around my waist, pulling me closer still. "Then we're getting married," he said, his lips brushing against my ear before he gently nibbled on it. "Then we're getting married," I echoed breathlessly, my fingers tangling in his hair. "Then let's celebrate," he murmured, lifting me into his arms once more, carrying me back to bed—making me giggle all over again.

Something felt strange. At first, I thought it was Nikolai trying to wake me again to celebrate our decision to get married, but no. Suddenly, I struggled to breathe, a deep sense of unease dragging me from sleep. The room was still cloaked in darkness, and I knew I was right when I glanced at the clock: 3:46 a.m. Nikolai was still asleep behind me, his face buried in my neck, his warm breath a soothing caress against my skin. I hesitated to wake him, but something felt wrong. Deeply wrong. "Nikolai," I whispered, gently caressing the hand he had draped over my stomach. "Nikolai," I said again, louder this time, and he bolted upright, his sharp eyes locking onto mine, alert—as if he hadn't been asleep at all. "What is it ? Did you have a nightmare ? Are you in pain ?" he asked, his hand brushing over my cheek as his gaze scanned my body. I shook my head, unable to explain the feeling gnawing at my chest. "Something feels off. I don't know how to explain it…" We both froze when a blood-curdling scream shattered the silence.

Sienna.

"Sienna !" I screamed, bolting out of bed, but Nikolai was already at the door, gun in hand. He stopped me as I reached for the handle, holding me back, "stay here," he ordered, pushing me toward the bed as he cautiously cracked the door open. A choked gasp escaped me—shock, or maybe horror. A man dressed entirely in black, a mask covering his face, suddenly shoved the door wide open, forcing Nikolai back. "Nikolai !" I cried out, but he was already lunging at the intruder, slamming him to the ground. His fist crashed into the man's face with a sickening crunch—his nose, likely broken. Then came another snap—the intruder's arm twisted at an unnatural angle as he dropped his weapon. "Don't look," Nikolai growled through gritted teeth. I barely had time to shut my eyes before another sharp crack echoed—the man's neck breaking. Gunshots rang out from the hallway, and I jumped. Instinct propelled me forward, stepping over the lifeless body to run outside. Sienna ! The boys !

But again, Nikolai stopped me, pulling me back inside. "Stay here, Selina !" he commanded, pushing me down onto the bed before stepping out and slamming the door shut behind him. Leaving me alone. With a corpse.

Chapter thirty-two
<u>Nikolai</u>

I closed the door behind me, tightening my grip on my gun. I didn't know what was happening, but if a single hair on my family's head had been harmed, I would burn them all alive. It had been Sienna's scream we heard. From the children's room.

The children.

I moved swiftly in that direction as gunfire echoed throughout the house and outside. I ducked just in time as a man appeared on the stairs, his gun aimed at me. He fired, and the antique vase Elif had bought three years ago shattered beside me. *Blayt.* I fired back. The bullet hit his knee, and he tumbled down the stairs with a grunt of pain. I climbed to my feet, groaning as shards of glass bit into my legs. Note to self: next time, put on joggers before leaving the bedroom. Fighting in boxers was far from ideal. Just as I passed the staircase, a sudden weight crashed onto my back, knocking me down again and sending my gun skidding across the floor.

For fuck's sake—how many of them were there? And how had they gotten in? I drove my elbow toward my attacker's throat, but he dodged, wrapping an arm around my neck in a chokehold. I slammed the back of my head into his nose, making him recoil just enough for me to break free and flip onto my back. This time, my foot connected with his face. As I pushed myself up, he raised his gun—and the shot rang out. But it was he who collapsed, a bullet hole between his eyes. I looked up to see Sasha at the top of the stairs, his gun still aimed, blood dripping from his brow, chest heaving. "Sienna ? The boys ?" he asked, panting.

I grabbed my weapon and rushed toward the children's room, my stomach twisting at the sight of the door wide open. Nausea surged as I spotted bloodstains on the floor. A man lay sprawled on the mattress where Mikhail had been sleeping, his mask torn away, a scar slashing across his cheek, his throat slit—likely the fatal blow. I stepped inside, gun raised, Sasha close behind. Then I heard the crying. I braced myself for the worst—for blood, for bodies, for losses that would tear us apart. I was prepared for everything. Except what I saw.

The children were huddled in the farthest corner of the room, pressed together like frightened chicks behind Mikhail, who stood in front of them, arms spread wide. A man loomed over them, a knife inches from my eldest son's face. The only thing holding him back was a bloodied hand gripping the blade's edge. Sienna's hand. Sienna—terrified, crying—pushing back a man twice her size. A gunshot exploded. The man crumpled, collapsing onto Sienna and the children. Before I could react, Sasha vaulted over the mattresses, reaching them first. I followed, heart hammering. "Mikhail !" I shouted as Sasha hauled the corpse away, freeing the children and Sienna.

"Sienna ? Sienna, look at me. Come on, *moya angel*, focus on my voice," he said, trying to coax her out of her daze. She was trembling, her injured hand clutched against her chest. I scanned the boys, checking for injuries. They were shaking, crying, but they were alive. Unharmed. Thank God. "I'm fine," Sienna murmured, trying to sit up, clutching her wounded hand, but she couldn't even lift herself. "Boys ! Sienna !" Selina's voice burst into the room, and she flew to their side. I clenched my jaw to avoid cursing aloud. She walked into the fucking room as if it were a stroll through the garden. We didn't even know if there were more intruders. She dropped to her knees, wrapping her arms around the boys, trying to soothe them as they sobbed harder at the sight of their mother.

"Oh, Sienna…" Selina whispered, gently taking her sister's hand, now slick with blood. Footsteps thundered in the hallway. Sasha and I were instantly on our feet, guns raised toward the door. "Elif ! Wait !" Grigori's voice rang out, and we lowered our weapons just as Elif stormed in, barefoot in a nightgown, her eyes shimmering with tears, her face pale and my fury burned hotter. "Boys !" she cried, gathering them into her arms as Grigori and Roman charged in behind her, armed and breathless. "Sienna, you need stitches," Selina said, examining the wound, her lips trembling. "I'm fine," Sienna repeated, but her voice was fainter now. Then, her face drained of color.

"Sienna ?" Selina cupped her cheek as her sister's eyes began to flutter closed. "Sienna ?!" Sasha's voice cracked with panic as he knelt beside her, cradling her face in his hands just as she slumped into him, unconscious. "Sienna !" Selina and Sasha shouted at once as I knelt beside them, checking her pulse. "What's happening ? Is she losing too much blood ? Is it her insulin ?" Sasha demanded, pulling her limp body against him. Selina lifted an eyelid, checking her sister's pupils with the practiced calm of someone trained. Then her hand froze at the back of Sienna's head. She pulled her fingers away—soaked in blood. Sasha tilted Sienna forward, and I saw him freeze at the spreading stain on his shirt. "He strangled her. Slammed her head against the wall multiple times," Mikhail said suddenly, stepping forward, eyes bright with tears. "I tried to stop him. I took the knife auntie dropped and... I stabbed him in the thigh," he added, twisting his hands nervously.

I pulled him into my arms, holding his trembling frame close, "you saved her life, son. I'm proud of you," I whispered, rubbing his back. Selina choked on a sob, "she needs to go to the hospital. She might have a concussion," she said firmly. Sasha didn't hesitate. He scooped Sienna into his arms and ran from the room. But Selina hesitated, looking between the boys and the door. "Go," I told her. "I'll stay with the boys. Roman—get changed. Don't leave her side." We still didn't know what the hell was going on. Better to have two Ivanovs watching. And Sasha wouldn't look away from Sienna—not even for a second. Roman nodded and left. Selina returned to the children, kneeling before Mikhail. "Thank you for saving my sister," she whispered, pressing a kiss to his cheek. "Thank you."

And Mikhail—my brave son—finally let the tears fall, wrapping his arms around her. "I was scared. I was so scared, Mama," he sobbed, his body shaking. I stood, my thoughts already turning to vengeance. But I needed clarity. I needed focus. "Everything will be okay," Selina whispered, hugging each boy in turn. Rafael and Andrei clung to her, refusing to let go. "Come, boys," Elif said, gathering them into her arms—solid and unshakable in the storm. Selina gave them one last reassuring smile before hurrying to change as Grigori stepped into the room, his face grim. "The house is secure. The cleaners are on their way. The offices are clear—we'll move the children there." As they led the boys out, Andrei and Rafael wrapped themselves around my legs, sobbing. "I don't want Aunt Sienna to die!" "She won't," I told them, kneeling. "Your mother is with her. She'll heal her."

She'll heal all of us. And I will destroy whoever did this.

Selina

I stepped down first and opened the car door for my sister, ready to help her out—but before her foot even touched the ground, Sasha scooped her into his arms and carried her toward the house, just as he had done a few hours earlier. To my great surprise, Sienna didn't protest. Instead, she rested her head against his shoulder and closed her eyes. I closed mine too, drawing in a slow breath of crisp morning air. The sun had begun to rise, painting the sky in breathtaking shades of blue and pink. A strong arm wrapped around my shoulders, pulling me from my thoughts, "you'll catch a cold," Roman murmured, drawing me close as we walked toward the entrance.

"It was him, wasn't it? Antonio sent those men?" I asked, my voice barely above a whisper. Roman stopped, his gaze fixed on the horizon, but I saw the way his jaw clenched. "We're not entirely sure yet," he said, rubbing my shoulder. But under my persistent stare, he finally sighed. "Yes. I think it's very likely. Maybe he was trying to take Rafael again. To pressure you." I nodded slowly, pressing my lips together as we continued toward the house—the house that could have become our tomb last night. If Sienna hadn't screamed. If I hadn't woken up. If Mikhail hadn't been so brave. I shook my head as we stepped into the hall. Nikolai appeared from the kitchen, now fully dressed in a sharp suit, as composed as ever. My eyes immediately dropped to his legs, where I'd seen several cuts earlier. "Don't worry, *Solnychko*. The doctor stopped by. We're fine," he reassured, pulling me into his arms.

I clung to his jacket, breathing in his scent to steady myself. I heard Roman's footsteps fade as Velma and Sena called him from the kitchen. "The boys?" I asked, still pressed against his chest. "They're asleep in Grigori's office. We set up inflatable mattresses. Elif hasn't left their side," he said, kissing just behind my ear. I nodded. Everyone was safe. Well… almost. "Sienna?" he asked softly. I sighed and stepped back slightly, "when he strangled her…" I closed my eyes, inhaling deeply. Just speaking the words, just picturing the scene… Nikolai's grip on me tightened "…her vocal cords were damaged. She'll be able to speak normally in a few days. She needed sixteen stitches in her palm. Her head's fine—just a mild concussion. But…" I shut my eyes as tears welled up, "she could have died, Nikolai."

He cupped my face, resting his forehead against mine. "I know, Selina. She protected the children with her life. I'll never forget that image of her." a tear slipped down my cheek, and Nikolai kissed it away. "But she's here," he murmured. "Our family is safe. You're safe." I opened my eyes, losing myself in the depth of his gaze. And for the first time, when I thought about Antonio, it wasn't fear I felt. It was rage. Dark, searing rage. For the first time in my life, I wished for someone's death. Not when he tortured me for eight years. Not even when he violated me. Never. But now? Now, I wanted him six feet under ground. Nikolai gently led me into the kitchen, where Velma and Sena stood with Grigori and Roman, who was devouring a sandwich like a starving man. "You should eat too, Shelina. It's going to be a long day," Roman said around a mouthful, making me smile despite myself. "Swallow before you speak, you idiot," Grigori grumbled, smacking the back of his head.

"Come, Miss Selina, eat," Velma urged, placing a plate in front of me with a smaller sandwich. But as I reached for it, my breath caught at the sight of Sena's bruised face. Looking closer, I noticed the bandage peeking from beneath Velma's sleeve. "Oh my God. You're hurt too," I whispered, stepping closer and cupping Sena's face to examine her injuries. "We're fine, Miss Selina," Sena said gently, lowering my hands. "Thanks to Miss Sienna, we're all fine." She pressed her lips together, and I frowned, "she feels guilty for not waking sooner. It was your sister's scream that roused the entire house," Velma explained, slipping an arm around her. "I think it woke the whole damn neighborhood. Those bastards went straight to your floor," Grigori added, arms crossed, leaning against the counter. Like Nikolai, he had changed into a dark suit, but exhaustion still etched all our faces.

"You reacted quickly, *moy brat*," Roman noted after swallowing his final bite—honestly, the way this man ate was something else. "It was Selina who woke me. Without her, we'd probably be riddled with bullets," Nikolai said, slipping behind me to lift me onto a barstool in front of the sandwich. He never missed a beat. "The Floros sisters, huh ? Walking danger detectors," Roman chuckled—just in time to get smacked again by Grigori. A detector that had worked for me. But not for my sister. She had been too young to see the danger coming. And it had dragged me into something far worse. But unlike what she believed, I had never blamed her. She was just a child and she was under my responsibility. I should have protected her better.

"Eat, *Solnychko*," Nikolai whispered, pushing the plate closer. I obeyed, even as my throat tightened. I needed strength. For the kids. For Sienna. For Nikolai. For our family. So I ate—not for myself, but for them. But I had overestimated myself. Halfway through, I set the sandwich down, took a sip of water, and said, "I can't eat anymore." Before Nikolai could protest, heavy footsteps thundered down the stairs. Sasha stormed into the hall, a rifle nearly as long as my leg in hand. Nikolai cursed and bolted after him, followed by his brothers.

I trailed after them, stopping near the doorway as they all stood at the base of the stairs, arguing. Grigori gripped Sasha's rifle, trying to wrest it away, but Sasha refused to let go. I had never seen him like this. He was seething. And despite myself, I took a step back. So much rage. So much hate. "For fuck's sake, calm down," Nikolai growled, grabbing Sasha's shoulder. But Sasha shoved him off, locking eyes with his brother. "Calm down ?! You want me to fucking calm down ?!" He grabbed Nikolai's jacket with both fists. "She can barely speak ! Sixteen stitches, Niko. Sixteen fucking stitches!" Tears prickled at the corners of my eyes. And then I sensed someone approaching. "What's going on ?" Elif asked breathlessly, taking in the scene.

"I... I think Sasha wants revenge. For Sienna," I whispered, my heart aching. He loved her. Sasha Ivanov loved my sister. Even if neither of them realized it yet. And when the time came, he would burn the world for her. And I wasn't sure anyone could stop him.

"And we will make them pay," Grigori said calmly. "But not like this, *moy brat*. Where do you think you're even going?" "I'm going to find Lorenzo. He must know who did this," Sasha growled, pacing as he raked his hands through his hair again and again. "You're not thinking straight," Nikolai snapped. "Do you honestly believe that if Lorenzo had known anything, he wouldn't have warned us? We already contacted him. He's digging. He'll find out." Nikolai grabbed his arm again, but Sasha yanked away—only to stumble on the first step and fall hard on his back. I gasped as Elif, still barefoot and in her nightgown, rushed to his side. The brothers just stood there, stunned, "hey, hey, breathe. Calm down," Elif murmured, her hand on his back. When he didn't respond, she began rubbing gentle circles. "I can't," he choked, trying to rise, she cupped his face, turning it to hers. "I know you're scared, Sasha. I know what it feels like. When Grigori got shot, I thought my heart would stop. But charging into battle like this won't help Sienna. Don't you want to be here when she wakes up? Make sure she eats?"

Her thumbs brushed his cheeks and Sasha closed his eyes and inhaled deeply. Then he pulled her into a hug, clutching her tightly. "We'll spill their blood, Sasha. I promise," she whispered, leaning into him. And he stared past her, his gaze fixed on the horizon—cold, unrelenting. "Well, my beautiful wife, your wishes are coming true faster than expected," Grigori said, checking his phone. "Lorenzo just sent me an address. He's waiting." Sasha grabbed his rifle from Roman and stalked toward one of the cars, his younger brother close behind. Grigori kissed Elif and headed for the driver's seat as Nikolai turned to climb the steps. He reached me in seconds, "be careful," I whispered as he held me. "I'm not going anywhere. Not while my fiancée is waiting for me at home," he said. He kissed me and I blinked up at him "fiancée ?" I repeated, breathless and he smirked. "Second drawer in our room. Put it on. You said yes— no going back now, *Solnychko*."

Before I could respond, Grigori honked, "and finish your sandwich !" Nikolai called as he climbed in, leaving me stunned in the doorway. "Fiancée, huh?" Elif teased, bumping my shoulder. "I…" "Well, I've got a wedding to plan !" she exclaimed, hurrying inside to drag Velma and Sena into a bridal mission. Oh God. These women. I darted into the kitchen, grabbed the rest of my sandwich, and hurried upstairs. To my relief, the corpse was gone. The house was spotless. No blood. No bodies. Even the damaged furniture had vanished. I exhaled and sat at the edge of the bed. Setting the plate on the dresser, I opened the second drawer with trembling fingers. Inside, nestled in velvet, was a small midnight-blue box. I opened it slowly and my breath caught. A gold ring with a deep blue sapphire, encircled by four tiny diamonds.

Our sons. And the sapphire… his blue. Nikolai's blue. A sob escaped as I slipped it onto my finger and it fit perfectly. I pressed my hand against my chest. Wearing it felt like carrying all of them with me—on my hand, in my heart. And no matter what Antonio did, he could never take that away. Never.

Chapter thirty-three
Nikolai

Twenty-six hours later

We had been in that warehouse for over fourteen hours, and it had been twenty-six since we'd left home. I missed Selina. I missed the boys. I should have been with them, reassuring them the way Grigori and Sasha had when they returned earlier, after we secured the package. *Soon*, I told myself. *Very soon*. I finally signaled to Roman from my chair in the middle of the warehouse, where a table stood covered with various tools. "Finally !" my brother exclaimed, striding toward the trash bin. He unlocked the padlock keeping it shut, then tipped the bin over. Antonio Rasili tumbled out, covered in garbage, vomit, and substances I didn't care to identify. His hands and feet were bound.

"You motherfuckers ! I'm going to kill you ! Do you hear me?!" he screamed, thrashing against his restraints. I stood, calmly sliding the magazine into my gun after cleaning it. "You know how we Russians are, Rasili. We just wanted to return the favor—welcome you the same way you welcomed my brother." I approached him, my gun resting casually in my hand, and knelt beside him, eyeing him from head to toe. "So ? How does it feel to spend an entire night in a trash bin ?" I asked, jaw tightening. I should have enjoyed this. I should have relished the thought of torturing this bastard. But all I felt was rage. Bottomless, consuming rage that threatened to explode with the smallest crack in my self-control. And that crack came fast—because the son of a bitch started laughing.

"So, she told you about our little lovers' quarrels ? My sweet Selina... did she tell you about the time I tied her to the bed while she begged me—" My gun was jammed down his throat so fast he choked on it. "Nikolai," Roman's voice echoed behind me, calm but warning. My hand trembled around the weapon. My jaw clenched so tightly my teeth ground together. *Calm down, Nikolai. Not yet. Not like this*. I finally pulled the gun back, and Antonio coughed and wheezed like the pig he was. My gaze flicked to his bound hands as slow smile curved my lips. In one swift move, I grabbed his wrists, yanked his left hand aside, and fired twice—blowing off his index and middle fingers.

His scream was glorious, "you owed me two fingers, Rasili," I said, rising and wiping the blood from my face with a rag. "Tourniquet him. I don't want him dying too quickly," David obeyed while I cleaned my gun. "Keep talking, Tony. Please. I haven't been very creative lately. Tell me more about what you did to my fiancée." I leaned against the desk, crossing my legs as Rasili writhed in pain, "fiancée?" he croaked, bloodied and pale. "What the fuck are you talking about ?" his eyes widened, horror spreading across his face. "Ah, right. No one knows yet." I smirked. "She accepted my proposal last night. In our bed" I watched as confusion gave way to disbelief, then horror. "We're getting married, Rasili. Probably within the month. I've wasted enough time."

His eyes locked onto mine, trembling, "you're lying !" he shouted, trying to stand. Roman shoved him back down with a boot to the chest. "Selina is mine !" he screamed, kicking and twisting like a worm on a hook. "You're lying !" Was she screaming like this when he broke her fingers ? Did she tremble like that when he beat her ? "Bring the basin," I ordered David, stepping forward anger taking over again. Roman forced Rasili onto his knees while David and Marcus positioned a large basin in front of him. He kept screaming, not from pain—but from pure rage. I gestured to Roman, who punched him square in the face without a word.

"Level two, Antonio. You're getting closer to the final boss," I taunted, sliding my gun back into the holster and stepping behind him. "Ever tried diving, Tony ? Ever done it without an oxygen tank ?" I grabbed a fistful of his hair, yanked his head back, and lowered myself to his level, "I'm going to take every breath from you—every gasp you stole from my wife," my voice was a growl, low and deadly. "I'll haunt your nightmares the way you haunted hers. You'll beg me, Antonio. You'll beg to die" then I shoved his head into the basin. He thrashed. I didn't let go. The sound of Selina's sobs in the bathroom echoed in my mind. Her tears. Her trembling body.

I yanked Antonio's head back. He gasped, coughing violently, "how's the water ?" Roman smirked, pulling up a chair. "Do you like the taste ? Our dogs needed a bath after running through the woods." "Selina…" Antonio gasped, but I shoved him back under before he could say another word, "you don't get to say her name. You don't get to talk about her. You don't even get to think about her." I growled, twisting my grip on his mutilated fingers. He thrashed harder. I pulled him up again and he coughed so hard I thought his lungs might rupture. Was Selina like this too ? Gasping ? Panicking ?

I shoved his head down again, harder this time. A snarl escaped me. He was going to die by my hands. My phone rang, Roman raised an eyebrow. I threw Rasili to the floor and caught the towel Roman tossed to me, wiping the blood and water off my hands. When I glanced at the caller ID, the fog of anger cleared. "Yes, *amore mio?*" I answered in near-perfect Italian, signaling David to gag the bastard as Rasili's eyes latched onto mine. "Are you okay?" Her voice was soft. Familiar. In the background, I heard laughter—children, Elif calling out to them not to run on the stairs. This. This was the life I wanted. Selina's voice. The children's voices. Elif's, my brothers', our nephews'. Our family.

"Everything is perfect, *Solnychko*. And you? How are you? Did you like your ring?" I glanced at Rasili. His rage was boiling. "It's… it's perfect. The ring is perfect. You're perfect. Everything is perfect, Nikolai," she whispered shyly. "When are you coming home? I can't escape Elif, Velma, and Sena's attacks anymore. They've already ordered over twenty wedding dresses for me to try on. Twenty, Nikolai!" I laughed, unable to help myself, "I'm sure every dress will look perfect on you, Selina."

"It would be nice if you could actually be here to see me try them on," she grumbled. I blinked. Did she just pout? "*Moy solnychko…* did you just pout, *moy lyubov'*?" Silence. "I… no. You must have misunderstood, Nikolai. But you better be here for dinner, *amore mio*. See you tonight!" she said, then hung up quickly and I stared at the screen. The lock screen lit up—Selina on the swing, the boys on either side of her, all laughing. "Well, it looks like we'll have to cut this short. My wife is waiting for me for dinner," I said, tucking away my phone. I turned back to Antonio. "I'll leave you to have fun until dinner, *moy brat*. I need to pick something up for my wife and sons. Red or white roses, Tony ? What do you think ?"

Antonio's gag muffled his screams. "Wrong answer. Her favorite flowers are dahlias." I slipped on my jacket and grabbed my keys. "Don't worry, *moy brat*, we'll keep him entertained," Roman grinned, hauling Antonio back into the chair. "Isn't that right, Tony ?" At the door, I turned back as Antonio squirmed, his fury boiling in his eyes. "I'll be back to wish you goodnight… forever, Tony. Right after I say goodnight to my wife—in a very different way." And with that, I stepped out. His muffled screams echoed behind me. This was only the beginning for Antonio Rasili. Only the beginning.

Selina

The scent of my chocolate cake drifted through the house as I turned off the oven after checking its doneness. It was perfect. The kids were going to love it. "Is the sauce to your liking, Miss Selina ?" Velma asked from the stove, where she had taken charge of the pasta sauce. I walked over, grabbed a spoon, and tasted it. "Yes, it's perfect ! Thank you, Velma." She smiled softly, turning off the electric burner while I joined Sena to finish preparing the salad. "Let's go easy on the tomatoes—Alexei doesn't like them much," I said, still grating the carrots. Sena nodded and set the tomatoes aside. "Is there something for Sienna to eat ?" Sasha's voice suddenly cut through the air as he entered the kitchen, heading straight for the sink to put down the glass of milk he'd brought to Sienna a few hours earlier.

"Yes, I made her some soup. It should have cooled down by now," I replied, wiping my hands on my apron before moving to the counter where I'd left the soup to cool. I prepared a tray, added a bit of mashed potatoes with Velma's sauce, and headed toward the door—but Sasha suddenly appeared in front of me, hands outstretched. "You should get some rest too, Sasha," I told him as I handed him the tray. There was no point in arguing. "I will… when she's capable of annoying me again by talking non-stop," he muttered before disappearing down the hallway. I gave up after a few seconds. He and Sienna were exactly the same— stubborn and often foolish. I grabbed another carrot and resumed grating, my thoughts drifting back to my earlier conversation with Nikolai. I didn't pout. I never pouted. Why would I even do that ?

A car pulling into the driveway broke my train of thought, and before I realized it, I was already in the hallway, abandoning everything under Sena's amused laughter. I wiped my hands on my apron, unable to stop myself from brushing my fingers over my ring. I opened the front door, ready to throw myself into my fiancé's arms—but froze when my eyes met not blue ones, but dark. For a moment, it felt like I was looking at a younger version of Roman. He was younger, but just as tall and nearly as muscular. His gaze studied me in return, pausing for a millisecond on the ring on my finger before a smirk stretched across his lips. "You must be Selina. Nice to meet you. I'm—"

"Tarik !" Elif suddenly exclaimed, rushing past me before throwing herself into the young man's arms. He held her tightly, lifting her off the ground. "*Ya tak skuchal po tebe, moy malysh,*(I missed you so much my baby) " he murmured, his voice breaking as he pressed a kiss to her cheek. And suddenly, the resemblance struck me again. He had Elif's cheekbones. The same eye shape. Even his hair was a slightly lighter shade than the Ivanov brothers'. "*Ya tozhe*, Mama,(me too)" Tarik replied, pressing a kiss to his mother's forehead. His mother. Oh my God—Elif had a teenage son ?

They finally pulled apart, Elif's smile stretching nearly ear to ear, while Tarik gazed at her with shining eyes… filled with love. The same way my sons looked at me. And just like that, warmth bloomed in my chest, as it always did when I thought of them. Tarik's eyes found mine again, and he approached carefully, stopping at a respectful distance before offering his hand. "Tarik Ivanov. I'm the eldest son of Grigori and Elif. Nice to meet you, Selina—future Ivanov," I couldn't help but smile as I gently took his hand. Despite his youth—seventeen at most—his hands were already calloused, yet warm, his grip firm but gentle. "Nice to meet you too. I didn't know you had another son besides Dimitri and Ivan," I said, glancing at Elif, who grimaced. Tarik slid his hands into his pockets and stood beside me. "Well, Mother, I expected that from Father, but you ?" He shook his head, clicking his tongue, and a new smile tugged at my lips as Elif shifted uncomfortably.

"I'm sorry, *moy malysh* (my baby). With everything that's been happening lately, we haven't really had time to sit down and talk," she sighed, giving me an apologetic look. My smile faded slightly as memories of the previous night resurfaced. "I took the first flight when I heard what happened," Tarik said, returning to his mother and pulling her into his arms again. "Father said everyone was okay, but I wanted to be here—for the family." Elif smiled softly, caressing his cheek. More excited voices suddenly echoed through the hallway. "*Moy brat !* " Ivan yelled as he sprinted toward his brother, closely followed by Dimitri, who immediately started crying.

Tarik lifted both of them at once, kissing each in turn. Hearing the commotion, my sons appeared and rushed into the hall. While Andrei and Alexei ran straight to Tarik, Rafael clung to my leg, as he always did when meeting someone new. Mikhail, however, stopped beside me, arms crossed behind his back, his gaze locked on his cousin. I smiled softly, recognizing the admiration in his eyes. He was impressed. He looked up to Tarik. They probably weren't that far apart in age. "*Moy brat* ! How are you ?" Tarik asked, extending an arm toward Mikhail. My son took it in a firm grip, pulling him into a hug like their fathers did. My smile widened.

"And you must be my new little brother—Rafael ?" Tarik knelt in front of my son. After a moment, Rafael stepped out from behind my leg and nodded, shyly extending his hand. Tarik grinned, taking his tiny hand before lifting him into his arms, "come on, let's check out my car. I brought you all some stuff from Detroit," he said, heading outside where his driver was unloading his luggage. "I'm really sorry, Selina. I should've told you," Elif said, offering a regretful smile. I shook my head and took her hand. "No, you're right. With everything going on, you haven't had time…" "No," she interrupted, squeezing my hand. Her lips pressed into a thin line, and suddenly, she looked... fragile. "Elif...?"

"Tarik was my brother's name. He sacrificed himself to help us win the war against the Italians sixteen years ago," she said, her voice distant. And just like that, Grigori's words from the day we arrived made perfect sense.

We're about to enter another war with the Italians after everything we've been through, Elif...

Oh my God. Her brother had been killed by the Italians. And yet, she had welcomed me with open arms, without hesitation. "Oh, Elif, I'm so sorry. I understand now why Grigori feels the way he does about our presence..." "...No, that's just because he's an idiot sometimes," she said with a soft smile, looping her arm through mine as we turned toward the boys, who were excitedly opening boxes near the car. "Tarik... wasn't born alone," she murmured, sighing as she pulled her phone from her pocket and showed me a picture. A younger Elif, radiant, lying in a hospital bed—with two babies in her arms. "Twins," I realized, looking back at her. She nodded. "A boy and a girl. Perfection. We later discovered that my little Elena had sickle cell disease, like my mother," she continued, tears welling in her eyes.

Sickle cell disease—a genetic blood disorder. It caused fatigue, excruciating pain, swelling, vulnerability to infections... and for young children, it could be fatal. "She cried every night, Selina. Every night. She suffered so much, and there was nothing I could do. Only medications to ease her pain. And on her fourth birthday, she..." Elif's voice broke as she closed her eyes, a tear slipping down her cheek. "Grigori was devastated. Tarik cried for months, feeling the absence of his sister. Even now, I think he still searches for her, as if something is missing from him. I want to keep him close, Selina. I know I must sound like a lunatic, but Tarik… he's different for me," she said, her jaw clenched, her gaze fixed on her eldest son.

"And you, Elif ? How did you survive such pain ?" I asked softly, wiping away the tears that had escaped despite my efforts. She looked at me in surprise, pressing her lips together. She had married young, raised three boys while tending to a husband who, from what I'd gathered, hadn't been the most gentle man. She'd lost her brother, then her daughter, and she lived each day with the fear of losing another loved one. How could she be this strong ? "I… I don't know. I had to keep moving forward, for Tarik, for Roman and Sasha, who were still so young. But… for a long time, I didn't want any more children. That's why there's such a big age gap between my sons. But when Ivan was born, I slowly started to feel a sense of peace again. Even though there will always be an emptiness—the place of my little Elena." She smiled sadly, and I couldn't stop myself from pulling her into my arms. "You are so strong, Elif," I whispered, and she hugged me back just as tightly. "We have no other choice. The Ivanov women must be strong," she murmured, pulling back to look at me. "Nikolai couldn't have made a better choice, Selina. I'm so happy for you both." "…Thank you, Elif. Thank you for everything."

"Alright, enough with the emotions ! Show me that ring again," she said suddenly, grabbing my hand and inspecting the ring with utmost scrutiny. She offered a few critiques—mostly about the sapphire being too small, which made me laugh—while outside, the children's joyful shouts echoed as they marveled at the gifts Tarik had brought them.

Chapter thirty-four

<u>Nikolai</u>

Grigori adjusted my bow tie while Roman kept trying to run a brush through my hair, determined to make it look neater—even though it was already perfect. "Roman, I swear I'll shove that brush so far down your throat it'll take miners to dig it out," I growled, snatching the comb from his hand and swinging it at him, but he dodged. "Leave him alone, Roman. Getting married isn't easy," Grigori chuckled, turning to grab my navy-blue suit jacket after fixing my bow tie—but he froze when he saw Elif leaning against the doorframe, one eyebrow raised.

"Oh really ? And what exactly is so hard about marriage, Grigori ? Taking care of a grumpy man who sometimes speaks before thinking ? Or maybe it's carrying a child for nine months, nursing him, and raising the sons of that same man, only for them to grow up to be just like him ? Or perhaps it's cleaning up after that man and his brothers, who act without thinking half the time. But wait ! I did all of that !" she exclaimed, stepping toward my brother in her deep green satin dress that accentuated her complexion and long dark hair cascading down her back. "So tell me, Grigori Ivanov, what's so hard about marriage ?" she murmured, and at the same time, Roman, Sasha, and I grimaced. These two, seriously.

"You look stunning, *moy kotyonok*, (my kitten) " my brother replied, completely ignoring the question. No—

actually, that idiot probably didn't even register it. That was the Elif Ivanov effect on her husband.

She rolled her eyes but sidestepped him, grabbed my jacket from the hanger, and walked toward me with a warm smile that melted my heart. I turned my back to her, bending slightly so she could help me put it on, then faced her again. She smoothed the lapels of my jacket with gentle hands, letting out a contented sigh. "I told you, didn't I ? To keep your eyes on the horizon so you wouldn't miss your sun," she said, and I couldn't help but smile, remembering that moment. It had been during Rasili's gala when she told me those words. And when I looked up, Selina was there, stepping into the hall as if by magic. "I always tell them that they should listen to your advice, but their skulls are too thick," I said, smiling before kissing her cheek. She gently pushed me away, raising a playful eyebrow. "Cut the charm, Niko. You're all as dumb as each other."

"That's why we marry women who are both beautiful and intelligent, isn't it, *moy brat* ?" Grigori chimed in, wrapping his arms around his wife from behind. Elif allowed it, shaking her head but smiling slightly. "I hate to break up the moment, but shouldn't we have taken care of Rasili before you got married ?" Roman asked, flopping onto the couch next to Sasha. Antonio Rasili was still locked up in one of our warehouses in California, and I had thoroughly enjoyed visiting him almost every night. So had Roman—and especially Sasha, who had taken days to regain his calm and composure. In fact, not until Sienna started feeling better. We had never seen him like that before. Not when Grigori got shot, not when he and Roman nearly died in an ambush, not even when Roman was kidnapped almost two months ago. The impulsive ones in the family had always been Roman and Grigori. Sasha and I were the calm ones, the strategists, the ones who planned and thought things through. Seeing him like that—blind with rage, unable to think rationally or foresee the consequences of his actions—had shocked us all. And I remembered what Selina had whispered to me that night when I came home after capturing Antonio. Lying in bed, her warm body pressed against mine, she had murmured, "He loves her. He loves her, and he doesn't even know it."

Thinking back to how Sasha had reacted, Selina had been right. Because I knew I would have reacted the exact same way if even a single drop of Selina's blood had been spilled. And I had no doubt Grigori would've been the same if anyone dared hurt Elif. "No," I answered Roman's question. "We can't kill him until we know how he's been tracking Selina and Rafael." That bastard was stubborn. No matter the torture, he refused to reveal how he did it. And even if we killed him, someone else could use the same method to harm my wife and son. I would never let them live under a constant threat. Roman nodded slowly as I stepped toward the window, watching the preparations in the garden of our Sochi estate.

Selina had insisted on a small, intimate wedding in a place that meant something to us. "All the people I love are here, Niko. I don't need anything more," she had told me two weeks ago when I asked if she wanted to invite anyone else so we could issue them security badges. We were nearing the end of summer, and the garden was in full bloom, lush and vibrant. Flowers, greenery, and the fountain Elif had installed stood at the center, around which the boys were running. I pressed my lips together, remembering our conversation with the kids about our wedding weeks ago. "You're really getting married ?!" Andrei had asked excitedly, bouncing on Selina's and my bed, while Alexei snuggled against Selina with a huge smile that nearly brought tears to my eyes.

After a few moments of silence, Mikhail had nodded. "I knew it," he'd said, lifting his chin proudly. Selina had laughed. But Rafael's reaction had been anything but amusing. After staring at us for a long moment, he had burst into tears. "No !" he had cried out, making Selina flinch at his outburst. "Marriage is bad! The monster wanted to marry Mama !" He had kept sobbing, and I'd had to pull him into my arms to calm him while Selina gently explained what marriage really was and what it meant. I had spent an hour reassuring him that his mother would never face any monsters again. Only then had he finally smiled and gotten excited about the wedding.

He would heal too, just like his mother would heal from the past eight years. The long years we'd share from now on would heal everything. Scars would remain, memories would linger, but our love would help us move past them. "Aunt Sienna said Aunt Selina is ready," Tarik announced as he entered, dressed in a black suit like his father and uncles. When we had set the wedding date two days after his arrival, he had decided to stay until the big day before returning to school in Detroit—a school where all fifteen-year-old boys in the *Bratva* trained and honed their skills in various fields until they turned eighteen. Tarik was sixteen, in his second year of training. By the end of the four-year program, he would be ready to take on different missions to contribute to the organization's growth—a choice we would guide him through. Unlike what had happened with Roman, who had ended up fighting in the Middle East.

I exhaled slowly as anticipation built inside me. Why ? I didn't know. I was marrying the woman I loved. I knew she would say yes. I knew we would spend the rest of our lives together. But I couldn't stop my hands from trembling as the moment drew closer. "Okay, alright," I muttered, shaking my arms to get rid of the slight tingling in my fingers. My brothers burst into laughter, and Tarik grabbed his mother before she could smack them. "It's going to be fine, *moy brat*. Need any advice for tonight ?" Roman asked, laughing even harder when I shot him a death glare. *Bastards*.

Selina

I slipped my trembling hand into the white lace glove with my sister's help, while Sena ensured that my long veil was securely fastened into the bun at the nape of my neck. I blew at the strands of hair framing my face, feeling like they were constantly falling into my eyes. And it felt like my corset was suffocating me. Maybe I shouldn't have chosen a wedding dress. A simple white summer dress would've been enough, wouldn't it ? "For God's sake, Selina !" my sister exclaimed, grabbing my bare hand, which I'd unknowingly been waving in the air. "Stop fidgeting, and for heaven's sake, stop stressing so much—you're as pale as a newborn's butt."

She slipped off my engagement ring, helped me put on my second glove, which reached up to my upper arm, and then slid my ring back onto my finger. "He's not going to leave you at the altar. The man is ready to go to war just to marry you, Selina," she added, gently adjusting the curled strands against my cheeks. Her light green eyes studied me from head to toe, taking in my delicate heels, the slightly flared wedding gown with the slit running along my left leg, which was also covered in white lace stockings to match my gloves. She swatted my hand with a sharp look when I tried to loosen my corset. I gave her a small smile as she finally stepped back after adjusting the delicate sleeves of my dress, which rested elegantly on my shoulders.

"I don't know why I feel like this," I whispered, clasping my hands over my stomach and running my fingers over my ring. I was marrying Nikolai—the man I loved, the man who loved me despite my past, despite my burdens. "It's normal to be anxious on your wedding day, Miss Selina," Sena said, handing me my bouquet of white dahlias. I inhaled their scent deeply, closing my eyes.

Calm down. Calm down. It's just Niko and you.

"Could you give us a moment alone, please ?" my sister suddenly asked, smoothing out the deep green fabric of her dress. It was the color we'd chosen for my bridesmaids—Elif, Sienna, and Sena. I couldn't help but notice how the high neckline of her dress concealed her throat, which still bore faint traces of the attack. Luckily, her voice had recovered quickly, and she'd moved past the fact that… she'd killed a man by slitting his throat, as if it were something she'd done before. I pressed my lips together, holding back the questions that had haunted me for the past three weeks. Questions I didn't dare ask out of fear—fear of discovering things I didn't even want to imagine.

Sienna approached with a small box in her hands, "what is that?" I asked, frowning as I leaned toward it. My breath hitched, and I covered my mouth with my hands the moment I saw the gold locket inside. The very same one *Papà* had given *Mamma*. With trembling fingers, I picked it up, running my thumb gently over the carved designs. Small green gemstones formed the shape of a bird perched on a branch. I carefully opened it, and a sob escaped me as I saw the wedding photo of *Mamma* and *Papà* inside—the same photo my mother had worn close to her heart for twenty years.

On the other half was a different photo—a new one. *Nikolai*. His lips curled into a subtle smile as he stared straight into the camera. It was a picture I'd taken just a few days ago while we were playing a board game with his brothers, my sister, and Elif. "I thought having his picture in there would make you happy," my sister murmured as she retrieved the locket and stepped behind me, fastening it around my neck. It rested just above my collarbone. "I… I thought you had sold it. To survive after… after I was no longer there to pay the rent and everything else," I whispered, turning to look at her. She gave me a sad smile, "I had to sell a lot of things, Selina. But this… I couldn't." She reached out and brushed her fingers lightly over the locket, "it helped me survive, just like you said. I kept it close when I walked through hell to find you. It made me feel like they were there, with me."

I suddenly grabbed her hand just as she was about to step back, "tell me, Sienna. Please, tell me," I begged, my eyes pleading with hers—but she shook her head. "I will never let you live with that, Selina. And… I don't think I could live with myself, looking you in the eye, if you knew what I've done these past eight years." "Sienna…" "No, Selina. You're getting married today. It's supposed to be one of the happiest days of your life. Don't ruin it." I shook my head but didn't argue. Just for this once. Just for today. I let it go. But I would find out the truth about my sister. I had to.

Chapter thirty-five

Nikolai

Twice. I had only cried twice in my adult life. The first time was when my parents died, when I was sixteen. The second was the night I had to commit the irreparable with Irina. And I knew that today would be the third—something I desperately wanted to avoid in front of my brothers and sons. But the sight of Selina walking toward me, her arm linked with her sister's, was too much to bear. Suddenly, I felt a gentle nudge on my shoulder before a handkerchief appeared in front of me. I took it under Grigori's amused gaze, straightening up as I inhaled deeply. She finally reached me, and I extended my hand to take hers under Sienna's scrutinizing gaze—a gaze that sent a very clear message: *Hurt her, and I'll rip your balls off.*

I smirked at her before gently pulling Selina closer as Sienna joined Elif. My wife-to-be finally lifted her eyes to mine, and my heart stopped. Her cheeks were slightly flushed, her wide eyes shining, her lips caught between her teeth. "You look stunning," I murmured, tucking a loose strand behind her ear. "So do you," she replied, her breath hitching as she squeezed my hand. "I think I'm a little nervous… I've never done this before." She gave me a soft smile, and I swore my soul left my body just to go thank the heavens for this gift. I chuckled, taking her other hand and pressing a kiss to her knuckles. "You're doing just fine," I reassured her, and she relaxed slightly, slowly starting to enjoy the day.

Selina laughed heartily as the boys bounced excitedly around the cake we were cutting—our cake. My wife. Selina Ivanov. *My wife*. The mother of my sons—and maybe even my daughters, though female births were rare among the Ivanovs.

I pulled her closer, pressing a kiss to her temple as she sucked the frosting off her thumb, gazing up at me from under her lashes. She gasped when my hand slid from her waist down to her backside, giving it a gentle squeeze. "Nikolai !" she whispered, glancing around at our family seated at the long table, laughing and chatting. "You started it," I replied, squeezing once more before she swatted my hand away. "I can't wait to take off those lace stockings," I murmured against her ear. "While my hands take care of that corset…" She lifted her beautiful face to mine, her expression confused, "how are you going to take off my stockings if your hands are busy with my corset ?"

I didn't answer, simply flashing a wide grin. Her eyes widened as she realized what I meant, suddenly, she lifted the cake knife, eyebrows furrowed. "You keep your teeth away from me, Nikolai Ivanov. Especially from my thighs." I grabbed her wrist, brought the blade closer to my lips, and licked a bit of frosting off the tip, watching her pupils dilate as she nervously licked her lips. "These thighs are mine now, Selina Ivanov," I murmured, taking the knife from her before turning back to cut another slice of cake, her stunned gaze still fixed on me. I handed her a plate, but before she could take it, the sharp sound of gunshots froze me in place.

My brothers were already on their feet, scanning the garden for any sign of danger. But there was nothing.

The noise had come from beyond the walls. "David, Marcus, stay here," Grigori ordered before moving toward the garden's exit, followed closely by my brothers. "Niko," Selina whispered, grabbing my arm. I kissed her forehead. "Stay with the children. I'll be back soon." I quickly followed my brothers, with Tarik right behind us, his expression dark. We reached Samy, who waved us over at the western edge of the forest surrounding our estate. We pushed forward, quickly arriving at a group of our men gathered around something—or rather, someone. "Stay back, bosses," Yuri warned. "She has a bomb on her." A bomb ? That close to the house ? "I'm sorry, please," the woman on the ground sobbed, lying on her stomach, her thigh bleeding—probably the reason for the gunshot. "She's going to kill my daughter." "Who ?" Sasha asked, stepping forward, but Grigori held him back. "Alia. Alia Rasili." And my blood ran cold. "She kidnapped my daughter and said she'd kill her if… if I didn't detonate the bomb the moment I saw Madame Selina. Please, she's only four years old !" The woman's sobs grew more frantic, but all I could hear was the buzzing in my ears.

A bomb. For Selina. "Madame Selina knows me," the woman continued. "I was a maid at the villa she lived in with Mr. Rasili in Rome. My name is Sonia. Please, I need to save my daughter !" "How did Alia know where we were ? How are you tracking Selina ?" I snapped, striding toward her despite my brothers' protests. I grabbed the front of her jacket, where the bomb was strapped, and lifted her slightly off the ground. She screamed in pain, sobbing harder. "I don't know ! I swear ! She… she was looking at a tablet. It had two red dots showing this location ! But I don't know how she did it !" She hiccuped through her tears as Roman and Sasha grabbed me, pulling me back. *Two red dots.*

"GPS trackers," Tarik muttered, rubbing his chin. "Maybe in their belongings ?" he looked at me. I shook my head, "we replaced all their things. That's impossible." Sonia's sobs grew louder. "She's losing too much blood. We need to tend to her wound," Roman said, moving toward her, quickly examining the bomb strapped to her. "I'll handle the bomb and get her to our hospital, and I'll see if I can find her daughter," he stated. Grigori opened his mouth to argue, but Roman cut him off with a knowing smirk, "I'm the only one who can do it, and you know it."

We didn't argue—because he was right. "Be careful," I muttered, casting one last glance at the now unconscious woman before turning back toward the house. "I have an idea," Tarik said as we entered the mansion, quickly running upstairs. Grigori, Sasha, and I headed to the garden, where the rest of our family was waiting. "Grigori, what's going on ? Where are Roman and Tarik ?" Elif asked as she approached her husband. I made my way to Selina, who was watching me with worried eyes, "I'm here," Tarik called, returning with a small device in hand—it looked like a detector. "What's going on, Niko ?" Selina asked, grabbing my hand, her fingers trembling. "I think I know how the Italians have been tracking you," Tarik said, stopping beside us as I eyed the device. "This is a detector designed by the school to locate even the smallest tracking devices. Can I use it on you, Selina ?"

"On… on me ?" she asked, stepping closer to me, confused. And then it hit me. My blood turned to ice. "You think he implanted a tracker in her body ?" I asked darkly. Tarik nodded grimly. I clenched my jaw, looking down at my wife. *Fuck.* "Selina…" "I… okay," she whispered, taking a step toward Tarik. Her wedding dress trailed behind her. I hated that this day had been tainted by that bastard. Again. "Raise your arms, please," Tarik instructed, running the detector over her right hand, then her arm, and finally over her left hand and arm. The device remained silent, and I began to relax as he moved it over her torso and legs.

Finally, he scanned her back. When the detector reached her neck, it let out a piercing beep, and we all froze. "It's probably the pendant," Sienna said, stepping closer. Selina tried to remove it with trembling fingers, when she couldn't, I did it for her. "It was my mother's ; it's precious," she told me, glancing over her shoulder. I nodded, carefully placing the pendant into the inside pocket of my jacket. Tarik ran the detector over her neck again, and it emitted the same sharp beep. Selina gasped. "Damn it," Tarik muttered, stepping back as my wife brought her hand to her neck, turning toward me with tearful eyes. "He tagged me like an animal ?" she whispered, her lips quivering. In her white dress, she looked like an angel fallen from the sky. My fingers tingled as I reached for her delicate face. "I… I don't even know when he did this. What else has he done to me without my knowledge ? And Rafael ? Oh my God !"

"Hey, hey, calm down, *Solnyshko*, calm down," I tried to soothe her, though I knew she was probably right. Sonia had mentioned Alia watching two points on the tablet.

The other point had to be Rafael. That son of a bitch. That damn son of a bitch. "We need to remove those trackers. They might have microphones, or even devices that could harm you," Sasha said, placing a comforting hand on Sienna's shoulder as she quickly wiped away her tears. "I'll call our doctor right now," Elif said, rushing inside with Grigori following closely behind. I held my trembling wife against me, "it'll be okay, Selina. Everything will be fine." Everything would be fine as soon as I cut the breath out of that bastard. And I would—tonight. Then I'd come back to my wife for our wedding night.

Chapter thirty-six
Selina

Two. They removed two trackers from me—one in my neck and another from the sole of my left foot. And a third from Rafael's right armpit. Yes, he had tagged my baby, and I didn't know when or how. He must have drugged us, knocked us out, touched our bodies without my knowledge. What else might he have done to me ? How many times ? "Mom, why did Rafael get another shot ?" Andrei asked from his bed in our house in California. We had returned that morning, right after the doctor assured Nikolai we had both recovered from the minor surgeries. I didn't want to stay in a place Antonio already knew. I placed the bedtime story I had just read to the boys on the table and froze, staring at my three little ones nestled in bed, looking up at me.

Rafael didn't really understand why he needed local anesthesia for the procedure. He hadn't noticed anything—Roman had distracted him with a game while I cried silently the entire time, held tightly by Nikolai, who never left my side. "Uh… it's… his last vaccine didn't work. His body is so strong that it rejected it, so we had to do it again," I lied, clenching my fists as their wide eyes fixed on me. "Wow ! You're so strong !" Andrei exclaimed, hugging Rafael, while Alexei nodded and patted his back, making me smile despite myself. "If you want to get stronger, you need to sleep now," I told them, kissing each of their cheeks before pulling the blanket up to their chins. They giggled beneath the covers. "Goodnight, my angels."

"Goodnight, Mom," they replied in unison as I left the room, smiling—though the smile faded the moment I shut the door. Leaning against it, I closed my eyes. Breathe in, breathe out. *Calm down, Selina, calm down.* But I couldn't. He wasn't here. I had thought I was safe. I had thought I was free. But even now, he still had his grip on me, on my body—and on my baby's. My breath shortened, my vision narrowed, and my limbs felt heavy. I jumped when a loud noise echoed from downstairs, followed by shouting—including Nikolai's voice. I moved cautiously toward the stairs, gripping the railing as I descended. "What do you mean they recovered him ? How did they know the location ?!" Nikolai roared. "I don't know, dammit ! David says two of our men are dead, and Marcus is seriously injured. They're heading to the hospital," Roman replied darkly.

At the entrance to the living room, I saw Roman pacing, Nikolai rubbing his face, Sasha furiously typing on his phone, while Grigori and Elif spoke in hushed tones. Elif noticed me first and frowned, "Selina ? Sweetheart, what's wrong ?" she asked. Before she even finished the sentence, Nikolai had an arm wrapped around my waist, lifting my face to his, concern etched into his features. "Talk to me, *Solnyshko*," he murmured. I tried to speak, but my tongue felt heavy. I couldn't seem to breathe. My legs gave out, trembling, and Nikolai caught me before I collapsed. "Selina !" Sienna cried, rushing in from the kitchen. "She's having a panic attack," Nikolai growled, lifting me off the floor and placing me on the couch. He sat beside me, pulled me close, and pressed my cheek to his chest. "You need to calm down, *Solnyshko*. Focus on my voice," he whispered, rocking me gently.

I tried to listen, but the buzzing in my head was too loud. It drowned everything out. "I… he… I want him gone," I finally choked out against my husband's chest. His arms tightened around my trembling body. "I can't live like this anymore…" "Shhh. Everything's okay, Selina. He won't touch you again. Never again," Nikolai promised, soft but dark. My sister reappeared with a glass of water and helped me sip it as I struggled to breathe. "You'll be fine, Selina," she reassured me, rubbing my back. I nodded slowly as the fog of panic lifted, leaving me exhausted and embarrassed under all their watchful eyes. "I'm sorry…" I began, but Nikolai rose, gently pulling my face to his neck. "We're going to bed. Sasha, Roman, I want a full report of what happened tonight," his two younger brothers nodded, and Nikolai was already carrying me up the stairs. "You're okay, *Solnyshko*," he whispered, kissing my forehead. He set me on the bed, closed the door with his foot, then knelt in front of me to remove my slippers and socks.

He lifted my left foot carefully, pressing a kiss to the inside of my ankle. I shivered. His gaze darkened as he examined the small bandage beneath. My hands slid to his cheeks, guiding his face toward mine before I kissed him softly—then pulled back. "I love you, Nikolai Ivanov. My friend, my confidant, my protector, the father of my sons, my husband," I whispered against his lips, my thumbs caressing his cheekbones as our eyes locked. "I hated these past eight years. I regretted every day, every hour, and every minute. But I'm ready, Nikolai. I'm ready to relive every second of that torture if it means ending up here. In your arms. As your wife. As the mother of our sons." He exhaled slowly, as though he'd been holding his breath for years, "ah,

Selina. My everything," he murmured, before kissing me—this time, more deeply.

I soon found myself lying on the bed, my hands sliding from his face to his neck, then down his arms to his elbows as he braced himself on either side of me. "This is our wedding night," I whispered between kisses, he hummed in agreement, his lips trailing down my neck. "We could... maybe go somewhere ?" I suggested, my voice wavering. "To clear our heads—and the boys' too ?" He suddenly pulled back, eyes gleaming with interest, "a honeymoon ?" he asked, and I couldn't help but laugh at how eager he looked. "Yes, a honeymoon," I replied, massaging his forearms where the sleeves of his shirt were rolled up. He smiled—and I knew, even in ten years, that smile would still make my heart race.

"The Maldives are way too popular !" my sister exclaimed as we scrolled through endless images of stunning turquoise waters and dreamy overwater villas. "What about Sri Lanka ? Grigori and I went there two years ago—it was paradise," Elif chimed in, sitting to my left and placing a tray with three steaming cups of tea on the coffee table. I swore, this woman and her teas ! I figured it had something to do with her Turkish roots and her connection to *Karadeniz*. She once told me how, as a child, she used to play in the black tea fields with her brother and cousins. "I don't know. I'd never really thought about a honeymoon. I don't even know why I suggested it to Nikolai. Especially at such a critical time..." "Oh, sweetheart, you'll soon realize there's never a moment in your life as an Ivanov that isn't critical," Elif said with a laugh, shaking her head. "So enjoy every second now."

"She's right. If you keep waiting for the 'perfect moment,' you'll never live," my sister added, her eyes still fixed on the screen as she continued scrolling. I sighed. They were right. I couldn't keep living in fear. Even though the future felt more uncertain than ever, I wanted to live it—with Nikolai, my sons, and my family. "Maybe a lesser-known island?" I finally said. They both nodded enthusiastically, grinning as they dove back into their searches with the determination of seasoned investigators. I checked my phone for the hundredth time, waiting for an update from Nikolai—but still nothing. He had captured Antonio and had been holding him for over three weeks without telling me anything. And now, last night, that monster had managed to escape, and Nikolai had left right after breakfast to figure out how it happened.

It wasn't until later that evening that he reappeared with Roman and Sasha. Sienna had gone out with Kenji, who had come to pick her up, and Grigori and Elif had also stepped out. "Nikolai!" I exclaimed, setting down my anatomy book and hurrying into the hallway as Roman headed to the kitchen and Sasha disappeared downstairs. "What's going on?" "Nothing important, *Solnyshko*. There's a delivery tonight, and we're just making sure everything goes smoothly with Sasha," my husband replied as his younger brother reappeared with two large-caliber weapons, handing one to Nikolai. "Is this about Antonio?" I asked, grabbing his hand to stop him as he checked the magazine. He smiled softly before kissing my cheek, "don't tire yourself worrying about these things, Solnyshko." For the first—or maybe second—time, I wanted to hit him, "don't tell me what to think, Nikolai," I said, clenching my fists.

And he had the audacity to smirk, "we'll talk about this tonight when I'm back," he said, kissing me on the lips this time before walking out, followed by Sasha, who waved at me. I stood there, watching my husband walk away, mouth slightly open. Yes, he was loving, kind, and gentle—and he could be understanding when he wanted to. But he could also be arrogant and sneaky. Never with me or the boys—only with outsiders. I wasn't stupid. I knew my husband wasn't an angel, even if he was one for me. I knew what he did. I knew how he did it. Unfortunately, sometimes his professional side bled into our family life. "Nikolai Ivanov!" I yelled at the door as he climbed into the car. "Get back here!" I stomped my foot and the idiot laughed loudly, started the engine, and drove off after waving at me.

That little bastard...

"Already fighting the day after the wedding?" Roman's voice suddenly came from behind, making me jump. I turned to find him devouring the chocolate pudding Velma had made that morning. "Your brother is an ass," I grumbled, crossing my arms. He grinned at my pout, which probably made me look like a sulking child, "he just wants your weal—" Roman began, but I cut him off with a raised hand. "I'm not a child. And especially not Nikolai Ivanov's child," I said firmly. He raised an eyebrow at me but said nothing. Just as he was about to reply, his phone chimed. He shoved his spoon into the pudding and checked the message. His expression shifted. "Damn it," he muttered.

"What ? What's going on ?" I asked, my voice tight with worry. He shook his head, slipping the phone back into his pocket. "Nothing important. I've got a car race tonight, but we're short a partner. My date just canceled, so I'll have to ask one of the girls at the track… though that's not ideal." He sighed, scooping another spoonful of pudding as I watched him, smiling softly. If only I could be that carefree. Just for once. And then it hit me. What if I could ? Just for one night ? "I'll go with you," I said, my smile widening. "Uh… I don't think that's a good idea. Nikolai—" "What did I just say ? I want to live too, dammit ! To do things I've never done before !" I insisted, letting my voice tremble.

His face softened immediately and he looked at me for a long second, then sighed and shoveled the last bite of pudding into his mouth. I smiled again, victorious. I was going to a car race!

Chapter thirty-seven
Nikolai

The last cargo truck disappeared into the distance as I crushed my cigarette beneath my boot. "Looks like the Chinese didn't dare after all," Sasha said, joining me at the warehouse exit. Earlier that day, while we were trying to track Antonio, one of our informants within the Chinese triads had tipped us off about a planned attack on the night's shipment. Many believed the Italians and Russians ran the underground in America, but the Chinese had their share of the market too—a significant share. A share they were eager to expand, just like everyone else. "Call Yuan. Make sure he hasn't been compromised," I told Sasha, referring to our mole who had warned us. Maybe the Chinese had caught on when we changed the delivery location. The first light of dawn began to creep over the horizon when my phone vibrated in the inner pocket of my jacket. The name on the screen read : *Chief Jeff.*

"Nikolai Ivanov," I answered, already suspecting what this was about. "Mr. Ivanov, your brother was arrested last night during a street race. Again," Jeff growled, his voice rough and annoyed. I closed my eyes and exhaled slowly. Roman was supposed to manage the bets and logistics at those races. But the idiot couldn't help himself—he had to participate. And subtlety had never been his strong suit. The cops loved these little chances to make us miserable. They knew they couldn't actually touch us—not if they wanted to keep breathing—but they enjoyed reminding us that they were watching.

"Handle it the usual way," I said, about to hang up. "And your wife, Mr. Ivanov ?" *My wife ?* "Excuse me ? My wife ?" My voice dropped to a dangerous low, and Sasha froze beside me.

"Uh… yes, sir. Your wife was with your brother when we arrested him," Jeff stammered, his confidence fading fast. I closed my eyes and inhaled sharply, my grip tightening on the phone until I could almost feel it cracking. *Roman. You're dead.*

"I'm on my way. Don't let them leave," I growled.

<u>Selina</u>

I fidgeted with my wedding ring, my eyes fixed on it, my legs shaking uncontrollably. Nikolai was not going to let this slide. I knew he'd never hurt me, but the anxiety curled around my ribs like a tightening rope. Across from me, Roman sighed as Chief Jeff called my husband, standing stiffly behind his desk. And to think—it had all started so well.

Six hours earlier.

We had left the city and driven under a bridge, where a whole new world had appeared. Brightly colored sports cars were lined up side by side, engines purring like predators. A crowd danced to deafening music that no one outside could hear. Some wore flashy suits. Others were nearly naked. Roman had parked his electric blue BMW M2 CS—he'd talked about it the entire ride—right in the center.

The crowd erupted in cheers. I had stepped out after him, adjusting the black crop top beneath my leather jacket—clothes borrowed from my sister's closet, and I had a lot of questions about her wardrobe choices. Roman exchanged hugs and handshakes while I took in the scene.

It wasn't my world, not one I belonged to—but God, it was thrilling. "The next race is ours !" Roman announced, drawing sharp glares from women who kept their distance. Afraid, maybe? "This isn't dangerous, right ?" I had asked, nervously biting my lip. Roman laughed, "you can't have fun without taking risks, Nana."

"Nana ?" I raised an eyebrow. He just winked, practically buzzing with excitement. Engines growled in the distance. Two cars roared down the line, taking a sharp turn before accelerating between the rows. Startled, I stepped back. Roman caught me just before I could fall. "Roman !" I shouted, as the cars flew past, but he just laughed, holding me steady. The cars screeched to a halt a meter away. The green one edged ahead as the drivers jumped out, already shouting. "You cheated ! You cut the last corner !" Roman stepped between them, pushing them apart, "come on, guys. Don't be sore losers," he said with a grin—different from the ones he gave me or the family. Colder. Sharper. The two backed off, climbing back into their cars without another word, though they continued to glare at each other. "Let's go, Nana !" Roman said, holding the door open for me as my earlier courage slipping further away.

"We're going on the same track ? With that corner ?" I asked. Roman kissed my cheek, "buckle up, Selina." I did. Fast. "Who are we racing ?" I asked. "Whoever dares face me," he said, starting the engine with a roar that sent the crowd into a frenzy. Out of nowhere, a bright red car pulled up beside us. Roman froze, gripping the steering wheel tighter, "neporochnaya malen'kaya devochka, (cheeky little

girl.)" he muttered through clenched teeth. I leaned forward to see the driver, but the tinted windows only revealed a shadowy silhouette of a woman. Suddenly, the car's engine roared even louder than ours. "An acquaintance?" I asked. Roman nodded. "Kind of."

A woman stepped between the cars, raising a white handkerchief. "Hold on," Roman said, hitting the gas before the cloth even dropped. I gasped, clutching the door, "Oh my God..." we sped down the road, side by side with the red car. "Not this time," Roman growled, shifting gears and pinning me to my seat. "Shouldn't we slow before the turn?" I asked, fear overtaking my initial excitement. Roman didn't answer, his face dark and focused. We entered the curve at dizzying speed. The red car kept up without flinching. I screamed as the cars scraped. Roman pushed harder, and we surged toward the final turn the rows of parked cars coming into view.

Both cars were neck to neck, and my stomach churned as Roman pushed the car even faster.
"Roman!" I cried, grabbing his arm with one hand and covering my mouth with the other. He clenched his jaw and, to my immense relief, eased off the gas. The red car shot past us, drifting effortlessly through the turn. Roman followed closely, but the race was already lost. The red car skidded to a halt after drifting to face us as Roman slammed on the brakes, stopping inches from it. He jumped out and drew his gun, "get out," he barked at the red car driver. I stumbled out after him, collapsing. Roman tried to catch me, but I hit the ground. "Selina!" He grabbed my arms, panic in his voice. "You're pale as a ghost. Blayt, I'm sorry." I shook my head, about to reassure him—but tires screeched.

The red car reversed, spun, and disappeared into the night. "Blayt," Roman spat again. Then— "the cops are coming ! They're here !" someone shouted. Panic exploded. Engines roared. Roman yanked me back to the BMW. Just as I was about to climb in, another car reversed—slamming into our hood. I screamed as Roman shielded me. "Sorry, Ivanov !" a voice called, the loser from earlier, he sped off. Blue and red lights flashed. Sirens wailed.

Present.

"Uh, yes, of course, sir," the police chief finally muttered before hanging up. "Alright, can we go now ?" Roman asked, rising from his chair. I stared at him, wide-eyed, as he motioned for me to stand. Since the arrest, Roman had been disturbingly calm and casual. From what I could tell, this wasn't his first time being detained. The officer gave him a smile I didn't like one bit before signaling to two others. "Escort Mr. and Mrs. Ivanov to a cell, boys," he said, and I felt my lips tremble. Am I going to jail ? I'd just wanted to do something exciting for once in my life—and now I was going to end up behind bars?

"What the hell?" Roman growled, pulling me close when one of the officers reached for my arm. "Mr. Nikolai requested that you both remain here until he arrives," the officer replied calmly. I winced. Nikolai is coming here? Oh God. "So what? We can wait right here," Roman snapped, shooting him a glare as he gently rubbed my arm to soothe my trembling. "Unfortunately, we're short on space and need the room," the officer said as he sat back down. Roman and I exchanged glances, scanning the almost-empty precinct. "I always knew you were an idiot, Jeff," Roman said through clenched teeth. "But putting Nikolai's wife in a freezing cell? That's a whole new level of stupidity." "I'm sorry, but I have no other choice," Jeff replied, looking falsely uncomfortable. "No, you're not sorry. Not yet," Roman hissed before shoving the officers aside and guiding me toward the stairs leading down to the holding cells. "It'll be fine, *moya sestra* (my sister), even if Nikolai kills me later," Roman sighed as we stepped into the basement, where the air turned colder. An officer opened the door to a cell, and I stepped inside, wrapping my arms tightly around my stomach.

"You'll go in the other cell, Mr. Ivanov," another officer said, placing a hand on Roman's shoulder as he attempted to follow me in. Roman slowly lifted his head, staring the man down with an icy, lethal glare. What happened next was a blur. In a flash, the officer was pinned against the bars of my cell, his arm twisted painfully behind his back. I gasped, covering my mouth, stunned. Roman leaned in and whispered something in his ear, and the man turned pale. My brother-in-law released him and stepped inside the cell with me. The other officer, who hadn't moved the entire time, quietly shut the door behind him, avoiding eye contact. "Come here. Sit down, *moya sestra*," Roman said, shrugging off his leather jacket and laying it on the cold concrete bench. I murmured a soft thank you and sat down, pulling my jacket tighter around myself as a shiver ran through me. Roman sat beside me and pulled me close, wrapping his arm around my shoulders.

"I'm sorry, Selina," he said, gently rubbing my arm. "I didn't expect them to come down on us tonight. And I shouldn't have gone so hard out there." I shook my head. "I loved the race, Roman. I've never felt so... alive. Except when I'm with Nikolai," I admitted with a small smile, my cheeks flushing. It was true. Nikolai made me feel alive—powerful, beautiful. Yes, I'd been scared tonight, but it was nothing compared to the fear I lived with under Antonio's roof. This was different. This, I didn't regret. "I loved it... until we ended up in the back of a cop car and your buddy in the rabbit costume got tackled and cuffed. Actually, no, that part was hilarious too," I laughed.

Roman chuckled, shaking his head, his laughter echoing in the cell. "Anton is... special," he said, still catching his breath. "Nikolai's going to hate me," I murmured, exhaustion crashing down on me like a tidal wave. "The only way Nikolai could hate you is if he lost his memory and someone told him you were an Italian spy plotting against his family. And even then, I think he'd still doubt it," Roman chuckled. I mumbled something unintelligible as sleep took over, comforted by the sound of Roman's steady breathing.

I frowned as dull noises began to pull me from my slumber. "I'd suggest you stay asleep, for both your sake and mine. I can feel his anger from here," Roman whispered, still holding me close, my head resting on his shoulder. I cracked one eye open and realized we were still in the cell. Despite Roman's warmth and his jacket draped around me, a chill ran down my spine, and my back ached from the hard bench beneath me. I closed my eyes again as the sound of rapid footsteps echoed down the corridor. My palms grew clammy, and I clasped my hands over my bare stomach. The footsteps stopped just outside the cell, followed by an oppressive silence. You could've heard a pin drop.

"Don't look at me like that, *moy brat*," Roman murmured, pretending not to disturb me. "I won most of tonight's bets." A sudden loud crash rang out, followed by a pained groan. "I didn't know you had such a death wish, Jeff," came my husband's icy voice, slicing through the silence like a blade. My breath hitched. "This is where regret starts, Jeffy," Roman said, his grip on my shoulders tightening. "And unfortunately, there's no cure for stupidity." "Open the door," Nikolai growled. The lock clicked open before the last word had even left his mouth. And someone got inside the cell, I knew it was him—I felt him. He stopped in front of me, his presence enveloping me, his gaze inspecting every inch of me. "It's not her fault. She didn't do anything wrong," Roman stated, withdrawing his arm just as others slid around me—one behind my back, the other beneath my knees. A second later, I was cradled against my husband's chest, surrounded by his familiar scent. Without a word, he turned and began walking toward the exit.

"Lock the door," he ordered through clenched teeth, "brother?" Roman called as the heavy door slammed shut behind us. "Get some rest, *moy brat*. You're going to need it when I come back for you," Nikolai replied coldly, ignoring Roman's protest. I pressed my lips together, guilt rising in my throat. It wasn't fair—Roman and I had both been involved. I opened my eyes, ready to plead, to ask Nikolai to reconsider. "I suggest you refrain from saying a single word," he muttered through his teeth, and I froze. His jaw was rigid, his eyes locked ahead. Yet, even in his fury, his hold on me remained gentle, reassuring. Slowly, warmth returned to my body as I nestled closer to his chest. We exited the station, where Sasha leaned against the car, eyes fixed on his phone. He looked up, scanned me from head to toe, then opened the back door without a word, visibly relieved that I was unharmed. Nikolai approaches the car ready to set me down, without letting me speak, without explaining, or even argue. As if I were a misbehaving child awaiting scolding once we got home.

The injustice of it all ignited something inside me, fueled by adrenaline. I squirmed in his arms until I broke free. He hadn't expected it and I caught him off guard. Sasha grabbed me, swift and steady, but not fast enough—my lower body hit the pavement hard, sending pain through my tailbone. "*Blayt'*, Selina !" Nikolai snapped, bending to help me, but I shoved him away. Once I steadied myself, I also pushed Sasha aside. "I'm your wife, Nikolai !" I shouted, pointing a trembling finger at him. "Not your maid, not your sister, and most definitely not your child !" His eyes widened in disbelief—under any other circumstances, it might have been comical.

"I am Selina Ivanov, and I refuse to be treated like some clueless airhead ! Do you hear me ?!" I shouted, standing my ground as his gaze darkened. I sensed Sasha shifting uncomfortably, subtly gesturing to onlookers who had likely stopped to witness the spectacle. "And if Roman stays, then so do I ! We were arrested together. If he's punished, I should be too !" I added, folding my arms defiantly across my chest, ignoring the instincts that screamed at me to get into the car and keep quiet. Nikolai stared at me, utterly silent, as though I'd grown a second head. Then he began walking toward me, and I instinctively stepped back, his gaze was intense—the kind he usually reserved for the privacy of our bedroom. I backed up until I hit the car door behind me. Trapped. He raised his hand, trailing it along the line of my jaw before gently cupping it and tilting my face toward him. I held my breath. His eyes burned into mine, dropping briefly to my lips, then to my surely reddened, frozen nose. "You don't need to ask, wife," he murmured against my lips, voice low and deliberate. "The first thing I'll do when we get home is punish you so thoroughly, you won't be sitting for a week."

Before I could react, his lips were on mine—rough, commanding. By the time I caught my breath, I was already seated in the passenger seat, and he was buckling my seatbelt. He turned to Sasha, who was once again scrolling through his phone, "get him out. Call one of the guys to pick you up. I don't want to see him until tomorrow night," Nikolai snapped and slammed my door shut. Then he circled the car, climbed into the driver's seat, and started the engine. His threat lingered between us—and instead of fear, it sent a shiver down my spine for an entirely different reason.

Chapter thirty-eight
Nikolai

I couldn't help but smile as I watched my wife squirm in her chair the next morning during breakfast. She carefully avoided my gaze, and the few times our eyes did meet, her cheeks flushed an adorable shade of red—completely understandable, considering how much she had enjoyed her punishment. Fortunately for her, the boys weren't there to witness this scene. Earlier that morning, I had received a call—unexpected, to say the least, but not entirely unwelcome. My sons' grandmother, Agata, had asked if she could keep them for the weekend. I had been ready to refuse outright, but Selina had thought it would be good for the boys to maintain a bond with Irina, despite everything that had happened. And since Nina would be there, I knew she would keep a watchful eye on them.

So, I had agreed—on the condition that Rafael went with them. I didn't want to separate him from his brothers, not when they got along so well. They would look after each other. Nina had come to pick them up in the morning, and despite their initial reluctance, Selina had managed to convince them by reminding them of the vacation we were planning for next week. "Are you alright, Selina?" Elif asked suddenly from the other end of the table, her eyes still red from Tarik's early morning departure. My wife froze, lifting her gaze to my sister, opening and closing her mouth without answering. I burst out laughing, drawing Elif's attention. "Leave my wife alone, Elif. She didn't have an easy night—her first street race, then a stint in a holding cell with Roman, and finally, a well-deserved punishment," I said, taking a bite of bacon. Sienna choked on her orange juice, coughing so violently it seemed she might tear her lungs out. Elif stared at Selina wide-eyed, while my wife turned redder than a peony. "I can't believe you just said that," she hissed through clenched teeth as Sienna struggled to breathe. Sasha handed Sienna a glass of water, which she accepted without looking at him, her unwavering stare fixed on her sister. "Sienna…" "A street race ?! And a holding cell ?! What the hell, Selina ?" Sienna exclaimed. My smile faded as I saw my wife's expression shift. She was truly angry.

"That's not like you, Selina—" "Maybe it is !" my wife shouted suddenly, pushing back her chair as she stood abruptly, her dark eyes locking onto her sister's. We all froze. "Maybe this is who I want to be ! Maybe I want to stop worrying about everything—about whether I'll survive another day ! About whether Antonio has planted something else in my body ! About whether he's going to come after Rafael again ! Or worse—you! Where were you these past eight years, Sienna ? And why the hell do you have clothes that belong to a whor—" "Selina," I cut in, rising to my feet as well. A heavy silence fell over the room as the two sisters held each other's gaze. Selina's breathing was ragged, her shoulders tense, while Sienna remained perfectly still, her face unreadable. The only thing betraying her emotion was the single tear slipping down her cheek.

Selina gasped, covering her mouth with her hands as she shook her head. "Sienna…" "I need some air," Sienna muttered, wiping her cheek before walking out, her movements stiff but controlled. Selina started to follow her, but I held her back just as Sasha murmured, "I'll handle it," and followed after Sienna. "Oh my God ! What's wrong with me ? Why did I say all that ? Nikolai…" she sobbed. I pulled her into my arms, casting a helpless look at Elif, who had moved closer. She simply shook her head, just as lost as I was, before gently rubbing Selina's back and guiding her toward the couch. I watched them, still confused.

Selina

Roman smirked at me from the couch across the room, but his grin quickly faded when Nikolai shot him a murderous glare. Two days had passed since our arrest, and only now had Nikolai agreed to see him. After a long argument the night before, where I had refused any physical contact with my husband, which had only worsened his mood. The sound of hurried footsteps echoed down the stairs, and my sister appeared in the hallway dressed in sportswear, her hair pulled back in a ponytail. "I'm going for a run on the forest trail."

"Sienna—" I tried to stop her, but she was already out the door with a brisk "See you later." I sighed, sinking back onto the couch. Since my emotional outburst, we hadn't spoken. She had been avoiding me like the plague, and I couldn't blame her. Nikolai took my hand and gave it a gentle squeeze as I inhaled deeply, trying to keep the tears brimming behind my eyelids from falling. "She won't talk to me," I whispered, closing my eyes. "Give her time, *Solnychko*. Everything will work out," my husband reassured me. "Yeah, your sister is far more forgiving than my brother, Selina," Roman interjected, immediately drawing Nikolai's attention—a grave mistake.

My husband was on his feet in less than a second, but I grabbed his arm. "Nikolai !" I cried, but he didn't even glance at me. "You took my wife to a damn street race !" he growled through clenched teeth. "Because I asked him to," I replied, even though he wasn't addressing me. "She could've been hurt ! And as if that wasn't enough, she got arrested !" he shouted. I silently thanked God that no one else was home. Then again, I wasn't sure if it was a good thing, considering how close Nikolai was to tearing his brother apart. "It wasn't his fa—" "I know. I'm sorry, *moy brat*," Roman interrupted, lowering his gaze to the floor. I stared at him, stunned. "I shouldn't have taken her. It was a mistake," he continued, apologizing while Nikolai watched him in silence for a moment before exhaling sharply. "For the next month, Sasha will handle the races," he said darkly. I saw Roman clench his fists, but he said nothing, simply accepting his punishment. "Uh, I'm right here, you know? You do realize I'm not a damn chi—" I swallowed my words when Nikolai's dark eyes landed on me. "Oh, trust me, *Solnychko*, I know that very well," he murmured, stepping toward me. Before I knew it, I was seated again. "I'll go pick up the boys from Agata's," Roman announced before making a hasty exit. My husband stood before me, hands on his hips, "what ?" I challenged, crossing my arms and furrowing my brows. He knelt in front of me, spreading my legs gently to settle between them, his hands resting on my hips.

"Selina, what's wrong, *moy lubov'* (my love) ? If you're upset about what happened… I'm not mad at you. I'm not angry," he said softly. "I know you're not, Niko. I just… I don't know what's wrong with me. Lately, I feel like I've lost control of everything," I admitted, burying my face in my hands as tears threatened to spill again. "Hey, hey, Selina, look at me," Nikolai said, gently grasping my wrists and pulling my hands from my face. I tried to pull free, shaking my head, but he held me—firm, yet careful. "You're breaking my heart, *moy lubov'*. Look at me. Talk to me," he pleaded. When I finally met his gaze, the lump in my throat tightened further. "I'm sorry, Nikolai. I don't know what's happening to me. It's probably the stress from the past few days—with the trackers, and the bomb, and Sonia…" I sniffled, my thoughts drifting to the woman who had witnessed my suffering for years. But how could I blame her ? How could she have stood against that monster ?

Suddenly, my husband lifted me off the couch with ease and sat down with me on his lap. He cupped my face and began to kiss me—my cheeks, my forehead, my nose, my neck—gently, tenderly. And just like that, the sobs came. His tenderness, his unwavering care, shattered what little composure I had left. I clung to his shirt, burying my face in his chest as he stroked my hair, my back, the sides of my thighs. "Let it all out, *Solnychko*. Let yourself go. I'm here to catch you. I will always be here." His voice was a whisper against my ear, and in that moment, I silently thanked God for giving me this man.

The car finally came to a stop at the foot of the stairs, and I rushed out before it had even fully parked. The moment the doors opened, Andrei and Rafael leapt out, running toward me as I hurried down the steps to meet them. I wrapped them in my arms, inhaling their scent, biting back a curse when I felt fresh tears prickling at my eyes. I tried to pull back to kiss them, but Rafael tightened his hold around my neck, sniffling softly. "*Angelo mio*, what's wrong?" I asked gently, but he didn't answer. He only clung to me harder.

I frowned and glanced toward the second car pulling up behind Roman's. Alexei and Mikhail stepped out with him, but my attention snapped back to the first car door just as, to my disbelief, Agata emerged—accompanied by an older man. Nikolai had told me she was no longer welcome near our home. So what the hell was she doing here? Just then, my husband appeared at my side, his presence grounding me. I straightened, Rafael still wrapped around my leg, while Andrei instinctively moved behind his father. "Gelb wants to discuss business with us, but I have no idea what the hell that woman is doing here," Nikolai muttered, his body tense. "She has no right to be here." He made a move to step forward, but I stopped him with a hand on his chest. "Let's not escalate things, Niko. Please," I whispered, locking eyes with him. I saw the storm within him falter as he took in the exhaustion on my face. I had spent over an hour earlier crying in his arms, and he had held me through it all, whispering softly, kissing my hair, grounding me.

He exhaled slowly and pulled me against him, his arm wrapped securely around my waist. Roman came to flank my other side, effectively shielding me as the couple approached. "Nikolai! Good to see you," the man—Gelb, I assumed—said, extending his hand. Nikolai shook it after a brief instant. "Congratulations on your marriage. And you must be Selina," he continued, offering his hand to me. But before I could respond, Roman smoothly stepped in front of me, while Nikolai pulled me further back. "Come, Gelb. Grigori is waiting for you in his office," Roman said over his shoulder. As they headed inside, Nikolai guided me and the boys upstairs.

"Stay with the kids until they're gone, okay ?" His voice was firm but filled with concern. I nodded silently. He kissed my forehead gently, promising the boys a football game later. Normally, that would have had Andrei and Rafael buzzing with excitement. But this time, they remained utterly silent. "I'm going to take a shower, Mom," Mikhail said, kissing my cheek before disappearing into the hallway. "I'm going to start a new book in the library, Mama," Andrei added, waving before following his brother. That left only Rafael and Andrei. The two who never stopped talking. And yet, now, they sat side by side at the edge of the bed, silent, their gazes fixed on the floor. I knelt in front of them, placing a hand gently on each of their knees. "So ? How was your weekend ?" I asked softly.

Nothing. "Hey, my loves. What's wrong? You know you can tell me anything, right?" I murmured, brushing my fingers gently across their cheeks. Andrei was the first to lift his gaze. His eyes shimmered with tears before he suddenly burst into sobs, flinging his arms around my neck. "Mama!" At the same time, Rafael began crying as well, his small hands covering his face—just as I had done in Nikolai's arms hours earlier. "What's going on here?" came my sister's voice from the doorway, her expression reflecting the same confusion and concern I felt. I turned back to my sons, stroking their hair as my own desperation grew. "Rafael? Andrei? What happened, my angels? Please, tell me," I pleaded. Sienna knelt beside me, resting a comforting hand on Rafael's thigh. "Hey, little monsters," she said softly. "Sometimes, being brave means trusting your family. We'll protect you. I promise."

Rafael wiped his eyes with the back of his hand, sniffled, then took a deep breath. With heartbreaking resolve, he reached for the zipper of his hoodie and slowly pulled it down. And my entire world shattered. Dark bruises marked his delicate neck—familiar bruises. The same kind I had seen on my own skin too many times before. Sienna gasped beside me as my breath caught in my throat. Andrei hesitated before pulling off his sweater, revealing more bruises along his arms.

"A… Alexei and Mikhail—do they have marks too?" My voice sounded foreign to my own ears. "No. She only scolded us," Rafael sniffled. Only *scolded* ? "Who ?" Sienna asked sharply, wiping the tears from Andrei's face. My sons exchanged a glance but didn't answer, and they didn't need to. Because I already knew. "Stay with them," I told Sienna, rising to my feet with eerie calm. She called after me, but I didn't stop. I didn't tremble. I didn't rage. I didn't feel anything. I only wanted to see fear in Agata's eyes. The same fear she had planted in my sons. I wanted to hear her beg.

Chapter thirty-nine
Nikolai

Elif, perched on the armrest of Grigori's chair, barely refrained from rolling her eyes at Agata's monologue as the latter sat across from the desk. I struggled just as much, standing behind my brother while Sasha cast me a look from the doorway, waiting for my signal to throw them out. What was meant to be a meeting about securing our northern border had turned into Agata's endless speech about her supposed love for her grandsons. "I can't imagine living without my three grandsons," she said, dabbing at a nonexistent tear on her cheek. "Four," I cut in suddenly, arms crossed, drawing everyone's attention. "I have four sons." Elif nodded silently, while my brothers kept their eyes locked on Agata and Gelb—never take your eyes off the enemy.

I straightened abruptly at the sound of hurried footsteps outside the office, followed by Roman's voice. The door burst open, slamming against the wall, and there stood my wife, with Roman just behind her, his expression tense. "Selina?" I asked, unsure, taking in her face—an expression I had never seen before. Cold. Her breathing came quick, her eyes darted around the room before locking on Agata. Then, the coldness melted into a fury I never thought I'd see in Selina. She stormed across the room. Agata stumbled as she tried to stand. Selina snatched the Chinese marble sphere from the coffee table, and everything happened in a blur, she swung it with force, striking Agata at the temple. The old woman collapsed as weapons were drawn. Gleb raised his gun at my wife, only to freeze when Sasha and Roman had theirs aimed at him. Elif and I rushed toward Selina, now on top of Agata, hands wrapped around her throat. "Is this how you strangled my son, huh ?" she screamed, her voice raw, as Agata turned an alarming shade of blue.

I wrapped my arms around Selina's waist, trying to pull her back, but she threw her head backward, hitting me square in the chin. I grunted but held on. "Is this how you crushed his arms ?" she shouted again, letting go of Agata's throat only to seize her forearms, making the older woman sob. "Selina !" I finally managed to drag her away, but she thrashed wildly in my arms as Elif knelt beside Agata to check on her. "Don't even think about it," Roman growled. Out of the corner of my eye, I saw Gelb freeze mid-step, clearly realizing that getting closer would be a mistake. I turned my wife in my arms until she faced me. "*Solnychko,*" I whispered, and she froze, her tear-filled eyes finally meeting mine.

My chest tightened at the sight of her tears, "she touched them, Nikolai," she breathed. "She hurt our sons." A heavy silence fell, thick and suffocating as tension crackled in the air like a brewing storm. "What ?" I asked, my voice dark, deeper than I recognized. Selina trembled in my arms. "She hurt them the same way I was hurt. They have bruises. They were so scared, Niko," she sobbed, and a ringing filled my ears. I shifted my gaze from my wife to my ex-mother-in-law, now propped against the bookshelf, blood trickling from her temple. I glanced at Elif, and without a word, she stepped in to take my place, wrapping her arm around Selina's shoulders as I walked slowly toward Agata, reaching behind my back for my gun. "Nikolai," Gelb said, his voice sharp—but he didn't move.

"You touched my children?" I asked, voice hollow. She shook her head, but I pressed the muzzle beneath her chin, halting her breath—and her excuses. "You touched my children?" I repeated, pressing harder as her lips sealed shut. "They're just children!" she burst out. "They need to be raised properly!" Selina's sob echoed painfully in the room as I flipped off the safety, my vision tinged in red.

"Nikolai," Grigori called out, stepping forward, "no," I growled. First she'd slapped my wife. Now, my children. No one touched my family and walked away. "Nikolai!" A new voice cut through the air, and Elif gasped. A small hand grabbed my wrist, and a slender body stepped between me and Agata. I looked down to find Nina's tear-streaked face, her jaw bruised, a dark ring blooming around her eye. "Please," she whispered, her voice trembling. I clenched my jaw, "please," she repeated, eyes closing as she exhaled a weary sigh.

I flicked the safety back on and lowered my weapon. I grasped her wrist and pulled her toward Elif, who embraced her protectively. Gelb rushed to his wife, who is now weeping uncontrollably. I turned to Grigori, standing motionless behind his desk. He gave a stiff nod. I faced the couple again. "You will never see my sons again. You will never set foot in our homes. You will never have a hand in any of our businesses," I said coldly, shoving my trembling hands into my pockets. Gelb opened his mouth, ready to argue, but I cut him off. "And Nina stays here. If you ever lay a hand on her again, I swear it will be the last thing you do, now get out."

I turned my back to them as Sasha and Roman moved in to escort them, their protests echoing through the hallway. I gathered Selina into my arms. "Nikolai, Selina... I'm sorry. I tried to stop her, but—" Nina's voice wavered as Selina suddenly pulled her into a hug. Both women cried silently. "Oh, my babies," Elif murmured, rubbing their backs as Grigori came to rest a hand on my shoulder. "Mama ?" a small voice called from the doorway. I looked up and saw Rafael and Andrei standing with Sienna. Selina quickly wiped her face, forcing a smile, "my angels," she whispered, opening her arms. They ran to her without hesitation. I knelt beside them and gently pulled down Rafael's collar as he buried his face against his mother's chest. My stomach turned at the marks around his neck. Then, I rolled up Andrei's sleeve. More bruises.

Behind me, Elif swore under her breath, ready to finish what Selina had started, but Grigori held her back. Sienna, on the other hand, was gone. And for once, I hoped she caused real damage. And prayers answered because screams erupted outside. I tensed, but Elif shook her head, "we'll handle it," she said, striding out with Grigori following. "I'll take them to the playroom," Nina offered, motioning for the boys. They each gave me a hug before following her, "thank you, Nina. For everything," I murmured as she closed the door. I turned to my wife, still sitting on the floor, staring at the blood-stained marble sphere.

"I could have killed her," she murmured, more to herself than to anyone else. I knelt, cupping her face in my hands. She looked up at me, her red-rimmed eyes full of anguish. "What came over me ? I could've killed her, Nikolai. Oh my God..." she sobbed again. "No, Selina.

You did what any mother would've done to protect her children." She shook her head, "you don't understand, Niko. I swore I'd never raise my hand against anyone. I swore I'd never become someone's monster." I pulled her into my arms as her tears soaked my shirt, as her pain cut through me. "Everything will be alright, *moy lubov'*. I promise," I whispered into her hair, breathing her in.

A gunshot suddenly rang out from outside, "*Blayt'*," I cursed as we bolted toward the hall. The Ignatievs' car sped away, another shot shattering its rear window. "Sienna !" Selina screamed, running outside just as Sasha snatched the gun from my sister-in-law and lifted her off the ground, though she continued to shout. "I don't give a damn about your business ! That bitch needs to die, you hear me ? Let me go this instant, *Hardman !*" "She's not wrong," my other sister-in-law muttered, arms crossed. Grigori glared, but she only shrugged, "nice shot, by the way," Roman said, staring after the car. "We should hit the range together, huh, Sienna?" He turned to face her—then froze. "Sienna ?" Sasha called out as her body went limp.

"I think… I think I need an injection," she murmured, clinging to his arm. "Oh, shit," Elif muttered, stepping closer. Selina sprinted back inside as Sasha carried Sienna to the couch, laying her down gently and elevating her legs. Elif brushed the hair from her forehead. "Roman, get her water," she ordered gently and he rushed off. "I'll call the doctor, just in case," Grigori said, striding toward the terrace. Moments later, Selina returned with a syringe. Sasha rolled up Sienna's shirt, exposing her stomach, and Selina injected the insulin quickly before collapsing beside her, clutching her hand. "I'm so sorry, Sienna. I'm so, so sorry for the other day," she whispered, pressing a kiss to her sister's hand as tears ran freely. I had to be the worst husband in the world to make my wife cry this much.

"You've got that same look you used to get when you smacked me on the back so I'd stop crying before Mom came in," Sienna chuckled weakly, and just like that, the room softened. "You cried over everything, you little brat," Selina replied, finally smiling. And just like that tension melted from my chest. Sienna laughed again and gripped Selina's hand to sit up. I helped her as Roman returned with the glass. "I added sugar," he said, eyes worried, "thanks," she murmured, sipping. "It's me who should be sorry, Selina. I… I'll tell you everything. Just give me a little more time, okay?"

Selina nodded and pulled her into a hug, eyes meeting mine over her sister's shoulder. I smiled softly and brushed away one of her tears. Yes. It was time we all took a vacation.

Selina

The sand was warm beneath my toes as I dug them in, watching the waves gently roll across the shore. The weather in the Philippines was glorious—even after sunset, the air remained soft and balmy. I smiled when strong arms wrapped around my waist, pulling me against a firm, heated chest. "Want to go for another walk?" my husband murmured, pressing a kiss to my neck. It had been nearly two weeks since we'd left for our honeymoon, and three days since we arrived in the Philippines. Tomorrow, the rest of the family would be joining us to spend a few days of vacation together. I missed the boys terribly. Even though we video-called at least twice a day, every single day, the longing was unbearable. This trip would be good for them—to help them finally move past what had happened with Agata a month ago. We had waited a few weeks to make sure the boys felt safe before leaving for our honeymoon. Honestly, I hadn't wanted to go, not when they were still so shaken. But Elif and Sienna had practically shoved me out the door.

Actually, no—they had literally thrown me out. Most of my things had already been packed in suitcases in the trunk of the car, and they had pushed me outside before slamming the door in my face. "No, I'd rather enjoy our last evening alone with my husband," I replied, turning in his arms and wrapping mine around his neck. "Hmm, is that so?" he murmured, his hand sliding beneath my skirt to grip my thigh, making me jump before bursting into laughter. "Yes." "My wife's requests are my commands," he declared before scooping me into his arms and carrying me toward our cabana as I laughed even harder. His eyes gleamed with happiness.

"Mama! Papa!" the twins and Rafael shouted excitedly the next morning from the boat approaching the shore, waving with all their might. I jumped up and down, waving back at them while Nikolai chuckled beside me, his arm wrapped securely around my waist, preventing me from throwing myself into the water to reach them. The two small boats finally cut their engines. Roman was the first to jump off, wading through the water up to his knees with Andrei on his back. He then helped Rafael, Alexei, Mikhail, and finally Nina down. Since the events of a month ago, Nina had been living with us, and as I expected, I had come to see her as another sister—just like Elif. She was kindness personified, endlessly patient and so understanding it felt almost surreal. And the boys adored her. They had told us how she had stepped between them and Agata when things had turned violent, how she had shielded them even when her own mother struck her with a cane. I think I spent the entire following week thanking her and sitting by her side as she recovered from her injuries.

From the second boat, Grigori was the first to jump, carrying his two sons in his arms. Sasha followed, helping Elif down and finally, my sister, determined to climb down on her own, turned her back to him. But when she struggled, Sasha simply grabbed her thighs and lifted her onto his shoulder in a seated position. She shrieked in protest while he grinned, unbothered. I ran toward my boys, ignoring the scorching sand beneath my feet, too overwhelmed with joy to care. "Oh, my babies !" I cried, pulling my three little ones into my arms, tears welling up despite myself. Nikolai embraced his brothers tightly. "We missed you so much," I whispered, straightening to pull Mikhail into my arms as well. He had been standing slightly behind the others, waiting patiently for his turn. "You look beautiful, Mama," he said, kissing my cheek before wrapping his arms around me. "Oh, my angel, you've grown even taller," I smiled as the rest of the family joined us.

The following days became some of the most precious of my life—water sports with the kids, sunbathing with the girls, family dinners on the beach under the moon, and the countless intimate moments shared with Nikolai. His touch, his kisses, his gaze—I wouldn't change a single thing about what we had lived together.

I squinted when the shutters of my room suddenly flew open. Groaning, I covered my face with my pillow—only for it to be snatched away. "Rise and shine, girl!" my sister exclaimed, smacking me with the very pillow she had just stolen. "Five more minutes," I grumbled, burying my face into the mattress. But my little sister was worse than a pit bull. "We're supposed to meet Elif for lunch on the beach," she said, launching herself onto me. I couldn't help but smile. "Mmm," I hummed, finally opening my eyes, despite my sore muscles, I felt like I was in paradise. Nikolai, even at his age, was surprisingly… fit. He had left a few hours ago to meet his brothers. "Nikolai really needs to stop torturing you every night," my sister muttered with a dramatic sigh. I was about to laugh when we heard the front door creak open. We both turned, and I frowned at the sight of Rafael.

"*Angelo mio*?" I called gently, but he quickly turned away, his eyes dark and unreadable. What the…? I jumped out of bed, grabbed my robe, and hurriedly slipped it on before rushing out of the cabin. I spotted him heading toward the main hut—the communal space. "Rafael!" I called after him, but he didn't stop. He pushed the door open, and I heard my husband's voice asking if he needed anything. "Stop torturing Mom at night!" my son suddenly shouted. I froze in the doorway. My husband and his brothers sat around a table, all staring in stunned silence as I felt heat rush to my face so fast it felt like I'd burst into flames. A long silence followed—until my sister burst into laughter behind me, loud enough to be heard across the island. Unsurprisingly, Roman joined in, laughing like a donkey as he slammed his fist on the table, nearly choking. Sasha smirked, patting Roman's back to help him recover. I didn't dare look at Grigori, but I caught him in my peripheral vision, smiling behind his hand.

"Oh my God," I groaned, burying my face in my hands as the two idiots continued cackling. Suddenly, I heard my son squeal, and when I looked up, he was hoisted over Nikolai's shoulder. My husband strode toward me with a smug smile on his face. I glared, ready to scold him, but I barely had time to react before he tossed me over his other shoulder. "Enough of your nonsense. Leave my family alone," he declared, carrying us both back to our cabin. And despite everything, I couldn't help but laugh.

Later that day, I traced my fingers along Nikolai's forearms as we sat on the beach under the moonlight. His nose brushed against my neck, his murmured words sending a shiver down my spine. "Andrei promised to make me a necklace with the seashells we collected today," I said, sighing as I melted into his chest. "Yes, he asked me for paint to decorate some of them. I'll buy some in the nearby village tomorrow," he replied, and I felt him smile against my skin. "Mikhail and Alexei want to go diving again tomorrow. I'll go with them—and Sienna too." He hummed against my neck, making me smile again. "I can't wait to go home in two days," I continued, ignoring his lips trailing lower toward my collarbone. "Do you think we could get a cat? I love cats." "Mmm," he hummed again, clearly ignoring me.

I sighed and turned in his arms, straddling his lap. He groaned. "Would you listen to me for a second?" I asked, raising an eyebrow. "But I am listening, *moy lyubov'*. I'm listening with all my senses," he murmured, playfully nipping at my jaw. Despite myself, I tightened my thighs around him. "We've spent two whole weeks together, Niko. How can you not be satisfied yet?" I whispered against his lips. His arms tightened around my waist, nearly knocking the breath out of me. "Satisfied ? With you ?" He kissed my cheek. "Never. Not even in ten years." A kiss on my forehead. "Not even in fifty." A kiss on my nose. "Not even in a century, Solnyshko. I'll never be satisfied when it comes to you. I'll never get enough of your voice or your laughter, never enough of your scent or your softness. Never enough of your taste or your warmth," he murmured, kissing me deeply, his fingers threading through my damp hair from our evening swim. I moaned against his lips, my hands gliding from his shoulders to his strong neck, into his wet hair. I tugged, and he pulled back with a low growl.

"A cat ?" I repeated against his lips. He groaned again, trying to reclaim my mouth, but I tightened my grip, lifting an eyebrow beneath his burning gaze. "For fuck's sake, ten if you want," he relented at last, breath hot against my lips. But I tugged on his hair once more. "And I'm starting work at the hospital as a nurse when we get back," I added with a sly smile. His gaze darkened even more and I yelped as I suddenly found myself on my back, pressed into the warm sand. One of his hands pinned both of mine against my stomach, while his broad shoulders settled between my parted thighs. "Nikolai," I whispered. "Unfortunately for you, I don't respond to blackmail, *Solnyshko*—especially not when you're the prize," he smiled before disappearing between my thighs, making me shiver and moan more than once through the night.

I woke with a start, a cold shiver running down my spine. Carefully extracting myself from Nikolai's arms, I stepped out onto the small terrace where the pool shimmered in the dark. I rubbed my arms as goosebumps covered my skin, my gut twisted, my heart raced, and nausea rose. Another panic attack ? No—it felt different. I sighed, gently tapping my chest, trying to ease the pain, but it was no use. Grabbing a cardigan from the chair, I left the cabin and headed toward the boys' cabin next door. Just as I was about to climb the steps, I stopped. Several footprints marked the sand in front of the door. That wasn't unusual—they'd been running around all day. But these were adult-sized. And the boys had forbidden anyone else from entering their cabin.

My heartbeat pounded in my ears as I heard an engine roar in the distance. I ran toward the beach, sharp pebbles digging into my bare feet. A boat was pulling away from the shore. "No ! No ! Papa ! Mama !" Andrei's voice carried through the air. I saw Rafael struggling with one of the men, while two others hauled Alexei and Mikhail—unconscious—into a cabin on board. My heart stopped. "Andrei! Rafael!" I screamed, pushing myself harder as the boat drifted farther away.

"Mama !" Rafael cried as my feet sank into the water. "Rafael ! Andrei ! Don't be afraid, I'm here !" I kept wading deeper, breathless, voices shouting behind me. "Selina !" I began to swim, but the boat grew smaller and smaller, a speck on the horizon. My body, drained from running, could no longer keep my head above water. My sons, my babies… no. Panic seized me. I thrashed against the waves, but the water pulled me under. I tried to reach them—I couldn't. Water rushed into my nose and mouth. I fought. I didn't want to give up. My sons. My husband. My sister. My family— Cool night air hit my face, and I gasped, choking on the water that had nearly killed me. "Breathe, Selina. Breathe," Nikolai's voice urged, just as breathless as I was. "Come on, Solnyshko, breathe." He pulled me toward the shore. Roman appeared beside us. In moments, the three of us were on the beach, gasping for air.

"Andrei ! Alexei !" I cried, trying to stand, but my legs wouldn't move. I crawled on my knees back toward the water, but an arm wrapped tightly around my waist. "No ! My sons !" I screamed, thrashing in his hold. I had to save them—I had to find them. "Selina, calm down. We'll find them, I promise you !" Nikolai said, holding me tighter. But I heard nothing. Felt nothing. Only the crushing, burning need to be with my babies. "Mikhail !" I kept calling, my sobs turning into hoarse cries. My voice broke, faded into a whisper—until everything went black.

Chapter forty
Nikolai

I looked at my wife's motionless body on the bed in our cabin as Sienna gently stroked her hair. "Andrei," she murmured again, and I felt myself falter. "The helicopters are here," Roman said as he reached the door of the cabin where I stood. I didn't dare enter—didn't dare approach her or touch her. Once again, I had failed in my duty. Failed in my promise. They had come silently in the night, killed six of our guards, disabled the engines of our boats to keep us from following them, and kidnapped the twins—Rafael and Mikhail—who had been sleeping in the same cabin. Right under our noses. Without us sensing a thing. Or almost nothing. Because my wife had known. A mother always knows—always feels it.

"Let's go," I said, stepping forward toward the helipad where Sasha, Grigori, and a dozen of our men were waiting, dressed in the same dark uniforms as mine and armed to the teeth. Elif was there too. "Lorenzo confirmed Antonio is on the yacht, but a helicopter is on its way to pick them up," Sasha said, handing me two guns which I strapped to my back. "Be careful. We'll meet in Singapore or Sochi," Grigori added, placing a firm hand on my shoulder. "Bring my babies home safe… and come back in one piece. All of you," Elif whispered, kissing Roman on the cheek, her eyes glistening as they landed on me. "Stay close to her until I return, will you?" I asked. She nodded and embraced me. "I won't take my eyes off her until you're back. I promise," she murmured against my neck. With a heavy heart but unshakable resolve, I climbed into the helicopter, which took off, followed by the second one.

Soon, we were flying over the sea, leaving behind the paradise island where I had lived the best days of my life. "Roman will lead the operation," I said through my headset as we neared the yacht's coordinates—where the boys and Antonio were supposed to be. It was the most logical choice—he was the only one with enough field experience and had led countless operations before. My brother nodded from across the cabin.

"Based on our satellite images, it's a two-deck yacht with a bridge and captain's cabin. Delta team takes the bridge and captain's quarters. Beta clears the lower deck. Alpha sweeps the main deck. Check your earpieces. Follow orders without hesitation." We all nodded, testing our equipment one last time. "We're at the drop point," the pilot announced an hour later. It was the location where we would jump to avoid being detected by the Italians. Roman opened the side door and jumped into the water without hesitation. One by one, we followed, plunging into the dark, cold sea. I gritted my teeth at the impact, sharper than expected. Without surfacing, I swam toward the coordinates flashing on my digital watch—just a few meters from the drop point. After about ten minutes, the yacht finally appeared before us.

"Delta, port side. Beta, starboard. Alpha, stern," Roman instructed through the comms. I followed him toward the stern, both of us part of Alpha. Sasha moved off to the right with Beta. Silently, the four of us climbed out of the water. Roman signaled us to stay low as we heard footsteps approaching from the lower decks. In one fluid motion, my brother slid beside the door, and when a guard stepped through, he grabbed him by the throat. The man reached for his weapon, but I caught his arm, twisting it as I landed a punch to his face. Roman then snapped his neck without a word. He dragged the body under the stairs and covered it with a tarp before drawing his weapon and leading us down the stairs. We followed, guns raised. At the bottom, Roman raised two fingers— two guards were approaching. I nodded and holstered my gun, switching to silent.

He grabbed the first guard and shoved him toward me while punching the second in the face. I caught the man in a chokehold and stabbed him in the ribs repeatedly until he went limp in my arms. "This is Delta. All clear," came the voice of the Delta team leader. "This is Beta. Second-floor hallway clear. Room sweeps in progress," Sasha followed. Roman raised his weapon and advanced down the corridor. "This is Alpha. Room sweeps in progress." I followed closely, ears tuned for any sound— any sign of my sons. My grip tightened on the pistol. I would find them. I had to. We reached the first door. Roman took the left, I the right, and David stood center, weapon drawn. I reached for the handle, ready to breach, when static suddenly crackled in our earpieces.

"Evacuate the yacht immediately ! It's a trap ! There's a bomb ! The children and Antonio aren't on board !" A woman's voice—unfamiliar, frantic—screamed through the interference. I froze, trying to process her words, then turned to Roman for a decision. But he stood frozen, as if struck by lightning. "You," he whispered, bringing a finger to his earpiece. "Leave the yacht immediately ! The bomb could go off any second ! You're all going to die ! Roman !" The same voice again—piercing, desperate. And it snapped my brother out of his trance. His wide eyes met mine just as he grabbed my arm. "Evacuate ! Evacuate !" he shouted, dragging me toward the stairs. We climbed two at a time, hearts pounding. But everything felt slow—like time had bent around us. My thoughts raced. Was it true ? Were the boys really not here ? Was I abandoning them when I'd been so close? But even if I didn't trust that woman, I trusted my brother. So I followed him without hesitation when he leapt into the water.

A searing blast scorched my back just as I hit the surface, and my thoughts immediately went to Sasha—he had been on the second floor, even farther from the exit than we were. His name tore from my throat the instant my head broke above the waves, but there was no response. "Sasha !" I called again, straining to hear his voice amid the shouting of our men and the crackling splinters of burning wood. My eyes scanned frantically for him, for any sign of his team. Nothing. "Sasha !" This time, Roman yelled too as he reached me, pulling me farther from the yacht. "Here !" Finally, my younger brother's voice cut through the chaos. He emerged from behind the smoking vessel, dragging one of our unconscious men to the surface. A rush of relief surged through me as I swam toward them. "You're hurt," I said, noticing the blood trickling from the side of his face. "I hit the railing when I jumped. It's nothing—just a cut on my brow," he panted, barely out of breath, as two of our men took the unconscious soldier and hoisted him onto a floating plank. "I called the pilot. He's on his way," Roman said, slipping his radio into the pocket of his jacket. "What the hell was that ?" I demanded, looking between my brothers. But before either could respond, Roman signaled for us to remove our earpieces.

"David, take over communications," he ordered. David nodded and moved off to relay the orders. "Someone infiltrated our comms," Roman said. "We might still be compromised." I nodded slowly, then turned to Sasha. "Did Lorenzo betray us ?" I asked, my rage simmering just beneath the surface. "No. Impossible," he said firmly, wiping the blood away from his eye. "Lorenzo would never betray us. But that woman… Who was she ?" He turned to Roman, and I, too, waited for his answer. Who was this woman he had trusted without hesitation ? Roman exhaled deeply, running a hand through his soaked hair, avoiding my eyes. "I… I'm not sure," he admitted. I narrowed my gaze. "You followed the orders of some woman, abandoned the mission, and you don't know why ?" I asked, stunned by his uncharacteristic behavior. Roman never acted without reason. He never made rash decisions. "Her voice," he murmured, finally meeting my eyes. "I recognized it. It was her." And instantly, I understood. The woman who had saved him years ago, during that mission in the Middle East. The owner of the pendant he never took off.

"For fuck's sake, Roman !" I growled, clenching my eyes shut. "What if she was lying? What if my kids were on that goddamn yacht?!" "She saved our lives, *moy brat* !" he snapped. "Without her, we'd be fish food right now!" I clenched my jaw, forcing down my frustration. I needed to focus. I needed to find my sons. I needed to bring them back to Selina. Back to my wife.

"Fine. I get it. But whoever she is—if she knew about the trap, then she might know where the boys are. We need to find her," I said, just as the sound of approaching helicopters roared above us. Hold on, boys. We're coming. I'm coming.

Selina

I shook my head and pushed away the bottle my sister offered me. She sighed but didn't insist. I watched the travelers rushing in all directions through the bustling hall of Singapore's airport, and I felt nothing but anger. I was angry that life continued as if nothing had happened, while my children were no longer by my side. Angry that I hadn't woken up sooner. Angry that I had failed to save them. I was angry that Nikolai hadn't reached them in time either. Angry that he had nearly lost his life today—along with his brothers. They had almost died. Antonio had nearly killed them. I pressed a hand over my mouth, trying to suppress the sudden wave of nausea washing over me. I took a deep breath and closed my eyes, but the image of my sons on that boat resurfaced instantly. Tears welled up, and I leaned forward, burying my face in my hands. I wanted to hold my boys. I wanted to see their smiles. I wanted my husband to wrap his arms around me. I wanted to feel his warmth, breathe in his scent.

"Selina ?" Elif's voice pulled me from my thoughts as her hand gently settled on my shoulder. I sat up straight, quickly wiping away the tears as she took the seat beside me. "How are you feeling, sweetheart ?" "I feel a little nauseous, but I'll be fine. Everything will be fine as soon as my boys are home," I said, meeting her dark, searching eyes. She hesitated for a moment before asking, "When… when was the last time you had your period, Selina?"

I frowned at the question, confused, while my sister leaned in, listening intently. "I… what? I don't know. My cycle's never been regular," I replied, still not understanding where this was going. "Oh my God. Do you think… do you think she's pregnant?" my sister whispered, and I froze. Pregnant? Me? My hands instinctively moved to my lower abdomen. A baby… Nikolai's and mine? Suddenly, memories from the past few weeks flashed through my mind—the constant nausea, the exhaustion, the mood swings. The uncontrollable emotions. "I don't know," I murmured, staring into the distance. My throat tightened, as if the entire world were closing in around me. "I need to go to the bathroom," I said, pushing myself up on shaky legs. "I'll come with you," both women offered at once, but I shook my head. "No… I just… I need to be alone. Please," I added when Elif looked ready to protest. After a brief hesitation, they both settled back into their seats, silently watching me as I walked away. Out of the corner of my eye, I spotted familiar faces—our bodyguards, strategically positioned throughout the terminal.

As I finally reached the hallway leading to the restrooms, I suddenly collided with an Asian woman. She caught me just in time before I stumbled to the floor. "I'm sorry—" "Antonio is waiting for your response," she said in Italian, slipping a phone and a folded piece of paper into my hand before continuing on her way without a second glance. I froze, my mind reeling, struggling to make sense of what had just happened. Her words echoed in my ears. My hands trembled as I pushed open the bathroom door and locked myself in a stall. With shaking fingers, I unfolded the paper.

Cara mia,

We are waiting for you with our son and the Ivanov brats. Get on the plane I've arranged for you and join us. Call the number on the phone for detailed instructions. I promise I will return the little Ivanovs to their father once we are reunited.

Your loving husband,

Antonio.

It was too much. I pushed up from the toilet, lifted the lid, and vomited what little food I had managed to eat on the plane that morning. My throat burned. My eyes burned. My entire body burned. A sudden knock on the stall door made me flinch. "Are you okay in there ?" a woman asked. I swallowed my sobs, forcing myself to stay composed, "yes, thank you," I replied, flushing the toilet. I sat back down, waiting until I heard her footsteps fade away before turning on the phone. Only one contact was saved. It had to be the number for instructions. Should I have called Nikolai ? Gone straight to Grigori in the main hall ? But what if Antonio had people watching us ? If he found out I'd told anyone, he would hurt my sons. No. I couldn't take that risk. Another wave of nausea surged, but I forced it down. I stepped out of the stall, dragging myself to the sink. I rinsed my mouth, then splashed cold water on my face. "You know it's a trap, don't you ?" The voice behind me made me jolt.

I spun around sharply. A woman stood by the far wall, wearing a black cap and a matching mask. Her dark hair fell in soft waves just above her chest. She was the same woman who had knocked on my stall door earlier—I recognized her voice. "Wha... what ?" I stammered, clutching the counter behind me, pressing the phone and note tightly to my chest. She pushed off the wall and walked toward me with unsettling calm, "Antonio is using your children to lure you in," she said. I tensed, holding my breath as she snatched the note from my hand before I could react. "Hey !" I snapped, lunging to get it back. She dodged me effortlessly, scanning the words. "Give it back!" I shouted, stumbling in my rush. I braced for impact, but a firm grip caught my arm and steadied me. I looked up into eyes so dark it was nearly impossible to tell where the pupils ended. She handed the paper back with a sigh, then crossed her arms.

"He won't send the other three boys home," she said, as if reciting a weather report. "Best-case scenario, he turns them into soldiers—forces them to fight against their own family. The twins are still young. Easy to mold. As for the eldest, he'll use drugs to brainwash him. Worst case ?" She met my gaze. "He kills them in front of you. To punish you." Her voice was calm. Measured. Emotionless. I grimaced, trying to hold it together. But it was useless. I lurched back to the toilet and vomited again. Cool fingers lifted my hair, and I sighed as fresh air brushed my neck. "I'm sorry to be so blunt, Selina," she said gently as I sobbed, "but you need to understand the gravity of this situation." "Who... who are you ?" I whispered, sniffling like a child while she helped me sit again. She handed me a tissue and knelt in front of me, resting her hands on my trembling knees, "let's just say... I want to be your friend," she said softly, her eyes steady beneath the brim of her cap. "Why ?" I asked.

She hesitated, staring at the ground for a moment before looking up again. "A long time ago, a woman saved my life. At first, I thought I was just lucky. But later, I realized it wasn't random. It was so I could save others in return. That's what I promised her. That's what I've sworn to do until my last breath." There was no doubt in her eyes. No hesitation in her voice. And I didn't need anything more to know she was telling the truth. Because I recognized that look—the one I had seen in my own reflection, every time I swore I'd survive just one more day for Rafael. "I know it's a trap," I whispered, shaking my head, "but... I have no choice. I know Antonio won't harm Rafael, but the twins and Mikhail... they're not safe as long as they're with him." I exhaled sharply. "And we have no other leads. My husband and his brothers nearly died..." "I know," she said, watching me carefully. "And it doesn't matter if it's a trap. If you want to go, then you'll go, Selina."

A chill ran through me. It felt like I was standing before something immovable. Something unstoppable. And for some reason, I trusted her. "We're going to save your sons, Selina," she said calmly. "And we're going to end that son of a bitch Antonio. Together." She held out her hand. I pressed my lips together, studying her. She stood like stone. Unflinching. Like nothing could bring her down. I took her hand and rose to my feet. Nothing would bring me down either. Not until I'd saved my sons. Not until I'd seen Antonio dead.

Chapter forty-one

Nikolai

The lights of the manor in Sochi finally came into view as the helicopter I was in with my brothers approached the landing strip. Roman nudged Sasha, who had dozed off beside him in the co-pilot's seat, as he gently landed the aircraft on the tarmac. I saw several silhouettes approaching the helicopter, but I didn't dare look— afraid I might meet my wife's gaze. Ever since I had heard her sobbing on the other end of the line when we called to inform them about the trap on the yacht, I hadn't called again. And now, like a coward, I remained seated inside, avoiding her disappointed eyes. As I scrambled for an excuse, the side door suddenly opened, and my heart stopped.

I leapt from the cockpit, and my breath caught again at the sight of Sienna crying a few feet away as Sasha rushed to her and pulled her into his arms. "What's going on?" I asked, turning to my sister, who looked pale. Roman joined us, wrapping an arm around her shoulders. "Nikolai, I'm so sorry. I don't know what happened," she said, a tear slipping down her cheek. "Where is Selina?" I demanded, cupping her face and wiping away the tear. "We were waiting for the jet to be prepped in Singapore. She went to the restroom and… and she never came back, Nikolai. We went to check, but she was gone," she said, gripping my wrists with her ice-cold hands. "Grigori stayed behind to search for her. We didn't want to tell you until we had more information, but he hasn't found anything. He's on his way back," she added, pressing her lips together.

I stepped back, my hands shaking, my vision narrowing. First my sons, and now my wife. *Fuck. Fuck. Fuck.* I grabbed my hair, trying to think, trying to find a solution, but I couldn't even hear my own thoughts. I turned toward the helicopter and slammed my fist against the hood again and again. I felt nothing. Heard nothing. I just wanted to find my wife and my children, to hear them laugh, to hold them close to me. Arms wrapped around me, pulling me back, but I fought them off. I was weak—a coward who had failed to protect his family. I shoved Sasha away and pushed Roman when he tried to restrain me. I was a madman—untethered, lost. I froze when a much frailer body embraced me, trembling with sobs. "Please, Nikolai, please," Sienna begged, her tear-streaked face pressed against my chest. "You have to save them," she whispered, lifting her eyes to mine—eyes so much like my wife's, her face resembling Selina's so closely it made my stomach twist.

Where was she? Had she been kidnapped? Threatened? Were they hurting her? Was she scared? And my sons? My mind finally began to function again, slowly rebooting. My arms tightened around my sister's trembling frame, and I gently rubbed her back. "I will bring them home," I vowed, my voice like stone. "I swear on my life, Sienna—I will bring them back."

"I don't have any leads yet. I'm waiting for a call from one of my informants inside Rasili's circle," Lorenzo said over speakerphone as we paced around the dining table, Sasha's phone on speaker between us. "I'm coming to join you, Lorenzo. Let's check with the dock workers—maybe they overheard something during deliveries," Sasha said, shoving his hands into his pockets. "And I'll go to tonight's race. Someone there might know something—some of them rub shoulders with the Italians," Roman added, grabbing his jacket from the back of the couch.

"We'll find them, *moy brat*. Don't doubt it," he said, clapping me on the back before heading out, followed by Sasha, who gave me a knowing look. I nodded, and they both left. "I'll contact Capo Marino. He must know something," I said, pulling out my phone, but Elif grabbed my arm. "Niko, we haven't spoken to him in years. Calling him now to ask for a favor is like handing him a loaded gun," she warned. I shook my head and took her hand. "Marino leads *Cosa Nostra's* army. Lorenzo reports to him. If Lorenzo has any information, then Marino must know more. And if he wants my soul in exchange for telling me where my family is, then so be it," I said, locking eyes with her. She studied me for a moment, finally realizing how serious I was. With a sigh, she let go of my hand.

I stepped onto the terrace and closed the door behind me before dialing Marino's number. Dawn was breaking, casting a pink hue across the sky—the same color as the dress my wife had worn the first time I saw her. I closed my eyes as the line rang. I clenched my jaw, ready to hang up, when suddenly Marino's voice echoed through the receiver. "Capo Marino speaking," he said, his deep voice always reminding me of my father. If he were still alive, they'd be the same age now. Dark thoughts stirred, but I pushed them away. Focus, Nikolai. Focus. "This is Nikolai Ivanov," I said, shoving my clenched fist into my pocket. "Ah, a little Ivanov calling me. To what do I owe this honor?" he asked, his tone light as I heard a chair scrape—he was probably standing. "I need a favor," I said through gritted teeth, waiting for his answer. The kind of answer that could change everything. A long silence followed, and despite myself, I held my breath, gripping the phone like it was the last thread tethering me to reason. "What's the subject?" Relief swept over me, "Rasili."

He let out a long sigh, while I held mine in, "to think he's become an international problem. Should I be proud of the reputation he's giving *Cosa Nostra* ?" he muttered, irony thick in his voice. "He has my wife and my sons," I said, gripping the railing so hard my knuckles turned white. Pride and ego burned in my throat, but I swallowed them. For my wife. For my sons. "I see," he murmured, waiting for me to say more. "Do you have any information on their whereabouts ?" I asked, trying to keep my voice steady. "You're asking me to betray one of my own, Ivanov?" "I'm asking you to help me find my family, Marino." A heavy silence stretched between us. I heard whispering in the background. A woman?

"Marino…" I prompted. "What I was going to say before you started spitting hellfire was that Antonio Rasili has been disowned by his father. Rasili senior kicked him out—said he wouldn't shelter a traitorous slut dragging the family name through the mud. Don't get mad! I'm just repeating what I heard," he added as my blood boiled. "So, Antonio is acting alone. *Cosa Nostra* isn't involved in this, Nikolai." I shook my head, though he couldn't see me. "No, Marino. If I don't have my family back by tomorrow, this will become a war between *Bratva* and *Cosa Nostra*." "Are you threatening us, Ivanov?" His tone sharpened. "I'm warning you," I growled. "The last war will look like child's play if Rasili so much as touches a hair on my family's heads." I slammed my fist against the railing. More whispering echoed on his end. "Marino…" "Antonio has no access to *Cosa Nostra's* resources. Don't waste time searching beyond reach—he doesn't have the means to flee to the U.S. or even Italy," he said. "That's all I can tell you, Nikolai. I hope you find your wife and your sons," he added before hanging up.

I set the phone down on the cold stone and braced myself against it, shoulders hunched. And then, it happened—a tear. Followed by another. And another. I clenched my jaw until it cracked. I tried to breathe, but the air wouldn't come. I tried to think, but the world blurred around me. All I could see was Selina crying. All I could hear was the memory of her pain. All I could imagine was what Antonio might be doing to her now. And my sons—were they cold? Hungry ? Afraid ? Of course they were afraid. "Nikolai !" Elif suddenly called from inside. I heard the panic in her voice and rushed to her, quickly wiping my cheeks. "What is it ?" I asked as I reached her and Sienna, both hunched over her phone. "I just got a link," Sienna said, her voice trembling. "It came with a message: Follow this if you want to find Selina and the boys." She pressed the link. A map appeared, marked with a red dot. "Baku, Azerbaijan," she read aloud. "Do you think that's where they are ?" Elif asked, lifting her worried eyes to meet mine.

I held out my hand, and Sienna gave me her phone. I scrolled through her messages to find the number that had sent the link. I tried calling, but it was unreachable. "How do we know if this is real?" Sienna asked, her reddened eyes darting between me and the phone. A thousand thoughts rushed through my mind—real or not? We all froze when the phone chimed again—a new message from the same number. A voice message. I pressed play and almost flinched when I heard my wife's voice.

"Sienna, I'm sorry I left like that, but I had to... I have to find my babies. Antonio contacted me, promising he wouldn't hurt any of them if I came to him. Now, listen to me carefully, sorella mia—the person sending you my location only wants to help me. Help us. Trust them, okay? And come find me. I know you'll come. I know Nikolai will come. I'll be waiting with the boys. I love you. And... tell Nikolai that I love him too. That I thank him for every moment he's given me since we met. That I thank him for teaching me how to live again, how to love and be loved unconditionally."

Her voice trembled, and I didn't miss the sound of her sob as the message ended. "Oh, Selina... what have you done?" Sienna breathed, shaking her head and burying her face in her hands. "She walked straight into a trap, knowing it was a trap," Elif sighed, wrapping an arm around Sienna's shoulders. I stared at the phone in my hand, my wife's words looping in my head—her trembling voice, her sob. To love and be loved unconditionally. I forwarded the link to my own phone and switched to autopilot. Skirting around my sisters, I headed to the basement. The helicopter was still outside—I would use it to get to Baku. "Nikolai! Nikolai, wait!" Elif called after me, but I ignored her. I reached the weapons room and began to gear up. Already dressed in my combat clothes, I didn't need to change. I just grabbed a waterproof jacket and threw it over my black compression shirt.

"Nikolai ! You can't go alone ! Wait for your brothers ! Grigori will be here in an hour at most, and Sienna is trying to reach Sasha and Roman!" Elif insisted, following me. I shook my head, "there's no way I'm leaving my family in that son of a bitch's hands for another hour." I zipped up my jacket and headed for the exit, but my sister stepped in front of me, gripping my sleeve. "I can't… I can't lose anyone else, Nikolai. Please," she pleaded, her panicked eyes locking onto mine. I hated seeing her like this. I hated even more that it was because of me. But I couldn't. I couldn't wait for my brothers and leave my family behind. "I have to go get them, Elif. I… I have to," I said, my determined gaze meeting hers. Tears spilled from her eyes as she realized she wouldn't be able to stop me. Finally, she nodded and stepped back. I pulled her into a hug, pressing a kiss to her hair. "I'm bringing them home, Elif. We're all having dinner together tomorrow night. I promise you."

She sobbed into my chest but nodded again. "I know. I know you will," she said, stepping back and wiping her tears. "But if you want me to let you go feeling even a little reassured, then I need you to do something for me." I looked at her, confused, as her own determination settled in.

Selina

The car glided through the dim streets of an unfamiliar city, in a country I had never set foot in, flanked by two equally unfamiliar men. They had awaited me near the private jet and had not spoken a single word since. Not one. Discreetly, I adjusted my bra, where I had hidden the tiny phone Ferna had given me at the airport. I doubted it was her real name, but at the time, I hadn't dared ask.

Twelve Hours Earlier…

I splashed water on my face for the umpteenth time and accepted the tissue the woman handed me. "Thank you," I murmured. "So… are you really going to help me?" "Of course I am, Selina. With everything I've got," she replied, brushing my damp hair back the same way Sienna or Elif would have done. "Quick, before Antonio starts suspecting anything," she said, pulling a small phone from her dark jacket. "This one's modified. Undetectable by any tech in the world. It's got GPS so I can track your every move. I'll send your location to your sister—she'll show it to the Ivanovs, no doubt," she explained, handing me the tiny device. "And if they search me?" I asked, gripping the phone, no larger than my palm. "They won't. I'm sure that psychopath has forbidden anyone from touching you. Still, hide it in your bra. Even if they try, they won't dare go there."

She opened her own jacket and lifted her shirt. I frowned as she began unwrapping something from around her waist. "Lift your sweatshirt," she said, kneeling. I obeyed. She wound a heavy fabric around my stomach. "Sorry. I wanted to bring you a bulletproof vest, but it wasn't discreet enough. This will have to do. At least the little one will be safe."

"The... the little one?" I echoed, confused. "I think your sister and Elif are right—you're probably pregnant. That'd explain the mood swings. Otherwise, I can't see why you'd follow that idiot to a street race," she muttered the last part more to herself, but I heard it. "You mean Roman?" At the mention of my brother-in-law, she stiffened. I saw the grimace behind her mask. She'd said too much. "You know Roman?" I asked, but she said nothing. She stepped back, pulling out another phone—hers, I presumed. "We need a recording. I'll send it to your sister, so she'll trust me. Say something that proves you're doing this by choice."

She handed me the device with the voice recorder already open. I spoke the only words I knew would reach Sienna. "Remember—pretend this meeting never happened." She took my hands. They were warm but calloused, nothing like I had imagined. "I'll be with you every second, Selina. I'll track you constantly. Even if they find the phone, I'll find another way to reach you. And I'll send your coordinates to the Ivanovs—to your husband." I bit my lip to keep it from trembling, but I couldn't stop the tears from spilling. "I'm scared," I whispered. "I'm so scared. I can't go back to him. I can't." My sons were in his clutches—perhaps hungry, thirsty, terrified. And I stood there, shaking, unable to face Antonio again. His eyes, his touch, his scent—they all made my skin crawl. Then her arms wrapped around me. I collapsed into her warmth, breathing in a soft jasmine scent as I sobbed harder. "I didn't survive past thirty by being brave all the time," she murmured. "It was often fear that pushed me forward. If I'd let it control me, I wouldn't be here. You're one of the bravest women I've met. You'll get your sons back. You'll go home."

I pulled away, sniffling like a child, ashamed of my swollen, tear-streaked face. "You're older than me?" I asked, squinting at her. To my surprise, she laughed. "That's what you took from my poetic, motivational speech?" "Sorry," I grimaced, making her laugh again. But her laughter died as she touched her earpiece, "understood," she said, bringing her hand to her mouth. "Your sister's coming. I'll create a distraction. You take the left hallway, exit through the emergency door, then call the number Antonio gave you, okay?"

I exhaled slowly, pushing back the tide of fear and doubt. "Okay," I nodded, slipping the phone into my bra with trembling hands. "You'll be all right. And don't forget—we're here. Every step of the way," she said, heading for the door. "Wait !" I caught her hand. "What's your name ?" She hesitated. "Ferna. You can call me Ferna," she answered, squeezing my hand gently before stepping out. A moment later, I followed—but turned left toward the emergency exit, Antonio's phone tight in my grasp.

Present...

The car jerked to a stop. Dusk had settled as I stepped out, dodging the man who tried to grab my arm. "Don't touch me !" I snapped, backing away. My eyes scanned the shadows, desperate to catch a glimpse of my sons. But only warehouses surrounded us. Just as I opened my mouth to call out to them, a sickening dread curled in my gut. I couldn't breathe. He was here. I felt it. I knew it. "*Cara mia*, there you are," the demon's voice rang out between the silent buildings. I exhaled shakily. *Stay calm, Selina. Calm.* Nikolai would come. He always did. I turned toward the voice, and there he stood in the doorway of a warehouse, arms spread wide, that monstrous smile nearly reaching his ears. I clenched my fists. "Where are my sons ?!" I shouted. And thank God, my voice did not tremble. Inside, I was shaking, but outside—I stood firm.

"Come now, *Cara mia*. Looks like you've grown wings since your little Russian honeymoon," he said, cocking his head, making my stomach turn. Everything about him repulsed me. The way he spoke, the way he smiled, the way he looked at me. I felt nothing but disgust and hatred for him. For everything he had done to me these past eight years. For the trauma he had inflicted on Rafael. For what he had done to Sienna eight years ago. For all the horrors he had put me and my family through. He had kidnapped Roman and tortured him. He had forced me to be separated from my son. He had nearly killed Sienna. And most recently, he had almost taken the lives of my husband and his brothers. Not to mention all the men he had slaughtered when he attacked the shipments. Rage surged within me—a hatred so overwhelming I could barely contain it, "go to hell," I spat, hurling the words with venom, spitting at his feet.

He lowered his gaze to the ground, and I sensed it coming before I felt it. The slap whipped my head to the side, but I did not fall. I did not waver. I would not let him break me—not anymore. I turned back to him, met his dark gaze, his face twisted in fury. And then I did something I never thought I would dare. I slapped him back.

Hard.

Hard enough to make my hand tingle. Hard enough to make him stumble backward a few steps. Hard enough to leave the red imprint of my fingers across his cheek. "You will never break me again. You will never control me again," I declared, kicking him in the shin, making him grunt in pain. Then I punched him in the throat— just as Roman had taught me—cutting off his breath. "Never again !" I screamed, over and over, until his men seized my arms, dragging me away from him. Antonio clutched his throat, coughing violently, and I couldn't stop the hysterical laughter bubbling up at the sight of his son-of-a-bitch face and the red welt on his cheek. "You're pathetic, Antonio Rasili! Nothing but filth! A dog on a leash held by your father ! You trapped me in the worst way, using my sister ! She almost got raped because of you !" I shouted, screaming until the tears flowed freely, struggling against the grip of the men holding me.

Antonio stared at me, wide-eyed, one hand on his throat, the other still pressed to his burning cheek. "Ah, Selina, I'm going to take such pleasure in breaking the wings you've grown," he hissed, then lunged toward me and struck me again. This time, I collapsed to the ground, the metallic taste of blood spreading in my mouth. "Your sister should have shut up and satisfied my cousin instead of stabbing him with a pair of scissors ! Though I must admit, that video has served me well, hasn't it ? All these years you submitted to me, fearing I'd expose her as the murderer of my cousin—one of the Rasili heirs. Do you know what they'll do to her once they find out the truth, *Cara mia* ? Tortures you can't even imagine. But let me show you." He grabbed a fistful of my hair, yanked me to my knees, and struck me again, slamming me back to the ground. I spat out the blood pooling in my mouth and glared up at him with all the hatred I possessed. He froze, his hand raised, and for the first time, I saw it in his eyes—an emotion foreign to him : *fear*.

"I'm going to kill you, Antonio. And while you rot in a pit, Rafael and I will live happily with my husband and my sons." "I am your husband !" he shrieked, and before I could shield myself, his foot smashed into my side. But to my surprise, the pain remained superficial—the protection Ferna had given me worked. "It's me ! It's me !" he bellowed, kicking me again and again. One blow landed squarely against my chest, and I gasped. I shut my eyes as his foot arced toward my face—but the blow never came. A thud echoed in my ears. Then a grunt. I opened my eyes and gasped. A slender figure straddled Antonio, raining punches on him. "Mikhail !" I sobbed as I rose, just as the sound of more shouting filled the air.

"Mama !" my sons screamed, racing out of the warehouse, two men in pursuit. "My babies !" I cried, trying to stand and reach them, but I barely managed to get on my knees before Andrei hurled himself into my arms. "Let me go, bastards ! Let go !" Mikhail shouted as one of the men picked him up and threw him to the ground. "Mikhail !" I cried, but he stood again, placing himself between Antonio and me. "Why did you come, Mama ? Why ?" Rafael wept, his little hands cupping my cheeks—hands that no longer seemed so little. He had grown so much with the Ivanovs. "You shouldn't have come, Mama !" Alexei sobbed, clutching my hand and showering it with kisses, making me cry harder. "Go, Mama, you have to go," Andrei insisted, backing away, his tear-filled eyes locked on mine. "He's going to hurt you. Go, Mama," he pleaded again.

But I shook my head, pulling them all to me, "how could I have abandoned you ? Never. Never would I have left you," I whispered, feeling my heart break as their trembling bodies clung to mine. "How touching," growled the devil, now standing before Mikhail. I stood too, pulling the little ones behind me, trying to reach for Mikhail, but he refused to move, "Mikhail…" "Stay behind Mom," he said without breaking eye contact with Antonio. "I told you to keep them inside !" Antonio roared, turning to the men who had chased the boys. "Sorry, boss, they attacked us when they heard the screams," one stammered—and those were his last words. Antonio drew his gun and fired several shots into the man's chest. I screamed, reaching for Mikhail's shirt to drag him back, but he wouldn't budge.

If anything, he stood taller—arms spread to shield us. Antonio sighed and raised his gun again. "You hit almost as well as your father… but not as well as your uncles," he sneered. "You promised to let them go if I came ! You promised !" I cried, trying to step in front of my son, but he held me back. Antonio laughed darkly. "Ah, *Cara mia*, your naïveté is still what I love most about you. To see that, despite all your suffering, you remained so pure… it excites me beyond words!" Nausea surged, but I swallowed it down. *Focus, Selina. Stay calm. Ferna is here. Nikolai is coming.* He always comes.

"Enough games. It's time to go home. Pity—you'd have made a fine soldier for the *Cosa Nostra*, boy. But you look far too much like your bastard of a father," he sneered— and I understood. Adrenaline shot through me. The gunshot rang out, and I shoved Mikhail just in time to the ground. Not fast enough. "Mikhail !" I screamed as his blood blossomed across his shirt. The bullet had pierced his shoulder—not his chest—but it was still grave, especially for a boy his age. "Mikhail," I repeated, pressing both hands to the wound, making him moan. "It's going to be okay, my baby, it's going to be okay," I wept as the boys surrounded us. "Mama ! Here, Mama !" Alexei cried, tearing off his T-shirt and handing it to me. I pressed it firmly against the wound.

"Everything will be fine, I promise you," I whispered, tears blinding me, my hands and clothes drenched in my son's blood. "Don't cry, Mama," Mikhail murmured, but I shook my head. "Shh, my angel, don't speak. Don't tire yourself," I whispered, stroking his hair. "Seems these damn Ivanovs are unkillable," Antonio growled as he stepped toward us. "Let's go, *Cara mia*," he said, grabbing my arm and yanking me upright—but a hand latched onto mine, holding me back. "Mikhail," I breathed, seeing his fingers tighten around mine. "Don't touch my mother, asshole," he spat. "Unkillable and stubborn," Antonio muttered, tugging harder on my arm, prying me from my son's grasp.

"Alexei ! Press on the wound ! Hard !" I shouted as Antonio dragged me away. Alexei obeyed, while Rafael and Andrei clutched at my shirt, trying to pull me back. "Let go of Mama !" But nothing worked. Antonio dragged me toward a car, my feet skidding over the gravel. "Let go of me ! Let go of me !" I screamed, fought, clawed, bit.

Ferna was here. Nikolai was coming. He always found us. He would always find me.

Chapter forty-two
Selina

Antonio approached the car as I screamed, joined by my sons, who still tried to stop him. Andrei grabbed his thigh and bit down hard, making him grunt in pain. He shoved him off and struck him at the temple with the butt of his gun, drawing a thin trickle of blood from my baby's brow. "Andrei !" "Let go of Mama!" Rafael kept screaming, pounding his fists against Antonio's back, but he ignored him entirely. "Don't worry, kid. We'll be home soon," he muttered as he opened the back door of the car. Panic surged through me. I could not let him take me. I could not abandon my sons. They needed me. Suddenly, I stopped resisting. The moment he yanked me forward again, I stumbled into him, throwing us both off balance. He groaned as his head slammed against the car's frame, but I was already up again, grabbing Rafael's hand and pulling Andrei with me. We sprinted toward Mikhail and Alexei, but before we got far, Antonio seized me by the hair and yanked me back.

I screamed in pain. "I hope you'll be just as feisty in bed, *Cara mia*," he murmured against my neck, his voice thick with lust. "That really turns me on." The wave of disgust that surged within me gave rise to an explosion of fury. "The thought of you naked makes me sick, asshole ! And your dick isn't even a third of Nikolai's!" I screamed. I didn't care what I said anymore—I only wanted to wound him. If not with my fists, then with my words. He spun me around violently, forcing me to face him, but I couldn't help the twisted sense of triumph that bubbled up at the sight of his face contorted with rage. "You little—" "He makes me scream all night in positions you couldn't even imagine !" I spat. "All night long, because he has stamina you'll never even dream of with your pathetic weakness !"

His expression darkened, and his hand lifted to strike me, but he froze at the sound of screeching tires. A car barreled toward us, coming to a hard stop between the warehouses. In an instant, Antonio's men surrounded it, guns drawn and ready. My heart skipped a beat as I saw who stepped out. "Nikolai," I whispered. "Mikhail !" His voice broke when he saw our son lying in a pool of blood. He tried to run toward us but halted as more weapons aimed at him. "I'm okay, dad," Mikhail croaked, raising a shaky hand, and a sob tore from my chest. "Well, well, what a surprise !" Antonio sneered, yanking my hair to make me whimper again. "Let her go, Antonio," my husband said, stepping closer.

Antonio raised his gun—the same gun he had used to shoot Mikhail—and this time aimed it at Alexei, who still pressed his shirt to his brother's wound. "No !" I screamed, reaching for his weapon, but he yanked me back again. "Stay put, *Cara mia*. We're going to play a little game," he said with that smile that always stole the air from my lungs. "Let's see... do you love these kids like your own ? Or would you rather sacrifice them ?" He released me and gestured to one of his men, "give her a gun." One of them handed me a weapon. I looked at Nikolai, uncertain and he gave me a slight nod. My hands trembled as I took it.

"Alright then ! Kill him, *Cara mia*, or I shoot the brats," Antonio ordered. I could hardly breathe. "No..." I whispered, backing away, as if the distance could protect me from his ultimatum. "No !" I shouted louder, shaking my head wildly. "As you wish, Selina," he said, shifting his aim toward Alexei. "Stop !" I cried out, just as Nikolai did. "You need to make a choice," Antonio sighed, feigning boredom. "So, who do we kill?" Tears blurred my vision, my sobs turned into strangled gasps. "P-please…" "No ! I forbid you from begging that son of a bitch!" Nikolai roared. His eyes, blazing, locked onto mine. Then they drifted toward our children before closing briefly.

"Boys, close your eyes," he commanded and our sons obeyed without a word. Then he turned back to me. His face was unreadable—but I already knew what he would say. "Do it, *Solnychko*." And everything inside me shattered. I shook my head, "I can't. No," I breathed, barely able to speak. "Yes, you can ! I know you can because I know you better than this bastard ever will ! Because I love you like I've never loved anyone before ! Because you are an Ivanov, and in this family, we do what needs to be done. And our children always come first ! A broken sob tore through me. "Nikolai…" I whimpered, trembling. "Do it, Selina !" Antonio shouted, his patience fraying. "Raise your gun, *Solnychko*," Nikolai murmured

I looked at him, desperate, then at my sons—Mikhail bleeding out, Alexei pressing on his wound, Andrei's face bloodied yet still clutching his brother's hand, Rafael sitting close. All of them trembling. All of them afraid. All of them with their eyes shut tight. My arm rose slowly, trembling as I aimed at my husband. *My husband.* My breath came in sharp, shallow gasps. "A little more to the right, *Solnychko*." I sobbed but obeyed. "I'm sorry you have to do this, *moy lyubov'*. But it's going to be all right. Everything will be all right," he said, his eyes never leaving mine. "Nikolai, I... I love you. I love you so much."

"I know, Selina. And that's why you have to do this..." "Selina !" Antonio barked. But I did not look at him. I kept my eyes on my husband, my lips trembling and Nikolai nodded. And with ice-cold fingers, I pulled the trigger. The bullet struck him in the chest. His body jolted backward before collapsing onto the ground, motionless. "Nikolai !" I screamed, dropping the gun as he lay still. I tried to run to him, but one of Antonio's men seized me. "*Cara mia* ! Bravo !" Antonio laughed, clapping his hands, his gun still aimed at my sons. His eyes glinted with sick delight. I could not breathe. I could not think. I could not move, "Nikolai," I sobbed, falling to my knees.

"I'm so proud of you, Selina," Antonio purred, stroking my hair. "Now it's my turn to clean up the Ivanov filth once and for all," he said, turning back toward my sons and raising his gun at Alexei. "No !" I cried out in my broken voice. Another gunshot rang out—different from the others, so loud that I gasped. Blood sprayed across my face, making me flinch, and a scream echoed through the warehouses—the scream of Antonio, now on his knees, a hole in his hand where his gun had been. "Fuck !" he howled. His men scattered, searching for the threat. Then, three cars roared into view. A sob of relief escaped me as Roman and Sasha leapt out before the tires stopped screeching, weapons in hand, sprinting toward my husband's fallen body. He was alive—I knew it. I felt it.

I dashed to my sons, pushing them to the ground and covering them with my body. "It's going to be okay. Your father and uncles are here. They'll get us out," I murmured, squeezing my eyes shut. *Nikolai is alive. He is.* Bullets flew overhead, and each time one of Antonio's men neared, he dropped with a hole in his skull. "It's going to be okay. It's going to be okay," I kept whispering as my heart thundered in my chest. I screamed when someone grabbed me by the waist, struggling to break free—until I heard the voice. "Selina," he whispered against my ear, and I froze as his scent enveloped me. I looked up, unable to believe my eyes. "Nikolai."

"I'm here, *Solnychko*. I'm here now," he said, wiping the blood from my lips before turning to Mikhail. "It's going to be okay, son. You protected them well. I'm proud of you," he said, stroking his hair. My heart clenched as I saw my son's long-held tears finally fall as he nodded weakly. "I don't understand," I murmured, confused, my hands patting Nikolai's chest, searching for the wound. But there was none. He unzipped his jacket, and I gasped when I saw a black vest beneath. "What…?" "A bulletproof vest. We have Elif to thank for that," he said with a faint smile, and I exhaled shakily. Even from afar, she had protected us. I would never be able to thank her enough. "Mikhail!" Roman called as he reached us, still firing. He dropped beside us and examined my son's wound as Alexei lifted his shirt. "Nothing vital was hit," he said. "Yeah, thanks to Mom. She pushed me at the last second," Mikhail explained. My husband's arm tightened around me. "Sasha, extraction," Roman ordered, pressing his earpiece while rising to fire again.

A vehicle sped toward us, skidding to a stop. Sasha jumped out, hurled something toward one of the warehouses, and a few seconds later, an explosion shook the ground. "Are you all okay ?" he asked, lifting Andrei to inspect his wound. "I protected Mom !" Andrei declared, clinging to his uncle. "I'm proud of you," Sasha said, rubbing Rafael's back as the boy clung to his leg. "Come on, let's get you all out of here," Roman added, opening the back door of the car. "Watch out, Roman !" Nikolai warned as a man approached, but he was quickly shot down. "When did you find such a good sniper?" my husband asked, scanning the heights. "We didn't find anyone," Roman muttered, reloading as bullets ricocheted off the car.

"Ferna," I murmured, searching the darkness for her. "Ferna ?" my husband repeated. "*Blayt'*, they shot out the tires," Sasha reported, straightening from beneath the vehicle. "Shit," Roman growled, assessing our surroundings. "There ! That warehouse is isolated enough," he pointed to the smallest one, slightly apart from the others. "David ! Cover fire!" he shouted, while Sasha ran toward the warehouse, carrying Andrei and Rafael in his arms. "I'll take Mikhail," Roman said, and before I could protest, Nikolai pulled me up, Alexei slung over his shoulder. "Don't look back, Selina. Trust Roman," he said as we half-ran, crouching low. A grimace twisted my face as pain flared in my lower abdomen. I pushed the fear aside and followed my husband. We finally reached the warehouse. Roman followed, carrying Mikhail, and gently laid him on a couch against the wall before he and Sasha rushed back outside.

I knelt beside Mikhail, checking his pulse. "He's losing too much blood, Nikolai, we have to—" I winced as another wave of pain seized my belly. "Selina !" Nikolai exclaimed, wrapping his arm around my shoulders as our sons looked on, fear etched into their young faces. "Nikolai, I think… I think I'm pregnant," I said, uncertain. He froze, his gaze slowly dropping to my stomach. "And… does it hurt ?" he asked, concern darkening his eyes as he placed his hand over mine. "The monster hit her in the stomach !" Rafael blurted, frowning, and Nikolai stiffened beside me. "Selina," he said, his voice low and dark, but I shook my head. "We need to get to a hospital, Nikolai—for Mikhail and for the baby," I murmured, biting my lip to stop it from trembling. He gently cupped my face, and I flinched despite myself, the pain from Antonio's blows still burning on my skin.

"It's going to be all right, *moy lyubov'*. Everyone will be fine, and we'll go home, where we'll spend the next few years raising our little wild ones… and our princess." "Our princess ?" I asked, blinking at him. "It has to be a girl, Selina. With your green eyes and your soft hair," he said, pressing a kiss to my forehead. I couldn't stop the tears from falling. "I was so scared. So, so scared," I whispered, clinging to his jacket. "I know, *moy lyubov'*, I know," he murmured. Sasha reentered and pulled out his phone, dialing, "Lorenzo, where the fuck are you ?!" he barked, pinning the phone between his ear and shoulder as he reloaded his gun. "Hurry up, damn it ! We brought the bare minimum of men because you said the *Cosa Nostra* was going to take care of Antonio," he added before hanging up.

"Lorenzo will be here in less than five minutes," he informed us, then disappeared again into the night. "The *Cosa Nostra*?" I asked Nikolai, confused, as he applied pressure to Mikhail's wound. "Antonio acted without their approval. He attacked us on his own. They'll judge him, and he'll confess everything he did to you. They'll make him pay," he explained, lifting his gaze to mine. "But they'll wait their turn," he added, and I shivered at the cold finality in his tone. Screams echoed outside again, followed by more gunfire. "Lorenzo's here," Nikolai said, glancing toward the entrance. "It will all be over in a few minutes." I nodded, wrapping my arms around the twins and Rafael, their warmth a balm to my pain. "We'll be home soon," I whispered, kissing their foreheads. And as Nikolai predicted, the gunfire gradually ceased. Roman appeared at the entrance, wiping blood from his cheek. "It's over. We have him alive. Lorenzo has two helicopters on the way—for Mikhail." Nikolai signaled him to watch over Mikhail and pressed a kiss to my forehead before turning for the exit. "Stay here." "Nikolai—" "Stay here, *moy lyubov'*," he insisted before stepping out, removing his bulletproof vest. And despite the chaos around us, my throat tightened as I watched the muscles shift beneath his compression shirt.

Really, Selina ? Now ? Damn hormones.

"Are you all right, Selina ?" Roman asked gently, taking my hand in his—warm, familiar. "Yes. I knew you'd come," I said, squeezing his hand. "Of course we came. Family above all," he said, kissing the back of my hand as tears once more filled my eyes. *Damn fucking hormones.* "I'm thirsty," Andrei mumbled against my neck. I glanced around and spotted a fridge in the corner.

"I'll take care of it. Alexei, cover for me," Roman said, getting up and heading toward the fridge at the back of the warehouse.

I frowned as I heard shouting and growling outside. Struggling to my feet, I told the boys to stay put before making my way to the entrance—and froze at the sight before me. Antonio was writhing on the ground, Nikolai on top of him, punching him over and over again, blood spraying, bones cracking. "Nikolai, that's enough ! They want him alive. For Rafael, remember ? He has to confess at the trial—how he forced Selina to stay with him. It will prove she has the right to keep custody of Rafael ! Rasili Senior wants Rafael, no matter the cost." Sasha said. My breath caught. They wanted to take Rafael from me ? Antonio and his father wanted to steal my baby ? I startled as I felt a vibration against my chest. Reaching into my bra, I pulled out the phone Ferna had given me, frowning at the message on the screen:

<u>We have proof and a witness that will guarantee you keep custody of your son. You don't need his confession to keep Rafael. You don't need him... alive.</u>

Slowly, I lifted my gaze from the phone to Antonio—bleeding, coughing, groaning in pain. My eyes shifted to my sons, huddled together, frightened, exhausted, hurt. Then to my husband, so tense I could see his veins pulsing. His weary face twisted my heart. Antonio would never stop. He would never let us live in peace. And *Cosa Nostra* would never kill the heir of a great family. I slid the phone into my pocket and picked up a gun from one of the lifeless men on the ground. No one noticed me as I stepped forward, my stride firm. "So, *Cara mia* ? Are you going to kill me ?" Antonio chuckled as I raised the gun toward him. And to my surprise, my hand didn't shake. My mind was calm. I felt... at peace, as if I had always known this moment would come.

"*Solnychko*," my husband called softly from a few meters away. But I shook my head. I felt everyone's eyes on me, but no one moved. No one dared. A war might begin today because of what I was about to do, but I couldn't keep living with an eye over my shoulder—not with a family to protect. "I swore I would never become anyone's monster. I swore I would never let your darkness reach me. And I succeeded. I protected my heart and soul, and I gave them to the man who deserved them. That is the greatest victory I will ever have," I said, my voice steady and calm. His eyes darkened with every word. "But today, I will make an exception. For you, Antonio." "Selina, *Solnychko*, you don't have to do this. Just say the word, and he won't leave here alive, *moy lyubov'*," Nikolai said, taking a step toward me, his hands raised as if taming a frightened beast. "He made me shoot you, Nikolai. The man I love. In front of our sons," I said with a sad smile, shaking my head. "I will be your monster today, Antonio Rasili. The last face you will ever see. The face of a fulfilled woman who will live a life full of love with the man she adores, with the children she cherishes. And you ? You will be forgotten. You will be nothing but a bad memory." "You can't forget me, Selina ! I marked you ! You are mine ! Mine !" he shouted, trying to lift himself but failing—Nikolai had broken his legs. "You can't kill me, Selina ! You can't—"

The first shot went off almost on its own, startling me. My finger had barely brushed the trigger before the bullet lodged in his chest. The second shook my arm. The third, my heart. And with each bullet that buried itself in his body, I felt lighter. I kept pulling the trigger over and over until the gun clicked empty. Antonio's body lay still. He would never move again. He would never reach us again. He would never haunt me again. Never hurt me again. A warm hand wrapped around my wrist, gently taking the gun from my grasp. "It's over, *moy lyubov'*. You're free." "Yes. It's over," I nodded, leaning into him as his arm wrapped around me, his hand resting against my stomach, while two helicopters approached in the distance.

Yes, it was over. For Antonio. But for me, for my family… this was only the beginning.

Chapter forty-three
Nikolai

"Am I going to be a big brother?" Rafael whispered, sitting on my lap, drawing the attention of his brothers, who were seated on one of the many couches in our hospital suite in Sochi. Selina had lost consciousness in the helicopter, driving me insane. Between Mikhail, who kept losing blood, and Selina moaning in pain from her stomach, we all thought we were going to lose our minds—my brothers and I. My gaze fell on my wife lying on the bed, a monitor tracking her vital signs. The marks on her face reignited the rage that had been consuming me for the past two days, but now, there was no one left to take revenge on. Antonio was dead. My wife had killed him. My *Solnychko*, my Selina—so brave, so beautiful, so intelligent, so generous.

"I hope it's a girl," Roman said from his seat on the windowsill, his eyes never leaving my wife. His entire body radiated tension, and it would be that way for days—for all of us. They had touched our children, one of our women, our family, reminding us of our responsibilities, our duty as protectors. "A female presence will do you all a lot of good when you're older," Elif smiled, holding Andrei and Alexei close. "We're back with the treasure !" Sienna announced as she walked into the room, carrying plastic bags full of sandwiches, closely followed by Sasha, who was balancing a box of drinks. The kids and Roman perked up at the sight—and especially the smell—of food. From what they told us, Antonio had only given them bread and water twice. *Twice.* "Too bad Mika isn't awake. These are his favorites," Elif said, unwrapping a still-warm sandwich and handing it to Andrei, who couldn't stop touching his stitches.

Mikhail had made it through surgery, and thank God, he was going to be okay. The doctors had said he should regain consciousness within an hour. The door opened again, and this time, Grigori stepped in, followed by the doctor. "Well, well, a true family gathering," the doctor smiled as he approached the monitor tracking my wife's vitals. "When will she wake up ?" I asked, gripping her hand tightly. "Don't worry, Mr. Ivanov, your wife's vitals are strong, and the baby is developing well in its third month. Your wife and child held on despite the stress and violence they endured—they are both incredibly strong," he said with an encouraging smile, and I nodded. Yes, my wife was strong. Stronger than I would ever be, braver than I could ever be. "I believe that by tomorrow evening, you'll all be able to go home with Mikhail. But don't forget, the patients need plenty of rest," he added, jotting down notes in his notebook before shaking my hand and Grigori's, then leaving the room.

"Here," Elif said, handing me a sandwich. "See ? I told you we'd have dinner together," she teased, nudging me with her shoulder, making me laugh. "That's not exactly how I remember our conversation," I replied, taking the sandwich, though I set it down on the bedside table. I wasn't hungry—I wouldn't be until my wife and my son opened their eyes. "You saved my life. Again," I said, grabbing her hand. "And you saved my wife's soul. If I hadn't been wearing that vest, if she had… Thank you, Elif." I sighed, closing my eyes, haunted by the image of my wife just before she pulled the trigger. A memory that would stay with me until my last breath. "Oh, Nikolai, I'm so proud of you. You've become the man you were always meant to be," she murmured, snuggling against me. "I could never have become the man I am without you," I replied, holding her close in return. I met Grigori's gaze over her head. Despite his smile, I saw the worry in his eyes—concern for the upcoming meeting with the *Cosa Nostra* in the next few months.

Antonio's death would be difficult to justify. Selina had to gain custody of Rafael, or war would be inevitable. A war that would cost many lives—including Ivanov lives.

A month and a half later

The Italians looked at us as if we had murdered one of their own, ironically. From across the table, their glares burned with silent accusation as we waited for the arrival of Grigori and Capo Marino, the representative sent by the *Cosa Nostra*. "I heard you got your ass handed to you in your last race, Roman," said Michele, Marino's nephew, about the same age as my brother. Roman leaned back in his chair with an irritated sigh, crossing his arms behind his neck. "And I heard you didn't even last two minutes with a chick last time," he retorted. The tension thickened as the younger men exchanged increasingly hostile glares. Then, the door to our headquarters' meeting room in California swung open, revealing Grigori and Capo Marino. We all stood in respect. "Shall we begin ?" Marino asked, settling into the seat at the head of the table, while Grigori took the opposite end.

"Today, we are gathered to judge the circumstances surrounding the death of Antonio Rasili and the custody and inheritance rights of Rafael Rasili Ivanov," Marino declared, his hands clasped firmly on the table. "Do you have any evidence or witnesses to prove that Antonio Rasili held Selina Floros Ivanov against her will and subjected her to torture and manipulation for eight years?" he asked, turning to Grigori. "My wife is ready to testify via video call about what she…" "Unfortunately, her testimony cannot be accepted," Marino interrupted. "Without Antonio's word to counter hers, we cannot judge based solely on her claims." A low growl escaped me. We had expected this—but we had to play every card.

"Rafael is an Ivanov. He's not going anywhere," Grigori stated, leaning back and crossing his legs. "So we might as well begin discussing the terms of the war to come." Despite the weight of the moment, I couldn't help but feel pride—pride in a brother I could count on, no matter the cost. "You're willing to start a war over a kid who isn't even your blood, Grigori?"

"Rafael is my son. I don't give a damn about his blood, and I care even less about the war I'll fight to keep him. But let me be clear," I said, locking eyes with Marino, "Rafael will never return to the Rasili family. Even if I die in this war, he will never again live under the same roof with a Rasili. He will grow up with his mother and his brothers." Marino exchanged glances with his men, then slowly shook his head. "Antonio may have acted without our authorization, but he was still a Rasili. He was the heir of his family. His unjustified death must be punished," he declared, standing. "And since you refuse to hand over the culprit, we will have to settle this through war—"

"There will be no war," a voice interrupted sharply, cutting through the room like a blade. Gasps echoed as Sienna burst in, ignoring the guards' startled protests. "What the fuck, Sienna ?!" Sasha exclaimed, rising to meet her, but she raised a hand to stop him. "I am a witness. And I have evidence justifying Antonio Rasili's death," she said, stepping forward with unwavering resolve. She positioned herself between Grigori and me, while Sasha and Roman moved protectively behind her. "What the hell are you doing ?" I hissed, my eyes never leaving the Italians, who had begun whispering among themselves. "What I should have done eight years ago," she replied, folding her trembling hands over her stomach. "My name is Sienna Floros. I am Selina Floros Ivanov's younger sister. And… it's because of me that she was forced to live under Antonio Rasili's control." Sasha stepped closer to her, but she continued. "I was sixteen when I met Emilio Rasili, Antonio's cousin. He promised me an internship at a tech company. I was naïve enough to believe him. He arranged a meeting at a hotel, saying I'd meet my supervisor there. But when I arrived, he was the only one in the room." Her voice trembled, but she didn't stop. "He threw himself at me. When I tried to push him away, he hit me. Knocked me to the floor. Then he… he started crushing me. I panicked. There were scissors on the coffee table. I grabbed them. And then there was blood. So much blood. I don't know how long I sat there, frozen. Then my sister arrived. I hadn't called her—Antonio had. He used what happened to blackmail her. He threatened to show you the video he had recorded unless she obeyed him."

She stood tall now, her chin high. "So if you want someone to punish for Emilio Rasili's death, punish me. But do not go after my sister for Antonio's death, because this asshole deserves it. And don't you dare think of separating my nephew from his mother." "No one is punishing you," Sasha said firmly, pulling her back into the protective circle he and Roman formed around her. "Do you have the video he used to blackmail your sister?" Marino asked, now seated again. Sienna shook her head, "no. I don't know where it is. But I have a recording of Antonio." She pulled a small phone from her pocket and handed it to Sasha, who placed it on the table and hit play and Antonio's furious voice filled the room.

"Your sister should've shut up and satisfied my cousin instead of stabbing him with scissors! Although... that video served me well, didn't it? All those years she submitted to me, just so I wouldn't reveal that her sister was the murderer. My cousin—an heir of the Rasili family. Do you know what they'll do to her when they find out, Cara mia? Tortures you can't even imagine. But let me show you..."

The recording ended, leaving the room in heavy silence. I wished Antonio were still alive—just so I could kill him again. Judging by Sasha's murderous expression, I wasn't the only one. "I believe we now have enough evidence to justify Antonio Rasili's death," Grigori said, turning to Marino. The two men locked eyes. And now... we waited for the verdict. War or peace? Death or survival?

Selina

"It's not fair ! Everyone knows except me !" I pouted, crossing my arms, unable to see a thing with the blindfold tied over my eyes. "No, Mama, we don't know either!" the boys laughed from the back seat, making me smile despite myself. The car jolted suddenly, and my husband's hand instinctively found its place on my growing belly. I was nearly six months pregnant now, and soon, we would discover the baby's gender. I couldn't wait—we all couldn't wait. Since the meeting with the Italians almost two months earlier, we had remained on guard. They had accepted that Antonio's death was justified, and I had been granted custody of my son. But when it came to Emilio's death, they had said nothing. Sienna had returned home without consequence, yet the uncertainty lingered. I feared for my sister—but fear would never keep me from moving forward again. Never. I placed my hand over Nikolai's, squeezing it gently, letting the love I felt for him continue to anchor me, to warm me. "Dad ! Uncle Roman's car is gone !" Andrei suddenly shouted. "He probably took a shortcut, son. Don't worry," my husband reassured him as he turned down a quieter road. A few minutes later, we slowed until the car finally stopped.

The boys leapt out, shouting in excitement, while I unbuckled my seatbelt, feeling around for the door handle. But before I could find it, the door opened, and Nikolai's warmth enveloped me. We walked for several minutes to the sound of joyful cries from our boys and Elif's, the laughter of my sister and Elif, and the usual bickering between Roman, Sasha, and Grigori. "We're here," my husband murmured against my ear, sending that familiar shiver down my spine—just as he always did when he was near. "And where exactly is 'here'?" I asked, leaning into him. "I hope you'll like it, *Solnyshko*," he whispered, untying the blindfold. I blinked several times, adjusting to the light, and then my breath caught at the sight before me. "Strawberries," I whispered, staring at the endless rows of strawberry fields. "Strawberries," I repeated, feeling as if the baby inside me was just as excited by the sight of my favorite fruit. Or rather, our favorite fruit, considering how intense my cravings had been lately. "Strawberry fields for my wife and my daughter, who can't get enough of them," he said, pressing a kiss to my neck. "It could be a boy," I replied absentmindedly, still taking in the view. "Then he'll help me and his brothers finish building our chalet," he added.

I frowned. "Chalet ? What are you—" He gently turned me, and there it was—a beautiful chalet under construction, nestled slightly higher up the hill. "We've been working on it for over a month now !" Roman shouted, already running toward the building with Ivan laughing on his back. "Nikolai," I whispered, tears welling in my eyes. "You once told me about the little house in the countryside where you grew up with your sister and parents. I thought you might like this," he said softly. I turned in his arms, wrapping mine tightly around his waist and burying my face in his chest. "Don't cry, *moy lyubov'*. Everything I do—everything I will ever do—is for you, our sons, and our daughter. I will never let you shed another tear of sorrow," he murmured, kissing my hair.

Which, of course, only made me cry harder—*damn hormones* !

"Even if I were to cry from sadness one day, I know it would never be because of you, *amore mio*," I whispered, cupping his face in my hands. "You are my pillar, Nikolai. You are my savior, the love of my life, my last hope," I said, before kissing him.

And he kissed me back with such passion that words became unnecessary. He loves me. We love each other. And we would never let anything—or anyone—extinguish our hope.

Epilogue

She walked confidently down the long, dim hallway, her Shadow trailing behind her as always—especially in the darkest moments. The laughter of women, the smell of smoke, and countless other odors mingled in the air, making it heavy—almost suffocating. Several Stars and their Shadows greeted her and her own, some with faint smiles, others with discreet gestures—always subtle, always careful not to attract the Master's attention. At last, she reached his door. Despite herself, her heart raced. For the first time, she was going to defy him. For the first time, she wasn't submitting. She wasn't afraid. She pushed the office door open without knocking. The Master sat behind his desk, laughing with one of his guards and Stars who were clearly there to entertain him.

"Ah, my *Stella* ! You're back !" the Master exclaimed, spreading his arms with a smile that revealed his yellowing teeth. "Leave us," she said firmly, planting herself in front of the desk, her Shadow silent at her back. The guard looked at the Master, awaiting an order. With a flick of his hand, he dismissed the Stars and the guard. Some brushed their fingers against her hand, others her back as they passed—small gestures of support, of silent rebellion. The door closed behind them, muffling the noise outside. Only the Master, the Goddess, and the Shadow remained. "Listen to me—" "No. You're going to listen to me," she cut him off, her tone calm but cold. "From now on, I work on my terms. My hours. My clients." She pointed at him—an act she knew would enrage him.

"I think you've forgotten that I have in my possession—" "If you're talking about the video, it's useless now. I told them everything. They know." Her voice carried a mocking edge. "Impossible ! They would have killed you ! They would never let the murderer of one of their own live. You're lying !" She laughed, stepping forward until her hands were flat on his desk. She leaned in close, eyes locked on his. "Then go ahead. Send it to them. Let's find out if they already know, shall we ?"

The Master studied her, searching her gaze for signs of bluff—but she didn't flinch. When he saw the truth, his shoulders stiffened, his fists clenched against the armrests of his chair. "That's all I came to say. I'll return when I choose. And if you ever dare lay a finger on me again or the others, you know who I'd tell about your little secrets. And they won't let you live." She stood tall and turned toward the door, her Shadow falling into step behind her. "Sienna !" the Master barked, rising from his chair, his face flushed with fury. "The Ivanovs won't always be there to protect you! " She paused, then looked back over her shoulder with a wry smile. "It's not my back that needs protecting, Master," she said, dragging out the word with venom, before walking out.

"You should have told him you were quitting for good," the Shadow said quietly, now walking beside her—something strictly forbidden. The Shadow was supposed to stay three steps behind the Star, always. A crucial rule to avoid unsettling the clients. "Not yet," Sienna replied, her pace never slowing, her eyes sweeping over the young faces around her—some barely of age, others not even that. Just like she once had been. No, she wouldn't stop. Not until they were saved—the girls who were once her. So that they never became what she had been forced to become.

A monster.

About Gateli YOZREL

While others were solving math equations, I was crafting worlds.

My love for writing began in middle school—during math class, of all places. While my classmates hunted for the value of x, I filled my calculation notebook with characters, heartbreak, chaos, and dreams. Numbers never made sense to me, but stories always did.

I started sharing little pieces of my imagination on Instagram, then on Wattpad… but I never truly dared to expose my worlds to the light. Maybe out of fear. Maybe out of love—for keeping them mine, a little longer.

People have always said I was "in the clouds," detached from reality—as if that was a flaw. But for me, it's always been my superpower. Escaping into stories isn't weakness—it's survival. It's joy. It's freedom.

I'm a woman of simple joys: books, writing, green tea, red berries, and lately… pineapple (don't judge me). I love my parents, my sisters, my brother, and I love weaving emotions into words.

But more than anything—I live for your comments. Each one is proof that what I write touches your heart. That my emotions found a home in yours.

And that… is the greatest gift a writer can receive.

Also by

Coming Soon

The Last Chance, the Ivanov Brothers Book II.

Peace is nothing but an illusion in this world and Sienna knows it better than anyone.

Scarred by a past she keeps buried in silence, she moves through life behind a mask, determined to let no one get too close. Until him.

Sasha Ivanov is everything she fears, cold, sharp, relentless.

He doesn't back down.

He sees her. He seeks her.

And he's willing to do whatever it takes to keep her.

Caught between dangerous attraction, buried truths, and raw wounds, their bond breaks every rule, crosses every line.

And when faced with a man who never gives up, Sienna will have to choose:

Run again or finally let go... but at what cost?

Sienna & Sasha.

Acknowledgments

First and foremost, I want to thank myself.

Thank you for not giving up despite the doubts.

Thank you for not walking away when the obstacles felt insurmountable.

Thank you for pushing forward, even when those around you said this was nothing but a waste of time.

Thank you for surviving the emotional blocks, for learning the beauty of solitude, and for finally understanding the importance of you.

To my sisters—Lena and Nis—thank you for believing in me when I couldn't. Your love and support carried me through.

To my best friend, Mel—thank you for standing by me, for never doubting this dream, and for always cheering me on. You have no idea how much that meant.

And finally, to all my readers on Wattpad and my followers on Instagram—thank you. Your unwavering support, your comments, your encouragement… I see you, I feel you, and I love you.

This book exists because of all of you.

With all my heart,

Gateli YOZREL

www.ingramcontent.com/pod-product-compliance
Ingram Content Group UK Ltd.
Pitfield, Milton Keynes, MK11 3LW, UK
UKHW021307250725
7080UKWH00030B/278